CANARYVILLE

Also by Charlie Newton

Privateers
Traitor's Gate
Start Shooting
Calumet City
Symphony for the Devil

CHARLIE NEWTON
CANARYVILLE

BLACKTYPE PRESS

Published by BlackType Press, Austin, Texas
www.charlienewton.com

Edited and designed by Girl Friday Productions
www.girlfridayproductions.com

Cover design: David Drummond
Interior design: Paul Barrett
Project management: Devon Fredericksen
Editorial: Tiffany Taing
Image credits: iStock/Steve_Gadomski (front cover),
Shutterstock/ARENA Creative (back cover)

ISBN (paperback): 978-1-7344368-4-6
ISBN (ebook): 978-1-7344368-3-9

Library of Congress Control Number: 2021906267

It was the Law of the Sea, they said. Civilization ends at the waterline. Beyond that, we all enter the food chain.

Hunter S. Thompson

CHICAGO

2011

TWO DAYS BEFORE ST. PATRICK'S DAY

Chapter 1

LT. DENNY BANAHAN

Do hard-ons make you stupid?

Are we grading on a curve?

Anatomical life lessons may not seem like a discussion we need to have, but stay with me. It's 11:00 a.m. on the Saturday before St. Patrick's Day. If history is a predictor, hard-ons and stupid will be today's primary currency.

A thirtysomething crime-scene tech pounds my Crown Vic's hood and levitates half my lunch. She stabs two fingers into her ample chest and booms: "*My* goddamn husband, Oswald the accountant, is *hard-wired* to fuck secretaries? That's what you're telling me? Dick-on-patrol is a goddamn law of the universe?"

Sad, but well . . . yeah. "Diane, c'mon, don't stroke out—"

"Yes or no, goddammit! You're Denny fucking Banahan—big-swingin'-dick lieutenant—you're paid to have answers."

While it's true that I'm paid to have answers, I'm five nine, 187 pounds. *Big* and *swingin'* are not often attached to my name. I glance to my right for counseling assistance.

My sergeant, ex–defensive lineman Jimmie "the Gent" Daniels, palms both sides of a '60s Motown pompadour that adds three inches of vertical to what would otherwise be the impeccably tailored cube of

Chicago's best detective. Jimmie shrugs and declines to opine. Proof, yet again, that for all forty-nine years of his life, Jimmie Daniels has been smarter than me.

Our maritally challenged colleague makes five inches with her thumb and forefinger. "How much goddamn blood can fit in that? Not enough to make *me* eat rocks. I'm a goddamn primate; I move blood around . . . I . . ." Diane begins to stutter.

"Diane, this is been-divorced Denny, okay? You file the papers on Oswald, hit the gym eight or ten times, find a nice young thing who appreciates the *incandescent* wonder of you, and you're prepaid to happy-ever-after."

Teeth nip my fingertips.

My hand jerks up and speckles my face with hot sauce. Seated directly beneath my Harold's Chicken wing, a one-eyed terrier licks her lips and yips once. Her name is Chi-Town Bega (Rutabaga), the princess of Stony Island Avenue.

I frown at my dog. "We've been through this nine times; no people food."

Bega barks once and adopts perfect posture. I wipe hot sauce off my face with the back of my hand. If street mongrels had a category in dog shows, Bega wins them all. "Very nice." I reach for the package on my hood, Darwin's brand Turkey and Veg Dinner (I keep a cold case in the trunk).

"We have manners. We have nutritional standards. Are we clear?"

Bega yips. I toss the chicken wing in the trash barrel, open the Darwin's, and lay it at Bega's paws—

Jimmie stiffens, hand already inside his jacket.

I pivot fast.

The doorway of Harold's Chicken pukes out three of the thirty thousand made members of the Almighty Black P Stone Nation. The point men are six foot, prison lean, wearing hooded sweatshirts. Stenciled big across both chests is RED SUMMER over a black fist. Both gangsters balk hard at Jimmie going for his .45 and me coming to my feet. One gangster jukes left, the other right, both speed-reading a future none of us may have.

Alone in the doorway is the third P-Stone, calm as cold water. His name is RayLen Starks, age twenty-six, six foot four, 220 pounds. A street-evil, stone fucking killer.

Bega scoots 180 to face RayLen—

RayLen sneers the one lip that works, lifting a nose I broke, and eyes me, then Bega protecting her Darwin's.

RayLen says, "Man, why the fuck you feed that rat?"

Jimmie stiff-arms his .45 at his nearest P-Stone. "Got left."

"Got right," shouts Diane.

I step in front of Bega, close the distance on RayLen. Jimmie and I popped RayLen for a home-invasion murder when he was a minor, and again two years ago for a Gangster Disciples drive-by. RayLen beat both murders—two elderly witnesses disappeared; the others recanted.

I tell him: "My dog's eating her lunch, okay? I'm eating mine; you're eating yours."

"Nigga, please." RayLen throws his Coke can into the alley. "Your *rat* eat here, sleep here every fuckin' night; rather be homeless than a white muthafucka's bitch." He nods behind me at Diane. "Like her."

Diane says, "Uh-huh. Dog's too pretty to be your mama. And *Mama* the only bitch you know."

My eyes tighten on RayLen. I reach behind my Smith & Wesson to the Illinois horse racing ID hooked into my belt. Hanging from the ID card's ring is a one-inch voodoo doll made from barn hay and racing silks. Without looking at Bega, I lower the doll to her nose. "Racetrack dog. Winner's circle. Ray-Bans. Sunshine."

Bega quits the low growl she's giving RayLen, barks twice, and wags her body against my leg.

RayLen spits on Bega's paws. "One-eyed bitch born in an alley, gonna die in one. All that's gonna fuckin' happen."

"Sixteen days, Ray. Me and my girl are retiring from your police department, then marching toward the Breeders' Cup. Shit, five years from now, you'll be telling everyone on death row you know us."

RayLen points across Stony Island Avenue at the twenty-four seven FBI tail car I've had for the last six months. "Uh-huh; only Breeders you seein' is twenty to life in Marion. FBI got you this time. *Grand fucking jury.* Double fuckin' homicide." RayLen makes a pistol finger at Bega.

"Day you go to prison, this rat-bitch is headfirst off the Magikist roof. Send you the muthafuckin' YouTube."

Jimmie's P-Stone moves—Jimmie slams him into the wall.

"Not this dog, Ray." I close all the distance between RayLen and me. "See, she's *my* dog. I don't have courtrooms and missing witnesses for that."

RayLen taps the two tears tattooed beneath his left eye for the murders he beat. "Magikist rooftop killed my mama's blood, Antoine and Odetta. Finally gonna get you. And rat-dog, too."

A siren wails in behind me. Tires screech-stop at the curb. A uniform charges past Diane to her banger. "On the fucking wall!"

RayLen doesn't flinch. He slow smiles to his gold incisors. "Rat-dog ain't leavin' and Denny fuckin' Banahan ain't leavin'. Magikist rooftop gonna get this bitch. FBI gonna get you."

Bega will ride in my Crown Vic all day, go to the vet, my office, a picnic with my girlfriend—pretty much anywhere—but she won't stay overnight in a fenced yard or a house; paces nonstop till I bring her back here.

On our left, another beat car splits traffic head-on and slides to the curb behind Jimmie. The patrolman jumps out, dash mic still in his hand.

Jimmie pats air with one hand. "We got it."

I lean into RayLen's nose. "Do not hurt my dog."

The patrolman by Jimmie shouts: "Lieutenant," and waves his dash mic. "They got a heater. Rubber boots. In Canaryville."

Heater in Homicide-speak means "high profile." *Rubber boots* means . . . what you think it means. RayLen adds chill to his vampire smile.

I step back, wave Jimmie and the beat-car patrolman to disengage their bangers, then point south. "Hit the bricks, Ray."

RayLen and his P-Stones pimp roll south. I glance Bega, wink *No biggie*, and point at her food. "Mangia."

Diane yells over Bega toward RayLen's back: "Got your mama's crack pipe. When she's done trickin', have her come by."

RayLen flips Diane the bird. "My mama be at Banahan's grand jury, see her brother, sister done right. FBI got Jon Burge and they gonna get Banahan." RayLen nods and keeps walking.

Jimmie points to the Third District car and the patrolman with the dash mic. "Want a brother to get that?"

"We're off duty, they can wait."

Diane shakes her squarish haircut, frowns, and says, "Check the TV, Lieutenant Cupcake's blowing the camera."

The fifteen-inch TV facing out of Harold's front window is a live shot of the Chicago River—dyed emerald green—and Lt. Gael Gilmartin, the youngest of the Gilmartin sisters, standing between the mayor and the superintendent for the "downtown" St. Patrick's parade. Diane doesn't care for Gael because Lieutenant Gilmartin is Canaryville tough, master's-degree smart, and can wear *out* a pair of pants.

"Good idea, Diane. Go to the downtown parade. Throw a potato at Oswald."

"Fuck you and him. And all the size 4 Gaels."

Bega barks once at Gael's name. (Gael named her.)

The moving banner at the bottom of the screen is where I focus: "Judge rules for federal takeover of Chicago Police Department." Not good news—for the city surviving a race-baited bloodbath or me facing the grand jury.

"Denny." Jimmie straightens from the beat-car's window and the heater call he decided to answer. His giant hand hugs the call mic against a Brooks Brothers lapel. "Commander wants us to roll, *hot*."

I glance the FBI car. "Commander Hanlin know who he called?"

Jimmie nods . . . too slow.

I fisheye Jimmie's trepidation, then: "Nah. I'm watching the parade. Have him call the Feds. Let 'em start running Canaryville's streets a few hours early."

Diane laughs for the first time this week and steps to my shoulder. "Commander Tight-Ass Motherfucker hates you. *Jesus, Mary, and Joseph* he does. Gonna give him a heart attack. I hope."

"If Hanlin dies, Feds may make you boss."

Diane spits. "No way I work for the G, other than picking up my check. If those dumbasses step into the Debate, Chicago'll be on fire by dinnertime. Empty-holster motherfuckers need somebody the Reverends wanna kiss, and she ain't me."

Reverends is an unkind reference to the Black, South Side preacher-activists like Jesse Jackson and Jeremiah Wright.

"The Debate" is the bitter reality of shrinking public resources and their reallotment.

Diane adds, "And fuck 'em, anyway, the G *and* downtown. You were the best commander on the job, and before that, the best lieutenant. Other than the slept-at-the-police-barn mornings." She wrinkles her nose. "Glad you stopped doing that."

"Always thought you and Jimmie would get me my own float."

"In the South Side parade." She points at the TV. "Downtown parade is for tools. Like Oswald."

Like all things "quintessential" Chicago, one St. Patrick's parade isn't sufficiently quintessential. We have two. The downtown parade is held on the Saturday before March 17. The South Side Irish Parade is held on St. Patrick's Day. Personally, I had all the Irish mythology I needed before I was ten, but for the record, Chicago isn't divided by the Cubs-Sox rivalry you always hear about, we're divided by where you eat your hot dogs and which parade you attend.

The downtown parade is just east of Michigan Avenue by the lake and any "acceptable" organization can march in it—Greenpeace, Muslims for Jesus, Black politicians (boycotting this year), personal-injury law firms, Jenny Craig—anyone who can pay the fee and walk the length of Grant Park.

To march in the South Side Irish Parade—the largest neighborhood parade in the world, pushing three hundred thousand—you have to be Irish. It was cancelled, forever, in 2009 after the annual "alcohol related" melee between the political factions of Northern Ireland resulted in twelve coppers being assaulted and fifty-four arrests.

All year there've been rumors that the South Side intends to march on the seventeenth, two days from now—parade big and angry through the Irish Riviera like they do in Belfast—to hell with the permit and consequences.

I make the parade a 100 percent. The Riv's never been big on outside permissions. The only rules applied there were made there, inside four contiguous neighborhoods born out of the livestock slaughter in the Union Stock Yards—Canaryville, Bridgeport, New City, and the Hardscrabble.

The TV in Harold's window cuts away from Gael with the mayor to a shot of the downtown parade. Jimmie hands the mic back to the beat car, then raises his arm and circles it at me.

My "day at the parade" has ended. For some compelling reason, Sergeant Daniels has decided the city cannot survive without him and me working overtime. Time to saddle up.

While it's absolute fact that Jimmie Daniels can sartorial, and his combination Jackie Wilson–Major Lance pompadour could front a '60s album cover with the Temps or Tops, at heart, Jimmie's a cowboy. Has 'em on his sheets at home—I kid you not. So, when he says it's time to ride, that's what you do. And where we're headed won't be good if putting me and my FBI tail in the picture is expected to improve it.

I point Bega at Jimmie and tell her, "Trouble at the ranch. I'll be back later. Stay away from RayLen; he's feeling it." I nod at the FBI car. "Them, too."

**

Flies feed on fluid pools and exposed organs. The gore belongs to a naked white male piled just west of the Norfolk and Southern Forty-Third Street viaduct. When I grew up here it was the Norfolk and Western.

I force my stomach calm; wave the flies out of my face. "Police" yellow tape strings the weeds. Fifty raw-boned, hard-eyed, paycheck-to-paycheck whites line the tape.

The victim's name is Dillon "Dill" Reem. I never liked Dill and I'm glad he's dead. Best I can tell, he was beaten to death, maybe two or three times, then gutted, then quartered—with ferocity, not precision. The body parts that are still recognizable as human were apparently beaten *after* the slaughter. You don't see that too often. As in I've never.

Next to Dill's exposed spine and entrails lies an attractive white female, one powder-burn bullet hole in her sweater, makeup still perfect, not a scuff on her stockings. Her name is Cissy Noonan. Dill and Cissy should not be dead, or together. They are, what we professional police officers would privately call, a prelude to a major fucking problem.

"Denny!" Jimmie points me at a gagging rookie patrolman within vomit distance of our gore *evidence*. I corral the patrolman before he can taint the crime scene or further disrupt Jimmie's virtuoso, stream-of-consciousness homicide investigation. The patrolman and I walk to the far corner of the yellow tape.

Pinching his nose, Officer Walter Johnson keeps his palm over his mouth and tries to tell me something. I stay at his shoulder but finger-tip his face forward. My clothes can't compare to Jimmie's, but they still cost money to clean.

"Walter, I warned you not to take this job. Remember?"

Patrolman Johnson nods, hand clamped over his mouth.

"But you wanted to be Easy Rawlins." I marshal as much Denzel Washington cool as a short white guy can own. "Easy Rawlins never gave back lunch he paid for. It's a rule if you work for me."

Officer Johnson takes three measured breaths through his fingers, then points at fresh gang graffiti on Canaryville's heavily defended, white-only end of the Forty-Third Street viaduct. Painted on the wall above three homeless white men is a twenty-four-by-thirty-six-inch poster-sized rectangle of blood red. The rectangle has a large black fist in its center and RED SUMMER underneath.

I know the story, and so does Officer Johnson; it's short and it isn't pretty: Forty-three Black men were lynched during 1919's Red Summer, two from gas streetlights on Halsted Street outside Chicago's Union Stock Yards. Both men were new employees of Chicago's meatpackers—shit-heel profiteers who'd recruited hard in the Deep South, promising good jobs and safety from the race hatred and violence of Southern Reconstruction and Jim Crow. These promises were made to Black fellows only two generations out of Civil War slavery. Probably just an oversight that the meatpackers forgot to mention "strikebreaker" to their new Black recruits as they helped them into the railcars.

The new tag has already been defaced. Spray-painted over it in white is a hangman's noose and the letters **PNDH** across it.

I glance at Dill and Cissy DOA thirty feet away, then back to the Black-versus-white graffiti—a possible connection to their double homicide that I'm gonna work overtime not to make.

"Fuck. Tell the detectives I said get photographs, then you get some paint. Don't wait on a city crew; there's a paint store on Thirty-Fifth by Morrie O's. Do that now, Walter."

Officer Johnson stares at the Black-versus-white story on the viaduct wall, like maybe he doesn't quite understand the possibilities.

Some puzzles solve themselves. "Red Summer," painted with a Black man's spray can, translates to the white citizens of Canaryville as: "Move out or burn out." The part Walter may not get is Canaryville's response—the white noose and "PNDH"—which translates to: "Project niggers die here."

I tell Walter, "Red Summer's the next course on the city's menu; that ain't news. And summertime's coming whether the Feds take over our police department tomorrow, or not. The Red Summer–PNDH argument killed three in January, nine in February, and eleven so far in March—ten of 'em white, thirteen Black. Come summertime, Walter, fire trucks and ambulances are all that's gonna matter. Go get the paint."

He leaves. I blink into the afternoon glare he was blocking. Thirty feet behind the commotion and *way* outta place is a female apparition that'd make a God-fearing witch burner back up—

Maureen Cavanaugh Cane, proprietress of the Malvern, a thinking man's pub *way* north on the leafy side of the river—five seven, lightweight leather duster, matching boots, midthigh skirt on dancer's legs, tasteful but tight sweater, narrow orange choker at her throat, and enough four-alarm red hair to start a fire.

Ms. Cane squats to assist a rag lady, semicrumbled between two dead cars, next to a grocery cart packed with other people's trash. The rag lady tries to stand again, but can't. Ms. Cane pats her calm, strokes stringy hair out of the old face, listening, stroking . . . then nods, stands, turns toward two Ninth District uniforms—

They stop working the perimeter of a double homicide, hide their left hands, and try to look pretty. Ms. Cane steps to the officers, points discreetly behind her, the crumbled rag lady no longer invisible. One of the uniforms leaves his post, walks with Ms. Cane to the rag lady, speaks to his collar mic, then offers Ms. Cane his card.

She smiles, accepts it, trades one of her own. The exchange has the look of a woman who intends to know if the promises made to the rag lady are kept. The look of someone who does not fuck around on her word.

Ms. Cane squats to the rag lady again, points to the uniform, then curls money and another card into the rag lady's palm.

My posture improves to "manly."

Ms. Cane stands, winks *Thanks* to the uniform, then walks toward me. Like she slow dances, shoulders back, the slightest cant to each hip, looking nowhere but at me. She stops when we're twenty-four inches apart, only the yellow tape, her sweater, a hint of Inis Ór perfume, and the heat from her skin between us. After giving me a three-count in her blue eyes, she leans into her West Belfast accent, the orange choker the only trace of where her politics fall on the Springfield Road.

"Well, Dennis?"

"Ah, it's grand you look, Ms. Cane."

Her eyes narrow at my use of her accent.

"Hey, no one's happier to see you than me." I wince at yellow-tape world. "Kinda unfortunate it's here."

She waits, then, "Is it our afternoon you're forgettin'? Or have I stopped being the girl you fancy?"

"*Shit.* Sorry. I was uptown having lunch with Bega, got this call—"

Maureen half turns, smiles at the two uniforms who smile back—I turn her back to me.

She allows herself to be pulled closer. The eyes bat; her chin rises, marshaling injury into temper. "Possibly, I came this far to see if it was a man in those pants . . . who's interested in being about the business of a man and a woman."

She matches my smile with her own—no more, no less—and we stand there. My smile widens; so does hers. Two teenagers on the porch wishing the light would go out.

For the record, Maureen's not just the "girl I fancy." She and I have bet her pub and my pension on a thoroughbred rescue farm. Our way home—something that before I met her had become harder and harder to see, but on her lips sounds so good it can run tears down my cheek . . . if big, bad Denny Banahan isn't careful.

A gloved hand waves me back to the slaughter. It belongs to a woman with a strong stomach and a man's haircut, a crime-scene tech Jimmie and I work with on "rubber boots" cases.

I tell Maureen: "Gimme a sec," and step to the tech.

The tech says, "If I didn't know better, I'd say the male swallowed a bomb."

"That'd be new."

"Jimmie says the male is Loef Brummel's top guy? The hit man who killed the horses in the barn fire at Sportsman's?"

"Allegedly."

I turn back to check Maureen, hoping she didn't hear that. Her blue eyes are cold, the smile gone. I ease the tech farther away.

The tech says, "What's left of the male's chest cavity is stuffed. Have a look."

"Just ate. How about you just tell me?"

"Inside is a 9 mm Browning automatic, leather wallet, wristwatch, neck-chain crucifix, and an Irish passport. The wallet belongs to Dill Reem. The passport is 1990; has his photo, but the name's Darragh O'Brien."

One sees a lot of fake Irish passports—they were the go-to choice for President Reagan's Iran-Contra perps and several other lower-profile misadventures. Dill's worldly possessions stuffed in his chest? Must mean something to the perp; would be swell if someone would call and tell us what.

The tech points at Cissy Noonan. "Jimmie said the female is Loef Brummel's *fiancée*?"

"Allegedly." Shoulder pat. "And you pronounce Loef's name Lāfe. Today would be a good day to piss him off a little less."

I glance at Maureen who seems to be processing that, and not particularly well, then pat the air with my palm, hoping she'll let me explain, yet again, that Loef Brummel and I were childhood neighbors; we're not "friends" as she describes us when she's suggesting my "neighborhood loyalties" are radioactive.

The tech squints at the sun. "If we're not done by dark, you better get reinforcements. Loef's not known for restraint."

"Probably a good idea."

"Jesus, Den. Who'd *dump* Loef Brummel's *fiancée* on a *parade day*? People gonna die wholesale down here. Not sure Jimmie and I and Walter—officers of color—should be here much longer." She winces at the slaughter. "With that. On parade day. In Canaryville."

"Sergeant Daniels is on the job he's paid to be on. You have a gun. And my permission to use it."

The odor around me sours toward stench, heated by the unseasonably warm afternoon. Jimmie hasn't weighed in yet, but the death scene *does* look like a three-way that went mental-patient. That's what I wanna hear—make Loef the perp. Two weeks ago, a sniper round missed Loef by an inch. Although assassination is an occupational hazard in Loef's line of work, it would piss a guy off, especially so if the perp was your top guy with a takeover on his mind. While he's having a backdoor romance with your fiancée. Who might have her own aspirations. Watch *The Postman Always Rings Twice* with Lana Turner, pretty much the textbook for three-way betrayal.

The sniper didn't kill Loef, so my Homicide crew and I didn't work the case.

But I am working this one. And the concept of a *nonracial* three-way that went mental-patient—any version, with Loef in it or not—would keep the motive hard-on related or Irish-gangster related. And that would produce *several hundred less dead people* than a connection to the Red Summer–PNDH graffiti.

I refocus on Dill.

We've had Dill in handcuffs six times, once for *allegedly* killing horses at Sportsman's and five other times for the murders of five US citizens, all five of whom were serious gangsters, men involved in drugs, money laundering, and guns.

But when serious gangsters kill each other they don't get this twisted. Being a gangster is about money. There's too much emotion here for this to be money, too much pageantry. It's either three-way that went mental-patient or it's Red Summer Black versus white. The passport requires that we have a look at Darragh O'Brien and his history, if the name's real. All of that history at least starts out white and Irish, and I'm thrilled to put my top ID guy (a girl) on it.

My phone rings. I answer.

James B. Loef, a.k.a. Loef Brummel, says, "Is it Cissy?"

We call this "the moment," a genuinely shitty part of this job. "Yeah, Loef, it is. I'm sorry."

Silence, just his breathing, then: "Don't move her, Den. Be there in fifteen minutes."

Most murderers don't want to return to the scene if Jimmie and I are there to watch their reaction. "Come to the tape, west side of the viaduct."

Silence. "How'd my girl die?"

"High caliber; once in the heart. Powder burns on her sweater."

"And she's not alone."

"No . . . she's not."

Loef Brummel clicks off.

I look at the ME bent over the soupy pieces of Dill Reem. The ME glances sideways at Jimmie recording his impressions—the nuance only a very, very few detectives can see in the violence—then up at me pocketing my phone on our hoped-for primary suspect.

The ME is inspecting the dents and damage, the animal ferocity of the beating before and after the butchering. He glances at the blood and bone splatter that should be above Dill on the backside of the viaduct wall but isn't, then at Cissy, then up at Jimmie drawing diagrams in his notebook. The ME is putting the puzzle together, the how and the when of it. And the inescapable conclusion that what he's looking at doesn't add up.

Jimmie folds his notebook and says, "Taking a minute." He nods toward our car.

The ME and I stare at the best detective in Chicago. I'm hoping Jimmie will say something funny.

Instead, Jimmie says, "Maybe Loef Brummel could do both . . . clean-kill his fiancée, then slaughter his top lieutenant . . . if he caught them in flagrante delicto and lost it. *Maybe.* But that confrontation would've been in a bedroom, not out here in the weeds. And when it was over, Loef would have no reason to dump them *here. On a parade day.*"

Jimmie nods to himself.

"This location, on parade day, is a message for an audience, and so is the Irish passport. But whoever sent those messages is having trouble staying inside the lines."

Jimmie pivots, chins at the fresh RED SUMMER Black-versus-white graffiti. "And if that someone isn't Loef crazed inside a three-way betrayal to take over his Irish rackets, then we've got something seriously wrong in Canaryville."

I nod. "And that'd be saying something." Then I turn toward Maureen to—

She's gone.

Chapter 2

STEVEN

I am God; hear me roar.

No, *God* is too almighty, too much responsibility. Who wants the headaches? The faithful always at your door asking for a handout?

The last of my watery Old Style goes down easily. Not because my mouth is dry, or my hands are unsteady. I'm a professional, privately trained, battlefield proven; ambivalence is my bible. Scorched body parts are merely wet squiggles on history's pages, a day's work for the civil servants to bag and sift, and the insurance men to value.

The empty glass hesitates at my mouth; a bit of veil between my intentions and the loud working-class tavern that surrounds me. To its plaster-and-wood walls, the Bayside Inn is chaotic with conversations and jukebox music, the hoo-ha of young and old quaffing away their afternoon, ever loyal to the opiate of the great proletariat.

Here in Canaryville, Karl Marx's simmering underclass of industrial workers are known to their detractors as *hillbilly* and *white trash*. I've seen the droopy eyes and rounded heads of Appalachian incest— these are not they. I see rural Ireland, the Catholic church, cruel winters, and rocks in the soil.

These are the sturdies who didn't die in the Great Irish Famine, or the steerage and slavery of the exodus to America. The same thick skin yellowed by tobacco and alcohol; clothespin wrinkles in their hand-me-down shirts, scars on their knuckles, and no doubt, straight razors in some socks and pistols in some belts. Their hard but convivial faces dance in a crowded portrait of interwoven emotion, of movement, of neighborhood saga—a Renoir of tavern life.

First, I erase their grand, seminal social identifications—the unfurled flags of the Chicago Bears, Chicago White Sox, and the Republic of Ireland. The latter, a hysterical construction of three color bars—the green for Catholics, orange for Protestants, and white for the "peace" between the two . . . that both congregations have labored judiciously to ensure never happens.

Then I erase the faces. And with them, the first communions, weddings, and mortgages; the spousal abuse, unemptied ashtrays, and flies comfortable on the window screens.

Only *blanks* with haircuts remain.

Atop the younger, sturdier blanks, the shopping-mall haircuts range from hooligan bristlers to cutesy mops. To several of these sturdy blanks, I assign aspirations beyond this neighborhood. With luck, a life sentence in rolled-up sleeves, pocket protector, and cheap tie.

The older, less-sturdy blanks favor practical haircuts—baldies and bobs—haircuts that require no $14 sessions at Ama Abella's Beauty Shop around the corner. I make these blanks the grandparents. Their aspirations were regular work in the garment factories, slaughterhouses, and freight yards; a union that could protect a fair wage; and a heated one-family apartment. Chicago's fabric of broad backs and fated outcomes.

Crowded together in the immigrant pathology, their array of torsos and legs and tilted shoulders speak the body language of belonging, appeal, and camaraderie. *The boat to somewhere.* An artistic composition that would require more scale than color to articulate. Acrylic on canvas, an unframed eight foot by twenty foot would do it. Not a mural, though; murals lend themselves to the hyperbole of *illustration*; background to some larger story, not *the* story. Scale, intensity—that's what's required—Pollock or de Kooning, Rothko or Golub, with a drug-fueled epigraph scribbled from Burroughs or Kerouac. *The* story in eight by twenty.

Critically speaking, not a painter's career-defining centerpiece, but an important work.

I allow the Bayside Inn a final opportunity to fill in detail—it won a close decision over Keef's 5x5 Pump to be today's star—but the Bayside adds little, busy with its own quotidian ebb and flow. The beer glass rotates in my hand. Does the Catholic God feel sorry for these parishioners, these parents and children, friends and lovers? Their proletarian dreams about to end?

Blink. How would I know?

Because, Steven, you *are* God, at least for this congregation; you deconstructed them, ended their lives. A memorable thought would be appropriate.

Really? For meaty pieces? Moving soup?

No, Steven. Inappropriate, little children with harelips talk like that.

Fine, then. *Children shouldn't be allowed in taverns.* And . . . the waitress is pretty. Waitresses should be pretty. And, I no longer have a harelip, thank you.

The jukebox segues from the Dubliners to the Pogues. A ruffian at the bar stares at me again; his shirt has a hangman's noose with **PNDH** across it. I'm a stranger in his local, eating a pub meal, reading the Chicago *Herald*. He's wondering, Is that man here to meet someone? Who? Why?

The answer has everything to do with his shirt's gallows embellishment. His shirt threatens a race war, and although my participation lacks any interest in the final score, I *am* here to help; here to incite the whites to attack their Black neighbors twelve blocks away, then incentivize the Blacks to retaliate, and "burn Canaryville to its foundations."

To the unenlightened, this may sound complicated, but in my world, this is freshman-year tradecraft and game theory. Sufficiently simple enough sleight of hand that even midget-mongoloid Charles Manson understood the concept.

The more complete answer regarding *my* participation is the politics of money.

My jobs are about money. I get paid, the client gets . . . more money than I cost him, or in this case, her. Lads with no pedigree work love, hate, betrayal, even religion—abortion clinics, incorrect God choices, and such. I have a pedigree, so I only work money.

This client believes her objectives are political. *Whatever.* Simply stated, all things political eventually translate into "have versus have-not," and that translates into money. I have sufficient understanding of her motives to be comfortably cautious. And I have a man in her camp who made the introduction, a fellow traveler from private-contractor world in Iraq. And I'm not God, I'm a sociopath. Scary Little Stevie Sociopath when I was young. Now that I'm grown, Mr. Steven L. Sociopath.

Sociopath is how I was labeled after my parents died. *Sociopath* is my genre bin in the record store, the name tag above my pocket in the cosmic butcher-shop scheme of things. The clinical truth is *psycho-path* probably fits better, but that's for the PhDs to masturbate over.

Lacking the Christian-values gene has always been a cosmetic challenge. Then and now, the absence requires constant vigilance when in public (the ruffian watching me). When I was younger, I wasn't up to the task. Mom and Dad saw me for what I am but were a bit late on the decision to institutionalize me. My honest responses and non-responses were viewed as cruel, rather than the more accurate indifference. For me, murder and mayhem isn't fun or entertainment, it's a job. I don't like or dislike the endeavor; probably how you feel about your job. If being an accountant paid better, or a railroad engineer or a hairdresser, that's what I'd be doing.

A few feet away, a young woman reaches soft hands across her table and smiles at her significant other. Beautiful teeth. The medical examiner will identify her by her dental work; the man toying with her cheap engagement ring will likely be ID'd by his oversized wristwatch. Their pieces will smell like burnt offal.

"Wouldya have another?"

Blink. I smile up at the young waitress, her face round and cherubic and happy to be my conduit to the Bayside's craic. "Please. Just have to step out to my car. Could you watch my computer?"

She winks and pats my shoulder when I stand. "Not to worry. Everyone in here's family."

***

I tug my surgical gloves tighter, start my Wisconsin rental car, flip open the cell phone, punch in the number, and pull into sparse eastbound traffic on Forty-Third Street. Money and pluck are about to kill a rather large number of friends and neighbors. Next of kin will rocket through emotions I don't have.

I look in my rearview mirror, punch send, and count: "One, one-thousand. Two, one-thou—"

Eleven pounds of C-4 shatter the windows into Forty-Third Street and blow the pitched roof off the walls. Ten pounds of wood screws shred the friends and neighbors. Thermite-propelled flames engulf the Bayside Inn before burning pieces of roof begin landing in the intersection. A blood-mist Bahamas-sunrise glows the street orange.

I continue eastbound at the speed limit. The smoke cloud engulfs the glow behind me. Three blocks east I catch the light at Wallace. No cops; no hero neighbors in my rearview mirror; I'm clean. Just stop at the self-serve carwash between here and Chinatown, change the plates back to Wisconsin so they match the stickers and paperwork, and yo-ho-ho, we've covered the nut for this summer. Two more Chicago jobs that will cover all of next year's nut, then we're off to Berlin for Oktoberfest and my first Nina Hagen concert.

I'll paint big in Berlin. I can feel it; eight by twenty will be a postcard. *Hello*, one-man show at the MoMA and Tate. Sotheby's and Christie's begging for canvas . . . happy to sell a few, have your people call my people.

My phone beeps as the stoplight goes green. I press the gas pedal and—

Flashing lights and a siren scream into the intersection. I jam the brake; a blue-and-white cop car skids around my front bumper, then races west toward the smoke and flames.

Ho! That was close. I ease forward, check Wallace to not get T-boned by another mindless cop, then press on toward the Norfolk Southern tracks and Wentworth where I'll turn north—

Roadblock; ahead of me on Forty-Third Street—police cars, lots of 'em, marked and unmarked. Yellow tape at the train tracks' viaduct. TV news vans . . .

Uniformed cops charge at me.

Then sprint past toward my burning rubble. Another cop approaches my car. He's pumping his arm, pointing me to take Canal Street south . . . back into Canaryville.

Behind him, talking at the viaduct's yellow tape, are two plainclothes cops I absolutely don't want to encounter here. I roll forward. The uniform pumping his arm bends to my window, one hand on his pistol.

I stare at the yellow tape. "What happened?"

"Where'd you just come from?"

"Back there." I thumb over my shoulder.

"Where?"

"Wallace. By Ama's beauty shop, my girlfriend. Dropped her off."

He stares. Doesn't check the Wisconsin sticker that won't match the stolen Illinois plates. His collar radio speaks to his ear. He straightens to look west at the Bayside Inn's smoke and fire filling the sky, then me.

At that moment, the urbane Black giant behind the viaduct's yellow tape turns to stare, right at me; I mean, right into my brain. I know all about Jimmie "the Gent" Daniels; feel him all the way to my spinal cord.

I stutter, then make a smile for the cop at my window, as in: *What?* Forgetting I should care that two blocks back from where I just said I dropped my girlfriend, a tavern full of friends and neighbors just disintegrated. He draws his pistol, steps back, and says: "Out of the car, please. Hands where I can see them."

My foot mashes the gas. I spin the wheel, duck below the seatback, and blast down Canal Street. No gunshot explodes the back window. I sit up, slam the brakes at the first intersection, wheel west, and mash the gas again. A ball rolls into the street. I veer; a boy darts out. I crush him on the bumper—"Shit!"—and mash the gas. At Wallace, I brake hard to miss a cop car screaming north, turn left after he's past, and head south.

Slow down. Get. Out. Of. The. Car. All the cops can trace is the fake name who rented it.

Yeah, but if the cops get lucky and find DNA, it'll be mine—if they take it that far—and they will know that you ran down the kiddo. So what, this car mashed a kid; doesn't mean the car belonged to the Bayside bombing. Could be a local drunk—No, he wouldn't have rented a car. A lost tourist, then. He'd been drinking, took the wrong exit off the expressway, panicked, then did a hit-and-run, and—

Fire engines charge at me on Wallace. I pull into the first alley, park under a white **PNDH** and noose spray-painted on the wall, leave the keys, and walk west, then south toward Forty-Seventh and a cab or a bus or a carjack if it comes to that.

I did my homework on Detectives Banahan and Daniels before I accepted work in their jurisdiction; always good to know who'll hunt you. The coincidence of them being within blocks of me when I'm at work is bad luck in the extreme . . .

My stride extends.

If it *is* a coincidence.

Chapter 3

DENNY

Lights flash through air that stings my eyes and nose. I cough hard behind my hand. Fire trucks vibrate the pavement, dancing the storefront glass that carpets the sidewalks. Heavy nylon-filament hoses snake past me through slosh and debris toward a smoking void that thirty minutes ago was the Bayside Inn. Three rescue teams pick through charred rubble for survivors we all know they won't find.

Partials of the Bayside's walls still stand. I wipe at my eyes. Radios squawk. A charred foot is removed from the rubble. No telling how many were in the Bayside—are in the Bayside—old people, kids . . .

"Denny." Jimmie taps my hip, then points at my cell phone. "Ringing."

I rewipe both eyes and pull my BlackBerry. "Banahan."

My secretary says, "Den, the superintendent and Deputy Superintendent Mahoney are en route from the downtown parade."

"Better get our new boss down here, too."

Silence, then: "Commander Hanlin was in the Bayside."

I glance the rubble. Hanlin was a prick, but he had a wife and kids. The smoke cracks my voice. "Ten four. The mayor coming?"

"His deputy and press secretary."

"Tell 'em it's messy." EMS begins unloading body bags from three vehicles. "On the high side."

"Ten four. I'm sorry, Den . . ."

My secretary's sorry because I'll have gone to school or worked the Stock Yards with half the surnames buried in the Bayside rubble. Two or three I'll have had a beer with in the last month; heard about their son or daughter, mom or dad.

I answer, "Thanks," then bite my jaw tight and stare at the sky. I stay in the sky for a two-count and the silent mantra that builds the wall between what you're looking at and a reaction you can't have. I drop from sky to Forty-Third Street's roofline. Then down to the familiar storefronts, their glass windows blown out from the concussion. Then to the yellow tape cordoning the intersection. Yellow tape is the final stage of denial on the bad ones; you—the person—is no longer present.

A fireman squeezes between me and a ladder truck, hand to his mouth, and he bumps me off balance. I stumble but don't lose the phone. He takes four fast steps, then pukes at the cab end of the truck. He spits, sucks fouled air, wipes at his mouth, and nods an apology. Puking or not, he and his bosses own the scene until CFD releases it. When they do, the Bayside Inn, and at least thirty or forty murders, will belong to the police.

This many noncombatants dead in one event will be the most any Chicago policeman has faced in my four decades of street murder. Old people, kids, whole families . . . Why murder whole families of blue-collar people barely scraping by? For what? Chicago isn't Jihad-world or Belfast; we don't do shit like this.

I cough bile, spit it, and glance down Forty-Third to the Norfolk Southern tracks, visualize the two bodies I just left on the Canaryville side of the viaduct. Then cut back to the Bayside, then to Loef Brummel at the tape. Loef Brummel's people—murdered at the east and west borders of Canaryville, maybe an hour or two apart.

Both crime scenes have Loef Brummel in them, but career gangsters in Chicago don't do this kinda shit to their neighborhoods and expect to go to work tomorrow.

The wind shifts into my face, thick with melted clapboard siding and scorched asphalt shingles and the sharp char of meat at a backyard barbeque where the Old Style got the better of the cooks. I stare at the fireman, then my phone screen and the name of the lost call: "Superintendent Jesse Smith." My ultimate boss. Jesse Smith has a strong stomach he'll need.

Three FBI suits approach the perimeter through the Ninth District uniforms. The suit I know, Special Agent Robert Stone, locks eyes with me, then bends under the tape. The ranking fire chief yells for him to get the fuck back on the civilian side.

Behind Agent Stone, a young Irish woman runs up Forty-Third Street with a shrieking baby hugged to her chest. The woman's feet slow as she nears Agent Stone. Her eyes go wide. She stops, then points at the Bayside. The scream is agony, loud and long.

To my right, a charred hand and oversized wristwatch wash along a fire hose toward the storm drain. I bend to grab evidence but the hand slips through my fingers into the drain. Further up the fire hose, ten feet from the tape, the new priest from St. Gabriel's drops to his knees, hands slowly rising to his face. Three hardhats run up behind him—construction workers with tool belts and framing hammers slapping at their thighs. They stop short, stunned horror in their faces. All three will have guns at home. Four beers from now they won't care about penalties or mortal sins, just the *who* and the *where*. Like almost everyone in Canaryville, they already believe with absolute certainty they know the *why*.

Red Summer: Move out or burn out.

Three more women cry out in the smoke. Jimmie weaves toward me through the firemen, notebook in his left hand, right hand wiping his cheek. Behind him, our detectives are bent over, photographing blackened heads and body parts before the paramedics place them in the bags.

Jimmie stops at my shoulder, eyes me carefully, and squeezes my arm. "We okay, Den?" Jimmie knows I have people inside, knows how my ma and da died . . . burned to death twelve blocks from here.

I nod at the rubble. "Commander Hanlin was in there."

Jimmie cuts to the Bayside, then back to me, *No shit?* in his face.

I nod again, then chin at Mayor McQuinn's chief of staff shaking hands with Agent Stone and the other FBI suits. Once a Fed, always a Fed.

Jimmie computes the political and chain-of-command possibilities. "Don't let Smith hand you this. Leave it to the Feds. Sixteen days, Den, and you're hauling hay for thoroughbreds in Darien."

The good news is, the first thing the mayor's ex-FBI chief of staff will mention to Superintendent Smith is that ex-commander Banahan is almost certain to face a grand jury, then a federal trial for the two civil rights–related *wrongful deaths* of Antoine and Odetta Starks at the Magikist building, and has far too much personal baggage and far too little media sensitivity for a case of this magnitude and timing.

While my ultimate boss is processing what he already knows about my shortcomings, continuing legal drama, and family history, the mayor's chief of staff will add that Lieutenant Banahan is only *tolerated* in the Riviera. His very presence under current conditions exacerbates the potential of a violent white response.

The mayor's chief of staff will support this with two inditements: (a) after I accepted Officer Matty Rzepecki's offer and became the police, I moved to Sixty-Ninth Street and became an Italian. Treason, yes, but there is the one worse sin. It would be: (b) twenty years later, I, *Lieutenant* Banahan, and the youngest of the beguiling Gilmartin sisters, then rookie patrol officer Gael Gilmartin, called off our engagement. A year later, I married a Black woman, the also-beguiling and brilliant Renatta McCray.

Do hard-ons make you stupid?

I shouldn't be the control group. I started out stupid . . .

The trick to being twelve in 1960s Canaryville is trying not to show off all the cool stuff you know. Not a biggie, unless your older brother is officially a "teenager." Luckily, my brother, Mike, is not an asshole. We're a team, "financial titans" the *Tribune* would report, if a *Tribune* reporter ever got lost and stumbled into the Riv. Probably wouldn't wanna do that, though, unless he had close pals in Canaryville or Bridgeport. Maybe if he knew the right guys at the Stock Yards, that might work, as long as he stayed across Halsted Street in Packingtown and out of the taverns, and didn't talk to anybody's sister.

As the financial titans of the Irish Riviera, the Banahan brothers don't have time to blab. When we're not in school getting the shit beat out of us by the Dominican nuns at Visitation CS, Mike and me are in the pop-bottle business. Two cents apiece, bagged and delivered to Koonce's candy store.

Prime pop-bottle time is shift change at the Stock Yards. The big bonus at shift change is the shrieks of animals on the killing floors sorta stop. Makes it lots easier to fake that the fear and dying doesn't bother you. No bonus on the odor, though. The Riv's "perfume" is unmistakable—blood, "burned cheese," and warm shit—sorta like the steel mills down in Gary but different, and our sky's not orange, and the Riv's odor only quits when the wind's out of the south or when your ma burns your hand-me-downs on purpose so Da has to fork over clothes money. Second-best pop-bottle harvest is sunrise till eight a.m., then three till dark, all day Saturday, and every Sunday after high mass at Visitation and St. Gabriel's if Ma and Da's fight ends without our ma crying. Like the animals crying, you have to pretend that Ma and Da's fights don't bother you either.

Mike spies an opening in the traffic and bolts across Halsted Street. I'm right behind—horns blare—I stop on the centerline, dodging between two cow trucks.

A driver shouts: "Outta the fuckin' road, ya ragbag scrounger."

I give him the finger. The truck misses me by six inches. More horns blare, like this isn't my neighborhood. Father Galwane slows his black Rambler going the other way and points me to the curb. "Outta the damn street, Dennis. And I'll see ya in Confession today for that finger."

"Yes, Father. Sorry." I dart in front of the third cow truck in the convoy, then jump the curb and bump shoulders with Mike on the curb in front of Koonce's.

Mike says, "You wanna fight a truck driver?"

"I could take him."

Mike shakes his head. "Da's right; Ma must've found you inside a cow."

I grab Mike's bottle bag and walk into Koonce's. The string bells rattle on the door. Mr. Koonce is, like, two hundred years old. He's behind his short counter, wearing his patched apron, giant hearing aid, and a grin full of false teeth. "Well, Dennis. And how's the business this mornin'?"

"It's grand, Mr. Koonce, and yours, sir?"

"Been no more trouble." He nods to the tape holding his window together. "Thank you. How's the eye?"

My left eye is black, blue, and yellow, swollen to a slit. "Couldn't be better." I stand our nineteen Pepsi bottles on the counter two at a time.

"And the hands?"

My knuckles are blotchy, like Ma's when she scrubs. "Hurt, kinda. Italian heads are hard."

"That they are, Dennis. Remember that. Stay out of Armour Square for a week or so, in case those older boys are mad."

"Yes, sir. If they'll stay outta here."

Mr. Koonce hands me thirty-eight cents. His candy store may not look like the First National Bank, but it's the only "bank" in the Riv—if you don't count Bathhouse John's loan sharks—and one of the two cornerstones of the Bana-Plan. Today's first thirty-eight cents will fill yet another paper roll of pennies. Fifty pennies to a roll, two rolls and you have a one-dollar bill. That dollar bill goes in our shoebox vault. The shoebox hides in our ten-by-twelve room in the Bana-Flat, one of six apartments off our entrance in the Byrne's Building, "a piss-stained, roach-farm 'outpost'" as it's called by the grownups, at Fifty-Fifth and Halsted, the far-far south end of the Riv.

Penny roll—dollar bill—vault. Simple as that, *if* you're a financial titan. I grab Mike away from the candy rack: *"Route 66."*

Mike looks at the white-wrapped Mars Bar the same way he looks at Pattie Maloney, but doesn't succumb. He uses both hands to make like Tod Stiles steering his corvette on TV's *Route 66*. "Bana-Plan. Tod and Buz."

I make fists like Buz Murdock, Tod's trusty sidekick. *"Route 66. Bana-Fam.* To California."

We do the Bana-Plan's one-nod-lock that carves our plan in stone. Pop bottles are gonna buy our family a Chevrolet happy ship—*See the USA in your Chevrolet,* just like Dinah Shore sings on TV. Ours will take us 2,448 miles to the City of Angels—96,384 bottles. That's 4,016 cases. In sunny California, Ma never cries, Da only drinks on weekends, no animals die, and the drunks from McDonald's Tavern don't piss on our mail in the foyer.

Mike steers us out Koonce's door and back to work. Mike gets to steer because he might could see over a Chevrolet's steering wheel. I'm happy to be Buz. Buz has the same "bad attitude" the nuns say I have. I could be Zorro, too, like on TV, but Ma and Da probably wouldn't want to ride horses all the way to California.

Coming our way is little Cullen Mahoney, two years older than Mike, half-size, and positive he'll be a police detective when we all grow up.

Little Cull says, "What's the noise, boys?"

"Bana-Plan."

Headshake. "Is that all you guys do?"

Mike shrugs and chins at the Superman comic Cullen always has in his front pocket. I scan for bottles. Mike says, "Goin' to the tracks. Come if ya want."

"Goin' to the store for my gran. Watch out on the tracks, coppers caught some hobos this morning. 'Bos tried to get one of the Gilmartin girls into the bushes."

Mike and I both nod. "Gotta watch the 'bos."

"Beat 'em baaaaaaaad," says Cull. "Matty Rzepecki threw one off the Forty-Seventh Street viaduct."

Matty Rzepecki is a Frankenstein, a giant, disfigured Polack copper who is equal parts scary and nice. *God* does not mess with Matty Rzepecki.

Cullen points at my eye. "Who this time?"

"Wops from Armour Square. Were robbin' at Koonce's."

Cullen makes prison bars with his hands. "Denny Banahan: Reform school at Charleytown. Probably Joliet, life without parole."

I say, "Cullen Mahoney: chief of police, gets me off."

We slap hands. Cullen starts walking west, stops, then points: "Watch out for the 'bos."

Mike and I climb inside the Norfolk and Western yard at Forty-Seventh Street for the day's next circuit. There's 'bos in the far bushes, but they're lying way low.

Mike says, "You watch, I'll grab." Mike and I harvest all the way to Fifty-Fifth Street, first time we've made it all the way in three weeks. God bless Matty Rzepecki.

By sundown, we make it back to the Byrne's Building. Da's three-sheets like usual. Ma's in the kitchen and not crying.

Before we help with dinner, Mike and I plant ourselves in our room with today's massive nine-roll haul. Above our beds is the Bana-Plan altar, a promo map CBS TV sent us for joining Tod and Buz's fan club. Every Friday night when *Route 66* comes on we take the map down into Da's living room and follow Tod and Buz like we're all with them.

In the map's lower right corner is a smiling family in their Chevrolet. Man, are they happy, just like we're gonna be once we're coated in California sunshine. Everything will be A-okay, you'll see. We already have the brochure for the brand-new Biscayne we're gonna buy.

A door slams across the hall.

You can tell it's the Farrells' door because the Byrne's Building's walls aren't thick enough to snuff a tea kettle whistling in the morning. Mr. Farrell is drunk (duh?). The yelling starts. Then the punching. One of them bounces off our wall. I duck; so does Mike. Mrs. Farrell starts her swearing and screaming, "I kill ya, ya fookin' bastard!"

Da's voice yells back from his living room: "Shut yer yammy, goddammit!"

Mike points me to a spot on the map, already almost to Oklahoma. "Today puts us at 18,350 bottles, total. Be in Tulsa by winter. Cassiopeia, Arizona, the winter after that."

"Yeah!" We slap hands. I stack the penny rolls under the spot. "Add today's haul, we got $367.00 of the $1,967.28."

"Piece-a-cake; 78,034 to go."

Before I pull out our shoebox vault, savings book, and Biscayne brochure, I tell Mike: "Banahans don't quit."

Mike answers, "Ever."

I dig out our vault, pop the lid, carefully remove the brochure, then the savings book—The vault's empty. Our $362.50 is gone.

Mike flies off his bed, grabs the empty box. "No-no-no. No."

I drop the lid, pat the closet floor, look under my shoes that used to be Mike's. So does Mike. He's frantic; checks under his bed, then mine. "Where, Den? Where'd you put it?"

"Right here. Where I always put it."

Mike jumps back into the closet with me, swats winter jackets and rain boots out of the way. He stops sudden, straightens on his knees, says, "Super. Ma said the super was here today."

Herman Mertz is the super, collects the rent, too. Loud, pie-faced Nazi who hates everybody in the building, mostly 'cause we're Irish.

Mike says, "Mertz knows the Bana-Plan; the bottles. Always telling us we're never going to California—"

"Mertz . . . he—" I can't breathe. "Mertz stole the money." Tears gush down my cheeks. Mike and I stare, frozen—

I don't wipe the tears. I push up off my knees, tell Mike: "Grab the bat; we'll go to Germantown. Catch him before he spends it all."

Mike looks at me like I'm four feet tall and twelve years old, which I am, then grabs the bat.

***

Herman Mertz is pissing in the alley alongside the Bavaria Haus restaurant, one frying-pan hand on the brick wall. He's twice our size, drunk, but not so drunk he doesn't recognize me, Mike, and Cullen Mahoney.

Mertz zips his pants, eyeing the bat in Mike's hand. "So, you boys come for the ass whippin' your piss-drunk old man don't give you often enough."

I say, "Three hundred sixty-two dollars."

Mertz smiles. "Tough guy, huh." He grabs his sack. "Come over here, little boy, and give this a kiss. I'll give you your money."

"Yeah, you will." I grab the bat from Mike, take three steps, and swing for the Nazi's balls.

***

Evangelical Hospital is at Fifty-Third and Morgan. The nurse says, "How old were the boys who beat you?"

My jaw's wired shut, so I can't answer. Mike and Cullen shrug, then wince at the pain from Mertz's boots. Mike says, "Can we go?"

"No. The police want to talk to you. They'll be here soon. Then we'll call your parents to come get you."

The nurse leaves. Mike tells me and Cullen, "Don't say nothing. Mertz promised to 'put your shit in the street' if we talk. We'll be living with the 'bos."

Cullen says, "That's stupid. We gotta talk. The police will arrest Mertz and get your money back—"

Mike says, "Ma ain't living in the street. C'mon." Mike grabs Cullen. "We'll make up a story—Wops or Ragen Colts chased us and we fell off the viaduct."

Every day for the next seven, we make a new plan to get the Bana-Fam money back.

We go zero for ten, and consider trying out for the North Side's epic-loser Cubs.

My jaw heals crooked; hurts all the time. I turn thirteen. School's out for the summer.

But even for financial titans on the rebuild, life isn't all work and emergency room visits. When the day refuses to yield more Coke and Pepsi bottles, the Riv has plenty of playgrounds. You can play chicken with the hundred-car slaughterhouse trains, then dodge the railroad cops who'll handcuff you to a pole for hours if they catch you, or beat you flat if they're in a hurry.

Another great spot is the stoplight in front of the Byrne's Building. When the convoys of semis rolling in from Kansas and Iowa stop, we jump on the wooden sides, ride up Halsted eye to eye through the slats with the baying cows, talking to 'em, trying to make 'em feel better for a couple of blocks.

If somehow we can't make Walt Disney out of all that, we walk Thirty-First Street, yelling at the Italians from our side of the street to chase us, then on the way home we can stick-fight with the younger Ragen Colts or the Orange Order Paddies trying to move in from Northern Ireland.

Being an eighth grader now, I know the Riv isn't Heaven, but until the Banahans pack up the new Chevrolet, the Riv is *ours*. And the super-enormo-bonus is, the Riv hasn't stopped growing pop bottles.

Today's a major pop-bottle day with the firemen on Union Avenue, but you gotta get there before anybody else.

We got two bags full, and are now standing out front of Keef's 5x5 Pump, a fireman's bar around the corner on Fifty-Fifth, a block from the Byrne's Building.

A westbound '58 Chevy four-door slow-rolls me—

Huh? No way. Negroes? A car full, eyeballing the 5x5 like they want to fight? Like Negroes can be where they are and not die?

In the back seat window, the brown face eyeing me has an arm hanging out underneath; the arm has a hand; the hand has a pistol pressed against the blue-painted door in broad daylight.

White fingers grab my shoulder and jerk me backward behind a fireman's work shirt and pants. Keef "Cold Deck" Gilmartin barks: "Get in the bar."

I don't move; Mr. Gilmartin stares bullets at the Chevy. It goes west, flips a U through the red light at Halsted, and heads back at us on the other side of the grass median. Gilmartin shoves me and my bottle bags halfway to his bar's front door. "Get inside, goddammit. Tell 'em to call the cops!"

I stumble the last few feet and into the 5x5's door. Mr. Gilmartin stands on the sidewalk, fists clenched, all alone, daring the car to shoot him. I drop the bottles, run back, and stand next to him. The Chevy keeps rolling. Mr. Gilmartin looks down his muscled shoulder and arm to me. He stares, then nods. "Go inside, get Loef Brummel, bring him out here. If you're gonna toe the line, Dennis, best you know what's on the other side of her."

That was the last afternoon I remember that didn't have *nigger* in it somewhere.

Chapter 4

Amid the smoke, slosh, and debris, a mob of cameras and microphones crowd the mayor's chief of staff. Behind him, forming the carefully planned background for his on-camera statement, are the chief of staff's three assistants, then Agent Stone and Stone's two suits.

Agent Stone will be called forward to make an epically moronic "reassuring" comment regarding tomorrow's FBI takeover of the Chicago Police Department—how the partnership between the FBI and the mayor will cleanse the police department of "systemic corruption" and save the city from racial immolation.

I don't like the FBI, with or without their grand jury. But the FBI is not moronic when it comes to politics, and I'm surprised they're represented here, now, no matter what the mayor is offering.

Stone receives a cell call, listens, then quickly pulls his men out of the shot. They reestablish to the side, their backs to the cameras.

I elbow Jimmie and nod toward the FBI exit.

Jimmie looks, reads Agent Stone's phone at his ear and Stone's added distance from the cameras. "Stone's bosses in Washington just did the math."

I nod. "No federal takeover of CPD tomorrow."

Why? No one in Canaryville will talk to Feds, about anything, ever, and the FBI knows it. The Bayside bombing would be a Fed career-ender— a front-page federal takeover of the first police department since Key

West in 1984, followed immediately by the Feds' colossal failure to solve a mass murder in a working-class white neighborhood with a volcanic temper, already pushed to its control limits.

More stunned neighbors arrive at the yellow tape.

And *not* solving the Bayside murders isn't an option. Somewhere between the first neighborhood-child's wake at McInerney's and the first mom-and-dad burial at Holy Sepulchre, the Feds, the city, and the mayor will face a square-mile Canaryville neighborhood of hard men and women who intend for someone, likely *lots of* someones, to die. Very few, if any, will be white.

"Denny." Jimmie's no longer next to me and waves me to him behind a fire truck. Standing at his substantial shoulder is CPD's top boss—my partner when we came out of the academy—Superintendent Jesse Smith, a 4XL Hohokam Indian with bad skin, lots of friends, and no fear. Next to him is sixty-four-year-old Deputy Superintendent Cullen Mahoney, our Chinaman—CPD-speak for a big-holster boss—exactly what Cullen Mahoney always said he would be and the guy you want to see on the street when you're in the shit.

Jimmie waits for me to join them all, then reads from his notes, beginning with the nine-year-old hit-and-run victim DOA at Mercy, then Loef Brummel's fiancée and top lieutenant executed at the Norfolk Southern tracks.

Cullen Mahoney glances at me.

Jimmie says, "Dill Reem, white male," then describes Dill hacked to pieces next to Loef's fiancée. Jimmie falters, starts again, but has to stop.

Superintendent Smith squints at Jimmie, a fellow giant he's known on the job for twenty years, says: "What?"

Jimmie winces at his small, tooled-leather notebook, held now with both huge hands. "Something . . . really wrong there." Jimmie inhales and tells his notebook: "My first impression at the tracks was *ritual* and loud. Dill's perp wanted to go ritual—tell us something—but got caught up and lost it."

"And?"

"Don't know. It's . . . confused, somehow. An act of . . . I don't know, of . . ."

"*What*, for chrissake?" says Smith.

Jimmie shakes his head. "Don't know. Denny felt it, too. Then I locked eyes with the probable hit-and-run perp thirty seconds after the Bayside blew. Denny and I ran here and haven't had time to talk."

"You saw the hit-and-run perp?"

"The Bayside blew. Thirty seconds later Patrol stopped an eastbound Chevrolet Cavalier at Canal, told the driver to exit the vehicle. The driver wheeled, then a car like his killed the nine-year-old on Forty-Fourth. We have the car—stolen plates, a rental. Should know from where, shortly."

Superintendent Smith squints. "You're saying the *probable* hit-and-run driver also did the double at the tracks? And maybe the Bayside? The guy is, *what* . . . driving the borders of Canaryville *killing* people . . ."

"Possible. Cissy and the Bayside bomb were both professional. The hit-and-run could be him, too—heat-of-the-crime collateral damage. But Dill's way out there, nothing about that slaughter says 'professional.' The patrolman who stopped the Cavalier is talking to our artist now. I'll do my sketch; they'll combine 'em or we'll circulate both."

Smith cuts to me. "The double at the tracks?"

I shrug. "Doesn't add up to one perp doing both Cissy and Dill, nor does it say career gangsters as perps—doesn't mean it isn't, but kinda hard to ignore that the double is showy, on a parade day. That's all I can tell you. Then . . . this . . . the Bayside happened. On a parade day."

Superintendent Smith doesn't look at the fire engines or the Bayside or the FBI watching me/us. He leans closer, fisheyeing me and my history, just like Jimmie did. "You okay?"

I nod small, smaller than intended.

A voice at the yellow tape screams obscenities at the mayor's chief of staff. Superintendent Smith stays in my face, then checks Jimmie concentrating on his notebook, trying to sneak through the heebie-jeebies. Superintendent Smith asks me: "Loef Brummel still own the Bayside?"

"He does."

Smith looks past me to the Norfolk Southern tracks. "Any evidence *of any kind* that Blacks are involved? The tracks, the Bayside, the hit-and-run?"

"Fresh Red Summer–PNDH graffiti under the viaduct on the Canaryville side near the bodies. If we include that, then 'showy on a parade day' could be construed as 'racial.'"

Smith barks: "By you?"

"Are there Blacks crazy enough to want a race war? Yeah. Could they pull off the Bayside and the double? Maybe. Dill was a serious gangster. Maybe they lure him in with a drug deal, or somehow Cissy does—could happen. But how's a Black guy plant the bomb in the Bayside? Where's he find the highly skilled white guy who can do it? Could be military, guys who were together in Iraq or Afghanistan."

Smith listens, erases every possibility that burns the city to the ground. "Then, at this point, other than Jimmie's *problems*, you'd say all three murder scenes are organized-crime related . . . Irish, Italian. But, being that today is a 'parade day,' you would not rule out politics . . . of some kind."

"I'd say that if you want me to." I point at Jimmie. "Hard to shake Jimmie Daniels. Organized crime or politics isn't going to do that."

The superintendent frowns, moves himself, Mahoney, and me out of the FBI's view and anyone else's hearing, then curls his fingers at me for more answer.

I add, "Between *us*, I'd say Jimmie's 'problems' represent a serious non sequitur if we want all three murder scenes under one organized-crime umbrella. Or any other umbrella for that matter. I've never seen a double murder that looked like that, and I've been looking thirty years."

Cullen Mahoney injects, "Could be a tag team—two men, maybe a man and a woman, pro and a head case—feeding off each other. Tag teams are almost universally white."

Smith looks at me to agree.

"You want me to believe your tag team—bright-and-shiny white people—could kidnap and murder a Canaryville mob assassin, hack him into roadkill, stuff his valuables in his chest, bag him, kidnap the female before or after, bring 'em both to the neighborhood, unbag the slaughtered body at the edge of plain sight, bring the woman out, execute her, change clothes, drive to the Bayside, blow it up, run over the nine-year-old, and vanish?" Headshake. "Sorry. I'm willing to see 'Loef Brummel' stamped at the east and west borders of his neighborhood, but I'm missing the combined message." I nod at the Bayside. "I sure as hell don't understand *that* message—sent the day of downtown's St. Patrick's parade—*unless* it's Black, and political."

The superintendent steps right at me. "Are you up to this, Denny? The politics? It doesn't sound like it."

I turn to Mahoney, then back to Smith. "*Me?* Are *you* okay? I got sixteen days. I'll help, but shit, this has to have star-power fronting it, not street and a federal grand jury for 'wrongful death.'" I squint at a boss who doesn't need me to tell him the politics of anything.

Smith and Mahoney glance each other, then at Jimmie . . . and linger.

"No. No fucking way." I jab my finger. "Don't even think about it. A Black man cannot front this and survive, not even Jimmie Daniels."

Both men focus on me.

Mahoney says, "Turn this assignment down."

"I just did."

Smith waves Jimmie over. I turn fast and point at Jimmie to stay where he is, then turn back to Smith. "You can't. Jimmie worked twenty years for my job, but when I was promoted you gave me Hanlin as my lieutenant instead. And when the *Herald* and the FBI decided I was the Antichrist for a disco-era cold case, you made Hanlin my boss. Jimmie's a goddamn *artist*; don't feed him to these fucking cannibals."

Smith waves for Jimmie.

I turn to Mahoney. "Please. Don't let him do it. You can't. Appoint one of the deputy supers, the chief of detectives, hell, the head of the parking authority—I'll help 'em. Anybody you name, I'll help."

Smith glares Mahoney silent. "It's you, Den, or it's Jimmie. We have the potential for a *very* bad situation to accelerate beyond our ability to contain it. I need you to behave *and* solve the Bayside. You fit the 'solve' half of that equation better than anyone we have. You know the territory and despite your . . . history . . . and possibly because of it, I would be derelict in my sworn duty if I didn't appoint you."

Mahoney frowns hard but doesn't contradict his boss.

I do. "Shit, why not *hang* Jimmie from a light pole? Your boy Hanlin's dead. In sixteen days you gotta give Jimmie my desk—*like you said you would before* the *Herald* hung me around his neck. Now you can shove him under the lights, he lasts the whole fucking night, you install yourself a new Hanlin." I close the distance between me and Smith. "Twenty fucking years Jimmie gave you; number six on the exam—"

Mahoney pushes his arm between us. "Temper, Dennis."

Superintendent Smith doesn't blink; he's fucked, just like whoever takes this case. Smith says, "My way, Denny—the goddamn *smart* way—or I cut you loose and promote Jimmie right now. We'll attend his funeral together."

And Smith would, the fucking savage. His job is to defend the city, accept the casualties.

I show Superintendent Smith my palms in surrender, but agree to nothing. Cullen Mahoney lowers the hand he has between Smith and me. I start to speak, but Mahoney gives me the look: Lesson one in the Cullen Mahoney rule book—when the threat is serious and the choices are bad, and you're on the wrong end of both, shut the fuck up, say nothing, and wait.

Superintendent Smith flexes at the tension in his thick neck, then straightens his collar and tie for his on-cameras. Without looking anyone in the eye, he says, "Keep this white, west of the Norfolk Southern tracks and north of Fifty-Fifth. At least past the morning news cycle," and walks away.

Jimmie stops the superintendent, re-straightens the superintendent's crooked collar, then the tie, then says: "Might want to give the National Guard a heads-up. The acting governor was a little late on the call last time."

***

Off camera, more body parts are pulled from the Bayside.

On camera, Superintendent Smith completes his statements in front of a tight-shot, brick-wall background. He answers shouted questions, then makes room for the mayor's press secretary to enter, exits the throng, steps inside the yellow tape next to the mayor's chief of staff. Their conversation is shielded by the chief of staff's city hall suits. It ends heated with both men pointing at me standing with Mahoney and Jimmie.

Deputy Super Cullen Mahoney scans our old neighborhood, the horror-shock in faces he's known all his life. "Hell to pay, Dennis. Be an amazing effort to stop the train that's coming."

Smoke and soot settle on his white hair and simple uniform.

"I know your temper and your love for our city, but I advise you again, step back from this, allow someone deserving their time on the cross."

My mentor, my Chinaman, a small man of quiet authority who, both times the Feds tried to bury me, risked his ass to save mine, and who may have to do it again.

I say, "It ain't Jimmie's turn on the cross."

Superintendent Smith returns to us, points to Jimmie just out of earshot, turns his broad back to the crowd and crime scene, and tells me: "It's yours."

"No. Give it to—"

"You have the blood in both camps—Black and white—and you'll do what the situation requires. No grand jury will impanel until the city stabilizes, and by then, your success may render you less attractive as a defendant."

Smith pauses so I digest the serious redemptive value that he sees, that may, or may not, be there, but absolutely could be.

"Pull whatever shit you have to, Denny, but in the weeds you're on your own. Clear?"

My eyes roll. "Yes, sir. Ten four."

"Out in the open, play it tight, by the book, and silent. Lieutenant Gilmartin at News Affairs, *not you*, will speak for the department."

Nod.

"I want a report—back-channel; you to Deputy Superintendent Mahoney—every hour."

Another nod.

The superintendent chins at the Bayside. "The federal takeover of CPD will stand down for an indeterminate period—a day or two, a week, possibly longer—but they're still coming, make no mistake. Find our perp while we still have a city to defend." Smith turns and says "Jimmie" as he reaches for Jimmie's shoulder.

Jimmie turns to us and Smith pulls him into our circle. "Sixteen days, Jimmie . . . you're the lieutenant if I'm still running CPD. As for him"—Smith nods down at me—"Red Summer and the Bayside may be Banahan's hammer on the grand jury. Save the city from self-destruction and our citizens are unlikely to indict a hero—Banahan goes to Darien with his broken horses, we all go to the Breeders' Cup instead of visiting him dead broke in Marion. Don't let him fuck the future up . . . for everyone."

Jimmie winces small and exhales. "Can I file overtime for that? Assuming I survive?"

My phone rings. I ignore it.

Smith turns to me. "I just bet my career on you, asshole." He pokes me hard in the chest. "And for the record, I promoted Hanlin to keep Jimmie out of the goddamn 'Banahan fire,' not the job." Smith waits in my face. "Your history's gonna boil up out of every open wound you touch. Friends and enemies—blue, white, Black, federal—the bastards are already taking numbers. This is your chance to put you and your Maureen at the right end of the next twenty years. Remember that."

Smith squeezes Jimmie's shoulder, but cuts me the glance we did as patrolmen before deciding to chase a gunman into the sixteen-story Robert Taylor Homes. "I'm doing what I'm paid to do, Denny; you do the same."

Smith leaves. Cullen Mahoney watches him go.

Mahoney turns to me; his eyes harden. "Don't just save Jimmie Daniels and the superintendent. May be noble, Dennis, but it's not smart." Mahoney finger-taps my shirt pocket. "Defeat *your* enemies first, *then* discuss everyone else's. Call me in an hour."

Mahoney walks to the yellow tape.

The Bayside Inn is now mine.

I huddle with Jimmie and eight stunned detectives and begin to direct Homicide traffic.

Beyond us at the yellow tape, the mayor's press secretary retreats from his on-camera. Shouts and microphones assault him but he's not coming back.

The microphones and shouts pivot to assault Lt. Gael Gilmartin as she steps up. They want answers about the medical examiner, Bomb and Arson, and the crime lab doing their forensics behind her.

Jimmie and I deploy our eight guys in two-man teams. Team One gets the double at the Norfolk Southern tracks. Team Two gets the hit-and-run. Teams Three and Four get the worst of it. They will can-vass the neighborhood, interviewing anyone who saw, or thought they saw, something. Worse still, on a crime scene of this magnitude, *every-one* you interview has a connection to a victim or several victims. The reactions will range from catatonic stares to spit-mouth *Kill the fuckin' niggers* rage.

Just as I finish with Team Four, a Ragen Colt standing nine feet from Lieutenant Gilmartin's media conference rips off a green T-shirt with a white hangman's noose, whips the shirt over his head, and screams: "Lynch 'em! PNDH! PNDH! PNDH!"

Officer Johnson confronts him. The Colt jumps into Walter's face, chants: "Lynch this nigger! Lynch this—" Walter grabs him and they go to the pavement. Two officers bolt past me. I crash into a deputy district fire chief in my way. The officers pry Officer Johnson and the white banger apart.

The deputy fire chief regains his balance, shouts: "Goddammit, Banahan!" and blocks my path. The uniforms cuff the banger. Two baton strikes and they drag him semiconscious toward a beat car. The deputy fire chief chest-bumps me and fans his arm. "Get these Black cops outta here."

Eight Ragen Colts rush to block the beat car's exit. Twelve uni-forms charge into the green shirts. The deputy fire chief stays between me and the fight. "Pull the Blacks off the scene. *Now.*"

I step left. So does he, then jams his arm over my shoulder at the four hundred faces lining the tape. "You're from here, or were. You know what Canaryville's thinking. Show some goddamn initiative to go with the balls your brother had."

At the beat car, the uniforms swing batons. Five of the eight Colts are on the ground. The other three are bent over cars by four of my detectives. The fire chief points at Jimmie. "Get him out, all of 'em. No goddamn reason to rub the families' faces in it."

I quit focusing on the fight and lean into the deputy fire chief's face. "I'm the police. Not the fire department. We don't apologize for dressing better than the population."

He inhales to bark more orders.

"Don't you have a basement to save?"

"Do your fuckin' job, Banahan, before—"

"I am." I shove him backward. He falls. I duck under the tape toward the fight. Two of the cameras with Lieutenant Gilmartin are pointed at the deputy fire chief and me, the others have twisted ninety degrees to record the arrests.

Gael watches with the cameras as all eight bangers are handcuffed. A brief crack shows in her game face, eyes dropping to the pavement, lost somewhere in the Canaryville of her youth that never changes and the long, painful night to come.

She recovers, points at the next reporter, listens, then answers. "It's not productive to *assume* anything. You don't know that this is related to Red Summer and neither do I. And you're goddamn right I'm upset. Chicago's my city—"

She winces at her profanity, girds, then points for the next question.

I start toward her, no idea what I'll say that could improve anything. A hand grabs my arm. The deputy fire chief jerks me sideways. Jimmie knocks his hand off my arm and steps big between us, facing me. "Be cool. Lotta cameras." Jimmie shows me his phone. "The hit-and-run was rented at the Milwaukee airport."

I take a breath, nod. "Rental counter video?"

Jimmie says, "No."

"Get someone up there."

"Already rolling." Jimmie looks at Gael engulfed in reporters.

Gael grew up around the corner working in her mom's beauty shop. Gael's movie-star looks, MBA, and high-profile career were her story an hour ago. Now, Lieutenant Gilmartin is a Canaryville girl who knows every name in the body bags. Any one of whom could be her sisters, mother, or father.

Beyond her, standing at the tape of an IMAX crime scene, is Loef Brummel, lights flashing across his face. Loef *is* the Irish Riviera, the raw-knuckle, stiff-back Canaryville-Irish of it that refuses to change, buckle, or move: five foot eight, wide shoulders, 175 pounds, facial scars from teenage acne and his father's bottle of Bushmills, good teeth but chipped, summer Donegal cap dipped on the left eye that Mike and I saw two Italians close with a bat in the summer of '63, then slow down long enough to regret it forever . . .

Summer of '63 . . .

Loef has me, Mike, and Cullen lined up on top of the water tower next to the fire station at Fiftieth and Union; high up as I've ever stood. Directly in front of us to the east is the Norfolk and Western Railway's vast Forty-Seventh Street maintenance yard.

In the fifteen-year-old weight class, Loef Brummel is the toughest kid who ever lived. Someday he'll run the Ragen Colts, the Riv's century-old "athletic club and benevolent association." The coppers call the Colts "gladiator school for white boys" and only occasionally mention the IRA flag in one of the windows.

Loef begins with, "From now on you live and die on: 'We got ours; they got theirs.' At school they're teachin' ya about *territorial imperatives*, yeah?" Loef points east at the railyard, then points ninety degrees north toward the river, then turns and points due west behind us, then south, then back facing the railyard. *"Everything* this side of those tracks is ours, *yours*, and from now on you act like it." He spreads his arms. "The Riv runs from the river on the north to Fifty-Fifth on the south; from Racine on the west to the railyard in front of you." He focuses us on the tracks. "Those tracks are the Riviera's 'beach.' Beyond the tracks east is the 'sea.'

"The beach is *yours*. Got it?"

We all nod.

"*Their* side of the beach is the sea. The sea is theirs. You don't give a fuck about the sea. Got it?"

Past our beach, the first four blocks of the "sea" are a mishmash of Armour Square, Comiskey Park (where the White Sox play) and its parking lots, and a thin strip of no-man's-land rubble I've heard the cops call Fuller Park. Those first four blocks of the sea are nothing much to worry about—Italians and Sox fans—we sneak in and out of there all the time, especially when the Sox are playing.

Loef points just beyond Comiskey Park to the brand-new sixteen-lane Dan Ryan Expressway. On the other side, built like a fortress, are two-and-a-half *miles* of sixteen-story concrete towers, one after the other. Loef says, "Stateway Gardens and the Robert Taylor Homes. Largest housing project in America. Forty thousand in there, maybe sixty dependin' on how many squatters they count. Highest crime rate in the goddamn country. You don't go there, ever." He stares at each one of us. "And they don't come here. Ever. Not a goddamn step into the Riv. Understand?"

"Jesus." Cullen points, "I heard coppers say—"

"Understand?" Loef shoves Cullen off his feet.

"Yeah. Jesus. Sorry."

I help Cullen up, keep him behind me, and look sideways at Loef.

Loef tells me, "Save that tough-guy shit for the nigger gangs." Loef points again. "Mile and a half between *us* and *them*. Over there, in stinkin'-shithole town, they got somethin' new. 'Super Gangs.' Not gangs like ours with twenty, thirty guys. Over there, they got *thousands*. And guns, too. You seen that in front of the 5x5." Loef pokes me in the chest. "Guns or not, this is *ours*. Got it? Every day, every night, all the time. We ever see one of you back down, we dump you over there." Loef points to the projects. "When they're done fucking your white coward ass, they eat you."

Chapter 5

Halfway into hour two.

My phone rings. It's the detective chasing the Darragh O'Brien passport. She tells the phone between Jimmie and me: "A Darragh O'Brien is thought to be one of the 1998 Omagh bombers in Northern Ireland—"

Jimmie and I register *bombers*. Red Summer as our perp now has a legit competitor.

"—Omagh was a five-hundred-pound car bomb planted by the IRA; 29 killed, 220 injured. No way you carry that passport if it's yours, or put your own picture on it if it's fake."

Makes sense. "Run Dill Reem from birth. Tell the ME to run his teeth. Get Dill's pieces in first, ahead of the Bayside casualties, or it'll be weeks."

"Ten four, Den."

Jimmie says, "If the passport's a fake, then the killer left it on purpose. Why leave a fake that points to an IRA bombing?"

"Don't know. Kinda has to be fake, doesn't it? If Dill was Darragh O'Brien, Dill's prints would've come back wrong and we'd have known years ago. So, why leave a fake . . . unless *leaving the fake* is the story? Reagan and Bush One used fake Irish passports for Iran-Contra. Used some bad actors like Dill to further the Feds' 'American way.'"

Jimmie walks through that Rubik's Cube. "Dill's a gangster, we know that for sure. No Western government could afford to own him as their operator. Maybe Darragh O'Brien just murdered Dill and Cissy; passport fell out during the thrash."

Neither of us put much stock in that. I say, "Something will come back; we'll roll from there."

A uniform sergeant from Nine frowns and lowers his radio. "Half the downtown parade's coming west to wake the Bayside. Gridlock will slow 'em down, but they're coming. Will be some serious assholes in that bunch. They'll only see the Bayside one way, one color."

I nod. Eight hundred locals now line the Bayside's tape—double from an hour ago—their faces a measure of grim I've seen before, but never in this volume. Breaking-news feeds, Twitter, and amateur video on YouTube will double the eight hundred within the hour. Only local cars in the gridlock are being allowed in, all other vehicles are being forced east, west, or north to "not impede rescue efforts."

The eight hundred locals at the tape know *rescue* doesn't apply. Some have brought chairs and blankets from home. Neighbors cluster together in small family units, cradling each other's heads or holding hands. The wailing has died down to just the new arrivals—the friends and relatives who didn't want to believe. Twice in the last hour an ambulance siren has bounced echoes off the buildings, parting the crowd for the EMTs to gurney out two grandfathers and a grandmother who succumbed to the vigil. For now, all the ambulances can do is get them to triage or medical emergency helicopters. Or add them to the victim list.

4:00 p.m.

Hour three. The crowd is eighteen hundred. Many of the new arrivals have progressed through shock and disbelief to whiskey. It'll be dark in an hour. Dark is jet fuel for street mobs. I call Cullen Mahoney back-channel and tell him, "Nothing new; just a white guy in a rental car who *probably is* the hit-and-run and who *might* have rented the car." Then I tell him what I'm looking at, the vibe and temperature, finishing with: "I'm calling the Ayatollah—"

"No. We're not; you're not."

"If the Bayside was Black against white, we better know now, not later. And *way* before Canaryville knows."

Mahoney and I argue about martyrdom and its limited value, my temper, history, and other failings. He tells me to put Jimmie on.

They discuss me and the Ayatollah as peace partners.

Jimmie buttons off and hands me my phone. "Mahoney said okay, but I make the call."

"Because?"

Jimmie glances at the firemen and reporters. "The deputy superintendent feels that due to the sensitive political nature of the requested action, it would be best to have another Black man make the initial contact."

"Not because I'm *me*."

"The Deputy may have mentioned your affinity for 'ball-bat diplomacy' when you feel your counterpart is guilty."

Frown. Some shit follows you forever . . .

As the 1960s heat up, I follow Mike and Cullen into high school at Tilden. Pepsi introduces nonreturnable bottles and the brothers Banahan have to modify the Bana-Plan to California.

Mike and me lie about being under sixteen and go to work weekends and nights under the union rules as "casual labor." It takes two of us to wrestle the quarter-sides of beef onto the trucks at the Stock Yards, so we only get paid as one guy. Plus we have to give our union rep a quarter of what we earn.

On the docks and in the trucks there's angry talk about the IRA fighting the Protestants in Ireland, but the really awful talk is about the "civil rights movement" that's going on in Alabama and Mississippi. And now coming up north.

Mike and I try to stay clear of the truly horrible stuff the older guys are threatening; we just wrestle beef all night, run home, shower off the blood, and get to school before our first class.

Every shift, the talk gets worse. Standing at the punch clock, I hear our union rep telling five men in bloody aprons, fathers of kids we go to school with, "There ain't no goddamn choice if you care about your kids havin' a roof. Meatpackers are gonna ship niggers from down there up here as scabs; break the union, same as they did back in the 1920s. Our answer's same as last time—light poles and rope—same Red Summer for them and the Jew owners who brung 'em."

At 12:25 p.m. the next day, I'm in the lunchroom at school, trying to convince a movie-star Gilmartin sister that I should be her date to this Friday night's dance. That I can clear it with her da.

"Da will have none of it, Dennis, even if I would. Which I won't."

"I'm a good dancer." Grin. "We both know you want to go." My fingers tap on her polished nails. "Say yes; I'll go by the fire station."

"You'd never return."

"So, if I don't die, you'll let me take you?"

Hint of Gilmartin, heartbreaker smile. "I suppose it's . . . possible."

The clock hits 12:30 p.m. Instead of the class bell, the PA announces that our president, John F. Kennedy, has been assassinated in Dallas.

For two days and nights, the entire Riv wakes America's first Irish Catholic president. Canaryville's porches and doors are a forest of funeral wreaths. IRA flags hang from four streetlights. Men under them say it was the Protestants who killed our president. The streets echo with wails and grief. On the third day, Washington, DC, buries our president after a funeral mass and parade.

That night, Mike and me get the call to go back to work in the Yards. At two a.m., fire engines start racing around, a bad sound in a clapboard neighborhood. We can't see the smoke 'cause it's nighttime, but the sirens are coming from the south.

At three a.m. the foreman pulls my shoulder, yells Mike out of the truck. "You boys get home. Them fire sirens was the Byrne's Building."

Me and Mike sprint Halsted.

Panting, we bust through the crowd still wearing our blood-soaked aprons, jump the hoses, and run into the smoldering—

Mr. Gilmartin and another fireman bear-hug us both out of the smoke, back through the fire hoses to their truck.

Gilmartin crushes my arms and chest. "Quit fightin' me, goddammit."

"Where's Ma?! And Da!"

Mike gets partway loose. The firemen pin us both with big bodies and huge hands. The Farrells are next to us, shell shocked, wrapped in blankets. Father Galwane shoulders in, helps Mr. Gilmartin hug me and Mike to the truck.

I rip out, run the crowd, shout: "Ma! Where are you? Da!"

The neighborhood faces are grim. Hands try to pat or grab me.

Mr. Gilmartin chases me down, grabs me off the ground and tight to him again, tells my ear: "They didn't get out, Den. They're gone; both of 'em."

***

Starting at sunrise, me and Mike sift the ashes. What's left of Ma and Da are an unburned piece of our Route 66 map, a scorched hem of Ma's curtains, part of our Biscayne brochure, and our baseball bat.

I hear Mrs. Farrell say it was Da's cigarette that lit the fire, and that "the piss-drunk bastard damn near killed my children with him."

So far, Cullen Mahoney's parents have kept child services from grabbing Mike and me to an orphanage. St. Gabriel's is gonna get us, and that's no better. I'm kinda numb, like trying to grab hold in the dark.

***

Ma and Da's funeral is today. Mike and me sit in the front pew at Visitation wearing borrowed suits that don't fit, holding borrowed rosaries we don't say, while Father Galwane says mass over the two gray caskets bought with money from a three-day funeral jar at the 5x5. A wreath from St. Gabriel's is up there, too.

The hearse from McInerney's leads four cars out to Holy Sepulchre cemetery.

There's nine neighbors, mostly women, standing the final service with Mike and me. The caskets, the ground, and the sky are all frigid November gray. Mike lays one of the singed pieces of our Route 66 map on Ma's coffin. Ma and Da are lowered in their holes. And then it's over.

Inside the rectory at Visitation more neighbors come by to tell us how sorry they are, what good people Ma and Da were, and that everything will be okay.

I nod, say "Thanks" when I can, then pull Mike to the bathroom and hug him.

He says, "What?"

"Get Cullen to fill in for me at the Yards."

"Why?"

"'Cause I may not be back right away."

Completely confused, Mike watches me sneak out the side door. I weave through the school buildings onto Wallace, then hop a CTA bus north. I'm the only thirteen-year-old on the bus with a baseball bat.

For three hours I hide in the cold between the parked cars across from the Bavaria Haus. Herman Mertz finally stumbles out. This time I don't ask him for our $362. Herman Mertz doesn't quite duck the first swing of my bat. He blocks with his wrists, up high to guard his head, but I hear the snap. I pound his knees. He screams, drops to the street. I pound his arms guarding his head, his ribs, and knees, and keep pounding until my bat breaks and a crowd pulls me off.

Mertz goes from the street to Grant Hospital, touch and go in ICU they said for two days. I go to the lockup in the Eighth District where the coppers keep me separate from the freight-'bos and killers, then to juvenile court, then the State Home for Delinquent Boys at St. Charles, just like Cullen Mahoney said I would.

My third day in, Patrolman Matty Rzepecki and his wrestler pal from the South Side, Golden Moose Cholak, come to see me. They say I did the right thing; say that the Mahoneys are looking after Mike, and that I can look them up when I get out.

The day-to-day damage of reform school isn't too bad—two broken hands and one stab wound—but the classroom education is pretty much "see Spot run." I get along okay with the ganged-up Black guys who don't want to punk me, not so well with the ones who do. To get through the worst nights without crying into my bunk pillow, I imagine Herman Mertz in his wheelchair, his house on fire, and nowhere to go. It only works some of the time.

SEVENTY-NINTH STREET

Chapter 6

Immediately south of the Irish Riviera, Chicago is Black, poor, and just as violent. Southbound through Englewood is the only direction that isn't gridlock.

Hard-eyed bangers track us from the sidewalks and street corners. The residents we're sworn to serve and protect peer from their windows. The porches are empty. Halsted from Fifty-Fifth to Fifty-Ninth belongs to the Almighty Black P Stone Nation. And it's thick with young Black gunmen showing the flag, looking to light up whitey if he's coming south thinking drive-by reprisal for the Bayside.

From Fifty-Ninth to Sixty-Third, Gangster Disciples are making the same show. Eight blocks of hair-trigger outlaws better armed than we are. There isn't one "civilian" on the street.

Jimmie stares into the rearview. "Got a car."

I twist and look over the seat at a black Ford a half block back. "Agent Stone on the job."

Jimmie stays in the mirror. "Man's too hungry. Shorties down here don't know from the G. Stone's budget and supercomputers won't matter after some ten-year-old shoots him for his shiny new car."

I nod. "Smith puts me out front on the Bayside sixteen days before I retire? Stone can't figure that."

Jimmie nods. "You *agreeing* to be out front is the only part Stone can't figure. Stone's a career Fed. He knows the mayor wants you out front. Mayor's betting you'll 'do a Denny'—the South Side goes Red Summer, Feds have to come in, National Guard at a minimum, mayor dodges responsibility for a race war he didn't know how to stop in the first place."

"How many of those dime-novel westerns you read a day?"

"Just don't do a Denny. That's all I'm saying."

We catch the light at Seventy-Ninth.

Jimmie stops the car and the Dr. Phil conversation. This is the ghetto. Time to pay attention. Home to Hall of Famer Alderman Leslie Constantine Gibbons, the man we've come thirty-six blocks to see.

For most of the 1960s, Leslie Gibbons marched with Martin Luther King Jr., stood with King against the dogs and the bullwhips from Selma to Montgomery, in Birmingham and Marquette Park. And was in the parking lot of the Lorraine Motel when Dr. King was murdered on the balcony. Twenty months later, Leslie Gibbons was shot with Fred Hampton in Hampton's apartment on West Monroe near Black Panther Party headquarters. Hampton died; Gibbons survived to do seven years at Joliet for his role as the political officer of the Illinois Black Panther Party. A major résumé.

Leslie Gibbons is a *long* way from my favorite person, but had I been born Black, I would've been a Panther, 100 percent. And I like to think I would've had the stones to stand where he did.

In the South Side's bars and factories, from Hegewisch to the Riviera, whites refer to Alderman Gibbons as "the Ayatollah" and routinely threaten his life. Gibbons doesn't take the threats lightly, having survived five serious attempts in the last twenty years, three of them by white men, one of them a retired firefighter who blamed Gibbons and ex-Panthers for the Maurice Warehouse fire-explosion that killed three firemen from the Canaryville station and eighteen others.

Jimmie turns east onto Seventy-Ninth Street. The more desperate spandex have been on the stroll since lunch, but sparse here compared to the Soul Street parade and the crack-pipe rangerettes of Sixty-Third Street. They know something bad happened up past Fifty-Fifth, but a girl's gotta earn.

The Ayatollah's office is just east of Halsted, within spitting distance of Louis Farrakhan's towering pole-mounted Nation of Islam sign. Gibbons coexists with Farrakhan, the Gangster Disciples, Jeff

Fort's Almighty Black P Stone Nation, CPD right around the corner, and some of the worst poverty in America. With the demise of the old First Ward, Gibbons is the city's most powerful alderman. Five years ago, he was one poorly aimed bullet away from being our new mayor.

Four Black gentlemen in black suits stand in front of the Ayatollah's office.

Jimmie brakes to stop. The Ayatollah's men lock on us. I flatten my badge midwindow. Jimmie double-parks, calls the Sixth District for a squad backup should things get ugly, then checks the roofs on the south side of the street for defensive shooters we both know are up there but can't see.

The Sixth District squad arrives, loops Agent Stone's FBI car, and stops at Jimmie's back bumper. I exit. Two of the black suits stare at my hands; the other two watch Jimmie exit the driver's side. Us being the police doesn't mean our intentions are honorable. Fred Hampton's wife has never stopped saying that the FBI's COINTELPRO operation and the Chicago Police Department executed her husband on the Black Panther raid *after* the gun battle ended.

For those unfamiliar with the sainted FBI's COINTELPRO operation, the Church Committee who finally investigated them called it: "a sophisticated vigilante operation . . . the techniques used would be intolerable in a democratic society."

Go figure, that episode never made it onto ABC's I-love-the-FBI TV show.

I cross the curb in front of the Ayatollah's office. One of the black suits steps forward. The other three flank him. I lead with my badge. "I'm the police. I'm investigating a homicide and I'd like to speak with the alderman. We called; he knows we're coming."

Intense brown eyes. Silence.

"I understand your job description, and your employer's concern for his personal safety. Unfortunately, that doesn't trump the law of the land. *Me*, I'm the law of the land; I have a serious problem and Alderman Gibbons can help."

Intense brown eyes. No fear. Commitment.

"Okay. How about, I don't care how many cameras or rifles you have on the roof behind me. Step inside and ask your boss to come out, or step *a*-side and I'll tell him myself. For the record, gentlemen, that is no longer a request."

The man in front does neither. He raises a phone to his ear and speaks.

We wait. A crowd gathers behind us.

Jimmie turns, hand on his .45. The uniforms exit their squad, hands on their weapons, speaking to their collars for reinforcements.

The heavy front door opens inward. Alderman Leslie Gibbons steps out. He's my height, dressed better, and calm, seriously out of sync with the tension. He eyes the uniformed officers, then Jimmie's broad back. Gibbons spreads two of his black suits, steps through, and offers me his hand. "Well, well, Commander; back in the ghetto."

I let "Commander" pass and shake the alderman's hand. "Home is where the heart is."

"Has yours finally found a place for us?"

"Right next to my picture of Saint Patrick." I nod thirty-six blocks behind me. "We have thirty-eight dead in the Bayside, forty-one total for the neighborhood, and sundown coming."

Alderman Gibbons processes the body count, then waits for me to tell him why I'm here.

"I need to know if anyone less white than me is fucking with the Riviera. And if so, I need their name and address."

"Because it can't be your Irish brethren killing each other over their various criminal enterprises?"

"I want it to be, but without proof, Canaryville's prepping for war. Saving white people from stupid isn't your job, but saving Black people is."

Two TAC cars screech-stop behind me. Four white men in jeans and body armor jump out. Seventy-Ninth Street morphs into a Baghdad checkpoint.

Alderman Gibbons frowns at the firepower. "*Stupid* is not the issue and never has been. The white men who run this city have a vision. That vision has a balance sheet. On the liability side, they intend fewer and fewer low-income Black citizens, fewer and fewer public services for those citizens, and fewer public servants in support."

"City hall shares that stuff with you, not me. I'm here to stop a war that doesn't have to happen."

"So, you're here to indict the policemen who watched our honor students Bernard and Latoya Osborne burn to death in their car. Or you're here to admit who murdered Antoine Starks and his twin sister, Odetta?"

I give Alderman Gibbons my professional *blank*.

"*No?* Then I'm confused, Lieutenant."

I half turn and point north just past Jimmie's back. "We had eighteen hundred at the tape in Canaryville when I left. There'll be five thousand when I get back. Maybe ten thousand. It'll be dark. They know who they want to blame."

"So, you're here to scare us into submission? Again?"

"I'm not here to suck your dick, if that's what you're asking, like Don Imus did Al Sharpton. I'm here to stop forty-one funerals from becoming a thousand."

"And how would a defrocked CPD commander propose to do that? Call in the FBI?" Gibbons nods to my FBI tail car.

"It won't be twelve hours at a conference table talking bullshit reparations with the victim nation. For a Red Summer that was ninety years ago."

"No, a reasonable conversation would be too noble of you, too cerebral. It wouldn't match your illustrious record. How many citizen complaints was it? Over four hundred? In one year?"

"*Maybe* I can help, Alderman." I focus on his eyes. "I'd like you to call your ward heelers, street captains, ministers—whoever—tell them to cut the Red Summer rhetoric and stay out of places they don't belong."

"Places they don't belong . . ."

"You know what I mean."

Jimmie turns halfway to Leslie Gibbons. "Alderman, please. The South Side's about to disintegrate. Denny can help. That's a fact, like it or not."

"Fact? The facts are Fred Hampton. Bernard and Latoya Osborne. Antoine and Odetta Starks—all murdered in this city, denied their civil rights by those sworn to protect them. But why should that matter? They were Black, constituents of *Lieutenant* Banahan's 'victim nation.'"

"So, file another complaint." I poke my badge. "Make sure you mention it was me who stopped the Klan from blowing up your house with your wife and kids in it."

"That's your *job, Lieutenant*. And while I thanked you repeatedly, do your heroics saving my family on that day somehow bring the Starks children back from the Magikist rooftop where they died? *On a St. Patrick's Day?*"

Gibbons steps back and opens his door. A frail woman steps out, Ida Mae Starks, mother of RayLen Starks. Gibbons says, "You remember Mrs. Starks, from the funerals of her brother and sister?"

I nod, soften my posture. "Mrs. Starks."

"Mrs. Starks is why I risk my life for this community. Far too many of our families bury their children."

"That's what they're doing at the Bayside Inn. They don't need caskets; they need buckets."

Alderman Gibbons hugs Mrs. Starks to his hip. "Your brethren in Canaryville require civilization, not buckets, a rung or two rise on the evolutionary ladder."

I nod away from Mrs. Starks toward the Gangster Disciples in his crowd. "And these rabid fucking monkeys are what? Yale grads?"

"*Monkeys?* Did you call my constituents—"

"Some of the crying's already stopped in Canaryville. Someone's already building the bomb for one of your churches and Red Summer rallies, maybe two or three bombs for the same Sunday—like *this* Sunday. Your Yale grads will answer, do a four-gunship drive-by on St. Gabriel's playground." I point east and west on the Ayatollah's Seventy-Ninth Street. "Four hours later there won't be a building from here to Fifty-Fifth that ain't on fire."

Alderman Gibbons stares, intent, expressionless.

"Wake up, for chrissake. '*Suddenly*' the Klan and the American Nazis have the money to run recruitment marches? You were here at last month's Christian Identity rally—Armour Square drew twenty-eight thousand; had to turn people away."

"Meaning the Black man should hide? Abrogate our right to freedom of speech? Accept the City of Chicago's blatant embrace of swastikas and pointed hoods to do its bidding?"

"If your Yale grads give whitey a reason, he'll converge on Chicago by the carload—angry, bucktoothed, camo'd-up motherfuckers without shirtsleeves or jobs, looking for a cause and somebody to blame."

"Freedom has a price; for them, for us." Gibbons yells over me to his crowd: "We have paid our share in blood and bone, on buses, at lunch counters, in fiery churches, and lonely oak trees—forty-three Black men dead in Red Summer! Burned at the stake! Stripped naked and lynched! Two on this very street!" Alderman Gibbons points at Halsted. "And yet here we are, unbowed believers in the United States Constitution, prepared to pay yet again. All over the world *the people* fight and win their freedom. We will win ours."

"Great speech. Your front yard will be ground zero for the race war you and the Reverends and Radio Free Ghetto have been promising for the last year."

"As always, the problems of the poor and the disenfranchised are of their own making."

"Some of 'em sure the fuck are."

Jimmie pulls me back a foot. "Whoa, Denny. C'mon—"

Alderman Gibbons smiles. "You were a racist Neanderthal as a patrolman—gifted with a career by a society that loves its one-dimensional solutions—and you are a racist Neanderthal now, here to scare the *niggers* into accepting Mayor McQuinn's twenty-first-century exodus as an irreversible fact."

"Remember that speech, too, when you punch 911."

Alderman Gibbons booms beyond me to the crowd of fifty: "RED SUMMER!"

The crowd roars back incomprehensible, but loud.

"WILL THE MEATPACKERS UNION LYNCH US? AGAIN!"

"NO!" roars the crowd and bunches toward us.

"WE LIVE HERE! NO EXODUS; NEVER AGAIN!"

The crowd roars, "RED SUMMER! RED SUMMER!"

Alderman Gibbons levels his eyes at me. "The mayor has already called. I told him the Bayside Inn was an act of domestic terrorism and asked that the Department of Homeland Security take charge of the investigation."

I start to argue, explain that the Feds won't be here until after the fires start. "You still go to Trinity? Huff and puff with Barack's guy, Reverend Wright?"

"I will be there tomorrow."

"Wear a vest under your Johnnie Cochran pimp tie."

***

Northbound from the Ayatollah, Jimmie says, "That went well. Maybe call the deputy superintendent, give him a heads-up."

"Tell him that the Ayatollah and me aren't friends? Or that Gibbons is using Ida Mae Starks as a campaign poster so he can be mayor?"

"Think we better warn Mahoney that 'monkeys'—in reference to the Gangster Disciples—and 'wear a vest' could be on the news tonight."

"Did I say that?"

"Someone did. Best I could tell, it wasn't you."

I pull my phone to call Mahoney; it rings before I can finish. One of my detectives says, "Church fire by you in Englewood. Ebenezer Mennonite. Witness ID'd a van, three males—work pants, boots, balaclavas, and gloves."

"White guys?" I crane under the windshield visor and search a dusk sky for the smoke.

"Don't know. Drove up, tossed three cans of gasoline through the church windows, fired two flare guns, and gone. FD found a noose on the walk."

"How bad?"

"Still burning. House next door, too. No casualties. Old folks hadn't arrived for service yet. Scared the few who had into ambulances, but didn't kill any."

At Seventy-Third, flame-light brightens the sky two blocks to the west. A bit of ash drifts across our car. Two CPD beat cars and a CFD cruiser scream toward us, inbound for the fire.

Jimmie brakes hard for three bangers slow-rolling across Halsted at Sixty-Ninth. I look right for the gunship trap, don't see it, and tell Jimmie: "Run 'em over. White or Black, everyone south of the river will be dead soon anyway."

One of the bangers points north. "Canaryville. Irish charcoal. *Burn, baby, burn.*"

At Fifty-Fifth Street, entry into the Riv is barricaded with police units. Between us and the barricade, Fifty-Fifth Street is gridlocked, bumper to bumper, east and west.

Jimmie pops the siren, flashes our dash light, wedges into the intersection to the centerline, but can't get through the westbound lane. In our windshield, on the northeast corner, is the ghost of the Byrne's Building and the Bana-Flat . . . gone long enough now that I rarely still see its ghost . . . all its windows open, my ma's hand-sewn curtains she had to wash twice a month; the Route 66 map above Mike's bed.

Today, I see the fire, then the funerals. Then Mertz unconscious in his alley . . . Then our light blue jumpsuits at the Illinois State Home for Delinquent Boys, the cockroaches, the predators on both sides of the bars. Thirteen-year-old Denny Banahan serves thirty-nine months and three days in and out of St. Charles and its limited-release foster homes . . .

When I get off the CTA bus in Canaryville, I'm seventeen and no longer a minor. I don't feel grown up, but I am. I'm headed to the union hall with the papers Golden Moose Cholak sent me. Midblock, outside the Darling rendering plant, the air is still too foul to breathe. Two older kids I don't know are pissing at the alley, kicking garbage at a mangy barking dog. They're wearing jacket colors of the Ragen Colts and IRA T-shirts underneath.

The big one sees me, says: "And who d'fook are ya, mate?" His accent is foreign, Ireland.

The other one zips his pants, shoves me hard. "Ya owe for walkin' here. Dollar apiece."

The dog hunkers down, keeps barking.

I tell the dog, "Easy, fella." Tell the two Colts: "I live here," and point at the dog. "So does he."

The dog false-charges the biggest Colt. He kicks the dog in the head. The dog flips to its back.

I drop the big Colt with a right hand; wait on the second one to charge, then drop him. Between them, they have enough money to buy the dog a decent meal from Koonce's. I wait while the dog inhales it, eyeing me the whole time. He runs away.

The two Paddies are my first official fistfight as a free adult.

The new steward at the meatpackers union reads me as underage, stupid for wasting his time. "Beat it, kid. Men workin' here."

"Maybe you could read these?" I show him the papers again.

He reads my papers and the sponsors' names on them. Then gives me a union button and a place on graveyard shift hauling sides of beef for Swift. "You start tonight at midnight. Quota's the same for you, no matter who you fuckin' know. Understand?"

"Yes, sir. Thanks."

He eyes me. "You that pop-bottle kid, aren't you?"

Nod.

He leans back. "Thought you died in the fire."

Next stop is the fire department on Union. Keef "Cold Deck" Gilmartin hides a smile, looks me up and down. "You okay, Den?"

"Got a job." I show him my union button.

He nods. "You know I been downstate, too. You gotta let Charleytown go. Put whatever happened there behind ya."

I nod back.

"And the Nazi in Germantown." Gilmartin wags one gnarled finger. "Go after him again, you go to Joliet. You don't wanna go to Joliet."

There is nowhere scarier than Stateville, the prison at Joliet.

Mr. Gilmartin stares, decides I might be able to live within Canaryville's relatively wide code of conduct. "We got you a room at the Wexford Rooms a block from your brother at the Mahoneys'. Nobody staying at the Wex will bother you—and you don't bother them."

I nod.

Mr. Gilmartin offers his hand. "Good to have you back, Den. You and Mike come for Sunday dinner."

Outside, Mike and Cullen rush me. Before I can hide it, I'm crying like the little-boy, pop-bottle kid I used to be.

***

I go to work at midnight—same men; same "territorial imperatives" as before—haul meat for eight hours, then enroll at De La Salle High

School, where kids with "problems" or "records" have to go to get a diploma. I want a diploma; do not want to be a bogtrotter-dumbshit, as the Paddies say.

Unfortunately, De La Salle is not in the Riv; it's on Thirty-Fifth Street on the wrong side of the Dan Ryan. *Their* side. Part of the curriculum is I have to get there and back five days a week without buying a ticket to Joliet.

My second night on the Swift docks, Loef Brummel sits next to me while I'm emptying the lunch pail Mrs. Mahoney gave me. Loef hands me a Belfast crumble muffin from the Wee Tram Bakery. "Welcome back."

"Thanks."

"The two Paddies you dropped yesterday. They're ours. Ragen Colts."

I nod.

"Can't do that, Den. Not how it works."

"Can't let 'em rob me, either."

Loef nods. "Agreed. You all set up?" He chins at my union button that he doesn't have, or need, to be here. Loef's working for loan shark Bathhouse John MacGrath.

"Yeah, I'm set up good. Moose Cholak and Matty Rzepecki."

"Bad motherfuckers, those two. But watch them coppers, Den. Not sure that's the way you wanna go. Gonna get tough here. Nigger gangs ain't playing. Cops can't help ya with 'em till after you're dead."

"And you can?"

Loef shrugs. "Maybe." Loef's nineteen now and, according to Cullen, already a made guy in the Irish mob. "Come by the athletic club. You should be with us. Have a look."

"Nah. Gonna finish high school, see what happens. Try to stay outta Joliet."

Loef nods at 'Joliet.' "That'd be good. Come by anyway, have a look. 'Cause I asked ya." He stands, pats my shoulder, and walks down the dock.

Chapter 7

On April 4, 1968, Dr. King is murdered in Memphis. Within an hour, riots break out all over the country. "Burn, baby, burn" is front page everywhere.

Across the Dan Ryan from the Riv, the super gangs from Stateway Gardens and Robert Taylor mass to jump the Ryan. The cops who live on our side say there's gonna be carloads of 'em, throwing Molotov cocktails.

Canaryville and the Riv on fire is not a hard picture to imagine.

The Riv goes combination Alamo-call-to-arms and Pancake Tuesday. The rest of the city is scared shitless of the super gangs; and if the truth were told, so are we—every tenement, six-flat, and clapboard bungalow in the Riv will go up if the Molotovs land.

By midnight there isn't a man in the Riv who isn't outside with a bat, knife, or gun. Cars wait at every corner to ram any vehicle with Blacks in it. Every fire-engine crew west of the Dan Ryan is at their station, ready to go.

The standoff and the barricades hold till sunrise.

At eight a.m. the first Molotov cocktail lands in the Norfolk and Western Forty-Seventh Street yard. Mayor Daley issues a citywide "shoot to kill" order for all arsonists. The Riv doesn't require the mayor's permission to shoot arsonists. As much as most of us hate being soaked in blood all day, the Union Stock Yards and the meatpackers union are the only reason most of the Riv's families aren't on welfare or living in the freight cars with the 'bos.

For the next thirty days, the Riv is locked down to outsiders. The armed men and barricades are 100 percent illegal and no one stops it.

And it works.

Canaryville doesn't burn.

⁂

Through the spring and into the summer of '68, Keef Gilmartin and his firemen work double shifts. The Riv and the Black super gangs fight bloody skirmishes. Nine die, six Black and three white. The Blacks die in two cars, both rammed, both with Molotov cocktails that burn them to death. The whites die burning a cross they'd planted out front of the Canaan Baptist Church.

That August, Mayor Daley decides Chicago can still hold the 1968 Democratic National Convention—Chicago PD and the Illinois National Guard will keep the peace. The mayor's the mayor, but he's wrong this time. Riots overwhelm the convention, but lucky for the Riv, the violence shifts out of the South Side and into the Loop—Chicago's downtown. For six days and nights, Chicago *is* the national news.

The Riv gets another reprieve, of sorts. The Ragen Colts, facing criminal convictions and prison, get the option of Vietnam, gearing up big-time after the Viet Cong's Tet Offensive. Most of the Colts won't come home. The ones who do will be stone killers. Some of them go to Northern Ireland to fight for the IRA. The others stay in Canaryville to fight for whoever will pay them.

⁂

I turn eighteen, graduate high school top five in my class . . . but then "my class" was predominately kids with "issues."

On our side of the tracks, the Gilmartin sisters remain elusive, but beguiling.

Cullen Mahoney joins CPD just like he said he would.

Mike and I have an apartment, furniture, but no car yet, and a mutt named Tiger we saved from mange and the alleys. We're all on the good road—

Then someone invents "long-haul refrigeration." You wouldn't think refrigerated semitrucks would end an era, but they do. The new technology allows the meatpackers to build slaughterhouses closer to the farms. At midnight on Friday, July 30, 1971, the Union Stock Yards—the heart, stomach, and intestines of the Riv—shuts down, never to reopen. The killing floors had been running continuous since the Civil War.

Me and Mike and ten other guys walk to Keef Gilmartin's 5x5 Pump for the wake. In one night, seven out of ten working men in the Riv are out of a job. None will admit it, but most of 'em are sixty days from some sort of welfare or enlisting for Vietnam.

One beer after sunrise I've imagined a foggy version of me in a marine uniform (the only service who will take guys with a record) and intend to join before lunch. A giant in a patrolman's uniform completely fills the door of the 5x5. He's backlit, glowing at his edges. Matty Rzepecki walks straight to me at the bar and says, "Outside. Leave the beer."

Oookay.

In the sunlight, Matty is even less pretty, and still the most frightening human being I have ever encountered—six foot six, two-ninety, bigger than the biggest guy in the NFL—road-map face from WWII Warsaw, hands like shovels.

Matty flexes his Frankenstein head and shoulders. "How long you been outta Charley?"

I blink at the sunlight, move a step so Matty will block all of it. "Since I was seventeen? But shit, Matty, you know that. You came to my eighteenth birthday and my graduation at De La Salle."

Matty nods. "Ain't nowhere to work now. No reason to be dead marines in the rice paddies. If you wanna be street coppers, not suits like your midget pal Cullen Mahoney, or a lame-ass fireman"—Matty chins at Keef Gilmartin's bar—"we got a spot for you. Work's gonna be hard, Den. Gonna take men to do it."

***

Me and Mike graduate the police academy on the same November day in 1971, standing either side of a pal we made there, an Indian kid named Jesse Smith who one day plans to be the superintendent. Cullen Mahoney gets us all posted to the Second District, "the Deuce," with Matty Rzepecki, home to Stateway Gardens and the Robert Taylor Homes—the absolute epicenter of the Black super gangs.

We're not idiots or Matty; we ask how we'll live through the weekend.

Cullen takes us up to the water tower where we stood with Loef Brummel almost a decade ago, across from the Forty-Seventh Street railyard. Cullen points at the projects—territory where we were never, ever supposed to go, and says, "Nobody will work the jets except Matty and his kinda guys. If you and Mike can keep each other alive, in five years you'll be sergeants. I'll be a captain. Trust me, I've been on the job three years; I know what I'm doing. We're good Irish Catholics. We'll run the city."

I look at Mike, then Cullen. "*Mike and me* are good Catholics?"

Cullen laughs. "*Good* may be a stretch, but what you're not, and never will be, is Protestants from the Shankill Road."

Jimmie sirens us from the centerline of Fifty-Fifth through the westbound bumpers, jumps the sidewalk, and snakes around the barricade into the Riviera.

Crowds jam the Riviera's walks and streets and unfenced yards. Work clothes and grim expressions mix with downtown's St. Patrick's parade caps and shirts, many re-stamped with **PNDH**.

Jimmie slow-rolls us twelve blocks north through the crush. Every fourth or fifth building has a bed sheet hanging from a roofline gutter, **PNDH** and white nooses are spray-painted big and bold. Feels like newsreels of Berlin in the 1930s.

At Forty-Fourth Street, the crowd becomes too dense to penetrate. We park under a **PNDH** bed sheet, hang our badges around our necks, and exit into the crowd.

Four mounted patrol officers weave toward us through the noise and bodies. The horses are nervous, one of whom I know. Samson is a seventeen-hands sorrel gelding my girlfriend, Maureen, and I rebuilt two years ago. I step in front of Samson; his rider I haven't seen before. He looks nervous, too.

"What up, Sam?"

Samson balks, then heads at me to move. I don't. He steps forward as I hold out my hand, inflates his nostrils on my fingers. His eyes register me and he nudges my fingers higher.

"Attaboy." I stroke him calm, then kiss his nose. "You know the drill. Nothing out here you haven't seen before."

Loud shouts on my right. Samson and his rider turn toward a five-man argument.

Jimmie and I shoulder through toward Forty-Third and the Bayside's yellow tape. Everyone we pass stares or glares at Jimmie's skin and his pomp. A large man in overalls brandishes a homemade **PNDH** flag with both hands. He barrels forward, doesn't see Jimmie, bumps him hard, bounces off, and into me. He yells, "Fuckin' nig—" sees our badges and doesn't finish.

Inside the Bayside's yellow tape, emergency-light towers cover Forty-Third and Emerald in silvery moonscape glow. The last of the bodies and body parts they bring out will be tenfold as horrifying under the lights, but we don't have a choice. Jimmie nods toward the rooftops—maybe two or three hundred up there. The internet psycho sites will be wall-to-wall video. I glance at Jimmie. The yellow tape should be pushed back to the city's borders.

My phone rings. Superintendent Smith says, *"Monkeys?* You called Alderman Gibbons a monkey? *On camera?"*

"Me?"

"Did you tell him to wear a vest to church?"

"No."

Silence. "The only reason you and I still have jobs is Alderman Gibbons went on record with the mayor to keep you. *Then* Gibbons called me privately to say he has 'monkey' and 'vest' on camera." Pause. "That's leverage, Denny, leverage we'll have to eat later, in case you've forgotten how the fucking game's played."

I stare at the grim faces. "Before you bust my ass on PC politics, you might want to come back down here and have another look. I make it three thousand, counting the rooftops and alleys."

"Maybe calling him 'nigger' would've helped."

"Gibbons will toss another bomb in here, figuratively or otherwise. *Monkey* and *vest* are Hallmark cards compared to what he's planning."

Silence. "Don't fuck with me, Denny. I'll put Jimmie up front before you blink. Your grand jury subpoena lands so fast Gale Sayers couldn't outrun it."

"'My way,' remember?"

"Keep being stupid and *your way* doesn't have many minutes left in it."

Click.

I look at Jimmie. He shrugs. My phone rings again, on the screen: "Deputy Super Mahoney."

Jean Jeffcoat from Fox News shoves a mic across the tape at me and a Fox camera lens cranes over her shoulder. "Commander—*Lieutenant* Banahan. Is it true—"

"No, Jean, it's not."

"Has Red Summer begun?" Ms. Jeffcoat is Black and probably risking her life being here. She shoves the mic closer. *"Lieutenant—"*

"Can't comment, sorry."

"Fox News has confirmed that members of the American Nazi Party and the Ku Klux Klan have threatened Alderman—"

"Sorry, talk to Lieutenant Gilmartin."

"Are white supremacists responsible for the fire at the Ebenezer Mennonite Church? A noose was recovered—"

"Jean, I'd get my ass out of Canaryville if I were you—"

Jimmie's large hand jerks me away from the microphone.

11:00 p.m.

The Riviera continues to ramp from shock into cold, naked hate. Beyond the tape, wolf packs weave through the vigil, brandishing ball bats and flags. Some have torches. All have bared teeth. I was here when the Riv went *Heart of Darkness* back in the mid-1960s, and I've seen the photos of 1919. Both times the rage built and built and built, then turned so fast napalm couldn't have stopped it.

I wipe my eyes, swollen from the corrosive air, emergency lights, and hour fourteen on the job. Jimmie yells into his phone, a rare bit of temper that's drowned out by radio chatter and heavy equipment working the debris. To my right, the ME and a crew of ruined-looking crime-scene techs, including Diane Winooski, log in body part number 162 and a metal fragment (number 7) that could belong to the "Bayside Bomber," so named by the Chicago *Herald*.

I lean into the fender of Officer Johnson's car. My BlackBerry is on his roof, charging from his cigarette lighter. Officer Johnson does not look healthy for a twenty-three-year-old, not that anyone looks healthy at the edges of emergency lights and mass murder.

I point at his roof. "When my phone's cooked, go home."

"My sergeant said to stay. With you."

"He did, did he? 'Cause I can't look after myself."

"Yes, sir, something like that. The language might have been stronger."

I curl my fingers at him. "Clarity, Walter, if you want to work Homicide."

Officer Johnson balks, worn from too many hours, too many stares. "This is a quote, sir, from my sergeant. 'The dumb Mick motherfucker backed a trainload of his coppers when they were jammed. Banahan don't fall to the brass or the G because this Polack policeman folded.' Unquote. Sir."

Walter probably tested smarter than me when he was nine, but he might not understand this millennium's concept of loyalty. "Other than your sergeant and maybe ten other guys, those days are over, Walter. Go home and see that baby of yours. He's who needs looking after."

"Yes, sir, as soon as you're done."

I pull my BlackBerry off Walter's roof, check the time, then call Deputy Super Mahoney at home. He answers, should sound sleepy, but doesn't.

I tell him, "Sorry for the hour, but you told me to call even if we had nothing. Which is what we have. Witness canvass came back empty on the double at the tracks. We have seven possible bomb fragments at the Bayside, but off the record, the crime-scene techs say they're meaningless. Looks like the perp might've used C-4, packed it with wood screws of several types, probably ten to twenty pounds that he bought a pound at a time. FD thinks he used thermite as an accelerant, but no proof yet."

"Loef Brummel?"

"Brummel did the interrogation interview for the double with no lawyer present. Unfortunately, even with the three-way angle, he was a stretch from *go*. He fits *target* lots better than *perp*—some version of a crime-world takeover. Loef's alibis are solid. And so far, he refuses to say what his fiancée was doing alive, or dead, with Dill Reem."

Mahoney coughs. "And the Bayside? Canaryville and the Riviera?"

"A mob, all white, maybe five thousand now, waiting for a spark. Good news is they have to go twelve blocks south or six blocks east to reach the front line of the people they want to murder. Unless someone from that target group were dumb enough to come across Fifty-Fifth Street or the Norfolk Southern tracks."

The deputy superintendent's silence affirms what we both fear.

I turn away from the emergency lights. "He's coming north, isn't he? The Ayatollah."

Mahoney says, "I fear he will. When he has sufficient cameras." Pause. "After you put on First Watch, go home, sleep. Tonight may be the last of it for a time. Patrol and SWAT will keep the peace, if they can."

"Ten four. I'll call you in the morning with whatever First Watch finds."

"Focus all efforts on the bomber. Either we find him, or a facsimile to feed Canaryville, or we have Red Summer."

Four detectives from my First Watch crew dip under the tape. I tell Mahoney, "Ten four," pocket my phone, and wave the detectives over. One points at a streetlight with a noose on it. "National Guard better be inbound."

Jimmie pulls one detective aside, then explains how he wants First Watch to deploy. Jimmie waves me to him. "Time to go home, Den."

Like Mahoney, Jimmie makes it clear this is not a suggestion. We cut Officer Johnson loose with promises we're done for the night. Jimmie and I bend under the tape, then squeeze past taut faces and defiant body language, around mounted policemen, and the wolf packs with their bats, torches, and dwindling regard for anything but reprisal.

In the car, Jimmie loops us south, then east into ghetto dark, toward my parked car. I pocket my BlackBerry on the last call I intend to take tonight. Seven of the Bayside surnames have had my cell number since

I've owned a phone. Throughout the evening I've spoken to them all—Walsh, Smith, Byrne, O'Neil, Doyle, Lynch, Murray. Each call was a tortured voice who wanted to know *why* their father or brother or sister was dead, or "When are you gonna kill the motherfuckers who did this?"

They "know" who did it—Blacks attempting to ignite a race war that they want. It's a picture that draws itself—Loef's fiancée, Canaryville families, a parade day.

Their picture should feel right. But it doesn't . . . Why, I don't know.

Across the Ryan, east of the Norfolk Southern's Forty-Seventh Street yard, Jimmie pulls into a CPD fenced lot that used to be sixteen-story projects. I pop the car door. Jimmie grabs my arm, eyes the FBI tail car at the gate, lights on that they want us to see, then stares at me.

"What?"

"In an hour, Den, it's fifteen days. You're in the barns with Maureen, talking horse-whisperer to cripple thoroughbreds who've never spoken to a human. Go home. Be cool. Don't get confused."

"Tell Gayle I said, 'Hey.'" I close the door.

Jimmie does a U, turns past the FBI car at the gate, then heads for his family. Once home—when we're on a normal schedule—Jimmie will put his gun and badge in his dresser drawer, take out the unopened bottle of E&J brandy he's had for six years and set it on the kitchen table between him and his wife. Gayle will ask him about his day. His kids won't. He'll ask about everyone's day, their lives, their world. After dinner and a two-mile silent walk, he'll retire. In the bathroom, Jimmie will try to cry, but rarely get there. He'll strip down to boxers, cut the lights, crawl into bed, and hold on to Gayle until she thinks he's asleep. Somewhere between that moment and tomorrow's alarm, Jimmie will dream the Dream.

The Dream is a no-man's-land I don't visit, no matter how bad the day was, a place where Jimmie has to go to compartmentalize the killer or killers he became, to keep that information on hand but out of sight. Like all of us who choose this job, Jimmie's end-of-watch ritual puts the blood behind him for the night.

My ritual is to key my car's ignition and head north—exchange the present for a five-foot-seven soul mate the cosmic river dropped on me like I somehow deserved her—then hold on and believe with both hands that Maureen Cavanaugh Cane and I will make it past my grand jury to the horses who do as much for us as we do for them.

But tonight, that's not what I do. I turn on the radio and stare across the Ryan. The Riviera's lights are a low glow that, fifty-fifty, will be flames before sunrise. A single gunshot *pops* to the west. *Pop, pop, pop* answers. I hear the Ayatollah's voice, then realize it's my radio.

WNTD's not broadcasting *The Blues at Midnight*. Tonight, the radio DJ is interviewing Leslie Gibbons. The tone is somber, like a prayer vigil with most of the candles already burned out. Leslie Gibbons is educating the DJ's audience on Red Summer.

Eyes shut, I visualize the streetlight poles at Forty-Third and Emerald hung with the short, festive banners of St. Gabriel Catholic Church, then imagine what I don't want to imagine hanging from the same poles.

The Ayatollah segues into why the bloodbath of a new Red Summer is a virtual certainty for Chicago. His reasoning is the simple "A plus B equals C" that's popular on the soundbite news shows. Eighty-seven years to the *day* after the 1919 Red Summer lynchings, Chicago announced our 2016 Olympic bid, and historic rebid. According to Alderman Gibbons, the mayor used the Olympic bids to scrape city-owned Black neighborhoods on the East Side. Residents and their rep-resentatives were promised "new" neighborhoods when the Olympic bidding was complete.

In September 2008, Wall Street crashed. Chicago was already mired in a serious West Side gang war (Hispanic). On October 2, 2009, Chicago lost its bid for the 2016 Summer Olympics in the first round. No "new" Black neighborhoods were built.

On my radio, the Ayatollah shifts gears and booms: "This mayor stole our neighborhoods! He and his developer cronies got our land; we got the Pharaoh's exodus."

Yup, and some version of that is exactly what happened. North Side liberals, university lawyers, and an endless array of rainbow-colored urban planners from DC to San Francisco accused the mayor of "bulldozer gerrymandering" and "merciless urban colonialism." Translation: The city stole Black lakefront land in the name of the

Olympics, hoping to expand the city's underperforming tax base. And avoid bankruptcy.

Chicago's Olympic era officially ended with two Black college kids—Bernard and Latoya Osborne, brother and sister—burned to death in their car. Two as-yet-unindicted police officers from the Ninth District watched the Osbornes' car fire. It was one day after a Canaryville woman and her daughter were abducted, raped, and dumped dead on the Norfolk Southern tracks. The white woman and her daughter had DNA from seven Black males, all with gang affiliations and serious criminal records, five of whom remain at large.

Gibbons booms again: *"Restoration or Incineration.* Convict the police who murdered our children. Rebuild our twenty thousand bulldozed housing units. Reinstate our lives, our schools and communities: or give us yours!"

Yup. *Move out or burn out.*

I glance back across the highway toward Armour Square at the north end of the Riv. Last month, the church of Christian Identity held a Stop Ethnocentric Entitlements rally in Armour Square Park; drew twenty-eight thousand; had to turn participants away. The *Herald-WNTD* poll estimated the average age at fifty-two. The theme underneath the religious and patriotic fervor was, and is, *Whitey's all done paying the guilt tax.*

The Ku Klux Klan and the American Nazi Party have marched twice in the city. Both said they were here "in defense of the citizens the city won't defend."

I key my ignition, roll past the FBI car at the gate without looking at Agent Stone, then head west for the Ryan. Stone knows where I'm going.

My BlackBerry rings "UNKNOWN." And again, "UNKNOWN." And again.

"UNKNOWN" calls me every fifteen seconds until I shut the phone off.

THE MALVERN
PUBLIC HOUSE

OLD TOWN

Chapter 8

Sixty-nine blocks north of Canaryville, the North Side isn't grief stricken or rallying to commit mass murder. Up here, for those revelers the downtown parade didn't finish early, "St. Patrick's" Saturday night is still on the climb.

The Malvern is jammed. I wedge through raised pints and bagpipe music, don't see Maureen, then order a Guinness from a thirtysomething bartender who works Vice in Eighteen. She curls red lips, reaches across the bar, and covers my hands with both of hers.

I say, "Yeah. Not good. Thanks."

Maureen's doorman taps my shoulder. "Dennis. A woman outside, cryin' a mess; says you gotta talk to her."

I glance between the fern baskets at the Wells Street windows, then the door. All I can see are heads and shoulders. "She alone?"

"Came off the bus alone. From Canaryville. Tried to bring her in, but she'll not stand in a Loyalist public house."

Odd, anyone hunting me this far north. Could be one of my detectives said maybe I'd be here. I glance the windows again. Odd; but often you're the only name they know, the only connection to the past when it was all still okay. If they can just find you, you can fix it.

I ask the bartender, "Hold my stool?" then point the 2XL doorman to the door and follow him out.

Most Chicagoans would call the Malvern a North Side yuppie pub. Accurate enough, but it would be more proper to call it a Loyalist or Protestant pub frequented by yuppies. Not that it makes a difference to me—yuppies need a place to drink and Northern Ireland's alphabet soup of Protestant factions are beyond my understanding or interest.

Maureen's *from* Northern Ireland and, other than that, not involved in the alphabet soup. What I know (from my childhood geography and our parades) is that if you're Protestant, like Maureen's family was, then you're Orange or Loyalist and favor keeping the six counties of the north—often referred to as Ulster—as part of the United Kingdom. If you're Catholic, you're Green or Republican and favor reuniting the six counties of the north with the rest of Ireland.

Favor has killed a whole bunch of people over the last fifty or one hundred years, but very few here in the US, and none that I've had to work. The Irish in America are a lot like other immigrant groups who've left troubled places. After two or three generations, the learned hatreds and prejudices are still under the skin, but few are still swallowing regular doses of the old-country poison. There are the drunks, the pub-rebels who can blather you to death. And there are legitimate extremists—fundraisers and fire-breathers tied umbilically to the politics of back home. And like many extremists, some can be hair-trigger violent.

Outside the Malvern, the old woman alone on the sidewalk is more shape than person, hugging herself into her shoulders. I've known Mrs. Shaughnessy since I could walk to Koonce's candy store. Her life's had one marriage, three funerals, and two high school graduations. She was a hotel maid downtown for forty years till her knees gave out. Last year her hotel company went into bankruptcy, her pension went south and the medical with it. What she's got left is one good grandson, the other a Ragen Colt, both probably in the Bayside when it blew.

Mrs. Shaughnessy grabs my shirt. "*Dennis. Please.* You brought Bill and Charley back before . . . when there was trouble. They're good boys, you know they are. Please. Just this time, again."

"Mrs. Shaughnessy, I—"

"God bless ya, Dennis." She crumples, hugging my waist. "*Please.*"

I pull her up, my hands gentle under her elbows. "Mrs. Shaughnessy, c'mon, up you go. We're okay; I'm here." She trembles against me. I lean her against the headlights of a parked Escalade SUV; glance at Agent Stone's car across the street, then try to look in her eyes but she won't let me. "Take a breath."

She pants, eyes shut tight; fingers curled desperate into my shirt.

A voice in the dark: "Hey! Asshole!"

I jerk to red lipstick and a two-hundred-dollar hairdo craning out the Escalade's driver-side window. The driver's door pops open and a girl in a minidress rounds the fender. "Seventy thousand dollars! Get off my hood!"

Mrs. Shaughnessy cringes fetal into my chest. I ease her to the next car, shielding her from the Escalade's owner. "We're okay, Mrs. Shaughnessy. I'm here. Easy. Easy." I lean her against the next car's far fender and keep my hands on her arms. "When's the last time you saw Bill and Charley?"

"Dennis, please. Please." Her eyes are open wide and raw red. "They were not in the Bayside. Couldn't be. I can't lose 'em. Their father's gone, you know that."

"I know. I know. When did you see your boys last?"

"Dennis, please." She buries her face in my chest. "Bring 'em home, Dennis. Please."

I hug Mrs. Shaughnessy as gentle as I can. Her knees buckle and she mumbles against my shirt. Mrs. Shaughnessy knows I can't bring her boys home. I know I can't. And there's no worse part of this job.

**

Walking ten blocks of the Malvern's neighborhood doesn't magically undo a mass-murder day, nor does it shake Agent Stone's tail car twenty feet behind me, nor does it change my history with the cycle of violence that defines my job, neighborhood, and DNA . . .

Like our ma and da, Mike never did make the Route 66 trip. He died at twenty-two, our first year on the job, going in first with Cullen Mahoney on a liquor-store holdup in the Deuce. Full name in the papers; big wake, bigger funeral, his star on the lobby wall at Thirty-Fifth and Michigan. When coppers die on the line it typically matters outside our family for five news cycles, sometimes a week, then it's over. What remains of Mike is a statistic on the urban scorecard and a granite-slab rectangle next to our parents at Holy Sepulchre.

And a shoebox vault he'd made—like the last one we'd built when I got out of Charley. Mike's had a photo each of Ma and Da, the unburned piece of our Route 66 map, our Biscayne brochure, a returnable Pepsi bottle, and the scorched hem of Ma's curtains. Now I have it all, and Mike's original CPD uniform patches.

Reapproaching the Malvern, I slow; Stone's passenger window drops. He says, "Troubled, Lieutenant? Happy to discuss it, if you'd like."

"Sure. Know where Mrs. Shaughnessy's boys are?"

Agent Stone shrugs.

I flick my toothpick in his window. "When you know, maybe we'll talk."

***

Inside the Malvern, I drain the Guinness with my left hand, drop the glass on the coaster, and answer my BlackBerry. The District Eighteen beat car I called to pick up Mrs. Shaughnessy says they have her at her neighbor's house. The neighbor says she'll keep her the night. I tell the patrolman "Thanks" and that I'll stop by the neighbor's tomorrow.

He says, "Anytime, Lieutenant."

The bartender from Eighteen pats my hand and says, "Let me buy LT one."

I nod; may nod four or five times before the hour is over. Or maybe I'll find Bega, get her some Harold's Chicken she shouldn't have and me a six-pack, sit us in the 1960 Chevrolet Biscayne Bana-Ship for another stationary practice run out to Darien. We'll listen to Cameron Smith DJ the blues on the radio, smell horse tack, and wait for Maureen to get off work.

Framed in the long mirror of the back bar, Maureen steps in from the restaurant hallway, sans the leather duster, dressed as she was earlier today. She is—to use a phrase that's likely fit her since grade school—pretty fucking spectacular.

Maureen's arm is entwined with a dapper old fellow shuffling on a gnarled blackthorn walking stick. She carries his carryout box from their once-a-week dinner. His pace is slow, unsteady, but his smile is all pride and possession. A man in full. Some women can absolutely do that, make a man forget his frailty, his failures, or worse.

As Maureen walks her man through the crowd, I begin a smile I'm surprised I have, consider "woman" as refuge, as defender, as keeper of the flame. Maureen the Lionhearted. The hair, the shoulders, the hips; posture that has presence, much of it earned working horses ten times her size all her life. *My* girlfriend. After a lifetime opining to the contrary, there are—no question about it—women worth dying for. Ask the old fellow Maureen's with; he'd tell you the same thing.

Maureen waits while her doorman helps with the old fellow's topcoat. She buttons him up, hugs him goodbye, and hands the doorman the carryout box. The old fellow kisses her cheek. She keeps his gaze and taps a fingertip to the orange choker at her throat. He taps his cane on the floor, nods to the sound, and Maureen's doorman helps him outside.

Maureen *hellos* back through the crowd. I swivel to face her, three feet between us when she stops, shoulders back, chin up. Her blue eyes read mine a mile deep, concern written into her face, and an unusual hint of age. She hesitates, then pitches forward and hugs my neck with both arms. My world becomes jasmine and lavender.

Her lips land on my ear. Breathy across it, she says, "Ah, Dennis, ya smell of the smoke and sadness." Her fingers grip into the back of my coat, a tremble in the warmth of her breasts and shoulders. "God believe me, I couldn't be more sorry."

I squeeze back, let the power of her run through me. Her arms don't let go, all of her pushing sympathy and protection through our clothes. She exhales deep, then extends backward from my shoulders. Her strong fingers feather into my hair. The stare is penetrating, searching . . . hypnotic. She quits the search, slides onto the stool next to mine, hip to hip, elevates her leather boots across and over my knee, and hooks them under my leg. Her right hand reaches inside my coat and grips my shirt.

"Promise me, Dennis; tell me you're done with it."

"I love you."

Maureen flips red hair off her face, and eases her cheek into my neck.

I say, "Before you get mad—"

"No." Maureen shrinks back. "I'll not have an explanation. Canaryville wanted a war with the Blacks; now they have it. She can avenge her own ghosts."

"And she will. A lotta innocent people are gonna die."

"Chicago has thirteen thousand policemen. You're one, and mine. Leave this war to the department's brave-hearts who left you to the wolves rather than defend you."

"Two weeks from now it's you, me, and a barn full of *happy*." I point up at the top of her back bar and our rescue farm's soon-to-be raced jockey silks. "Promise."

"My da promised the Troubles weren't ours. At Down Royal, at the Curragh, at every racecourse in Ireland we raced. But that's not how we finished. It's a lie you're tellin' me, same as his, and damn you both."

Damning her dead father is not something Maureen has done before. I reach over her knees and look square in her eyes. "No. Baby, I don't lie to you, ever. I have to do this, *for us*, or I wouldn't."

Maureen has buried all but one of her family. Her lips flatten and her jaw sets so hard it creases her eyes. My fingers slip into the waist-band of her skirt. "C'mon. We'll get the Bana-Ship, pick up Bega . . ."

"We will if you use that phone in your pocket. Tell the brave-hearts you've a woman to look after, promises you've made and intend to keep."

"Baby, I—"

"If you love me, us, our future we've worked for, accept what one man cannot change and hand me your star."

The bartender asks for Maureen's attention.

I don't hand Maureen my star. She frowns, waits, then leans across the bar to listen to her bartender. I glance the back-bar TV.

The screen is filled with adobe-brown buildings, Border Patrol uni-forms and National Guard and police in riot gear, all clashing with civilians. The camera cuts to an aerial shot of packed streets, rooftop mobs waving homemade flags, and street-level skirmish lines.

The camera cuts back to eye level. A white minister stands mid-riot surrounded by full-alert security men. The minister is cut over his right eye; he's speaking to a semi-cringing reporter the way a calm, controlled battlefield general would to a shaky war correspondent.

The overlay reads: "Bishop Haswell Burke, Church of Christian Identity."

Maureen answers her bartender's question, then leans back, checks the TV I'm looking at, and explains. "The good bishop's immigration rally on the border went rippin' mad." She pulls my fingers out of her waistband and holds them up between us, then wraps my fingers in both her hands. "Your star. I'll not allow—"

Maureen's brother, Pádraig, bumps her boots as he passes, nods at me, and doesn't apologize to her. He's six foot with heavy bones, deep-set eyes, and hard features. Maureen bends away to hear another urgent question from her bartender.

I consider Pádraig's back . . . Pádraig is a player in security-world, works the mega nightclubs and rock concert venues, and does VIP stage control for public spectacles like today's downtown parade, the Taste of Chicago, and the Christian Identity rally—staged by the very same fellow who's midriot on the TV.

Cissy Noonan also worked in concert-venue world, before someone killed her this morning at the Norfolk Southern tracks.

I refocus on Pádraig. His company is built on what he calls the "European model," recruiting from the football hooligan firms of Belfast, East Berlin, and Glasgow, absorbing the more farsighted into a "capable, controllable confrontation force." That's corporate-speak for the insurance companies. When the gloves are off, Pádraig's Europeans aren't much different than the Ragen Colts, Hells Angels, or Gypsy Vikings here. He who controls the door to a thousand-person nightclub, by default, controls who sells sex and drugs inside. Pádraig's lads may look less "outlaw" in their black Stone Island bomber jackets, Donegal caps, combat pants, and shined, steel-toed boots, but truth be told, they're as tough a hand-to-hand crew as exists in the city.

I'm not a fan of Pádraig, for a number of reasons, but I'm in the homicide business, not the security and vice business. And he's Maureen's only living relative, a year younger, and now a US citizen. Pádraig was military. After that he joined the Garda—Ireland's national police force—got jammed on an IRA confrontation in a North Dublin bank robbery that killed two IRA gunmen (Catholics), and agreed to retire to America if the IRA wouldn't kill him. Maureen asked me to help him; I did.

I raise my voice above the bagpipes and singing. "Pádraig?"

He turns, stares, then chins *What's up?*

I wave him back to speaking distance.

"You guys work the parade today?"

Nod.

"Cissy Noonan there? Handling the VIPs?"

Pádraig looks at Maureen, then me, and shrugs.

"You know Cissy, right? She works the same rock venues you do. Dill Reem been seeing Cissy? On the side? They an item?"

"Heard she was dead." Pádraig points at the TV. "Today."

"She is. So's Dill. Was she seeing him?"

Maureen's leg flexes on my knee. I glance at her, asking with my eyes if she'll *please allow me a chance to end the case before it kills the city*, then back to her brother.

Pádraig says, "Cissy's a Catholic girl. Her bedroom's not somethin' I'd be party to."

"Know a guy named Darragh O'Brien?"

Stare. Pause. Slow headshake.

"Think he's from Omagh. IRA guy."

Maureen barks, "Dennis. You'll not bring the Troubles in here—"

The side door to the Malvern opens wide and fast, the outside lights blocked by a long leather coat and two more behind it. Loef Brummel leans into his steps as he approaches, stops at a distance that might be conversation, looks Pádraig a step back that Pádraig doesn't take, then a barback completely away, then says: "Outside, Den. Be better than in."

Two of Maureen's bouncers have followed, but stay at a respectful distance. Like most of Chicago connected to things Irish or criminal, they know who they're looking at and don't want to die. Three of Pádraig's crew materialize from the tables. They have hands inside their coats and pre-gunfight posture.

Maureen removes her legs and releases my hand. Loef Brummel in person in the Malvern is a first—a South Side crime boss in a part of town that isn't his—and not on a good night.

One of Loef's crew sides him; the other has stayed at the side door. No doubt there are more outside. I swivel to face Loef square, but stay on the stool, not much I can do if six guys start shooting. "Your lawyer out there?"

"Comin'?" Loef glances Maureen. "Or hidin'?"

Maureen lowers her chin, sliding forward an inch. There isn't an ounce of Maureen that won't die fighting if she's protecting what's hers to protect. Best you hit her first or you'll be blind in both eyes.

I touch the outside of her knee, then tell Loef, "We ain't off the record. Not if you popped Dill." Out of courtesy, I don't mention Cissy.

"Was four hours with your detectives." Loef's eyes are frigid, expressionless, paying no attention to Pádraig's crew, just me. "My alibi was across the river, Father Crosby and two Sisters of Providence."

"So I hear. My condolences. Across the board."

Loef nods. Maureen says, "Mine as well, Mr. Brummel; an awful thing. The whole of it." Her sympathies are genuine, but so is her posture.

Loef stares at Maureen, her orange choker, then cuts to Pádraig and measures him like pro fighters do before the bell. Loef nods small, then turns for the door. Maureen stands to side me. I tap her back onto her stool. She mouths *Careful* at me, then turns and waves her bouncers to her.

Loef and I walk out onto Wells Street. His two men follow.

Two more of his Canaryville crew are outside at the fenders of a Chrysler 300C; neither look pleasant or comfortable. Maureen's bouncers appear at the pub's door. Pádraig's men don't.

The black Escalade that belongs to Princess Yuppie Fuck is still there, but empty. Agent Stone's Ford is across the street. It isn't empty. Loef checks the street in both directions, turns his back to Agent Stone's Ford, and speaks with careful diction.

"Riv wants answers, targets to focus the grief. Now, tonight. Before she gets away from us."

"I'm not in the *target* business, Loef. Why were Cissy and Dill together, dead?"

Loef eyes the Malvern's front door, then the alley, then cuts back to me, but doesn't answer.

"Who's Darragh O'Brien?"

"The Bayside, Den. Targets. Now. Tonight."

Fifty-fifty any explanation is a mistake, but I do it anyway. "Fire department, Bomb and Arson, and the crime lab are working the bomb forensics. We have a rental car abandoned near where Tommy O'Boyle's boy was killed. Plates were stolen, switched after the car was rented at the Milwaukee airport. Driver's MIA, but we're looking."

"Black or white, the man who rented the car?"

"Patrol stopped the same make and model a block away just before the hit-and-run. The *driver* of that *similar* vehicle was white."

"Meanin' the renter wasn't?"

"Don't know yet. The rental was a pass through—grab any car, use the company card—gate agent's cameras were broken. The account's driver's license and credit card may be bogus. The gate agent went on vacation and hasn't answered his phone."

"And?"

"*And* your name's everywhere there's blood and money. Superintendent and the mayor's people want to make the Bayside and Cissy part of the same move; something done for, or about, Loef Brummel. Package both as an all-white, organized-crime takeover."

"But some of it don't fit."

I nod. "So, if it isn't your top guy Dill making a move on you that you outplayed too late to stop the Bayside . . ." I look for something in Loef's face that says it is. "Then who clean-kills your fiancée, slaughters one of your crew, then same day blows up your bar?" I keep looking for guilt that should be there. "No offense, Loef, but you sure Cissy and Dill weren't . . ."

Loef fixes me with the straight-razor stare that was already lethal when we were boys. "Dill was a hardman, a gack now and again, but stupid? *No.* Fuckin' my girl? *No.* Takin' a five-block walk to do some dope-business with Vice Lord bangers? *No.*"

Harsh. But reasonable, other than the part about *my girl.*

"Could've been a move-up, couldn't it? Pushing you out?"

Loef scans the street, his men on either side of us, then Maureen's bouncers in the doorway. He says, "Cissy's a girl, not a queen. The Bayside's a pub, not a fucking castle. Killin' it don't make you boss of shit—even if you get me, there's no surviving the Bayside burning when she's full of neighbors . . ." Loef shrugs at an answer he doesn't have. "You, your crew, their families, all of ya are dead the first day you say you're runnin' the Riv."

I don't bother with an explanation of the Illinois criminal code that Loef won't hear. I say, "We're expecting you to keep Canaryville out of the ghetto once the Bayside wakes start."

Loef reads my face. "CPD knows somethin' *ghetto*?"

"No. But you and I grew up on the same block. And like you said, I know what your neighbors are thinking. I know where they want to *focus the grief.* If I don't identify a perp—Black or white—a bunch of this city, including the Riv, will be ashes and crying mothers."

"That's a fact."

"So, you want to confess to Dill and Cissy?"

Headshake.

"Then what were they doing together and why?"

Loef's eyes narrow. He adds emphasis and diction: "I don't know."

"But *I* need to know. Now, like ten hours ago. And then I need two days to get us past St. Pat's, no matter *what* the ghetto says, or does."

"If your bangers *whisper* they did the Bayside, we start hangin' 'em from streetlights."

"No, Loef, we're not doing that."

"Ain't up to us. Not ninety years ago, and it ain't now." Loef nods his men to their car and his Chrysler 300C. "Your woman's still alive. I'll see to the Colts and the worst of the banshees till morning. I don't hear something from you by breakfast, the rest of the day's outta my hands."

"Tell 'em I said it ain't gonna happen. 'Cause it ain't."

"Remember where you're from, Den. Who your people are." Loef steps in to me but without threat. "Your brother, Mike, died for this fuckin' city and it was Englewood niggers who killed him."

A dog growls from the dark, deep in the alley behind me. Loef turns toward his car, stops halfway, turns and says, "And your parents, God rest 'em . . . The German's electrical wiring killed 'em, not your da's cigarette, and you did what you should've. You understood eye for an eye then, and you understood it when Mike bought it, don't forget it now when it ain't your people we're burying."

My teeth grind. Loef turns to walk away. I yell: "Cissy and Dill. They died *today*; talk about today."

Loef looks to his right as he passes the Malvern's arched front door, fixing on my girlfriend standing there. Loef and his men climb into their cars and pull from the curb.

I cut to the Malvern's front door and Maureen, shoulders squared, chin down, eyes narrowed on Loef Brummel's taillights. She stares Loef's Chrysler up the block until his taillights fade, then slowly rotates her head to Agent Stone's FBI car. Her appearance in the doorway was for Loef, making sure he knew that if I go, Loef better get her, too. Above Maureen in red, chiseled deep and ragged into the masonry is:

Every Country Gets the Circus It Deserves.

Below it carved into the door reads:

Spain gets bullfights. America gets Hollywood. Italy Ireland gets the Catholic Church.

I met Herself, the proprietress of the Malvern, on the morning she carved her doorway, a four-homicide, sixteen-degree, sunrise Sunday. Maureen Cane was balanced atop a barstool, a claw hammer in one hand, a chisel in the other. At her feet, a heavy camping knife lay next to a bottle of Tullamore Dew. Blood from Maureen's hands was flecked on her face and frozen on her fingers. Her blue eyes were cried-out red.

After the last smash with the hammer and chisel, she jumped off the barstool, dropped the chisel, and took two slugs of the Tullamore Dew. The drink or the cold wobbled her. She pulled two tubes of crimson lipstick from her jeans pocket, then scrawled the solid wood door with the last two lines. I stepped closer into her peripheral vision and asked the side of her face how well she knew my victim, a young woman from Ireland who, according to her green card, worked inside.

Maureen Cane turned slightly and considered me through rivulets of red hair obscuring her face. "And were ya busy at Sunday church, constable? When my girl required your protection?"

I answered that I didn't spend much time in church.

Ms. Cane suggested I step out of her way if I wished to avoid injury.

I did. She picked up the knife and with both hands began carving the last two lines she'd scrawled. The wood splintered into her fingers.

She hacked each letter deep into the door, the cuts as raw as her eyes and hands.

I watched, confused. *Guilt-grief? Rage? Pinning a threat to a door? A wake?* All responses I'd seen played out for an external audience—present and future—or for an internal jury who knew the guilt-ridden truth. But this business felt different. Like, outer-space different.

It took another six minutes before I realized it was *her* who was outer-space different. After the last stab, Maureen Cane allowed the knife to slip from her hands and clatter on the frozen sidewalk. She grabbed the Tullamore Dew, took a third gulp, stepped back, bent her neck, and screamed the words she'd carved at whatever version of God she saw high above her building.

I waited. The Tullamore Dew stayed clamped in her fist. Her head lowered and she focused on the door, not my question, her lips mumbling, "Ireland gets the Catholic church . . . always and forever." Her knee faltered and she steadied against the barstool.

I reached to help but stopped short, then asked a second time about my victim, Maureen's employee from Ireland. Maureen turned just her head, breathing frozen vapor between us. Her mouth trembled and tears rimmed her eyes. The tears froze on her cheeks. She didn't speak.

I was a Homicide lieutenant; I'd seen soul-naked before—dead-spouse IDs, blaze-gutted homes, blindside betrayal—and this was close, but not the same. Or maybe this was as naked as women like this one knew how to be. In her anger and sorrow, there was absolute defiance. Her shoulders were set strong, backbone rigid . . . like she was on a battlement wall somewhere, done running, daring the other side to fix their bayonets, and come the fuck on.

One stunning woman. But while *stunning* is always in short supply, it wasn't new. Carmalee Greco at Sacred Heart's grammar-school dances; the Gilmartin sisters anywhere. And since then, I'd also seen tough-as-nails denial, repeatedly, but this? This woman was on fire. She *glowed* with it. I, quite literally, couldn't take my eyes off her.

When Maureen finally spoke, she was looking right at me, she tapped the quote she'd just carved into the door, said: "Erica Jong."

I attempted conversation instead of police work. I said that Erica Whoever seemed a perceptive lady, but she likely had too much education for slaughterhouse work—Hollywood's spin factory was the *symptom*, the movie trailer before the big show. The real circus—the one with the swords and the lions—was out here on the pavement.

Maureen looked away to the wood she'd just clawed and carved. She told the jagged carvings and me that she'd sponsored my murder victim, the deceased, Bintleigh Grace of Belfast, into the USA, had known her and her family all her life. The door was Bintleigh Grace's tombstone.

I figured I could remember that, so I didn't write it down.

We stood there. Maureen turned all of her to face me, looking at me different than I'd ever been looked at, into places I didn't know I had. After what seemed a nanosecond, or a lifetime, Maureen extended her bloody splintered hands, scarred and man-strong. I asked why the scars and why the strength. She said, "Horses." I removed the splinters. Her eyes kept the tears. But she never flinched.

Blink.

Loef Brummel's car disappears into Wells Street traffic.

Maureen stares hard at the FBI car, then steps out of her doorway, passing the small tables and window flower boxes that front the Malvern. She checks the alley shadows before she crosses. The dog doesn't growl. Maureen doesn't stop until there's no space between us. Her hands rise from her hips and flatten on my chest. Her skin radiates heat.

The fingers slide slowly to my neck, then lace behind it. Her red lips part and she bores deep into my eyes, searching for proof she and I are where we're supposed to be. Maureen presses all of her against me, breathes so I can feel it, and whispers, her lips on my ear, "The long grass, Dennis. Our future's there. Canaryville and the Blacks, this business here, with men like Brummel, will kill us."

I don't ease her off my chest.

A woman who doesn't scare easily, says, "It's a bog wind blowin' all around you. I know better, but I'll not leave you to her. She'll take me, the same as you, and whoever's in her path. You need to know that."

A slowing southbound four-door passes us and stops in front of her pub windows. Indiana plates. St. Patrick's parade revelers exit from three doors. One of the men wears a green sweatshirt with "PROVOS" over a nationalist flag and an AK-47 crossed into a Catholic crucifix. He sees the bouncers at the front door, the orange pocket squares in their sport coats, and stops. The bouncer shakes his head but doesn't move.

Maureen says, "The long grass, Dennis."

I focus over her shoulder. Five miles south is a bloodbath-mix of crushing sadness and lynch-mob rage, that *may* annul the FBI's grand jury if I can stop the reprisals. And *no* grand jury would truly be the long grass. I hug Maureen to me. "I know Maureen Cane. If I run from a war I can stop, she won't want me for long."

Maureen says, "I want the man I'm holding now. If he'll not allow misplaced loyalty to kill him."

"Baby, I'm not built to run. I'll win and all will be forgiven."

She stiff-arms away, her blue eyes hurt but defiant, then points hard at the Provos/IRA T-shirt. "I lost a father and a husband to that fight. I'll not marry another to lose him to the Blacks and the Catholics of Canaryville, and theirs."

"Two days, that's all. I'll win. No more citizens have to die; FBI and US Attorney drop the grand jury. I promise."

Maureen slams into me, tears running down her cheeks. Her fingers dig into my back, holding on, a rare demonstration of weakness, the second one today. "Dennis, *please*. Don't make me choose between you and us. Give this up. You have to."

I stare at her tone, her shoulders trembling in my hands, the absolute certainty of disaster carved in her face. Something is way out of line here. It's like I'm looking at a table of tarot cards and an empty chair after the reader bolted.

Chapter 9

STEVEN

I killed thirty-eight people yesterday. Thirty-nine, if you count the nipper. I made money and endured not a drop of goo under my fingernails. In a few hours, I'll earn again. There might be a bit of mess this time. Everyone, please watch your step.

The Chicago *Herald*—Chicago's waste of wood—has, in their *special edition*, headlined me with: "IS THIS THE BAYSIDE BOMBER?" atop a police-artist sketch that is an embarrassment to a matchbook art school. The newspaper called me a monster, and wondered ad nauseam how a human being could do what I've done.

Please. Mix sufficient blood and entrails into the ink and the *Herald* has a reason to turn the presses on tomorrow.

Early in my career I used to debate the difference between my field of commercial endeavor and the more common freedom fighters, ultranationalists, superpower collateral-damagers that also sell newspapers and their advertising. But no more. Media is murder and the übermorality of state is nothing but an existential blank check.

And, alas, few of our fellow twenty-first centurians will ever understand that, or see deeper than an insurance claim adjuster. Call me immodest, but I've been gifted with the painter's eye and a curator's discipline, especially so concerning smoking rubble. Photographs in particular.

The art required to capture the power and precision of an explosion—after the fact—requires vision one rarely encounters. Anyone with an Instamatic can shoot for the six-o'clock carnage effect, but the truly great smoking-rubble photographs rival Georgia O'Keeffe's flowers for sexual imagery. But to see the blossom for what it is, a fellow traveler must have the painter's eye.

"A-ha!" the doctors would say. "The very same eye as Walter Sickert—allegedly—and John Wayne Gacy!"

Thank you, no, they are not me; I work in acrylic. When Walter was not slashing through Whitechapel, allegedly; or Gacy—born on St. Paddy's Day ☺—was not sodomizing runaways in his basement cemetery, both worked almost exclusively in oil, and quite possibly the drying time drove them mad.

All kidding aside, where Sickert, Gacy, and I *do* intersect is our impact on the public consciousness. While we're operating in your neighborhood—picking your flowers so to speak—the neighbors and next of kin lurch out of their sleepwalking existence to hammer their windows shut and nail crucifixes to the doors.

My work at the Bayside Inn certainly has pushed that button. As I said, my work always does, but the ripple effect here has been mega prodigious. I had no idea Chicago was quite this deep into racial fragmentation—Black-white-brown. Give the nuns here machetes like those three penguins in Rwanda—yes, yes, I know, somewhat of a stretch and not smoking rubble, but what a series those photographs were, nun hackers, blood-spattered habits—a Pulitzer every one. I mailed copies to my childhood shrinks, asking for an explanation that never came. Little Stevie Sociopath is straitjacket-for-life, but Rwanda is . . . *what?* Understandable? Nuns there can join the party there because it's . . . African? Won't that sound PC on the talk-show circuit. Probably why no one explained African nuns hackin' for Jesus.

I'd love to explain, and could, but, alas, I'm not Little Stevie anymore; I'm a professional—and unlike the delusional "American Terrorist" Tim McVeigh who wildly flattered himself a professional—I actually am. I do not succumb to temptation. I work; I paint; I *comment.*

***

Between its streetlights, Ashland Avenue is dark. My client material-izes as she approaches the shadowy bus-stop bench for our meeting.

On my phone is the clandestine video of her—sent by my man in her camp as "proof of contact." The first frame is a mural in Belfast, the corner of Malvern Street and Shankill Road.

Shankill Road, for those unfamiliar with urban warfare, is the Protestant-paramilitary artery of Belfast. And has been for ninety years. Fifty of her buildings—from Boundary Street to Woodvale Avenue—are muraled with dead gunmen, petrol bombs, and impris-oned British patriots. Day and night, the two-story paintings shout *Loyalist* and *Ulster* at half of West Belfast's working-class pubs and council housing.

I've been there; did the *tour de mural*. Not great, but as primitiv-ism, I'd give them a well-intentioned "ho hum." Midway up the road from this one is an orange-brick reformation church.

The video starts: Inside the church, five men in nondescript pea-coats and field jackets guard the doors. Each has a short-barreled submachine gun. The nave they guard radiates violence, not salvation, a consequence of a bitter, internal power struggle within the Loyalist UVF—the Ulster Volunteer Force.

Two hundred members sit the pews. The Irishwoman who stands to speak is known to all. According to my conduit, she's three days free of Havana's Manto Negro prison. She has one hand, burn scars above her right eye and ear, and a history of catastrophic violence committed by and against her. Her clothes are modest—men's pants, high-neck sweater, a small orange scarf tied at her neck. Her diction is sharp, her intentions clear.

"For God and Ulster, I openly state my name on the record: I am Corrissa Howat. I am a Loyalist, a Protestant patriot in the ninety-year war with the IRA. If our Northern Ireland is to remain British, safe from the Catholics and their murderous benefactors in America, it is us in this church, the heart of the Ulster Volunteer Force, who must carry the fight.

"Should the UVF bow to the peace agreements signed by the cowards who led us while I was incarcerated—"

Cowards grates through the crowd.

Respect, not fear, keeps fists on knees and weapons in belts.

Howat points her arm-stub at five men wearing balaclavas and forage caps. "Allow the Brigade Staff's peace agreements to stand and it will be the heads of your children, not shamrocks, that the Catholics brandish for their Falls Road parades."

A voice in the crowd shouts: "No man here lays down his guns without protections."

Howat shouts back: "There be no protections! Allow London's Parliament the room to lay us defenseless before the wolves and that day will come. As we sit silent, Parliament's accountants and taxmen tally the cost of Ulster remaining under Britain's flag. They and their Catholic 'peace partners' on the Falls Road plot the Final Solution for our six counties of Ulster.

"Be clear, gentlemen, we will no longer be Northern Ireland. We will be Jews on an island unified under the Catholics—Nazis by another name—our history in Ulster will be erased, with it our heroes, our martyrs, our schools, even our streets. There will be no record of what our generations died for and we willingly surrendered."

Have to admit, pretty darn good. They'll need better muralists to do her justice.

I pocket my phone and step out of the shadows.

Corrissa Howat watches me approach. We arrive at the bus-stop bench from opposite sides. She tosses a McDonald's bag on the bench and, in the same motion, slides her one hand under her jacket.

Ms. Howat looks the part of a budget Irish revolutionary, sort of a proto-Protestant Joan of Arc gone bad. *Pretty* might have been part of her childhood, but now the eyes are hard and fit coarse features that modern imagery associates with hunger or madness. She isn't slender, she's corded; *coiled* is more accurate, a formidable woman whose zealotry has replaced her reproductive juices.

She says, "The remainder for Target One. Half payment for Target Two."

I'm not happy about the afternoon's close call and am compelled to share. "The . . . mess . . . at the train tracks on Forty-Third Street?"

"And what of it?"

"Did you have a hand"—small smile—"in it?"

"And if I did, it'd be none of your affair."

"The timing nearly resulted in my capture. Extracurricular activities—scheduled but withheld from me—are not acceptable within my rules of engagement. They will not be tolerated. They will not go unaddressed."

Ms. Howat points at her paper bag. "You and I begin and end there. My use of your efforts is not, and never will be, subject to your rules of engagement."

Hmmm. "As you wish, madam."

She checks her watch on the arm that has no hand. "You are prepared for tonight?"

My small smile remains pasted. "My preparations aren't your purview, only the outcomes." I point at her paper bag. "In four hours, make sure the remainder is where it's supposed to be."

2:00 a.m.

Target Two is a defrocked priest accused of molesting children many years ago when it was still okay. He is, at this moment, taking his nightly neighborhood perambulation. His crimes must've been bad if the Vatican actually punched his ticket instead of moving him across the street. From what I know of my client's unfortunate family history in both Ireland and Chicago, I suspect there might be a deeper sin in Target Two's backstory other than the occasional fling with a pubescent.

My psychiatrist at the hospital was quite attentive to me—handsome, virile pubescent that I was—took me under his wing and other appendages, got me started on this career, in fact.

Ah, the good old days when the state could still afford to be your angel . . .

Anyway, Target Two now lives in the Hardscrabble by the river, perilously close to the Hispanics, but still comfy within the insular safety of the Irish Riviera. Father "Augustine P. O'Dwyer" has neighbors who are unaware of his political history or his real name. He has disguised himself well, and may or may not still enjoy the pleasures of children.

Tonight, Father Augustine seems more complacent than what I have observed during his previous day and night rituals. Hiding successfully in plain sight for thirty years will cause such lapses in almost anyone—ask Adolf Eichmann.

Like Herr Eichmann, my target does not see his captor coming.

***

Now seated behind the wheel of Father Augustine's Ford Focus—a vehicle I would not recommend over a Toyota—I watch the second-floor windows of his apartment. Inside, the gentleman who introduced me to my client finishes up a modicum of housekeeping, elements of Corrissa the Revolutionary's story to which I am not party. Undoubtedly, the housekeeping includes breadcrumbs for the constabulary and media.

I have a twinge of concern about the breadcrumbs and their risk to me. That said, the gentleman leaving them is from my professional tribe. Although he no longer practices our profession, he knows the penalty for a second transgression regarding my security. My fingers drum the steering wheel. Do I smell my tribesman's participation in the mess at the train tracks? Do I care?

Hmmm. Yes, I believe I do. According to the media, one of the murders there was clean, the other a psychotic break. Not good to be involved with those types, even from a distance.

My tribesman exits onto the street, walks past me in the Focus, and touches his Donegal cap.

Okay, we are a go. I pop the lights and drive off toward the Union Stock Yards and Father Augustine's date with destiny. He's dressed for it: naked, tied, and blindfolded in his trunk.

I make Ashland Avenue, then turn back east, cut the headlights, and creep through what remains of the dark and cavernous Union Stock Yards. More than nine hundred million cattle, sheep, and pigs were killed here, pouring so much of their blood, grease, and waste into the river that those renderings poisoned Chicago's water supply and forced the city to reengineer the river to flow backward. I steer Father Augustine's car past dark warehouses, some new, some old, then empty lots where the animal pens stood for a century, and finally onto Exchange Avenue. At the last alley on the left, I pull in and park behind the majestic, long-abandoned bank building at Exchange and Halsted.

Father Augustine thumps in the trunk. An unseemly, unnecessary attempt at conversation. I resist the urge to scold him.

Ever the professional, I grab my flashlight and a suitcase and exit the car. At the building's back door, I take a moment to enjoy the drama to come, then dial in the combination of the Realtor's key box. The key works; the door creaks open.

Inside, the air of the dark rotunda is stale, fetid with partially desiccated rats and their droppings. It's comforting to know the Union Stock Yards is still processing animals.

I drop the suitcase, heavy with its forty feet of rope. It echoes. Small shapes skitter. I return for Father Augustine and open the trunk. Balled fetal, he has watered himself. His mouth gums at his gag.

"There, there. All in good time. First, we shall depart this stinky mess you've made." I help the bound and blindfolded Father Augustine out of the trunk. His vinegary male parts drag over the trunk lip. Father Augustine stumbles on his feet, shivering and dizzy from his undressing, the confinement, and the ether.

"Very good." His private parts seem lost in the moonlight. I try not to look but they're so small, shrunken to a walnut cluster. "You're frightened. I understand. Nothing to be ashamed of."

Father Augustine radiates fear through his wobbly confusion. I remove his blindfold. "Is that better?" His eyes are saucers; so egregiously large it hurts to look at them. I replace the blindfold and lead him inside. Our footsteps echo, as does the door when I shut it.

"The Irish boys you *allegedly* abused long ago are upstairs. Possibly they will accept your apology, but I can promise nothing; it is in God's hands. And there's that rumor about the bomb, not sure how He's gonna handle that either . . ."

Father Augustine shakes his head hard from side to side, like he doesn't see how it is possible that his accusers are here in Chicago. I light my flashlight and run it over his body. He is not attractive, but still, there are many things I could do . . . have done . . . alone in the dark . . . with the terrified. Blood begins to flow toward my center; images and sounds make a painting in my head and an ache in my pants. But I cannot. Father Augustine—all of him—belongs to my client.

I cradle his chin with both my palms, fingertips massaging his neck. I kiss him lightly on the gag in his mouth, and we begin the long journey to the clocktower sixty feet above us.

Chapter 10

DENNY

The far northwestern quarter of the Riviera is 4:00 a.m. dark, exhausted from the last fifteen hours of the Bayside to the south. Jimmie and I are standing beneath the abandoned Stock Yards clocktower at Exchange Avenue. The silence is jittery, and should be, like a train that vibrates your feet before you see or hear it blast out of the dark.

The radio in my hand breaks the silence: "Roadblocks at Pershing are up, Lieutenant. FBI car is here but hasn't tried to pass."

"No cars come in till I say different; no pedestrians; no exceptions."

"Ten four, Lieutenant."

I turn toward the fireman waiting with his crew at their bucket and ladder truck. The fireman's bucket is already extended three stories into the night above us.

I inhale, wish there was another way, then signal *Showtime.*

The fireman ignites the bucket's Pelican 8K Lamp with a *pop.*

Half his crew winces and looks away.

The powerful light illuminates a tight ten-foot circle of red bricks midway up the clocktower spire of the Stock Yards National Bank. The spire could pass for a church steeple if prayer mattered more than money at a slaughterhouse.

Suspended in the circle is a naked man at the end of a hangman's rope. The eight-coil noose has grossly elongated the man's neck. His blood and fluids have settled into his lower extremities, distorting their shape and color. Forty feet beneath his ballooned feet, the contents of his intestines are splattered not far from my shoes.

A fireman in front of me makes the sign of the cross and mumbles, "Hell ain't big enough," then turns away into the crosshatch of deep shadows behind us.

As much as I need to look, I can't risk *this* drama, not here, and not now. I wave for the ladder-truck operator to cut the light. He does. Jimmie doesn't protest. I turn my back on the victim and stare two blocks south and a block east to the emergency lights that still glow above the Bayside crime scene Jimmie and I left five hours ago.

I look like three hours' sleep; Jimmie doesn't. Today, his runway ensemble is covered by a 'clamshell gray' Burberry raglan overcoat and a hint of Charles Street cologne. Three hours' sleep; Jimmie looks and smells better than I did at my wedding. He hands me our second cup of coffee. His hand is steady, but the eyes are worried.

Jimmie Daniels worried ain't good. I've faced more than a thousand death scenes as a detective. Vicks under the nose and one beer after the paperwork will cover all but the bad ones—someone's little girl, or a wheelchair whose front-door locks didn't hold—that kinda death scene never lets go of you. That's the way Jimmie looks now, and he shouldn't—not because a white guy is hung from a clocktower.

Puzzling? Yeah. How's it nobody saw this happen? The Bayside is three blocks from here . . . Okay; three blocks is a substantial distance in the pitch dark of the Stock Yards. Except last night half of CPD's Targeted Response Unit (TRU) was patrolling this neighborhood, its street crowds, and its families who vigil'd all night at the Bayside. Add the news vans and reporters; the wolf packs and ambulance chasers . . . Whoever committed the execution behind me and got away with it unseen was good, not lucky—

Shoulder bump. I turn back to face the clocktower and the sudden aroma of hot chocolate. One of my Second Watch detectives points at the hanged man. "Den, that has to come down. Posthaste."

I resist saying, *Well, fucking duh.* It's not his fault he was called in from his bed, same as me.

"The guy's collar, Den. The Riv can't see that. Not today. We'd have to call the Marines."

The man hanging naked above us has a priest's collar cinched deep into his neck. On a Sunday. In the heart of Canaryville. Three hours before the first bells at St. Gabriel's will ring to gather the grieving.

I glance at Jimmie making crime-scene diagrams in his notebook, the pen lost in his thick Black fingers. I don't have a good press release for who'd hang a naked priest at Exchange and Halsted, and I'm guessing Gael Gilmartin won't either.

Nobody here is accusing the ghetto, but we're all thinking it: two plus two equals Cleopatra Jones, Black as I wanna be; *burn, baby, burn.*

Face rub. The shave I didn't do scrapes my palms. Calling in the Marines isn't that bad an idea. My radio squawks again. I answer, "Banahan."

A uniform's voice says: "Car 916, Pershing and Halsted. We have two more cars at the blockade demanding to be let through. Bishop Haswell Burke, the church of Christian Identity guy—"

"I know who he is."

"What do I tell him? He has two news crews recording us."

I look up at the victim I can't cut down until the ME and crime-scene techs are done. And they haven't started yet because they're all working three blocks south or catching a few hours at the morgue on cots.

"Tell him to burn more Korans."

"Did not copy. Say again?"

"Tell Bishop Burke to make a Big Mac outta the Koran, Bible, and Torah. You and him have a Happy Meal."

"I'm sorry, Lieutenant, I don't understand."

Jimmie Daniels bends to frown into my face. I relent.

"Bishop Burke is from Florida. He's not the current boss of Halsted Street, I am. Tell the bishop and his cameras to turn the fuck around and get off my street."

"But the cameras—"

"Put your sergeant on."

Silence, then: "Sergeant Pulaski."

"Tell Bishop Burke to turn around or you'll impound his car. If he declines to cooperate, apply the same laws to him you would to any other asshole who thinks your uniform is a costume."

"Arrest him?"

"Shoot him if it's warranted."

"Ten four. Always a pleasure, Lieutenant."

I button off. Jimmie keeps the frown and says, "Maybe hop in the car, catch a few hours till you sober up."

I don't smell like alcohol; I smell good, like the few hours I spent with Maureen. I hoist my balls with my radio hand and pull my BlackBerry with the other. I can do technology: "Call the ME."

It calls, gets voicemail. I disconnect.

"Call the Twelfth District." The BlackBerry does; a female officer answers.

"This is Denny Banahan, Area One Homicide." I hoist my balls again. "Could you please send a uniform down the street to the morgue? Tell the ME to call me, right now, a-sap?"

"Hi, Den. Marie Gilmartin."

"Hey, sis. You . . . okay?"

"Grace a God, Da and my uncle Tommy weren't in the Bayside."

"Was bad-worried until Gael told me your da called her."

"Gael and I, and Da and Tommy, went door to door last night, seeing who hadn't come home. Hardest night of my life. Gael's, too."

"Do me a favor?"

Marie pauses. "If it's legal."

"The fire-breathers listen to your father. Ask him to do what he can today and tomorrow."

"Better you ask. You know, it'd be official. Da's . . . past you and Gael. You guys were ages ago."

"Right. Fire Battalion Chief Gilmartin is *never* forgiving me for marrying a Black woman instead of his daughter."

"There's that, yeah. And if the Bayside is Red Summer, Da won't be putting out any fires south of the Riv."

"Send someone down to the ME for me, okay? Talk to your dad, then come find me and we'll go see him together. Whatever's up, it isn't over, but I got nothing that says Red Summer."

Jimmie acknowledges a pretty damn good lie.

Marie says, "Ten four," and disconnects.

Jimmie points at the clocktower and snips his fingers like scissors.

I balk. "You're the acting ME?"

"No. But I can cut the rope. We allow the media that photo, this sergeant's calling in medical till the fires are out."

I know the truth when I hear it. "Have the fireman re-pop the light. We'll take the rest of the photos and measurements. If the ME doesn't show when we're done, then it's plan B."

5:30 a.m.

An hour ago, I called Cullen Mahoney, gave him the report, and went with plan B. I rode up in the ladder-bucket with a fireman. He cut the rope; the misshapen victim fell two feet into the plastic sheet covering my arms and the bucket's edges. Father John Doe smelled of intestines and ether and we all rode to the ground. I pulled the roadblocks at Pershing. Area One Homicide went to work.

My guys and the crime-scene techs are inside the deserted bank's rotunda, up in the cupola, and out on the clocktower processing the scene. The ME is down here on the pavement with me and the body.

The ME notes the smell of ether on the victim's skin. The ME's initial, off-the-record cause of death is traumatic asphyxia (suffocation; the noose did not break the victim's neck) and guesses the time as midnight to two a.m., meaning the victim hung at the Stock Yards entry, naked, for at least two hours in the pitch dark while much of the city's focus was only three blocks away.

The detectives I have on loan from across the river in Area Four are canvassing the commercial spots that would've been open. The residential door-to-door will have to wait till after sunrise and the first bells at St. Gabriel's. I don't want to initiate the canvass; nor do I want to wait. The Realtors who rep the crime-scene building are on their way here from Lincoln Park, a leafy part of town where they made it clear they'd much rather stay.

Jimmie and I trade theories, sipping coffee, trying to tie the Riv's three crime scenes and multiple perps together. This cup of coffee tastes no better than the others. Our theories that don't have Red Summer at their center are no better than the coffee.

Unfortunately, Black versus white will be everyone's answer. And it should be, because Red Summer covers all the bases, and so far, nothing else does.

We have no idea who Father John Doe is, if in fact he was a priest. Jimmie stops looking. His chin rises, flexing his neck, ears perked.

I scan Halsted's gray windows. None are open. The rooftops, teardown prairies (vacant lots), and narrow streets are deserted. They won't stay empty or silent for long.

Jimmie says, "Taking a minute."

"Again? Where you going? They got food and babes there?"

Jimmie doesn't smile.

"C'mon, it ain't *that* bad."

Jimmie points toward the streetlights where the two Black men from Mississippi were hung during 1919's Red Summer. "I hear 'em, Den."

Anyone else says that to me, I laugh in their face. Not Jimmie Daniels. If Jimmie says dead men are talking to him, they are. "You okay?"

Jimmie licks at his lips, eyes on the lights. "They're begging." Five seconds pass. Jimmie shuts his eyes.

A Crown Vic lurches to the tape and the doors pop. Two detectives from Area Four get out, both with doughnuts, one detective with more white shirt than his jacket will ever cover, the other with a mean streak that will one day have him breaking rocks for twenty to life. These detectives are not assigned to this case, although I know them both.

The one with the stomach stares up at the tower and barks, *"No."* He has a small digital camera in his hand. "You cut him down already?"

His partner with the mean streak, Detective Timothy Baskett, says, "But it was a priest, right? And naked, no shit?"

I nod at Detective Timothy "Fruit" Baskett, so named because it is rumored Tim takes it in the ass every now and then. Not from another guy, from his Belgian girlfriend who likes to strap on the biggest piece of equipment her genuine Adam & Eve leather harness will handle, then bang Fruit Baskett until she's done re-reciting her five citizenship-test questions (she passed). No, I don't know why; I asked once, but didn't press it; I *do* know that Tim attended Kinky Kollege at the Hyatt last October, "a pansexual institute of higher learning," because he brought my secretary a T-shirt. She filed on him for harassment.

Fruit Baskett looks past Jimmie and me, focuses on the Bayside emergency lights, and says: "Oh, shit, fuck-a-duck. *The priest is tied to the Bayside?* And Loef Brummel's double at the tracks? Oh, fuck. Hell comes to Frogtown."

Hell Comes to Frogtown is a pro wrestler cult movie.

Fruit's partner bites into his doughnut, then fans the powdery remainder 270 degrees. "Got the Riv surrounded, spics to the west, mayor on the run, CPD gonna fold to the Feds . . ." He nods at Fruit Baskett. "Ayatollah runs Red Summer right up the gut. Shit, this game's already over. Fire trucks are gonna run outta water."

I stare at Fruit Baskett's partner. "You have proof the Ayatollah's behind Red Summer?" I point at the body. "And this guy, too?"

"Well, fuck, Lieutenant, no offense, but who else would do that to a priest?"

"Satanists. Altar boys. Nuns."

Fruit's partner makes a quick sign of the cross with his half dough-nut. "God forgive ya, Lieutenant."

I frown at two loose cannons who could sink a lot of ships given current conditions. "You guys want something? The rest of us have shit to do."

Fruit Baskett says, "An hour ago, we crashed three P-Stones north of the river on Ashland driving a Ford Focus they didn't own. Had blood, piss, and ether in the trunk."

"Ether?" I don't look at Jimmie or the clocktower victim.

"Half a can. Car's registered to an Augustine P. O'Dwyer in the Hardscrabble, Thirty-First and Keeley. A brave old Irishman living within spittin' distance of the spics across the river; gotta love him." Fruit eyes his partner for agreement. "We had Patrol book the P-Stones on grand theft auto and went by the apartment; knocked, door's unlocked . . ."

They both swallow the last of their doughnuts.

I glance at Jimmie, stone faced, also pretending *ether* didn't ring his bell. He and I both know: A white priest, lynched naked by three Black P-Stones equals National Guard and city on fire.

I fake disinterest. "Why bother us?"

"Heard your vic here had a priest collar." Fruit pulls a framed eight-by-ten out of his car and hands it to me. "Photo of Augustine P. His closet had priest vestments in a hang-up bag, travel posters for Ireland, and some NAMBLA material—"

"Nambla?"

"North American Man/Boy Love Association."

I look up from the photograph that could match the bloated face of the hanged man on the ground. NAMBLA-related murder would be excellent; there's no Red Summer in NAMBLA—a completely new way for us to go—crazed Canaryville altar boy goes serial killer. I cut to Fruit's partner. He shrugs and doesn't make the sign of the cross this time.

"P-Stones say where the car's owner went?"

Fruit shakes his head.

"The P-Stones smell like ether?"

Fruit's partner says, "Like P-Stones."

Frown. "Where are they?"

Fruit says, "Patrol has 'em at Twelve."

I tell him: "Keep your Ayatollah-Red Summer theory between you and the doughnuts. We don't need gasoline on the Bayside fire." I pull my BlackBerry, punch "B," scroll to Buff Anderson, the TAC sergeant in Twelve, and hit call.

Two rings. Buff answers, "Tell me you're at the racetrack."

"Almost—"

"Banahan, you ain't that stupid. You're not working the Bayside."

I don't answer.

Buff mutters profanity, then, "So, the war's started? Feds got you carrying their ammunition?"

"You'll be down here fightin' when it starts."

"I'll be in Florida. Had my fill of the Feds last year with Bobby Vargas."

"Feds will be backing down for a bit, waiting for us to take the bullet or hand them a solution."

Buff says, "I don't work one day for the Feds. Not an hour. *And you*, FBI Prison Trophy"—Buff cranks his voice—"better watch your ass. You're their gift to Marion."

"Bayside's bad, Buff. Could get lots worse."

"Was off yesterday, packing up the house for the movers when we heard—the wife handcuffed me to the bed; hid my gun. Said she'd waited up every night for thirty-five years; almost lost me last year. No fuckin' way I was going in." Buff coughs. "I owe her, you know? And she already bought the suntan lotion. And she's right, thirty-five years of this shit's enough. Let these armchair geniuses build utopia on their own blood."

Like before, I know the truth when I hear it. "Fruit Baskett said he shipped you three P-Stones and a Ford Focus."

"Looking at the P-Stones right now. Fez and Pretty Ricky are asking them why Fifty-Fourth Street Africans are bangin' on our end of Brown Town."

"Tell your guys to stand down, okay? Nobody talks to the P-Stones. Be there in ten minutes."

"Feds let you drive by yourself?"

"So far. Don't mention I'm interested; don't want anyone getting the wrong idea . . ."

"Huh?" Buff loses the banter and makes the leap. "These guys are the Bayside? *Red Summer?* It's happening?"

"Hope not." I hang up and wave at Jimmie for the car keys. "Your minute will have to wait."

Jimmie flips me the keys. "P-Stones didn't hang our priest."

Fruit's partner says, "Why? 'Cause they're Black?"

Jimmie frowns. "Because you're wrong."

Fruit joins in. "You mean because my partner's white."

"No. Substitute *lazy* for *white.*"

"Fuck you, hambone. And your thousand-dollar shoes."

I turn my back to Jimmie and what I'm certain are the appropriate cordovans and ask Fruit: "How about you two gentlemen drive me to Twelve? Tell me what you have on the P-Stones." I point Fruit and his partner to their car, then turn and press car keys back into Jimmie's size 14 hand. "Gimme an hour."

Jimmie nods. "P-Stones didn't hang the priest."

"They had his car. It had ether."

"Yes, they had his car. But they didn't hang him. ME made the priest's time of death midnight to two. No way three Blacks were roaming *anywhere* in the Riv last night. I figure they jacked the car *after* the murder, somewhere north of the river, in which case they saw the killer. Or the killer dumped the car and they stumbled onto it." Pause. "They didn't slaughter Dill either. P-Stones aren't people, but they aren't *that*, either."

"How 'bout bombing the Bayside?"

Jimmie frowns. "Fifty-fifty. No command structure anymore. Lotta crazy on the shorties. Somebody could've paid 'em, but they'd have had the huge problem of getting the bomb inside."

I nod. "Call Fruit's LT at Area Four; tell him I want *our crew* to process the priest's apartment. Then round up whoever's slept enough to not screw it up. Strike that, grab R. Murph off the Bayside. Roger will be sober and church doesn't scare him. We're looking for . . . all the shit you know we're looking for." I wait for the nod I get. "Then you call Mahoney *back-channel* and tell him the bad news."

Jimmie says, "Father Augustine P. O'Dwyer?" Jimmie chins at the rope strand still hanging above us.

"That would qualify. *Somebody* has to tell Superintendent Smith that an Irish priest *might've* been lynched in Canaryville, and Mahoney won't want to be that messenger. You're big on the Cowboy-Indian stuff; Smith's a Hohokam, and a little short on the Denny love at the moment. Throw some *medicine man* in for him and maybe Superintendent Smith won't blame us."

6:30 a.m.

Fruit drops me at the Twelfth District station, a nondescript tan building at Racine and Monroe in Greektown. When we passed my perimeter at Pershing, what looked like another FBI tail car didn't ID me slouched in Fruit's back seat. Everybody seemed intent on Bishop Haswell Burke and his cameras.

Walking into Twelve, I don't see Marie Gilmartin at the desk, nor down the back stairs to the basement. The first door is to the old firing range and still stinks of burned gunpowder. Now the range is full of beat-to-shit metal lockers. Beyond the "locker room" is another door, also open, the combined Twelfth District TAC office and prisoner lockup.

The TAC office is a low-ceilinged square with reject desks jammed together in the center. Reject computers and printers cover the desks. The "lockup" is two metal benches in the corner with a pipe-backrest to handcuff the arrestees to. On one of the benches sit three Black men, two of them are early twenties—gang tats from a Fifty-Fourth Street Almighty Black P Stone set, vacant eyes, and not an ounce of fear. The third one I know; he and I have been to murder school twice. My old friend RayLen Starks.

"Denny." Buff exits his closet-sized office just left of the entry door, throws an arm around me, then introduces me to each of the eight young guys in jeans and body armor about to pull a double shift, one of whom I know from the racetrack, John "Fez" Kelyana. I shake hands eight times. Buff opens his arms to include them all. "The Wild Bunch, back when we were still the police."

One of the P-Stones harrumphs.

Always start with the one who wants to talk. I ask to borrow Fez's chair, then pull it to RayLen and sit so our knees touch. This way he can't kick me if he wants to go to the hospital ICU instead of county jail.

"So, Ray, yesterday, I'm out walking my dog by Harold's Chicken, you know? Minding my own business and these three street-pimp P-Stones roll up on me, talking all kinds of shit about my dog, me, and white people in general. Like eating greasy at Harold's gives these pimps the right. Know what I'm saying?"

RayLen doesn't remember yesterday or doesn't think I deserve an answer.

I point at his arm tat. "Just you on Fifty-Fourth or you still got peeps across the Ryan?"

He leans back against the handcuff rail, face slack. I don't lean forward.

"No? Your peeps move to Englewood when Stateway and RT came down? You know, back when I popped your ass for murder? Not the old woman you raped before and after; I mean the second time."

The brown eyes stare into nowhere. I glance his partners, both MIA in the same street defense.

"Jesus, Ray, your peeps didn't move up close to Canaryville, did they? Seeing distance from the Bayside Inn? The Irish bar that blew itself up yesterday lunchtime?"

Nothing. I tap his nearest knee. His eyes cut to mine.

I drop the happy out of my tone. "'Cause if your baby mamas stay by Canaryville, they best be white or they already dead. If you got Black babies who still in the Deuce or Englewood, they charcoal when the shit starts—unless the Reverends got their own fire trucks. 'Cause like the Reverends say"—I point over my shoulder at Fez and his Hispanic partners behind me—"Five-O ain't comin' to save no Africans, and your ass'll be in here."

RayLen's eyes fade back to blank. Either he has no people in the Ayatollah's neighborhoods or RayLen doesn't believe whitey can match "Move out or burn out."

I tap his knee again. "Forty-Third and Emerald. Bayside Inn. Ever been there?"

The banger to RayLen's right stiffens.

I slide my chair to him, our knees touching. He retreats into the void, his face empty. I tell his mask: "The car you're driving belongs to a murder victim."

All three wake up.

I pinch my thumb and finger "That's *life* in Stateville, and RayLen here came this close the last time me and him hooked up. *Life* for-fucking-ever, homes, unless our acting governor re-ups the death penalty like he says he will."

I'm close enough to smell ether on them, but don't.

"Kill a white man the way your victim went—Aryan Brotherhood ain't going for that. You're gonna die in your cell, or on the yard, or on the gurney. So we better explain how you're driving a dead man's car if you didn't kill him for it."

Three sets of eyelids flutter. I now have what passes for everyone's attention. A murder charge often accomplishes that if no one in hand-cuffs was expecting it.

"Maybe you jacked him. Left him wandering the street. Shit hap-pens; not your fault a bunch of Four Corners Latinos killed him. Brown Town's a bitch, Jim. Am I right?"

The P-Stone to RayLen's right nods a half inch.

I show him four fingers on one hand and two on the other. "We have forty-two dead in the Riv, all white. And 'cause Five-O pops you in the Focus owned by one of the decedents, it's gonna look like maybe you gentleman did *all* forty-two." I point at the walls protecting them. "This place won't hold ten minutes when them drunken, racist Irishmen come up here. You'll be hanging from the streetlights." I turn behind me to Buff's gang team, every one of them with *Holy shit—these are the Bayside bombers?* in their eyes. I wave for the *Herald* on the nearest desk. The front page is a six-column photo of the Bayside Inn and a three-inch headline: "MASS MURDER."

I show the headline to RayLen and his crew. "Any of you know how to read?"

All three stare, but remain silent.

I fold the *Herald* and drop it on their bench with the photo showing. "Me and the sergeant gonna get coffee. I'll be back in ten minutes. Between now and then, you decide to save your mamas and yourselves." I point at the walls again. "Or pick your light poles."

Buff looks at me, then tells his guys, "Stay off your phones. None of us want to be here if word leaks we have the Bayside bombers."

Three of his guys say, "No shit."

RayLen cold-eyes Buff, then me. "Muthafucka, you the one goin' to prison, talkin' that light-pole shit to us."

I nod. "Right. Like you'll be alive to testify."

Outside on Monroe Street, Buff squares up on me as soon as he's sure we're alone. "If my P-Stones are the Bayside, Twelve ain't the right jail. The Alamo lasted longer on its last day than this place will."

"Jimmie makes 'em no better than even money *if* they could get the bomb inside. Big *if.* Lotta crazy on the younger ones, though; somebody could've paid 'em. What Jimmie has *for sure* is a priest somebody stripped naked and hung from the Stock Yards clocktower. Your P-Stones are driving the priest's car. Fifteen hours after the Bayside blows three blocks away. That's judge and jury in Canaryville."

Buff looks toward his basement, then me. "Nah. Only way those shitheads bombed the Bayside *and* hung the priest is if this really *is* Red Summer. Otherwise, no fuckin' way. Not in their playbook."

"Something's wrong in Canaryville, way more than usual. We want the whole story to be altar boy goes nuts or Irish crime world, but can't fit it all in either bag."

"And *white versus Black* would hold it all, no fuckin' problem. Blacks have been laying for this fight since the Olympics toasted. Whites, too.

My teams worked that rally in Armour Square last month. Full house, twenty-eight thousand white people pumping their fists. Fuckin' Christian Identity guy, what's his name, leading the charge."

"Bishop Haswell Burke. Back in town as we speak."

"Pinhead Florida cracker." Buff spits in the street. "The wife's got a rack on her, though. Lord, take me to the river. Love to see those loose on baptism day."

I pat Buff's shoulder. "You'll do fine in Florida."

Back downstairs in Twelve, I take a final shot with the three P-Stones. "Okay. Who doesn't wanna do life for carjack murder?"

All three look at me and don't answer.

"Sunrise is coming, fellas. First bells about to ring at St. Gabriel's. That's a Catholic church in Canaryville." I point south. "*Angry* motherfuckers down there, Jim. *Marching* distance from here."

Nothing.

"You fellas remember the last time cops from the Deuce dropped one of your homies in Canaryville? 'Cause homie wouldn't cooperate? Brother lasted ten minutes. *Ten minutes.* And those racist fuckin' Irishmen beat him to death. And they wasn't mad about nothin' that day."

RayLen says, "Findin' a car ain't murder."

"*Findin'* a car? Okay, Ray. You *found* the car. So, maybe you *saw* the guy, or guys, who jacked the Ford Focus we caught you driving. And if you could describe the original driver real good, maybe I could find him and stop Canaryville from deciding to burn you and your mama and everyone you know to the top of their fucking Air Jordans."

RayLen says, "Yeah, we saw your driver. He the muthafuckin' mayor, you know? Had a pipe on him; rollin' concrete lookin' for rock."

I look at Buff. He shrugs.

I pick up the Herald and wave its "MASS MURDER" headline. "Maybe ship one of these felons north to Eighteen or Nineteen, try to keep him alive till this afternoon. Then get your guys outta here. Gimme a few minutes to leak the news that 'two Bayside Inn bombing suspects' are in custody. After alpha-dog Ray here watches his two homies beaten to death and lynched on live TV, he might remember what my Ford's driver looks like."

Buff's guys look at him to see if this is the old-school police procedure they've heard policemen accused of but never seen. Buff straps on a second gun and reaches for his fitted body armor. I call him outside into the hall.

Quietly, I say: "We keep RayLen and his boys here; let them think about what those streetlights will feel like." Buff doesn't nod. I point up the stairs at the rest of the station house. "Don't worry. Anybody upstairs connects our P-Stones to the Bayside, call me; I'll have Mahoney move 'em."

"Nah." Buff shakes his head hard. "Move 'em now, while we can. Word's gonna get out, always does."

"If Mahoney moves 'em now, it makes 'em guilty. Guilty triggers the white side of Red Summer and that equals streetlights."

Buff shakes his head. "I spent fourteen days in ICU last year 'cause of voodoo shit like this. Don't seem fair."

Watch check. Sunrise soon. "C'mon, man." I grin at him. "Join the club. Give Chicago one last chance to kill us."

Chapter 11

Police lights flash from curb to curb at Halsted and Twenty-Second, the Riviera's north border. I'm in the front seat of Fez's car, heading back to the clocktower. Behind the four-car barricade, riot police are deploying with shotguns to both ends of the bridge that spans the river. The heavy Indiana steel and pocked concrete "connects" the Riviera to the rest of Chicago. A news helicopter thumps overhead in the pre-dawn silence.

I call R. Murph, who should be at the victim's apartment by now.

He answers, "Murphy."

"Tell me Father A's killer is a white altar boy from Northern Ireland who's never seen a Black person."

"Nothing so far that says Black or ghetto, but nothing that says 'I love altar boys' either. If Fruit found NAMBLA stuff like Jimmie said, it isn't here."

"What is?"

"No sign of a struggle. No weapons. No phone. No computer—how do you do NAMBLA with no computer? A bible in Gaelic—the *Maynooth*, first edition; lots of passages marked with ribbons."

"Fits a priest."

"Could. A Chicago Auto Parts wall calendar from 1992, no marks. One vinyl album—*War* by U2, the Irish band from Dublin, but no record player. Lots of paperbacks, too many of 'em have *journey* in the title."

"Journey? And you think that means . . ."

"No idea. Maybe tryin' to be elsewhere?"

"Keep looking. Find me something for Gael's next on-camera. Out." I hang up. My phone rings.

Deputy Superintendent Mahoney's diction is precise, a style of speech he reserves for public hearings and executions. "Six minutes ago, the superintendent instructed the Command units to seal the Riviera. All nonresident traffic will be stopped at Fifty-Fifth on the south, the river on the north, Halsted on the west, and the Norfolk Southern tracks on the east. Are your P-Stones responsible for the Bayside?"

"Doubt it. Don't think they did the hanging either—Jimmie told you about the death scene?"

"He did." Pause. "Nine minutes ago, Alderman Gibbons informed the mayor, the superintendent, and the media that he will march into the Riv this morning. To the steps of St. Gabriel's."

"*Shit.*"

Mahoney says, "This could easily be the last of her, Dennis. Think before you act; do not hand the FBI the nails for *your* cross. No matter what happens, we're on the same side. And have been every day since you, Mike, and I learned to walk." Mahoney clicks off.

Huh? I know whose side we're on. Don't I?

The center squad in the blockade pulls back. Fez drives us through. I show my star to the first shotgun, point behind me at the blockade, and tell him, "The Riv's mine."

"Ten four, Lieutenant. We've been told."

"No FBI cars cross this bridge."

Fez accelerates the last of the road, past two tear-down prairies, then onto the Depression-era bascule bridge. Underneath us, heavy barges push inland from Lake Michigan on an urban river.

At the bridge's south side, we're officially in the Riv and immediately funneled down into the dark, diesel-fouled underpass beneath the ATSF switching yard. Trains vibrate above us until we're puked out into the light just long enough to glimpse the giant American flag at Archer Avenue, then roofed in again, this time by massive concrete columns and ten rumbling lanes of the Stevenson Expressway.

Crossing under and over against three major arterial currents is simultaneously jarring and claustrophobic. We exit the concrete columns at Twenty-Sixth Street. The transition is the same as when I was a kid; the world outside the Riviera is gone. And so are the "outside" rules.

In silhouette, the Riv is beginning to light. Trash blows everywhere from last night's crowds, but the streets have no people yet. We roll two blocks south; a WGN media van veers out of an empty side street followed by a similar vehicle from CNN. Fez brakes hard; I brace my knee into the dash. My BlackBerry rings. I tell Fez, "Call perimeter command, ID the vans. Arrest both crews. Strike that. Escort them out," then answer my phone.

"Banahan."

A detective I left at the Bayside says, "Heating up here, Den. Four hundred more on the tape and it ain't light yet. Been laying flower bouquets all night. Standing makeshift crosses with photographs stapled to the wood. Break your fucking heart. These folks want to know . . . something."

"Superintendent Smith just sealed the Riv. Alderman Gibbons is threatening a TV move on the steps of St. Gabriel's—"

"Gibbons can't do that."

"The Ayatollah knows we'll stop him before he gets to St. Gabriel's. No way he'll have to slide one Ban-Lon sock out of his Cadillac."

"No, Denny, no shit. He can't come down here, not in an armored car."

"Not up to us. The Ayatollah's show will happen. The only thing the superintendent and the mayor can pick is the place."

Fez stops us at the clocktower yellow tape. He says, "I know I'm not supposed to ask, but is this . . . *it*? Red Summer?"

"Why? You got somewhere else to be?"

"Like to tell my kids goodbye."

"You don't have any kids."

Fez points at the photo on his visor. "What about my boat?"

Fez hit the Pick Six at Arlington for high five figures; ransomed, then smuggled his family out of Damascus before Assad could kill him and them; spent the rest on a badly beaten thirty-eight-foot Scarab that doubled one of Sonny Crockett's fast boats in Miami Vice. Fez rebuilt and renamed his *Usual Suspects.*

I tell him: "Save me and Jimmie a seat. A mile out on the lake's gonna be a prime place to be." I exit and duck under the yellow tape. Fez flips a U.

Jimmie is at the front fender of his Crown Vic, studying his note-book. He looks up as I approach, and says, "What about the P-Stones?"

"My man, RayLen Starks."

Jimmie wide-eyes. "No way . . ."

I nod, start to explain, and my BlackBerry rings again. I answer, "Banahan," and glance at our clocktower victim still on the ground, noose still cinched into his neck.

Maureen's voice: "Dennis, it's . . . me. Not using my phone. The FBI just left my pub. Still parked out front; two cars, four agents."

"Four? Four's a lotta Gs for seven a.m. On a weekend. You call J. Edgar a swish?"

"They're buildin' for the grand jury . . . you and Renatta. And Loef Brummel."

My ex-wife is a civil rights activist and lawyer. Calling Renatta before a federal grand jury on the eve of Red Summer is either FBI desperation or a bombshell. Bombshell wouldn't bode well for *anyone* associated with her, including me.

"Why come see *you?*"

"For three hours the FBI asked me what you told me, what I knew. And Pádraig the same. They kept comin' back to the two Blacks at the Magikist building in Englewood." Pause. "The FBI says every word in the *Herald* is true—you shot Antoine Starks and his sister. Threw them off a six-story building in Englewood for killing your brother, Mike." Her voice cuts to a whisper. "And that *Loef Brummel* was with you."

Maureen and everyone else in the city knows what my grand jury will be about, but this is the first time anyone's said Loef Brummel was there. "Don't worry. Get some sleep; I'll call you back."

"They were *bold,* Dennis. *High* on it. Said they had a witness they'd be presentin'."

A bell tolls behind me.

"I'll handle it; have before. Get some sleep; call me when you get up and I'll explain. Love you."

The bell's first echo dies over Canaryville's rooftops. Jimmie quits his phone, scribbles quick notes in his journal, then turns toward St. Gabriel's, four blocks south. The bells continue to toll. There will be forty bell tolls in all, and then a last one for Tommy O'Boyle's boy.

I wag my phone. "FBI's at Maureen's pub. About the grand jury."

Jimmie blinks. "The rooftop was thirty years before you met her."

"Even money the FBI's there about her brother; no telling how much crime-world shit his security company's into." I put my hand up before Jimmie can brace me. "I know, I know, you warned me. Somehow, someway knowing him is coming back to bite me in the ass."

"Help a guy like that into the country 'cause you're in love with his sister . . . very definitely could come back—"

The bells toll a third time.

Jimmie blinks, confused. His eyes harden at a thought he doesn't articulate—about Pádraig Cane or maybe RayLen Starks. Jimmie circles his finger high above his shoulder, the signal that our loaner detectives can start the clocktower residential canvass.

For three minutes, the bells call the roll. Leaves blow across crime scene number four into the Stock Yards, into the shadows of the old slaughterhouse buildings and their corners that never see sunlight.

When the echo dies on bell number forty-one, Jimmie makes the sign of the cross, then lifts his notebook from the Crown Vic's fender, waits till he's sure he has my full attention, then reads me what he says he just got on Canaryville murder victim number forty-two: "Augustine P. O'Dwyer. Born South Derry, Northern Ireland, 1946. Ordained 1969; serves as a rural curate in Raphoe, then Malin Head, County Donegal, laicized 1980. Moved to Chicago, USA—"

"Laicized?"

"Defrocked." Jimmie frowns. "Altar boys." His eyes return to his notes. "Moved to Chicago, 1980, on a church-sponsored green card. No arrests, no traffic citations. US citizenship October 19, 1985."

"*Allah be praised.* Altar boys. Where's he work?"

"Don't know. We're checking."

"White serial-killer altar boy attacks Canaryville; Chicago doesn't burn."

"Would be nice."

"C'mon. We're gonna help R. Murph tell us that story. Before the fucking media pours gasoline every-fucking-where."

7:30 a.m.

En route to defrocked Father Augustine's apartment, we pick up an FBI tail car that isn't supposed to be inside Mahoney's barricades. We've got maybe fifteen minutes before sunrise tops the clouds above downtown's skyline and wakes up the Riv.

At the apartment, Jimmie knocks on the first-floor's door to do a witness canvass. I do the long flight of creaky stairs two at a time, duck the yellow tape of possible crime scene number five, and step inside Father Augustine's apartment.

R. Murph is in the bedroom on his knees, surrounded by stacks of papers. He shakes his head. "Nothing yet."

Not what I want to hear.

The rest of Father Augustine's apartment is cluttered, but clean, smells dusty, but isn't. The fridge has a crucifix above the handle, a Chicago Bears magnet, and a "to do" whiteboard with no notes on it. The furniture is dated, but not overly worn.

Watch check.

Three ashtrays but no cigarettes. A small stack of magazines: *Sailing, Poker Player,* the *Economist* (UK)—three copies of each, all without mailing labels. Three pictures on three different walls, all the same scene—a pre-framed, nonstatement, verdant-green landscape.

Lotta threes? I pull my trusty BlackBerry, open Google, and key in "333."

Nothing special in the links.

Jimmie appears at the apartment's open door, notebook in hand, says: "Mexican lady in 1A *thinks* she heard Augustine leave alone around 10:30 p.m. My Spanish isn't as good as yours, but I think she said it was not a normal time for her quiet, white-haired amigo to be up and out."

"How long's Augustine lived here?"

"Was here when 1A moved in, but that was only three months ago. I called the number she has for the landlord. The woman who answered said Augustine's been here since 2000."

I point Jimmie at the twenty-year-old, 1992 calendar on Augustine P. O'Dwyer's wall. "Been here since 2000, why hang a calendar from '92?" The calendar's front page has no dates marked, put out by a Bridgeport auto repair shop.

Jimmie says, "Came with the apartment?"

I use a pencil to raise the pages to our current month. March is announced with the semitasteful/suggestive bathing-suit photo of a young girl in St. Patrick's Day green.

"Probably didn't." I motion for Jimmie to look at the photo, tell him: "Renny-Mac MacGrath; age eighteen. Murdered daughter of Bathhouse John MacGrath."

Jimmie leans much closer, then adds: "Who was Loef Brummel's boss before an unknown assailant killed Bathhouse John and his psycho son on a houseboat in the Florida Keys in . . . 2003?"

"No Blacks. Irishmen, all."

"And Loef Brummel became the new boss." Jimmie straightens to full height. "So, we have a foreign pedophile priest defrocked for boys, but with a twenty-year-old girlie calendar. That *coincidentally* features a legendary Canaryville loan shark's daughter?"

I process a distant, but third, connection between Loef Brummel and a murder victim, then pull my phone and call him. Loef answers. I ask, "Know anyone from South Derry?"

"If you mean the Six (the six counties of Northern Ireland, not the pub), yeah."

"Augustine P. O'Dwyer. Age sixty-five? Might have been a priest."

"He your man on the clocktower?"

"Who said I had a man on the clocktower?"

"I got the same phone number since my parents; you're the one who moved to Sixty-Ninth Street."

Fuck. If Loef knows, the media already knows. "Augustine P. O'Dwyer. Know him or not?"

"Not the name. Maybe the man. What's he look like?"

"Country Irish, five eight, wavy white hair, saggy cheeks, pothole nose, 180 pounds that should've been 150."

"Know a hundred of 'em."

I glance at Jimmie who waves, *Get to it.*

Loef says, "This priest from Derry, he there in '72?"

"Don't know. Why's 1972 matter?"

Loef says, "'Cause '72 was a bad fuckin' year in Derry. Here as well, if you remember your brother, Mike, buyin' it; the forty-five funerals after the Illinois Central went off the tracks at Twenty-Seventh Street ... bad fuckin' year *that has nothing to do with me.*"

Heat rises on my neck. "Assuming you don't want to spend another half day in my office, spend a minute explaining what you mean or I'll send a car by to give you a lift."

Silence, then: "Send your fuckin' car whenever you're ready *assuming* you can find an extra when the shit starts."

I let the blood settle from "remember your brother," then ask Loef, "You do me any good last night with the banshees?"

"Any good? Had to listen to that fuckin'-monkey Ayatollah on TV every-fuckin'-where I went, talkin' about *his* people, the struggle, Red Summer. What about *our* people? Ayatollah better have an answer for them other than 'Irish charcoal.'"

"Grow up" comes out of my mouth before I can stop it. "C'mon, man, it isn't like you don't know the game. The Ayatollah will keep preaching napalm until you and the Riv do something stupid—*like your goddamn lampposts.* Two or three bangers end up swinging. Ghetto retaliates; maybe they hijack three or four gasoline trucks, drive 'em in on all these wooden buildings. All that'll be left from here to Fifty-Fifth Street is foundations. Feds come in, National Guard—you lose half the Riv to some federal agency's 'community revitalization plan' *because they got the money* and you got shit for votes. Rainbow City kumbaya lasts a year or two and all the whites move out. Ayatollah wins; the Riviera's Black."

"Riviera's Irish. You gave the niggers your house. Motherfuckers gotta be alive to move into mine."

I don't remind him that the Byrne's Building burned to its foundation when I was thirteen. "Army will be on every corner if that's what it takes—like Alabama and Mississippi. You're fucked if you let the Ayatollah, or anyone else, bait you into this fight."

"We're fucked; but they're dead."

"Blacks are 35 percent of the city; 80 percent of the South Side; better get used to it."

"Call me when you're done fuckin' around; we ain't got a lotta time. Gonna start bad today and get worse." Click.

I lower the phone, a bit of shake in my hand, punch "Derry Northern Ireland 1972" into Google. The first link is: "Bloody Sunday"—

I glance the U2 album; they're famous for the song "Sunday Bloody Sunday." I point Jimmie at the album. "Read me the song titles on that album."

Jimmie uses a glove, reads: "'Seconds,' 'New Year's Day,' 'Sunday Bloody Sunday'—"

"Denny? Lieutenant?" R. Murph waves me into the bedroom.

I show Jimmie my phone, the link: "Bloody Sunday–Derry, Northern Ireland, 1972," squeeze past, step around the couch without brushing it and into the bedroom. R. Murph points at a book of green matches printed with "The Bayside Inn"—

Fuck.

R. Murph says, "Definitely, our Father Augustine is connected."

"Because of matches? C'mon, anybody who drinks in Canaryville has been in the Bayside."

R. Murph opens the matches. Penned inside is: *Halsted Station. Blue hat. 10:45 p.m.*

Fuck. The Bayside blew at lunchtime. The matches might mean Father A was in the Bayside before it blew to meet whoever gave him the matches. Or not.

If 10:45 p.m. refers to last night—fifteen minutes after he left this apartment for the last time—then Father A went to the clocktower right after that meeting.

R. Murph points me back to the stacks of papers at his right knee. "There's more. His original green card. St. Gabriel's was his sponsor."

"Huh? He's a defrocked pedophile and St. Gabriel's *sponsors* him?"

"Yep. Happens all the time. That ain't news, but this might be." R. Murph spreads this week's copy of *Crain's Chicago Business*. Inside the front cover is a flyer for yesterday's downtown parade, a torn yellow-pages page that lists Chicago security companies, and a Xerox copy of the *Irish Times*—four columns of an article about the 2003 IRA bank standoff in Dublin eight years ago.

R. Murph doesn't know what he's looking at. I do—a CV for Maureen's fucking brother.

"Jimmie?" I turn away from R. Murph, pull my phone, find Maureen's brother's number, and call.

Pádraig answers on the second ring.

I walk out of R. Murph's hearing and tell Pádraig: "In eighteen minutes I'm calling your sister to tell her you're dead. Be out front of Rudy's Liquors at Sixty-Ninth and Ashland, alone, or you are."

I hang up and wave Jimmie to the front door. We creak down the long flight of steps and walk outside onto South Keeley Street. Jimmie waits for an explanation that matches my behavior.

I collect myself and say: "R. Murph found a matchbook from the Bayside. Augustine didn't smoke, at least not in this apartment. Fruit said they found NAMBLA material, but I don't see anything in there that says 'I love kiddie porn.' Guy doesn't have a computer."

Jimmie says, "Laptop. Portable."

Frown. "Okay . . . so maybe his laptop is hiding somewhere? Or the P-Stones sold it before Fruit crashed them."

Jimmie shakes his head at low, low probability. "Father Augustine probably doesn't have a computer."

"Then he isn't much of a NAMBLA guy."

"And Fruit ain't much of a detective."

I nod, say: "Let's get Fruit back here," turn my back to the FBI car across the street, then tell Jimmie what was between the pages in this week's *Crain's*.

Jimmie's face prunes. "So, ah, a parade flyer, an *Irish Times* article, and a yellow-pages list of local security companies is why you just threatened to kill your girlfriend's brother? I don't like Pádraig either, but . . ."

"Maureen's brother was a sniper in the Royal Irish Rangers. Sixteen confirmed in Iraq. And two in an IRA bank standoff in North Dublin. The Garda formally denied Pádraig was their shooter, but he was."

"You're thinking . . . what?"

"The *Crain's* is this week. Meaning, *this week*, Father A takes a copy of an eight-year-old Dublin article, tears out a phone book page that has Pádraig's company info, and adds the parade flyer—where Pádraig Cane will be."

Jimmie applies the 140 IQ under the pomp. "Father A went by the VIP stand to put a face with Pádraig's name."

"That's what I'm thinking. I'm thinking Pádraig's name somehow showed up in Father A's life. It shook Father A, so he had a look. Within a few days, he's hanging on the clocktower."

Jimmie nods. "Pádraig's the Bayside matchbook? Or the 10:45 meet?"

"Doubt Pádraig's a Bayside customer. He's a Northsider Protestant; Canaryville would be out of his range . . . and safety."

Jimmie looks away, then back. "Gets better. Pádraig's a sniper. The shot on Loef Brummel two weeks ago was what . . . three, four hundred yards?"

I nod.

"You're thinking Loef's connected to all three crime scenes—the train-tracks double, the Bayside, and the clocktower via the matches. Add the shot on him, and Loef has four homicide connects in two weeks."

"We got Pádraig right there, too. Pádraig knows Cissy Noonan—that ties him to the double. Pádraig's a sniper—could put him behind the rifle that fired at Loef. Pádraig's in Father A's papers—that ties him to the clocktower."

"The Bayside?"

"Don't have that. But three out of four . . ."

Wary creeps into Jimmie's brown eyes. He straightens his suit-jacket cuffs under the Burberry.

"What?"

Jimmie glances me at our FBI tail car. "I love her, but the FBI wasn't at Maureen's pub chasing their tails. They have something we don't."

"FBI was there for her brother. Timing's either about what we just found or some bad shit in Pádraig's security business."

Jimmie shakes his head. "If Pádraig was all the FBI wanted, they would've grabbed him alone. That's how the FBI works; hell, they've done it to you twice. I'm not saying Maureen's all the way in, or maybe even *knows* what she's in, but—"

"No." I wave off any possibility. "Not Maureen, not against me. Worst case—and it would be fucking bad—the FBI's threatening

Maureen to get to me. Telling her that Pádraig goes to prison for whatever he's into if she doesn't—"

"Agreed. The FBI wants to put you in prison for the rest of your life. Adding a few of your friends would just make it better. Those friends would be me *and* Maureen."

"She's not going to prison and neither are you. Not 'cause of my past or present. And for fucking sure not because of Pádraig Cane."

"Getting messy, Den. You need to calm down."

"Right after me and Pádraig clean some of it up."

Chapter 12

STEVEN

I'm still in Chicago and possibly shouldn't be. *Stay and Play* is for all-inclusive vacation cheapies, not men of the sword, men with their "likeness" on every TV and in every newspaper. Although, in this case, my "artist likeness" is probably helpful (to me), other than the eyes—a single but uncanny resemblance, likely thanks to Detective Daniels.

Why am I still here?

Target Three is part of my contract. *Mucho importante* in my line of work that the contract is completed regardless of obstacles. *Bust a deal and face the wheel.*

Too bad my client doesn't see her modifications and continuing extracurricular adventures as a default of our contract—in the World Court of Murder for Hire, I win that case hands down.

But there is no such court, only word of mouth in my community.

And my client has a mouth she's overly inclined to exercise. And she has the UVF merit badges for wreaking havoc on multiple continents.

Exhale. Now I must invest time and energy to control the narrative that frames this contract. For me to achieve the narrative that protects me and my reputation, Corrissa and her local accomplices must perish.

I succeed in my contract; they die in some unintended consequence, unrelated to *moi*.

My lip curls, wriggling across the surgery that made my new palate. A *lot* of extra work, this reframing. Unpaid and high risk. Mr. Steven L. Sociopath does not enjoy amateurs or threats in the workplace. Separately, they make him . . . unpleasant. Together, they make him far more—

Slow yoga exhale. I smooth at my nose and lip.

Never wise to overreact.

Mr. Steven L. Sociopath is a professional—*Bust a deal and face the wheel*. But I wouldn't want to taunt me. They did that at grade school. Taunting "Freak Face" is bad. I stole their bikes and ruined them into scrap metal. In seventh grade I took pets. In eighth grade I mailed Mrs. Graettinger her bully son's gooey underwear. The pet police were inflated to a "task force." Mom and Dad trailed me to the abandoned single-wide that had become my Berchtesgaden chalet, and I was shuffled off in restraints. Mom didn't even say goodbye.

Horn. I jerk to the rearview mirror of my new car. This time the horn is not carjackers. I crane into the mirror instead of accelerating. My teeth are properly white, but still quite scary. The usually supple lips don't want to relax. I tug the surgically rebuilt one into place and pat it flat. The horn sounds again.

Accelerating across the intersection, I check for carjackers who might be associated with the Negro behind me. The last group was quite a surprise. I was parking Father Augustine's Ford Focus north of the river and Black hoodlums attacked me. My God, what kind of city is this? I escaped, yes, but the shock, the indignity—I've always been racially agnostic . . . and they attack *me*?

My lip squirms, baring both incisors.

Possibly a bit of recreational gratification is required while I await my client's final modifications for Target Three. Something to ease the pressure. I could wander the Art Institute, masturbate in the impressionists gallery . . . except the best time is late in the day, and the museum is closed on Sunday morning anyway. I could go to a hospital, or a hospice, tour the tobacco ward, watch the Marlboro Men wheeze their last steps on the yellow brick road they built?

Funny, yes; productive, no. There is no grand canvas in slow suicide just because it has white sheets under it. We require a muse, a bit of sexual imagery, something that warms the cockles, so to speak. The Redhead? Make her a breadcrumb of the "unintended consequence" that will kill my client?

Hubba, hubba. Pádraig Cane's sister, Maureen, paladin-enchantress-inamorata of manhunter Banahan. Bound and gagged? But not gagged, we'd want to hear what she had to say: *Oh, please don't hurt me? Fuck me harder? I have money?* I've heard them all, recorded the really good ones, and I play them on occasion when I paint, when I want to finish *big*. And it never hurts to update the library. Or give the opposition something new to think about.

The light stops me at Division Street.

North into Old Town and the cozy Malvern Pub!

***

Ah, proximity. Foreplay!

On Wells Street, across from the Malvern Public House, my charred omelet is youthfully presented—an energy booster for the Redhead to come.

The jukebox explodes with "Video Killed the Radio Star." I ram fingertips into my ears, cringe into my shoulders, and—The window onto Wells Street frames a parked black car. Uh-oh. I hadn't noticed the black car. Or the two men in it. Government men? Not locals out for midmorning Sunday brunch. I ease my shoulders and face away from the window. The television screen above the bar runs a news-clip of the Bayside char and goo. I sneak a glance at the government car . . . the men are watching the Redhead's pub, not me. I cut back to the TV, feigning interest, scanning the barstools and tables for additional government men.

No G-men. Locals eating breakfast, half of whom haven't been to bed.

My pulse slows to normal. The TV does more Bayside "devastation" mixed with vignettes of the two men who hunt me. Detective Daniels is the more interesting, the more threatening of the two. When I researched Daniels and Banahan, I found them odd—Daniels, the Black, is the insider to the American dream. He has family, church, PTA. Banahan is the outsider, the knight errant whom the FBI will soon unhorse. Collectively, Daniels and Banahan are a storyline that America's haute bourgeoisie cannot afford to recognize—Black success on the rise and white corrosion; the collapse of empire.

I sneak another glance at the government car. They see something or they wouldn't be here. My pulse blips.

I recheck my diner's barstools but none of the pierced-and-tattooed, disaffected youth exhibit any interest in me. Nor do they seem to care about the big Red Summer–PNDH show about to boil over as my detectives' sensational backdrop.

Now there's a visual—Black and white massing at the border on their skirmish lines—the great Zulu-British confrontation at Isandlwana in South Africa. Ah, spectacle!

Yes, yes, Steven, pay the tab to these gothic morons, survivors-of-the-night. Find the backdoor exit and make a trek to the badlands where no government men meddle and the real combatants congregate.

I pull a twenty from my wallet. The best Black-versus-white skirmish line in Chicago would have to be . . . Fifty-Fifth Street. Have my picnic and watch the battle from the Black side of the esplanade—possibly the house with the room for rent I visited across from Keef's 5x5 Pump, the other "Catholic" pub I was asked to case as a backup for the Bayside bomb. Oh, yes, *perfect*. Second floor with kitchen privileges—I smell a hoedown.

Sadly, we cannot have the Redhead just now, but we can have a substitute. Someone we pick while we watch Chicago's Zulu and Irish maneuver for position in their coming conflict. Tension relief is important for a professional, keeps the mind clear and the hands steady. And there's the T-3 payday to consider. T-3 will pay for an upgraded studio space in Berlin, an oh-so-posh pad in grimy Neukölln with an east-facing wall of monumental windows, properly framing a modern master at the height of his Language of Love period.

Doktor Franken-Stevie!

The bartender is staring at me and my erect twenty-dollar bill. I plastic a smile and vow to be more careful. Even in this den of . . . whatever they are, I cannot afford to be anything other than "normal."

A siren blares outside. I cut to the window. Both men in the black car are exiting their doors. I snap back to the bartender, drop the twenty, and say, "Restroom?"

He points to the back.

Thirty steps down the bar and I'm at the bathroom doors. Just past them I bang through the kitchen door, sidestep a waiter, then a cook yelling Spanish at me. I bolt past him and his upraised spatula, kick the bar on the fire exit door, and jump into an alley. Clear. The knife slips into my hand. Hostage or unlocked door, whichever's first.

Another siren wails. A police car shoots past the alley's mouth and two rats run behind a dumpster. A door creaks open deeper in the alley to my left, young voices laughing—

Doktor Franken-Stevie grips his scalpel and exits stage left.

Chapter 13

DENNY

Jimmie weaves through traffic on Sixty-Ninth. I recheck the rear window for the FBI tail we lost three miles back driving through the Riv, then call Maureen a fifth time and tell the ringer: "Answer your goddamn phone!"

Maureen isn't perfect, and after my first year on the street, I know anything is possible if there's a beautiful woman in it. But Maureen's not femme fatal Lana Turner. We aren't living a remake of *The Postman Always Rings Twice.*

Maureen and I aren't. But her fucking brother? My teeth grind. I look at Jimmie. "How the fuck does this Mick piece of shit—"

"Easy, Den."

"If that motherfucker's got Feds on him, he's sideways in the deep water. His only way out is give the FBI . . . something, anything. Right? Why be at Maureen's? She's got nothing to do with Pádraig's business. The only fucking reason the G would be there is Pádraig's burning her. Burning Maureen for whatever sins she has 'cause she's with me." My hand pounds the dash. "How's that fucking happen just before she and I—"

"We're gonna ask. Nice and calm."

"Yeah. Nice and calm." Both hands rub my eyes and temples. Eighteen times Pádraig's committed sanctioned murder. He's the alpha dog in mega-club and concert/event world—sealed universes with controllable dynamics and wide margins for backstage behavior. No telling what kind of personal permissions those combinations can generate. Or what the FBI could tag him with. *None* of that has shit to do with Maureen.

And there the Mick motherfucker is—

Standing at the alley on Sixty-Ninth, midblock between Marshfield and Ashland, not where I told him to be, and he's not alone.

Jimmie parks the car.

"Stay put." I exit the car, stop eight feet from Pádraig, and point at his two bull-necked men in black pants and bomber jackets. "This is a homicide investigation, not a family argument or a rock-star appearance. Disappear, now. Or turn around and put your hands on the wall."

Pádraig says, "What, Dennis, is your fuckin' problem?"

I tell Pádraig's sidemen: "*Move*, gentlemen. Or you're going to jail, and today's shaping up to be a bad day to visit."

Both are large and fit, with close-shaved heads and flattened noses. They look at Pádraig for confirmation.

He says, "Get a spot of tea," waves them off toward Rudy's, then focuses on me.

I wait till both men cross Ashland, then step to Pádraig. He steps back deeper into the alley, almost to Fat Albert's overflowing dumpster, drops his chin, sets his hands and feet, and doesn't step back.

I say, "Your sister is the rest of my life. Nothing, not a fucking thing, will happen to her as long as I'm alive." I stare until Pádraig blinks. "Tell me about the sniper shot on Loef Brummel."

"Ask somebody who knows."

"Tell me about the Catholic priest."

"Priest?"

"The one you helped hang on the clocktower."

Pádraig's hands stay up. "*What?*"

I feint right, step in left, and bang a right above his belt. His elbow dips too late to cover and my left forearm smashes his head into the bricks. His left hook floats as he falls; my right grazes just hair, and Pádraig finishes on the pavement, shoulders against the bricks. He blinks at the blood in his eyes and blots with the back of his hands. I step in deep and knee him under the chin.

While I wait for his eyes to reopen, I take his 9 mm Glock (licensed), then his wallet, then search his pockets, not that I expect he came here with anything I could use. I rip open his jacket, then his shirt, and search for an FBI wire I expect to find but don't. I do find what might be raw-skin tape marks.

His eyes flutter; he rolls to his left, dry heaves, then raises his hands half-conscious like he'll fight from the ground. Tough mockers, these West Belfast hooligans.

His eyes blink till he thinks he's focused. The mouth tries to talk but can't; he tries to stand but can't do that either. Three more breaths, then, "Bloody . . . hell . . . Dennis?"

"Not jerking around, homes. Maureen isn't taking a fall with, for, or because of you. Whatever you're doing to involve her in whatever the fuck you're into stops right now or they'll never find your body."

Pádraig presses into the wall, flexing feeling into his neck. "Witnesses. Too many witnesses. My lads—"

"You and I argued, I left." I nod down the alley at Englewood ghetto. "Bangers burned another Irishman for today's Red Summer festivities."

Pádraig tries to stand again but his thighs and knees lack the brain-muscle connection that stops after a good shot to the liver.

He says, "Be a moment. Then we'll see to your abilities."

I step back, say: "Be right here whenever you're ready," put my hip into it, and kick him in the heart. Pádraig's eyes saucer, mouth gaping at the shock. He gasps again and again. His luck holds and his heart resyncs. He starts breathing again.

Pádraig has survived his first heart attack; with more luck, he'll live. I give him another minute, then: "Ready? The G likes informants in the family. Jam an errant sibling on a federal beef no working person can pay to defend, roll 'em, then start the party. How long you been with the G? What are you and them trying to use on Maureen? What's the FBI got?"

"No." Gasp, mouth wipe. "That'd be *you* suckin' those dicks."

"Okay. We'll do your move on Loef Brummel first." I check the alley both ways. "You think you're taking over in the Riv? You're a fuck-ing Northsider Protestant. How's that gonna happen?"

Pádraig feebles his hands up, a heavy silver ring on each index finger, sucks another breath. One bloodshot eye blinks semiclear, then the other. One hand wipes at the blood and water. The other hand slides for his Glock that he doesn't find.

The Glock's in my hand. "Father Augustine's looking to ID you because you're looking to ID *him*, right? You show up on Father A's radar and he wants to know who you are. He goes to the parade, IDs you working VIPs; twelve hours later he does a 10:45 meet at the Halsted L. With *you*. Next stop he's naked on the clocktower."

Pádraig feebles.

"Who was in the shadows at the L? Watching you put Father A's face to his name? So he could hang him in Canaryville." I aim his Glock at his head.

"You're making a move on Loef Brummel. Father A's part of it. Give me who's in the move with you, then how it fits with the FBI. Then you give me every goddamn word-angle-threat you and the Feds are building to hang around Maureen's neck. Every-fucking-thing. Or you're dead. Right here. Right now."

Motion at the alley's mouth. I pivot, aim, and duck.

Jimmie Daniels keeps coming. "For damn sure, don't shoot me."

Pádraig struggles to stand. I kick his legs out and he falls back to the pavement. Jimmie gets to us, removes his overcoat, and says, "Lotta ways to solve a problem. This isn't one."

"I told you to stay in the car; stay out of this."

"You implied it."

I aim at Pádraig.

Breathing hard, Pádraig eyes the Glock, says, "Your shit . . . is with Maureen . . . leave me out."

Jimmie interrupts: "What shit would that be?"

Pádraig sucks more air. "Banahan knows."

Jimmie says, "Okay, but I don't."

Pádraig doesn't fill in the blank for Jimmie or me.

Jimmie folds his overcoat over his shoulder and tells me: "Okay. Shoot him. We'll hack him up, dump him on the Norfolk Southern where he dumped Dill and Cissy."

I wave the Glock. "Last chance, tough guy."

Pádraig spits blood on my shoes. "FBI says you killed a buck. And his sister back in the '70s. FBI says Loef Brummel was with you." He wipes his mouth. "You been protecting him every day since; that you ain't a commander anymore because a that." Pádraig clutches a bloody hand to his chest. His eyes saucer and he gasps.

I kick his feet.

He breathes deep; his face pale, takes throaty seconds, then: "FBI says the two Blacks you threw off the roof shot your brother. In the liquor store. Got away with it."

"Sorry. The FBI doesn't work stand-alone murder. I know that; and since you're their bitch, you know that."

"There's more. To you and Brummel, they said."

Pádraig coughs and fights the pain in his chest. "You and him . . . and others . . . sucking the blood of the city." He pants twice. "You protecting him; him protecting you."

"This conversation's about *you*, asshole. You, Loef Brummel, Father Augustine, and the FBI. All of ya intertwined. Why?"

Pádraig coughs again. "FBI came at me on my visa." Blood dripples his lips. "Said I lied. Gonna revoke my citizenship. Deport me back to Northern Ireland." Another cough. "IRA and the murderin' fuckin' Catholics kill me if I go back."

"When'd the FBI *come at you*? The first time."

Pádraig sucks air, waits in my face. "Year ago December. When we came in off the Fiona Ness tour. And I told 'em to g'wan."

"You told the FBI to piss off and didn't mention it to me? Or your sister?"

"My business ain't yours. Or Maureen's."

"*Or Maureen's?* You two-bit Mick motherfucker. You *are* giving 'em Maureen. Aren't you? YOUR OWN SISTER. Wear a fucking wire on her; they roll her to get me. What're you assholes using to frame her and save your worthless fucking ass?"

I blink through possibilities—there is nothing Maureen knows about me, or that she's done with me, that could even remotely be considered illegal. If Pádraig and the FBI have a lever on her, it's outside of us.

"I gave 'em nothing. Give 'em nothing."

"And the FBI left you alone. Just went away. 'Cause that's what they do."

Jimmie shoulders between us. "Pádraig, I suggest you rethink your next answer. We're all in kind of a spot here, and your death, unfortunately, solves a number of problems my friend here has created. Sorry, but that's how it is."

Pádraig looks left and right for help that isn't coming. Chin up, he spits more blood and says: "Fuck both a you. You ain't the first Chicago nigger to threaten me."

Jimmie grabs the Glock out of my hand, shoves me across the alley, then tells Pádraig, "*This* nigger is attempting to save you." Jimmie points across the alley. "From him, from Loef Brummel the minute we tell him you're his and Cissy's shooter."

No reaction.

Jimmie leans in over Pádraig. "The FBI is in this with you. How do they fit with you and Augustine and Brummel?"

Jimmie jams his arm at me to stay back, to let him finish. I step around Jimmie's extended arm. He jerks me sideways and I stumble backward across the alley into the wall.

Jimmie says, "Pádraig, I can't keep Denny off you forever. Not another *day* if he thinks you're about to hurt Maureen."

"It's Banahan the FBI wants." Pádraig points across the alley. "Him and his Loef Brummel. Not me. And not Maureen. I don't know no fuckin' Catholic priest!"

I jump off the wall. "Hurt Maureen, I'll kill you—"

"Enough." Jimmie turns and blocks me with his size 56 chest. "You're done pounding on him."

I yell around Jimmie. "You're telling me what I wanna know. And your sister's gonna tell me where to bury you."

"FBI ain't rollin' me." Pádraig presses his shoulders against the wall to stand, but can't. "Don't know your priest. Took no shot on Brummel." He sucks air. Then, semibreathless, says, "I'll see you dead, constable. *Both* of ya. That's a promise. Long before the FBI's grand jury pins ya to the mast."

Jimmie chest-bumps me off balance. "Listen to me, Den. Our friend here may be hurt worse even than he looks. Either way, he should be in an ambulance. Now. Let the hospital patch him up; we can grab him after. He'll talk or we'll drop him on Seventy-Ninth Street."

Pádraig coughs blackened blood on the back of his hand. "Yeah, ya cuckold fuckin' wanker. Best hope I die."

Jimmie shoves me hard up the alley and follows. "The Riviera's about to blow. Mahoney and the superintendent have to talk to you and you aren't answering their calls."

"We're going to Maureen's." I stumble as I yell over Jimmie's shoulder: "I'm coming, motherfucker. Your sister catches a cold, tell the G and your partners to ship you to Mars."

9:00 a.m.

Maureen's phone goes to voicemail a tenth time. Jimmie squeals corners en route to her house. I leave her a tenth 911 message to call me before she talks to another person, including her brother.

At her house, Maureen doesn't answer her door. Jimmie hits our lights and we race to the Malvern.

No FBI cars out front. No one answers either of the Malvern's doors. Maureen could be anywhere, but I keep seeing her at the Federal Building, in handcuffs under the lights, reading transcripts from her brother's wire. God help her if she has sins Pádraig knew about that I didn't. And that's sure as shit the way it seems.

Jimmie says, "Anything you'd like to tell me?"

I rub my knuckles. "A distinct loss of composure. Really thought I'd do better."

"One would hope." Jimmie asks again, "I'd say something's bothering you."

"Me?" I stare at the Malvern. "Why?"

Jimmie frowns and shows me his phone. "Could we call the superintendent?"

I call Cullen Mahoney instead. Mahoney answers in one ring. "Dennis, there are rules for police officers. Occasionally we must follow them. Our current situation is one of those times."

"I was interviewing a possible connection to the clocktower and the shot on Loef Brummel two weeks ago. The connect wanted to fight.

We did; I won; Jimmie and I checked a fast lead that fell out of the interview, and now I'm calling you."

"It appears Mercy Hospital ICU has admitted a Pádraig Cane?"

"Yep."

The deputy super's exhale is audible, then, "And Maureen?"

"Coincidence. Got nothing to do with her."

Mahoney goes silent, then, "In one hour, Alderman Gibbons will lead a cortege of eight vehicles up Halsted to the steps of St. Gabriel's. Targeted Response Unit will interdict him at Fifty-Seventh. Hopefully, the alderman will spend his media opportunity there." Mahoney grumbles, then says, "Pádraig Cane is white, that's a start. How badly injured is he?"

"Not bad enough to die."

"Dennis. We knew you'd be challenged. If you're not up to survivable behavior, I'll remove you now."

"Won't happen again. It was about Maureen; the FBI might have her—"

"You just said Maureen wasn't involved."

I lie. "She isn't, but the G was at her pub for three hours; now I can't find her. Gotta be about her brother; hundred-to-one they rolled Pádraig on something. Pádraig's either working Maureen to get to me for the grand jury, or . . ."

"Or what?"

"This is a reach—*maybe* Pádraig and the FBI are sleeping in the same bed. There's smoke there, something out of line, and we're working on it."

Mahoney says, "Your lips to God's ears," then: "I'll look into Maureen's whereabouts in the Federal Building . . . through the channels that you can't. You instruct Homicide to *publicly* pick up Pádraig Cane as a person of interest in the clocktower hanging *and* the sniper shot on Loef Brummel. True or not, better we have Pádraig in our hands than in the FBI's."

"Ten four. Thanks. Patrol told Jimmie that Loef Brummel's pulling his crew together at the 5x5. I'm headed there. Brummel will listen to me . . . more than he will to any other policeman. If I can convince him he's backing a suicidal race war . . . He's our only real chance to muzzle Canaryville before—"

"No, Dennis, you won't do that. The 5x5 belongs to Keef Gilmartin. The battalion chief came close to killing you over Gael. Use your head; send someone else."

"I can handle it. And we want me to solve this, or at least slow down the explosion so someone else can stop it."

"No. Do not set foot in the 5x5. Not today. That's an order."

10:00 a.m.

Still no answer from Maureen.

Just ahead, on the north side of Fifty-Fifth Street, is the fireman's bar, Keef's 5x5 Pump. Jimmie U-turns at Union and double-parks out front. He pops his door; I grab his arm. "Thanks for coming after me. I'm sorry, you know, for being . . . me."

Jimmie smiles. "We'll find Maureen. And, for the record, I love her—think she's the best thing that ever happened to you. I just think she's in trouble—and so do you. We best open our eyes and help her."

"Thanks. No shit. And I'm sorry, okay?"

Jimmie smiles another half inch then nods toward the crowd outside the 5x5. "Think you can hold that thought while we're here? Always kinda wanted to be a Homicide lieutenant."

"Certainly better than unemployment or prison."

Jimmie cuts the engine. "Let me talk first. Then you ease Loef into Pádraig Cane, Father Augustine, and the FBI. Nice and easy, okay?"

"Only way I know." We exit the car.

Eight heads turn; five are Loef Brummel and members of his crew. Behind them, at the front door of Keef's, are three locals, two wearing PNDH shirts. Loef hard-eyes those three stationary, then turns to Jimmie, eyes frigid, sufficient murder in them to make three-inch headlines. "Bold, you workin' the Riv today, Sergeant Daniels. I'd be back in the car."

Jimmie shrugs. "Have to be present to do the job."

"Then you're down here to tell me who murdered my girl, then the Bayside, 'cause other than that, there ain't no fuckin' reason for you two to be here."

So much for easing into it. I step in and tell the scarred side of Loef's face, "Pádraig Cane. I didn't know you knew him till last night at the Malvern, but you do. And Pádraig knew Cissy from concert-world."

Loef stares, silent.

"Cissy hook you and Pádraig into something? Something that prompted the shot on you and two weeks later got her killed?"

Loef squares up on me.

I add, "Pádraig Cane might've done the shot on you. Might've killed Cissy and your top guy. Who's backing Pádraig to take over the Riv?"

"Ask him. I ain't the one fuckin' his sister."

Heat reddens my face. "Only warning you once—leave Maureen Cane out of our business."

"Because it's *Cissy's* wake we're holdin', not Maureen Cane's? Bait me today, Dennis, I leave ya in the river."

"We don't slow this down, the river'll be the only safe place between here and Indiana." I show Loef my BlackBerry, not my temper. "Great little gadgets, google up all sorts of stuff. Football scores, naked celebrities, 1972 Irish politics, U2 songs." I read Loef the text under the link "Bloody Sunday":

"January 30, 1972. Twenty-six unarmed civil rights protestors are shot by the British Army in Derry, five of them in the back. Fourteen died, half were teenagers. All of 'em Catholics."

"What the fuck do you care? You're Italian, down on Sixty-Ninth Street greased up with the Wops."

I paraphrase the rest. "Six months later, July 31, 1972, the IRA set off three car *bombs* in Claudy that maimed thirty Protestants and killed nine, three of 'em children. So, there's your recap of 1972 Ireland. Tell me why you seem to think that matters, here in Canaryville, now."

Loef points up Union Avenue to Tilden HS, a Canaryville high school that had metal detectors before the airports and courtrooms did. "Tilden's got history teachers. Ask them."

"Jail or talk. I'm running this, you aren't."

Loef steps back to his four men and whispers to one. The man hurries away and Loef returns to me. "Your man on the clocktower, he's from Derry, you said, right? There in '72?"

"That's what we think."

"He's *in* Derry when the biscuits murdered the fuckin' town."

"If *biscuits* means British Army, yeah."

Loef shakes his head at stupid. "The IRA's first retaliation for Derry's Bloody Sunday was the car bombs in Claudy you just mentioned."

"So what? We're not over there, we're over here, forty years later."

"The guy who set the car bombs . . ."—Loef looks behind him, then back—"was a Catholic priest. Father James Chesney."

"A Catholic *priest* set car bombs? That maimed thirty and *murdered* nine?"

"Ireland's bishop denied Chesney was IRA or involved; shipped him from Derry into Raphoe, County Donegal, then up the bogs to Malin Head."

Whoa, baby.

I turn to Jimmie.

Jimmie's already flipping pages in his Father *Augustine* notes. Jimmie reads: "Our Father *Augustine* was the curate in Raphoe, County Donegal, then Malin Head."

I twist back to Loef. "My priest on the clocktower and your priest who car-bombed Claudy were . . . what? IRA teammates? Lovers? NAMBLA partners?"

Loef doesn't answer.

I tell Jimmie, "See if Chesney's 1972 car bombs in Claudy match the Bayside bomb."

Jimmie scribbles two notes, pulls his phone, and steps out of hearing range.

Loef glares. "You wanna pin the *Bayside* on a *Catholic* priest? Because the obvious is too fuckin' obvious?" Loef jams his hand south. "Somebody ghetto paid bangers to kill Cissy, to kill your priest, me, and mine. Red Summer. Plain as fucking day."

"Where's Chesney now?"

Loef leans at me, voice raised: "Catholic church buried him thirty-one fuckin' years ago in Maghera. Same grave with his parents. So, yeah, Chesney probably didn't murder the Bayside *or* Father Augustine. *Ghetto-fucking-bangers did, Lieutenant.*"

"Nah, Loef, this is emerald-fucking-green. Cissy and your mad-dog Dill aren't ghetto related and you know it. Priest on the tower naked? Why's that ghetto? Hit-and-run by a white guy; the FBI having breakfast with Pádraig Cane—everywhere I go it keeps coming up Irish."

Loef barks: "You got three P-Stones driving a murder victim's car. Half a mile from the fucking body. If those bangers were Irishmen, you'd already be perp-walking 'em up Michigan Avenue. Give us Cissy's killers. And the Bayside bombers, or we give you dead gangbangers on every corner."

Not good. Loef shouldn't know about the carjack.

Jimmie steps back to us and changes the subject. "What we know as of just a few moments ago suggests that Cissy and Dill were together downtown at breakfast, possibly with a male Caucasian, and then"— Jimmie shrugs—"then nothing until we find them at the tracks."

Loef's eyes narrow to slits.

Jimmie adds, "Any help with who the Caucasian might be would be greatly appreciated."

Loef tells Jimmie, "You want me to say it was white people who killed Cissy? 'Cause none of your people coulda? Blacks don't do mosta the city's murders"—Loef does a 360 with his hand—"every fucking day?"

Jimmie's face and posture remain professional. "The rental car that killed the O'Boyle boy near Cissy's death scene had a *white* driver. The driver's likeness has been circulating in the media since last night, and by hand in the Riviera all day, today."

Loef unfolds a copy of the artist likeness. "Never seen this guy; none of my crew know him; no one within twenty blocks of here knows him."

"Have you shown it to Dill's people?"

"Are your P-Stones up in Twelve who murdered Cissy? And the Bayside?"

I answer for Jimmie, "District Twelve's outta our jurisdiction."

"Three hours ago, you were there. Don't fuckin' lie to me."

I step behind Jimmie and tell his ear. "Move 'em."

Jimmie turns, eyes me for calm, then turns away toward the curb and pulls his phone to call Buff.

Three feet separate Loef and me. I say, "I was at Twelve looking for a car that belonged to the clocktower. Buff Anderson has three P-Stones from Fifty-Fourth Street that they popped across the river in the *Four Corners*, not the Riv. His P-Stones have shit to do with the Bayside, and nothing to do with Cissy."

"Keep them fuckin' gangbangers safe, but let your neighborhood burn? Motherfucker, these lampposts fit you, too." Loef points at a broken streetlight. "In another hour or two, ain't gonna be nowhere to hide."

"Pádraig Cane has ties to the clocktower victim and to Cissy. Pádraig's a sniper, a good one. And Pádraig's dancing with the FBI. Lotta fingerprints. All *Caucasian* like the guy at Cissy and Dill's breakfast meet. Tell me why you don't want to see all that."

Loef stares. Doesn't answer.

Jimmie returns from the curb and shakes his head that there's a problem with the P-Stone move. He adds, "Ayatollah's inbound. ETA in six minutes. TRU and cars from the Seventh District are doing the stop at Fifty-Seventh."

Loef yells behind him: "Ayatollah's bringin' his bangers up Halsted. Get out the vote."

"Goddammit, Loef—"

Seven men take off. Loef turns and looks past me. I pivot to a phalanx marching up the sidewalk at us. Each man wears the creased black pants and white shirts of the Chicago Fire Department, five total. In front, removing his hat, is a man who fought twenty-seven bareknuckle bouts, eight hundred fires, and saved sixteen citizens from burning to death, Fire Battalion Chief Keef Gilmartin.

Gael's father stops two feet from me. "You ain't from the Riviera, not anymore." He punches his finger in my chest. "Peddle your love for murderin'-gangbangers at *their* wakes, *their* funerals, *their* goddamn weddings."

I feel Jimmie coming up fast to side me.

Gael's father rolls up the sleeve on his right arm.

"I'm working. Didn't come here to fight—"

"Then have your ass outta here."

"I'm the police, Mr. Gilmartin. I don't give a shit who you know that's dead or who your children are—"

Most of his punch grazes my temple.

The one I land hits Gael's father square on the scarred forehead. He staggers back and drops to a knee, wipes at the blood streaming around his eye, leaps at me with a left hook that skids on my shoulder and lands hard on my temple. Jimmie's chest keeps me standing. I bounce, swing, miss, get hit again, don't go down, and hammer Gael's father near the liver, then the jaw. His firemen keep him standing.

Jimmie pulls me back, stiff-arms his .45 over my shoulder at the firemen, and booms: "WE DONE."

Fire Battalion Chief Gilmartin spits blood. "The fuck we are."

Loef Brummel jumps in facing the firemen, his back to Jimmie's .45, both hands up and feet planted. Loef says, "Chief Gilmartin, it'd be a personal favor, you ta me. I don't ask lightly, given you have a fair grievance with Banahan."

Gael's father spits blood again and glares at me. "I'm sick every night knowin' your hands touched my daughter. God damn you for that."

I consider stepping around the obstructions and knocking the Irish motherfucker out.

Instead, I gently press down on Jimmie's gun arm, step forward and around Loef Brummel to face Gael's father from six feet.

"If I arrest you for assaulting a police officer, you lose your job. *Unless* those sworn members of your family come by my office and beg me to unwrite my report. You want the sainted Gilmartins begging me?"

Gael's father struggles against his men's hands. "Banahans are piss-drunks and cowards. We'll have our day, you and I."

"Right fucking now, we're gonna have it."

Jimmie says, "Easy, Den. We covered this possibility."

Deep breath, then another. I tell Gilmartin, "Sometime today, tomorrow at the latest, much of the city you've spent your life protecting will be on fire. A whole bunch of men and women you work with will be injured, dying, or dead. *Unless* you and Loef decide to help stop it before it starts."

"I'll not save the bastards who bombed the Bayside. To hell with you. And them. And their goddamn ghetto politics."

"It was a *white* guy, Chief, who ran down Tommy O'Boyle's boy. Brummel's got the police-artist's sketch in his pocket. *Same* white guy was driving away from the Bayside thirty seconds after it blew."

Battalion Chief Gilmartin orders his men to let him go. They do. He straightens his uniform with a jerk, pulls out a handkerchief, and pats the cut above his eye. His face is rage stretched to its limits. "My daughters don't beg. And one day *soon* I'll kill you for saying they do."

"I didn't mean it like that."

"And your piss-drunk father's cigarette burning his wife up alive? *Your mother.* Or was it gangbangers who killed 'em, and you did nothing about it? Banahans are your cowards. They're your goddamn beggars."

Jimmie bear-hugs me from behind.

Through bit-teeth I say, "Electrical fire."

Battalion Chief Gilmartin steps in and spits in my face. "Your own brother dead with the bangers. And your parents. And then you, married to 'em. The day the last of the Banahans dies will be a shinin' one for the Riviera."

Jimmie turns us away and tells my ear. "Gilmartin doesn't mean what he's saying; it's about you and Gael. That's all."

Inbound sirens scream on Fifty-Fifth Street. Lights flashing, two beat cars fly past, then turn south down Halsted. More sirens wail in from the west. I struggle against Jimmie's bear hug. "Let go."

"Are you good?"

"Let go, Jimmie."

He does, slowly. I wipe Gilmartin's spit from my face.

Gilmartin glares at me. His rage-bloated face morphs into the bloated Irish face in the noose; how Chief Gilmartin's gonna look when I'm done pounding.

Before I can punch him, a piece of the puzzle punches me: IRA hero Father Chesney, dead over *there* since 1980, where *everybody* knew him.

Defrocked pedophile Father Augustine arrives *here* in 1980, where *nobody* knew him, till today.

I yell past Gilmartin to Loef Brummel, "Get your ass back here. You're under arrest."

Chapter 14

STEVEN

The Zeiss VV60 riflescope is a delicate, precision instrument crafted with single-minded pride. It has one mission: bring target and projectile together. Like a love chapel. I raise the sleek black aluminum to my right eye.

Viewing the world through thirteen inches of German engineering dramatically reduces the societal clutter. In spite of the VV60's substantial cost, it should be a required teaching aid in an epoch of mindless distraction.

Sirens wail, punctuating my unexpected good fortune. In the VV60's crosshairs stand all the pretty horses a boy could want. Outside Keef's 5x5, *manhunter* Dennis Banahan is trying oh so hard to retire from public life before it catches and kills him and his redhead paladin. And, oh my goodness, there is his childhood friend and rooftop-coconspirator, Loef Brummel. A proud cock o' the walk, out in the open, I'm quite surprised to say. I lower the scope.

Hmmm? Another breadcrumb for my "unintended consequence" trail?

But even if I had the rifle, how would I exit, post impact? No, Mr. Loef is a temptation, the Last Temptation of Mr. Stevie. We don't succumb to temptation. We are a professional.

I raise the scope, avoid Mr. Brummel, and land on fearless firemen—one of whom seems to have substantial anger-management issues. I rotate past four men brandishing beer bottles, and—*Saint Paddy be praised*—there's my man-of-the-match: James "Jimmie the Gent" Daniels. The fates are literally throwing us together.

Or warning me.

Or both. Detective Daniels would have to be exceptional to catch me. But he's the kind of hoodoo man who could. I lower the scope. Add color to an all-white canvas? It wouldn't be art, or a social-sexual fling—Detective Daniels would be a professional move, removing risk, dropping a tasty, confusing breadcrumb to cover Corrissa's soon-to-be untimely demise. And I am a professional. I have a résumé. Résumés are important, critical.

But, alas, résumés are also breadcrumbs.

The end-zone crowd shouts *De-fense*.

I raise the scope. Detective Daniels could die from a gunshot wound to the head, fired from a great distance . . . Oh, yeah, while he's having dinner with his wife and three young children. Clean and crisp on my end; quite the picture on his end: three nippers and Mum, all with Daddy splattered over their faces. In the biz, it's called a JFK, and really the only choice given the time and planning constraints.

If I'd known he'd be here, it would have been *buttah* to take Detective Daniels now . . . but that would be poaching. Drama-less, and likely difficult to escape. Still, call it tension relief, résumé, or defense, the vision of Detective Daniels and his family safe at home, sharing brussels sprouts . . . then the brain splatter and shock frozen on everyone's faces . . .

I sight the scope until it's filled with Detective Daniels's left eye. The iris has an odd, inviting flicker—*planetary* would be the correct description. The astral home of Major Tom.

Wow. I hear David Bowie sing me Major Tom's agreement while I search for the perfect shade of brown. Peter Schilling sings his countdown in German.

Wow. Wow. Wow. Both artists at Hansa Studios. I am so *Berlin*.

Adrenaline pumps into my fingers. This is important, and brown is a tricky color, a tertiary combination of primary and secondary colors whose elemental value depends on what white adjoins it.

Depends on the white that adjoins it . . . My God, the muse has spoken: I must do Jimmie! But for your fabulousness, Jimmie, I do not exist!

I ease back on the scope's magnification. They call Jimmie Daniels "the Gent" because he dresses beautifully. Let's hope he does so at home; today has shaped up to be his big day.

Detective Daniels lurches out of the scope.

I lower the magnification to widen the field. Detective Banahan handcuffs Loef Brummel. I follow Banahan and Brummel to the back seat of a Crown Victoria. My mocha Major Tom reappears and slides in front to drive.

Midslide, Detective Daniels stops, straightens, and looks in my general direction, a block closer to Halsted, then seems to refocus—*wow*—straight at my window on the second floor of a soon-to-be foreclosed brick-and-frame house. A handsome man, erudite . . . and confused. He feels me, or something like me—we are connected again. *Tingle.* I like him even more.

I lower the scope to look at the police-artist sketch in my hand, the one Detective Daniels would have assisted in constructing—could be a distant relative of mine . . . other than the eyes; the eyes are mine. I'll wear the Vuarnet 113s from here on in.

I show the sketch to the large boy on whose lap I'm sitting.

His vacant eyes stare but don't see.

So few people *see.* It's no wonder the world is awash in poverty and degradation—the masses ram their genitalia at each other at every possible opportunity, creating more masses, creating more opportunity to ram. I do my part to thin the herd, but there aren't enough bombs or bullets to stop the fornicators. A plague—good old-fashioned biblical reprisal—is the planet's best hope. And luckily, there are government-funded programs that do nothing but work on that concept every day, all the time.

Enough. Hoodoo-man Detective Daniels has my picture. If he wants me to be part of the family, then so be it! By tonight, I will join.

The Black boy beneath me is cooling to cold. I'd exchange him for his Twinkie-loving tonnage-o'-mom, but she expired first and is no doubt colder still. And they both stink, a little.

Thankfully, now that sirens are wailing inbound from every direction, I won't have to stay much longer. A fire might be a nice touch? We have all the firemen right across the street. A tribute to their bravery?

I pat at the boy-chair beneath me. Leave him and Mom as murder victims to be investigated by the already overburdened police? Or drop a cigarette on the bed, give the swashbuckling firemen another shot at a hero moment?

I can mimic sensitive; I could do that.

Let's see, Mom would've been on the bed watching *The Biggest Loser,* cheering for the one-pound fat loss Tubbo the Manatee just scaled. A twelfth-Twinkie sugar rush knocks Mom into a coma. In slo-mo, her Salem menthol drops from her pudgy fingers . . . onto the evil Chinese poly-something bedspread . . . The rest, as they say, is mattress fire. Or *Burn, baby, burn.*

Chapter 15

DENNY

Jimmie wheels us off the curb at Keef's 5x5. Sirens wail in from east and west to deal with the inbound Ayatollah.

I lean over the seat and hit Loef with my epiphany: "Defrocked pedophile Father Augustine didn't die on my clocktower. Father James Chesney did."

Beat cars scream past us from behind.

"And Red Summer didn't kill him. Somebody found, then lynched, a world-class IRA priest-bomber hiding in Canaryville for thirty-one years."

More beat cars scream toward us, brake hard at Halsted, and veer south toward the Ayatollah.

Jimmie does speed-recall on what we know about the clocktower, smiles, and joins my club. "And gosh, the priest's here hiding on a Catholic-church-sponsored green card."

I déjà vu on a guy who was out front of Keef's 5x5 ten years ago. He was also *church sponsored* and *IRA*. Sirens were wailing like right now. *Big guy, an FBI snitch named David Rupert.*

FBI and *snitch* echo between my ears.

I ask Jimmie, "David Rupert? Remember him?"

Jimmie slows, waits for two more beat cars to scream past. "Truck company guy; hung out at the 5x5, raised money for the Catholic church and the IRA. Been in the Witness Protection Program since he testified."

"Right. FBI jammed Rupert on an underage female, rolled him, then worked him undercover. He testified *big* against the IRA over there. IRA bosses took it on the chin." I point Jimmie south toward the Ayatollah's march—where I'm sure Jimmie wishes I didn't want to go—but where I want Loef to be.

Jimmie turns. Dead ahead are flashing lights. Double-parked TV vans line both curbs. Between them, two black SUVs cover what's left of Halsted and block us from getting closer.

The SUVs have FBI government plates and numbers—

Except the FBI should absolutely not want their fingerprints anywhere near the carnage that's about to happen. Makes no sense, but here they are.

Out loud, Jimmie says what I just thought, then adds: "There's one way the FBI being here *does* make sense. They're in bed with Pádraig. Like they were with Rupert."

I point at the FBI tags. "Rupert got *paid*. Big FBI, federal *em-ploy-ee* money; federal *fingerprints* kinda money. As in, the FBI owned Rupert's ass and everything he did while he belonged to them."

Jimmie says, "If the Feds own Pádraig, they have a problem."

"Goddamn right." I glance at Loef. "FBI paid Rupert seven figures to betray the IRA and keep them from killing Tony Blair, the British prime minister. All of the assassination attempt planned and paid for right behind us in Canaryville."

Three, two, one . . . Jimmie sees the impossible punchline: "But nobody in Canaryville goes to jail."

"Right. Nobody *here* goes to jail. *Somehow* Rupert doesn't give up anyone in Chicago? Bullshit. Where all the assassination money was raised? He only gives up the IRA big boys in Ireland? And the FBI's all good with that? No fucking way. Never happen."

Jimmie nods. "Rupert didn't *testify* in Chicago, but it's a lock he gave up his Chicago coconspirators—because the FBI would've absolutely made that part of the deal."

I say to Loef, "You know what nobody going to jail here means. It means the FBI flipped the Chicago conspirators. And those guys ratted for the FBI the rest of their lives. Your boss, Bathhouse John, ran the Riv back then. Any assassination money Rupert helped raise before he rolled, and after, BJ knew about or took a piece of, or both."

I nod for Loef's agreement, which I don't get. I add: "Rupert's a *paid* FBI informant from jump street—he's paid to *inform*—but the most evil motherfucker in the Riv, Bathhouse John, your boss, doesn't go down to the Feds? They don't RICO him? How's that happen, Loef?"

Loef stares, silent.

"You know how. The FBI flipped Bathhouse John, too. Made him their rat. And those sanctimonious pieces-of-shit let him keep operating—"

I visualize Ms. March in the auto-shop calendar on the clocktower-victim's wall. "Fuckin' A . . . I just solved Renny-Mac's cold case murder. Rupert's IRA testimony and IRA Father Chesney hiding here is what killed her *and* Bathhouse John."

"You can prove that?"

"Not yet. But I can prove *this*: This whole fucking mess is about *Irish* bombings going back forty years; secrets that now tie Pádraig to you, Rupert, Chesney, and the FBI. Those secrets are coming back to bite you—Loef Brummel, successor to Bathhouse John—in the ass. *Those* fucking secrets are what killed forty-two people in the last twenty hours."

"Lotta legroom in that three-way."

"And more dead people." I look at the Ayatollah's procession of daytime headlights coming toward the barricade, then behind Loef at the Riv. "Every bit of this mess is Ireland-white and about to kill half the poor bastards you and I grew up with."

Loef chins south down Halsted. "It's Black and ghetto, and you know it. Look out your fuckin' windshield."

"Nah. It's Pádraig the Loyalist sniper, Rupert the FBI snitch, Chesney the IRA bomber, and the current FBI. That bunch and their story is the glue between the Bayside and the double that killed your fiancée. And you already know it."

"I do? You know me since we wore diapers. If your story were true, I wouldn't be huntin' P-Stones, would I?"

"Bathhouse John and his son are murdered in the Keys four years after his daughter, Renny-Mac, bought it. The son chopped and quartered not unlike your boy Dill. Maybe you forgot that? Know I did." I wave my BlackBerry above the seatback. "Like I said, amazing shit you can get on these if you can fit your fingers on the buttons. Our Father Augustine on the clocktower is Chesney the IRA bomber—get used to me knowing that."

Jimmie says, "If Pádraig's an FBI informant—"

"Then the fucking FBI knows the whole fucking story. But they ain't doing shit about it. Why? Because they're worried that Pádraig, *their guy*, is a perp in yesterday's Bayside massacre *and* this one about to happen."

Loef blinks once. Maybe a twitch—like maybe Loef *didn't* know?

Jimmie reaches for the shifter. "The FBI's in this; has to be. Best we re-hit the priest's apartment. Like yesterday—" Jimmie points me at the windshield. "Reporters inbound."

I turn. Fox's Jean Jeffcoat has broken away from the ring around Gael Gilmartin. Jeffcoat and her cameraman pass our front bumper to my open window. She jams a mic at me and says, "Lieutenant Banahan, did you decline to protect Alderman Gibbons? Is his life in immediate danger?" She glances at Jimmie. I power up the window. Jeffcoat doesn't withdraw her arm. Or yelp.

Jimmie straightens his already straight tie, smiles at Ms. Jeffcoat, applies his size 15 foot firmly to the brake, then drops the shifter into reverse.

More reporters break away from Gael.

Gael stares through them at me, her jaw set.

Ms. Jeffcoat speaks down her arm and through the window crack. "Is Alderman Gibbons a 'monkey'? Is that what you called him?"

Jimmie reaches to cover the mic. "Think we're news, Den. Better leave." Jimmie nods at my window. "Without her arm."

Ms. Jeffcoat cranes to look in the back seat, sees Loef Brummel in handcuffs and says, "Why . . . why's *he* here?" She does reporter math on yesterday's Black-church fire. "Did Loef Brummel order the bombing of Ebenezer Mennonite? Is he under arrest—"

Other reporters rap Jimmie's window with their mics. "Sergeant Daniels! Sergeant Daniels!"

Gael marches toward our windshield, loops the reporters crowding at Jimmie's side, and raps the backdoor window. Jimmie pops the locks; Gael pops the door, slides in next to Loef, and says: "Drive."

I drop the window to release Ms. Jeffcoat's arm and microphone, then shove both out. Jimmie hits the gas and we reverse up Halsted toward Fifty-Fifth. Gael looks at Loef, his handcuffs, then me. "Jesus Christ, Denny, any P-Stones see him, we're all dead."

"Thought I'd offer Mr. Brummel a look at what he's supporting."

Gael checks the Black faces trying to see in the car. "Tell me you didn't say 'monkey.' On camera."

"How you doing, Commander? Long time." I smile, hiding the welt her father gave me. "Just coming to see you."

Jimmie waves *Hello* into the rearview.

Gael doesn't de-ice. "Did you call Alderman Gibbons a monkey? Yes or no?"

"Well, Gael, I might have. He says I did, but Jimmie was there, and he says I didn't."

Jimmie waves again.

"My comment, *if* I made it, clearly referenced the Gangster Disciples in the crowd and was made after Alderman Gibbons suggested that *all* the residents of Canaryville, including your family, required significant elevation on the evolutionary ladder."

Gael taps Jimmie's shoulder. "Make the block; drop me at Fifty-Seventh." She glares at me. "Can you two . . . jagoffs be any dumber? The entire city's at stake—"

"We figured you'd want something to talk about. While we muck around in the blood and guts."

Her face shades to crimson. "Lives are at stake, Denny, lots of them."

"Really? Why would forty-two of your and my dead neighbors matter to me?"

"The FBI doesn't require incentive to eviscerate the department. Your mouth and your actions frame the rest of us as—"

"Alderman Gibbons and the FBI"—I point at the barricade—"*they're* who you'd prefer 'frames the rest of us'? 'Cause they have the microphone and the cameras, I should tiptoe around them and Loef here, and your father? 'Cause they're all yelling the loudest."

She notices the rising welt her father just gave me, glances at Loef, then me. "What happened?"

"Is there something we can help you with, Gael? We're kinda busy."

Her eyes flash. "Yeah. Shut the fuck up. Retire today. And if you don't go to prison, don't come back." She hits Jimmie's shoulder, says, "Right here," then glares at Loef. "If you care about Canaryville like you say, stand on the steps at St. Gabe's and tell Canaryville to stay out of neighborhoods they don't own."

Jimmie stops the car; Gael pops the door. Jimmie, Loef, and I watch her march up the street toward the reporters, shoulder-length brown hair swinging side to side, kind of a business-suit FloJo moment. Gael doesn't look back but does pull her right hand behind her pants, extending one finger.

Jimmie continues in reverse. "You're really good with women. Smart ones in particular. Really good."

I call my old secretary Leigha (a *smart one* who likes me), who is now my new secretary, and look directly at Loef as I ask her to find every bit of information possible on Father James Chesney's death and burial in Northern Ireland and Father Augustine's entry into the USA.

I hang up. A *whoosh* buffets the car sideways.

Jimmie and I look left—

Behind the tenements, flames explode forty feet into the sky. Dense black smoke engulfs the flames. Jimmie guns us into a power slide, spins the wheel to face north, and mashes the gas. "Damn, I knew something was back there."

I grab the radio. "House fire, looks like the seven-hundred block of Fifty-Fifth Street, south side."

Jimmie jumps the curb at the intersection, jams the shifter into park, pops his door, and sprints east toward the flames.

Black neighbors run out of the tinderboxes as he passes. I slide over behind the wheel and drop the shifter into drive. Jimmie's radio spits static, then "Shots fired . . ." and quits.

More Black neighbors run out of their houses.

I jiggle the radio knob, adjust the frequency, smack the radio's face with my hand, get static and nothing else. Sirens scream inbound somewhere behind me. Black smoke billows down Fifty-Fifth and swallows the Black people on the sidewalk, then our car.

I cough, jam reverse, *screech* us back onto Halsted—

Loef yells, "Look out!"

I slam the brakes. Loef bounces back into his seat. On Fifty-Fifth an eastbound Ford Bronco skids past our front bumper, leaps the curb onto the grass median, then crashes into a dead elm tree. The gas tank explodes. Hot metal bounces off our windshield and the dead elm tree falls across Fifty-Fifth. Two squad cars chasing the Bronco brake hard into the smoke and crash into the fallen tree.

On the median, the Bronco's driver staggers out of his burning car. He's on fire, his right arm ripped off and spraying blood. Keef Gilmartin and another fireman run from the 5x5 to the median, knock the man down, and roll him to extinguish his flames.

Black neighbors stagger out of the smoke into my fender.

The first fire truck on the scene charges in at us from the east, then jumps over the median that separates Keef's 5x5 from the rooming-house fire. I run through smoke to the crashed squads. Gasoline gushes from a ruptured tank. One officer is out of one squad helping the driver of the second squad out of his.

On the median, Keef Gilmartin strips his belt and cinches a tourniquet above the severed arm of the Bronco's driver. I jump in the first squad, try to start it but can't, then jump in the second squad to start it; it reeks of gasoline and won't start either. I yell, *"Gasoline!"* at Gilmartin. *"Gonna blow."*

Gilmartin and the other fireman drag the Bronco driver north out of the smoke to the Riviera side and yell for an ambulance. A second fire truck screech-stops behind me and does not kill the Black neighbors coughing blind in the intersection. I point at the crashed squads. "Gasoline!"

The firemen jump off their truck now engulfed in the smoke, strip hoses, and begin pumping water over the burning Bronco, the crashed squads, and the gas-puddled street.

More sirens sound from the west. They don't come to us. All of 'em turn onto Halsted toward the Ayatollah.

I run the block toward the house fire that Jimmie's in. Halfway to the fire the smoke spits out Jimmie Daniels and an elderly Black man Jimmie has cinched under his arm. Smudged and coughing, Jimmie hands the old fellow to a fireman with an oxygen tank, then bends at the waist like he'll toss.

I walk toward him. Jimmie doesn't toss, wipes at his face with the notebook in his hand, then walks past the elm, concentrating on the notebook. He scribbles as he walks, wipes at his eyes, then scribbles until he stops in front of me.

"And?"

"Two bodies. My old guy there said it's a mother and son. Second floor caved in with them." Jimmie coughs. "Smoke got me. Bodies were burned too bad for me to tell what they were. Firemen on the truck are guessing mattress fire."

I stare at Jimmie, then his notebook. "But 'mattress fire's' not what you think."

Jimmie coughs smoke. "Bodies looked . . . posed. Showy."

I lean away, don't have to add "like the clocktower and Bayside."

Jimmie points at *showy* in his notebook. "Think the perp left something in the boy's mouth."

"Like what?"

Cough. "ME will have to tell us."

I drag Jimmie and me toward our car and farther out of the smoke. "Talk to me."

Jimmie coughs, spits, "A Black mother and son would be noncombatants to our cases if we're all about things Irish."

"We're Irish, Jimmie. Hundred percent—here, Ireland, plus the FBI."

Jimmie blinks, imagining a six-degree connection that could tie the mother and son to things Irish. I follow his eyes across Fifty-Fifth to the 5x5. Jimmie says, "Mother and son die *showy* on the second floor across the street from an Irish bar . . ."

Shrug. Not much *showy* there.

"Where Loef Brummel—our guy with connections to everyone dead—just was. Standing out front."

I say: "Sniper." And run for our car.

When we get to Jimmie's Crown Vic, Loef Brummel isn't in the back seat. My handcuffs are.

"Goddammit." I kick the car, reach in, grab the mic, and call in a citywide on Loef.

A voice answers, "Ten four, Lieutenant."

I tell the mic: "Confirm—do we have Pádraig Cane in custody?"

Two firemen pop out of the thinning smoke. They wave us to them. I drop the mic; walk the thirty feet with Jimmie. The short one points at Jimmie, coughs, spits, says: "You asked what was in the boy's mouth. Kid's burned to charcoal but his teeth blocked most of the fire. What you saw was that paper that's been circulating, the wadded sketch of your hit-and-run guy."

Jimmie drops his chin. "Again, please?"

"We unwadded the sketch. The lips have cooked lipstick drawn on 'em."

The fireman says they put the sketch back in the boy's mouth for the ME to find, but since Jimmie had asked, they thought he ought to know.

Jimmie says, "Who else knows?"

The fireman thumbs at the fireman next to him.

I say, "Not a word. Okay? All you know is 'mattress fire.'"

The fireman stares at me. "The ME's gonna know. So will his people."

I wave that off. "I'll talk to them. We don't want either side of this street thinking the Canaryville hit-and-run and this fire-homicide are related. Not even a little."

Jimmie speaks before the fireman can say anything about the Bayside. "The house went awful fast, didn't it?"

"An accelerant." The fireman rubs his thumb to his finger. "Not much, but enough."

I bend my neck and stare at him sideways.

The fireman nods. "Yeah. Like the Bayside."

"No." I step closer. "Don't think that out loud. Really. No connection. None. Zero. Okay?"

The fireman nods small.

Jimmie pats his shoulder. "Much obliged. Thanks. We'll be up there in a minute."

The firemen leave. I do the math: "Ninety-ten, the rooming-house perp did the hit-and-run, and probably the Bayside and clocktower. If we've got Pádraig in custody, then Pádraig didn't do any of those."

Jimmie nods. "He's involved, though. Pádraig's scent's almost as strong as Brummel's. And if Augustine is IRA Chesney, then Pádraig's got a motive beyond just money. Pádraig's got a clear *anti-IRA–pro-Loyalist* history in that fight."

I punch my phone to see if we have Pádraig. A Ninth District car stops at our section of curb, his window down, hand waving for our attention. Before the sergeant in the car can say what he's about to, Jimmie points at the Bronco: "Who were our squads chasing?"

The sergeant answers from his car, "The guys who shot the Ayatollah."

I blurt: "Gibbons is *dead*?"

The sergeant says, "I'd pay double, but the Ayatollah ain't dying in this lifetime, at least not ours. His driver, Abu-Afghan-whoever was hit big; shooters killed a bodyguard and a bystander. Ambulances took 'em all to Mercy. Ayatollah was nicked. Wouldn't go to Mercy. Still on the scene; lotta blood but almost all from Abu the driver."

Jimmie asks the sergeant, "Shooters?"

"Three; balaclavas and gloves. That Bronco"—he points at the smoking shell—"T-boned the Ayatollah's Caddy as he crossed Fifty-Ninth. A follow car—late model Ford—blocked the Caddy from the front; fired twenty to thirty rounds through the Ayatollah's wind-shield." The sergeant shrugs. "Classic ghetto dance party."

I ask, "The guy in this Bronco, I couldn't tell, was he white?"

Nod. "Headed to Mercy's burn unit. Lost an arm; looked bad."

"ID?"

"One of the Shaughnessy brothers, the young one. Ragen Colt."

Exhale. His gran, who was at Maureen's, has one alive. Unfortunately, the wrong one. My phone rings: Deputy Superintendent Mahoney.

Mahoney says, "Five minutes, we're releasing Alderman Gibbons from the crime scene. No choice. His crowd exceeds one thousand; more coming from every direction." Static. "Dennis, I believe you stand the ground where our civic tragedy will begin."

"We gotta talk to him. There's five thousand white fire-breathers behind the Fifty-Fifth barricade. Gibbons can't come here. It'll be Gettysburg. He can't do it. He can't."

Mahoney says, "The alderman's speaking to the cameras now. Have a listen."

The voice of Alderman Gibbons booms through my phone: "I will crawl across Fifty-Fifth Street if necessary. And I will die in the Irish Riviera if that's what this march toward *equal treatment under the law* requires. God bless America. For all Americans."

I tell Mahoney: "*Die?* Motherfucker probably organized his martyr-moment in the car. Better call all the hospitals between here and Indiana."

"A moment, Dennis, they're bringing me . . ."

Faked "martyr-moment" or not, I warned Gibbons, and I warned these idiot white hillbillies. I fucking warned 'em—

Police helicopters crisscross overhead. Mahoney comes back and asks about the rooming-house fire just reported to him.

Across Fifty-Fifth Street from me, a Ragen Colt behind the barricade screams: "He's coming!" and jams his hand south over the police cars. "Ayatollah's got a thousand!"

Mahoney says, "Your rooming-house fire, the accelerant; is it the Bayside Bomber?"

"Could be. Could be the clocktower as well. Jimmie sees *showy* at all three."

"Is Loef's cooperation still achievable? If not, at least limit his ability to participate."

"We're on it." I don't mention I went to the 5x5 and had Loef in my car. "Send me some Patrol to pop the Ragen Colts, break their street-command structure."

"Ten four."

"And we gotta move the P-Stones locked up at Twelve. If Gibbons wasn't on his way here, those P-Stones would already be on lampposts."

"*Move them?* Those three P-Stones are how I might divert the alderman from St. Gabriel's. If the alderman is saving the P-Stones at Twelve, he'll be *outside* of the Riviera. Best for all involved."

"Unless you're a copper working at Twelve. Or a P-Stone, if Gibbons gets there too late."

"The alderman and his gangsters have to be somewhere, Dennis. Find Loef Brummel and engage his assistance. We have only a few blocks and a few minutes to keep this storm from overtaking us."

Chapter 16

Jimmie jumps us across the Fifty-Fifth median, out of the smoke, fire hoses, and dirty water. He stops at the curb fronting Keef's 5x5. Men with bats stand at the bar's brick corners, eighteen more on the sidewalk. Some cheer at the smoke.

I check the 5x5's roof. If there aren't men up there with rifles, there will be. Same on the ground. All these fellows have shotguns and rifles close enough to grab.

The faces I recognize are career street-criminals capable of killing policemen on a bad day, and today is every bit of that. None of them are Loef Brummel's crew and probably half aren't from the Riv.

Every copper inside the Riv has been told that Loef Brummel is Osama bin Laden; arrest him on sight, by any means necessary that doesn't kill him, then call me.

Before I exit the car, I try Maureen again. No answer.

My phone rings. R. Murph says, "Better come back to the apartment."

"Talk to me."

"Not on the phone."

I look at Jimmie, tell R. Murph, "Ten four. Be there in fifteen minutes."

Jimmie and I exit the Crown Vic, step through the flannel shirts, chain belts, and cigarettes to the 5x5's front door.

Inside, it's loud and smoky, vibrating with the violence of the Stock Yards era. A twenty-four-inch TV above the bar blares voice-over and helicopter video of one thousand Blacks massed four blocks south. Every man in the bar is glued to the screen, all talking at the same time. All of them have weapons—bats, hammers, lengths of pipe.

The TV screen cuts to a helicopter-shot two blocks west—whites in the Riviera surging south on Halsted to confront the Blacks at the Fifty-Fifth barricade.

The 5x5 cheers; fists pound the bar. "Project niggers die here!"

A half hour ago this place was full of Riviera men and their zealot auxiliary toasting the Ayatollah being shot to death. I lead us through the crowd. Eyes acknowledge me, but no one wants to talk. Jimmie follows, doesn't get knifed.

At the back door, I pull an ex–Ragen Colt off the wall at the pay phone and shove him outside. His partner reaches for me. Jimmie bear-hugs him from behind, walks him through the door, and kicks it shut behind them.

We put both men on the wall. I say, "Both of you are on parole. I make one call, you're violated back to Joliet. Give me Loef Brummel."

One shrugs.

The other says, "Ain't seen him."

"Really? I cuffed Loef out front, forty minutes ago."

Silence.

"I'm supposed to arrest you for being where you are, throw you in the tank. That'll be with gentlemen of color who are about to transgress *in volume*."

Neither answers or looks concerned.

I make the best "not fucking around" face I know how to make. "Find me Loef Brummel. Tell that motherfucker to call me, right now. That's your job. If he doesn't call, the next time I see either of you today, you're going to lockup in Six, Seventy-Ninth and Halsted. DOA after two steps. We clear?"

They nod, but it's not agreement. We cut them loose. They walk back inside where they're not allowed to be.

Jimmie and I duck around the brick corner to the street, then under a ten-loop hangman's noose added to the elm tree we walked under six minutes ago. The noose is stark, ugly, and real. I toss Jimmie my pocketknife to cut down the noose, because he can reach that high. He does, throws the noose in the back seat of our Crown Vic, and jumps in the driver's side.

We take Union north into the Riv toward St. Gabriel's. Loef will be close to the pain.

Deeper into the Riv's bungalows and three-flats, the streets and walks are jammed with mourners. Black funeral wreaths hang on the porches and in the windows. I hit redial a second time on Loef's last call. No answer. If we had the budget the FBI does, I could GPS Loef's phone. At Forty-Ninth, the crowd splits—

Twenty men wearing PNDH shirts and black armbands converge on our car, eyeing Jimmie behind the wheel. I pop the siren, pop it again and again. Jimmie slow-rolls through the PNDH shirts and armbands until we're dead-stopped by the crush at Forty-Fifth.

I climb out and onto the hood. If the streets are this packed in every direction for the St. Gabriel's service, then the crowd has to be the five thousand we guessed. The vibe is somber, respectful-of-the-dead but razor-taut, expecting the spark. Riot cars and officers dot the crowd. We're outnumbered a hundred to one.

The news that the Ayatollah didn't die is just now being reported inside and outside St. Gabriel's. In a matter of minutes, the Canaryville section of the Riviera will know what the Ragen Colts and PNDH street fighters already know up at the barricade—the Ayatollah and his surviving cortege, and at least a thousand Blacks, are marching on Canaryville.

On the first morning of the Bayside aftermath.

Before these violent, insular, blue-collar shanty-Irish can wail over their dead.

Not many insults can top that in the Irish culture.

I jump from Jimmie's hood into the street and call the unit commanders. No one's seen Loef Brummel. I tell Jimmie, "I'll make a loop on foot. See if you can get a goddamn answer on Pádraig Cane—do we have him or not? Then call Mahoney about Maureen; he said he'd run the FBI."

I wade into the crowd toward St. Gabriel's. At the outer edge, many of the mourners I pass still think the Ayatollah is dead. I hear, "God's will," and more than one warning that the Ayatollah's gangs are gathering for more blood. At Lowe, I can see the church steps rising above the crowd, and hear:

"MY FRIENDS. MY FRIENDS."

Bishop Haswell Burke has a megaphone to his mouth. Cracker found a way into Canaryville and the front steps outside St. Gabriel's. These are Catholics, on a death day, not his "Christian Protestants," and although they may agree with much of the ideology he preached at Armour Square, they're *Catholic* today.

"GOD IS HERE WITH US. RIGHT HERE. RIGHT NOW." Pause. "HE WANTS YOUR FORBEARANCE OF VIOLENCE. *BUT.* GOD DOES NOT WANT YOU TO KNEEL TO ANYONE BUT HIM. NOT TO THE THREATS. NOT TO THE DEATHS OF YOUR LOVED ONES. HE WANTS YOU TO *STAND!*"

I hit redial a third time on Loef Brummel's number. Loef answers with crowd noise all around him. I say: "You're under arrest. Plant your ass where I can find you, right now."

"One of your P-Stones is RayLen Starks? Tell me that's a fuckin' lie, Denny. Tell me you ain't protecting that murderin' fuckin' rapist."

"If RayLen's one of 'em, so what?"

"We're gonna drag RayLen Starks. Then we're hanging him and his two partners. Any part of that you and his mother don't wanna see, get the fuck outta town, now."

"You have to help put the goddamn fire out, Loef, not light it—"

"The fuckin' Bayside, Denny. *Our* people. Fuckin' *niggers* are gonna die. We're all done apologizing for their fuckin' history; they're dealing with ours now."

"Don't. You're a citywide. We won't be gentle."

"Bring the army you talked about. Ayatollah's got a thousand now, another two or three on the way. Your shift running Red Summer's all done."

Click.

Haswell Burke booms from the steps at St. Gabriel's: "STAND UP FOR YOUR NEIGHBORS. FOR YOUR HOMES. FOR YOUR COUNTRY."

Jimmie calls me. "Ambulance took Pádraig Cane to Mercy ICU, but he's not there, or he's lost somewhere in their triage. EMTs said he was hurt. Bad. CPD *does not* have him."

"Maureen?"

"Negative."

"Call Mahoney back. Tell him we're going to the clocktower-victim's apartment. We'll find something, anything that makes the Bayside perp white. Same for the clocktower. Add a white-ID from RayLen Starks at Twelve, then leak it all to the media."

"Mahoney won't want you feeding the media something we can't prove when the lions are at the gate."

"Tell him to have a listen:"

"GOD WILL DAMN THE PERPETRATORS OF YOUR SORROW. BUT YOU! YOU MUST *STAND* UP TO THE PERPETRATORS." Burke jams his arm south at the ghetto. "THESE ARE *YOUR* DEAD. NOT THEIRS."

I tell Jimmie, "Coming your way." I hang up, start wading through the crowd.

Back from the sidewalk, a TV's been set out on a table. On the screen is Gael Gilmartin midstreet, alone, in uniform, facing the Ayatollah and his thousand. Her officers are well back behind her, likely directed there by Gael to avoid the spark that kills everyone.

"Goddamn Joan of Arc," says one of the Irishmen watching the TV.

Another grabs his bat. "Known the Gilmartins since I was four. No fuckin' way she stands there alone for me." He bulls south into the crowd.

I call Buff Anderson at Twelve to warn him that he and Twelve are Mahoney's front line should Gael somehow survive and convince the Ayatollah to stay out of the Riv.

Buff answers, says he already knows—but because he's Buff—he pushed his TAC and gang teams out into the district, sent his secretary home, and now it's him, Patrol, and the P-Stones holed up in the basement. SWAT teams are en route.

"Put your phone next to RayLen's ear."

Buff does. I tell RayLen, "Loef Brummel just told me that you belong to him. That the uniforms guarding you, looking at you right now, are his. And they're giving you to Loef as soon as he gets there."

Silence.

I ramp into the lie. "We're not talking later today, RayLen. There's two hundred armed, murderous Irishmen moving north through

Bridgeport at this very moment. If you know what the driver of the Ford Focus looks like, describe him, and I can get you moved."

Silence.

"You're gonna die, RayLen, dragged naked behind a car till your skin burns off, then hung on a streetlight. I kid you not."

"Uh-huh. In front of the cameras."

"Remember the Rodney King riots? Cameras were all over your bros at that corner on Western; your bros killin' and stompin' like they were in the dark. These Irishmen aren't any smarter. They're not looking to loot a flat-screen TV; they got family blood on 'em."

Silence.

I wade five more feet of crowd to Jimmie's car, still talking at RayLen. "You got an hour, maybe two if you pray hard."

I slide in. Jimmie drops into reverse and turns to look over the seat. I quit RayLen and pop the siren as Jimmie reverses through the crowd. He says, "Talked to Mahoney. He knows about you and Keef Gilmartin throwing punches. Not happy."

"Yeah, well, it could've been worse. You could've shot him."

Jimmie mugs. "Mahoney's genuinely pissed. I hear *loose cannon* in his voice. He won't work with that."

"Goddamn civil war about to start, but my temper's the problem?"

"Mahoney said Gael Gilmartin has the Ayatollah talking to her on camera. Slows down his march, but the longer she keeps Gibbons at his crime scene, the bigger his crowd, the harder for him to control it. They lose it on Gael, on camera—"

I wave Jimmie to stop.

Jimmie nods, quits a scenario that no one survives. "Mahoney okayed us to Twelve but said if you start something there—with either side—you're done. He wants a call the *second* we have new, white-perp evidence from the apartment or a white-ID from RayLen Starks."

"Mahoney thinks I'm a genius, right?"

Jimmie continues, "Same for Loef Brummel or Pádraig Cane—the second we have either in custody we call Mahoney. Said all of it three times, Den, then told me to repeat it. And no media leaks unless he approves them. I believe he said, 'Not a syllable from Banahan or I pull him.'"

I keep popping the siren to part the crowd. "Hope there's something in that apartment."

Jimmie bumpers us into Thirty-Fifth. Lights flashing, he races full siren toward the Ryan.

11:35 a.m.

Climbing the last stair to Father Augustine/Chesney's front door, Jimmie stops, does a thumbs-up with his phone to his ear, then lowers his phone. "Mahoney, the master. *On camera*, Lieutenant Gilmartin was braced about the P-Stones 'holed up' at Twelve. She answered that the P-Stones were 'in protective custody, and that the situation outside Twelve was too volatile to move them.' Alderman Gibbons bit big; hasn't moved off Fifty-Ninth to save them yet, but he hasn't marched to the Riv either."

"That's why we carry our deputy super's luggage." I slap Jimmie's shoulder. "Mahoney, the master."

We open the door of 2B. R. Murph has now spent five hours inside the Father Augustine/Chesney apartment. Crime-scene tech Diane Winooski has spent two. I pull Diane out of earshot while Jimmie tells R. Murph our Augustine/Chesney switched-identity epiphany. If R. Murph has seen anything that disproves our epiphany, he'll recognize the breakdown before Jimmie finishes the explanation. Then R. Murph can tell us what he wouldn't say on the phone.

I put both hands on Diane's shoulders. "You holding up?"

She shrugs. "Bayside was bad."

I circle my finger at her crime scene. "What do you know about this apartment and its occupant that I don't?"

Diane points at an envelope. "Pay stubs, twelve of them."

Jimmie yells, "Den?"

I hold up my hand so Diane can finish.

She continues, "Augustine P. O'Dwyer is the bus driver at St. Gabriel's, has been for twenty years."

"Excuse me? Someone hung the *bus driver* from Canaryville's Catholic church? Ten hours after they blew up the Bayside?"

"Denny?"

I glare at Jimmie, then back to Diane. "The Catholic church in Ireland defrocks our victim for kids, then gets him a green card and a church job driving kids home from school? Twenty years ago someone at St. Gabe's was supposed to believe that?"

Diane shrugs. "It would seem so."

No way. Now I *know* our defrocked pedophile bus driver has to be Chesney. A Hall of Fame IRA murderer/hero with big friends on both sides of the Atlantic.

Diane points at an address book in R. Murph's hand. "R. Murph found it under the drawer, one of those old-timey compartments. Ran the phone numbers." Diane stops, then looks past me to Jimmie and Detective Murphy.

"Okay. And?"

Diane is not acting like Diane. She points, "Better R. Murph explains."

I turn, walk to Jimmie and R. Murph. "Address book? Anything with the name Chesney? IRA? Anything?"

Detective Murphy says, "This book has nine numbers from Northern Ireland." Pause. "I have a friend, a German I met when I was with the US Marshals; he runs the European Union's FAST teams for Germany—"

"Stop. Explain."

R. Murph explains FAST as "Fugitive Active Search Teams."

I glance at Jimmie, then back to R. Murph. He continues. "No way you'd want me to call the FBI in—so I called my friend. He ran the phone numbers—three numbers are IRA in Belfast, one of them nasty."

"Your German, can he run Chesney changing his identity to Augustine?"

"Already asked—your secretary gave me the heads-up before you got here. My friend won't break the law; German coppers don't cowboy." R. Murph shrugs *Sorry*. "My friend said he chased an IRA fugitive back in 1980. Guy killed a German MEK agent in the Rhineland—a dope for guns deal. Norbert—that's my friend—caught the IRA fugitive in Glasgow; guy tried to bargain, said he had 'proof' that MI5 and the Protestant UVF—the Ulster Volunteer Force—had killed the wrong Chesney, the wrong Claudy bomber."

Jimmie floats his eyebrows for me, asks R. Murph, "Ulster Volunteer Force?"

"Terrorists if you're Catholic. Ultrapatriots if you're Protestant. Stone killers, either way." Detective Murphy adds, "My German friend is a serious James Bond guy—no kidding; has all the gadgets. Wouldn't tell me how he knew—or whether he thought Chesney was dead or alive—but he's positive that it isn't Chesney they buried in Maghera with Chesney's family."

I pat R. Murph's shoulder, "Good work. What else?"

Nobody says anything. Two detectives and one crime-scene tech stare at me like my dog is dead.

"What?"

Jimmie shows me a phone number in his notebook, says: "I copied it from Augustine/Chesney's address book."

I blink at the number, then R. Murph. He nods. I look at Jimmie, then everyone in the room still looking at me. "Show me in the book."

R. Murph does. The number shouldn't be there. But there it is. I pull my phone, key in the number instead of using speed dial. It rings once.

A terse Cullen Mahoney answers his private line. "Have you helped me, Dennis, or made more problems to solve?"

"Father Augustine P. O'Dwyer, late of the clocktower, has been driving the bus at St. Gabriel's for the last twenty years. Don't know why his employment verifications didn't pop when we ran 'em the first time—could be because he's actually Father James Chesney, the *priest* who committed the 1972 Claudy bombing in Northern Ireland. Killed nine Protestants, three of 'em children."

"*What?*"

"Yeah. The real Augustine died in 1980. Chesney assumed his identity."

"You're *certain*?"

"Not a hundred percent, but I will be. Right now, I'd bet either arm on it."

"And how would you know this revelation?"

"German cop, an international R. Murph worked with. The IRA killed one of the German's guys."

"Major trouble if this is fact."

"Trouble? Shit, it makes the all-white lineup that much more believable—Loyalist-Protestant Pádraig Cane and somebody hung an IRA-Catholic bomber from the clocktower. Pádraig killed two IRA Catholics in Dublin. Fits him like a glove."

Long pause. Mahoney says, "I arranged Father Augustine's job at St. Gabriel's; I've known him for thirty-one years, since the day he arrived in the US. If he's an imposter, a *priest* who murders—"

"The church in Ireland says they canned your guy Augustine for kids. How the hell did that get past you and whoever runs St. Gabriel's?"

"It didn't. The church in Ireland investigated the sexual abuse accusations, found them baseless, but the temperament of the country—both times Augustine was accused—was the real issue of the day."

"*Huh?* Why defrock this guy if he didn't . . . I don't get it."

"Father Augustine was being continuously accused by the Protestants. The accusations were used to slander the church as unwilling to act. The church acted *publicly*, but privately solicited assistance for an innocent man. Or so the church told me. Possibly, it was a lie to gain my cooperation."

"Why didn't you tell me he worked at St. Gabriel's? Or that you knew him?"

"He's worked there twenty years, Dennis; how could your detectives *not* know?" Mahoney's tone hardens further. "I've attended mass at St. Gabriel's every Sunday I wasn't ill since 1953. She's an institution worth defending, whether or not this revelation is true. If Augustine *is* Chesney, my participation will be a trump card for the FBI at a time we don't need to give them anything else."

"No shit, a deputy superintendent of the Chicago Police Department implicated as a protector of a mass-murderer priest. *Jesus.*"

Mahoney says, "Bring your notes on Chesney/Augustine to my office; we'd best make a plan to defend ourselves and the department."

"*The department?* How about the city? Last I heard, Gael Gilmartin's the only thing between the Ayatollah and Canaryville. She weighs 120 on a pizza day; that ain't enough to stop a civil war."

"Nor am I; nor are you."

"We gotta drop this Chesney–IRA bomber story in the media."

"Yes, but not until we have the story in the form we want. Red Summer's been a long time burning. We'll select our fights, then have them on ground we can hold; not allow the FBI, the mayor, or Alderman Gibbons to choose."

I look at Jimmie. "Whoever's doing these murders is who's doing the goddamn choosing. I say we put Pádraig Cane and Loef in the same room—"

"Find them and that's what we'll do. And for now, his sister—your Maureen—is our best chance and she's at the FBI building."

You found her? Meet you there—"

"No, Dennis, do the P-Stones first. Secure their white-ID of Chesney's killer while we still have the opportunity, then bring everything you have on the Chesney-revelation to my office. We'll organize Maureen's . . . safety . . . another way."

"There's no safety in the Federal Building unless you're their tribe. Jimmie will drop you the Chesney evidence, then hunt Loef and Pádraig. I'll get the P-Stones to give me something white, then I'm going to the Federal Building. Fire me if you want."

"No, Dennis—"

I hang up, tell R. Murph to beg, borrow, or steal for the German's help, but prove Augustine is Chesney. We know he is, but everyone who matters will run or stall until it's too late to matter to Red Summer.

Detective Murphy nods.

I tell Jimmie: "Case of Glenlivet to whoever finds Loef Brummel or Pádraig Cane. Has to be *now* and *alive*. No 'accidents.' Bring both of 'em to me, not lockup. Nobody but me. Clear?"

Jimmie nods.

I say, "I'll brace Agent Stone, then you and me will take the Chesney evidence to Mahoney—"

"No." Jimmie blocks the door. "FBI, Den. We don't brace the FBI. You won't leave their building until the trial's over and you've served your ten years."

"Wrong. There's big leverage here—in Pádraig, Chesney, Rupert, and Bathhouse John—how they all connect underwrites FBI *ownership* of this horror show and the FBI can't have that public. I don't know what the ownership is, or how to prove it yet, but it's there."

"Don't go to the FBI building. Mahoney's right; Stone may be finally playing his cards; he may keep you."

I glance Diane and R. Murph, then back to Jimmie. "The FBI's in this with Pádraig. They're dirty, I fucking know it. They're not executing Maureen, or us, to cover their ass; not gonna happen."

Jimmie thinks . . . like he's recalling something, says, "I'm going home for a minute. Something you said. It's in the Dream file."

"What?"

"Don't know. Something . . ."

"If you say so. We need answers and you're usually the guy who finds 'em."

Jimmie's gone before I finish. Diane says, "Dream file?"

From the window I watch Jimmie exit the building, then squeal the tires until his taillights disappear. Back when Jimmie Daniels still drank and killed people, he wasn't near as good a detective. A lot more peaceful sleep pattern, though; sheets lasted the whole week, no fourth or fifth dimension to deal with. The daily E&J brandy hangover was a high price, but sleepwalking with murderers and talking to dead people isn't a freebie.

Now that he's no longer utilizing the twenty-five-ounce brandy anesthetic, Jimmie sometimes solves our murders in the Dream, in "blood metaphor" is how he describes it. He keeps a Dream file.

In the Dream, sometimes Jimmie rides with the Buffalo Soldiers—the all-Black Ninth and Tenth US Cavalry—against the Cheyenne and Comanche. Sometimes he's with Bass Reeves, a former Arkansas-Texas slave who escaped to freedom, lived with the Seminole and Creek Nation, and became the most successful deputy US marshal–manhunter in the Indian Territory. And sometimes Jimmie Daniels is Lakota Sioux, fighting against the gold-miner invasion of the Black Hills. He always kills the man or woman he's hunting. And most of the time they deserve it.

And although I believe with absolute certainty that Jimmie was physically born at 113th and Elizabeth ten years after I was born in the Riviera, Jimmie Daniels is actually from another century, maybe another planet.

And in that century or on that other planet, Jimmie accrued some grim karma. We ran into it the first time, eighteen years ago in July, at a wedding in Morgan Park on Chicago's West Side. Both of us felt the guns before they fired. The first bullet killed Jimmie's daughter, the ring bearer; the second and third shots mortally wounded the bride and groom. Ten rounds total; three shooters, all Appalachian and white. Shooters one and three escaped by firing into the wedding crowd. I killed shooter two, a woman.

The bride and groom were railroad police Jimmie had worked with in Kentucky during the war days of the coal-miner strikes. They were the targets.

Shooters one and three stayed missing for twenty-four months. Jimmie took a year from CPD, tracked them through back-holler Kentucky, into the fishing boats of bayou Louisiana, and finally into the Florida Everglades.

Like Bass Reeves, Jimmie was prosecuted for murder—Bass Reeves for killing a cook; Jimmie for breaking the back of one Caleb Wyatt in Florida. Bass won an acquittal and so did Jimmie, his in a nonjury trial before a female judge of mixed-race Seminole origin who chain-smoked rum cheroots on the bench and wore a Colt Bisley .38-40 under her robe.

Jimmie returned to CPD, a hero father to the rank and file. To his detractors, Jimmie was, and is, a murderer with a badge . . . and a file he keeps locked away with his daughter's death-scene photographs. When he can't dream it, he searches the photos for shooter three, the one who got away.

Diane asks again. "Dream file?"

"Long story. Not a good one," then glance R. Murph, then back to Mahoney's number on my BlackBerry. Nope, not a good one, either.

Chapter 17

Cullen Mahoney intercepts me outside the FBI's new palace at Roosevelt and Damen where I agreed not to be. Car to car he says, "Not our geography, Dennis. And certainly not now."

"Not leaving Maureen in there, alone."

Mahoney says, "Alderman Gibbons has decided against forcing his way into the Riviera. He's pointing his three thousand to Ogden Park three miles from Canaryville. Mayor McQuinn has agreed to meet Gibbons there in open forum in four hours."

The rush feels so good it could be drug related. I may call the alderman and thank him.

Mahoney continues, "While Gibbons and the Reverends swell Ogden Park into a bomb for this evening, Gibbons himself will march on the Twelfth District 'to save the three innocent Black men held there.'"

"Missed his calling; should've been P. T. Barnum."

Mahoney points north. "A mob of our neighbors has formed at the quarry in the Hardscrabble. They have bats and nooses and are at this moment attempting to cross the river on the old Loomis Street Bridge."

"Jesus. How many?"

"Two hundred, more than enough to assault the Twelfth District." Pause. "They'll not cross that bridge. If we have to shoot them all."

Before I can ask more questions, Mahoney segues to Augustine/ Chesney, his tone oddly fearful considering the civil war at Fifty-Fifth Street we just delayed and the bridge confrontation he just described. Mahoney's tone could be because of his involvement and where we're parked. Mahoney's been to war with the FBI over his own account; has the scars to prove it, and sooner or later the G buries their enemies.

Always.

Siren. An eastbound squad car shoots past on Roosevelt toward what's left of Little Italy. Mahoney says, "In theory, our story must pacify the whites, but not inflame the Blacks. Historically, one negates the other." Mahoney returns to me. "Some combatants have to have the fight. The combat is more important than the outcome. We do not want to be between them."

"Other than it's our *job.*"

"It was our job. When the problems of a city were of their own making." Mahoney nods at the FBI building. "I know I can't keep you from that building as long as your Maureen is inside. And I know you'll defend me, more than you should." He smiles small. "Don't go to prison doin' either and maybe we can still win a section of this fight."

* * *

Inside or out, the FBI building is ten stories of naked federal power designed by professionals to make you confess before they ask a question. Maureen's been inside for at least four hours, a total of seven with the FBI for the day. I've been inside for twenty-five minutes; that's twenty-four too many.

I lean across the table and tell Special Agent Stone, his three witnesses, and their tape recorders: "Maureen Cane will not wear a wire on me. Keep her the rest of the year, waterboard her every afternoon, and it won't happen. Her brother's a cunt. You own him, but that's as far as you get in the Cane family."

Four expressionless faces stare at me, one a middle-aged woman. My phone rings 911. I force myself not to answer.

Agent Stone smiles at the urgency that I try to hide, then nods at my pocket. "Extensive activity out there in your city."

"You could help, but why help stop a bloodbath when you can leverage it against me for your grand jury."

"That's what you think I'm doing?"

"Are you giving me Maureen, or not?"

Stone taps an unopened file. "What do you *really* know about Cullen Mahoney's background?"

"We've been through this twice. Mahoney and I grew up on the same block. If not for Mahoney, you believe the FBI would already have me in prison. And another fifty Chicago coppers."

Stone nods. "Not quite fifty. And Loef Brummel? You grew up with him as well?"

"All of us, the same block. None of this is news."

"And the Starks, Antoine and Odetta?" Stone opens the grand jury file in front of him, fingertips a document to midpage, "Shot, beaten, then thrown off a roof . . . on St. Patrick's Day, 1972."

I don't show Stone what I remember . . .

I've been the police for four whole months . . . It's 2:00 a.m. I'm on the roof of the Magikist building, six stories up. The giant Magikist lips glow the roof red. Under them is a green electronic holiday message:

Happy St. Patrick's Day, Chicago!

Bathed in the red and green are Antoine Starks and his twin sister, Odetta, early twenties, same age as me. Below them is a ghetto neighborhood that looks like shit even from this distance.

Down there, Antoine's a crime-world up-and-comer—armed robbery, protection, whores, dope. He's dressed in a powder-blue belted jumpsuit, matching hat and shoes. Odetta is less flashy, more political, tall under an immaculate twelve-inch Afro, and every bit as lethal. Last time she was arrested, her purse had an ivory-handled straight razor, two grams of cocaine, and a paperback copy of *Managing Your Own Money*.

Antoine is pacing, hiding the *wary* a successful street predator surely feels.

Odetta checks her watch, steps deeper into the shadows of the elevator tower. "Ease up, Toine. Bathhouse John the Irish crime boss of

Canaryville. He say he got this figured out good; for all of us. Don't hurt to listen—"

"Banahan's dead." Neon glints on Antoine's belted .380 palm gun. "Cops die. Everybody die. Had a funeral. Played their fuckin' bagpipes. Get the fuck over it. We wrap this shit up tonight, or whoever them Irish ofays send up here is getting a lipstick kiss off this muthafuckin' roof."

I wait till Antoine reaches his sister, then step out of the deepest shadows, aim a police-issue Smith & Wesson .38 my older brother, Mike, owned, and say: "On your knees."

Antoine and Odetta go stone-still, squint until they recognize the white man they're looking at. Neither drop. I shoot Antoine in the stomach. He blows backward, loses his Superfly hat, lands on his back, balls fetal, and starts screaming.

Odetta stays frozen, her intense eyes framed in oversized glasses.

I shoot her, too. She lands like her brother, bloody and screaming.

I belt Mike's .38, drag Antoine's writhing 180 pounds to the roof's edge, stare into his murdering-piece-of-shit eyes, punch him as hard as I can twice in the face, then Superman him into the night sky.

He covers the seventy feet in a four-count.

I do the same to Odetta—two hard punches that fracture her face, then Superman.

The .38 I just used to shoot them both I place on the parapet. The homicide detectives will know why. And they'll know where to look.

But they won't. They'll label Antoine and Odetta Starks an unsolved, "gang related" double homicide.

I glance north across the rooftops to the last lights of 1972's St. Patrick's Day celebrations—

In Canaryville, they won't call this murder, or revenge.

They'll just wanna know why it took me so long.

My BlackBerry rings 911. I tell Agent Stone: "We doing this again? Really?"

"It continues to be said, or otherwise inferred, that the Starks murdered your brother, Patrolman Michael Banahan. That they were the two Black armed robbers who fired first and got away."

My BlackBerry rings 911 again. I answer Stone instead, put the same answer in the record that I did the last time Stone interrogated me. "The perpetrator who murdered Officer Michael Banahan at 400 Liquors on January 1, 1972, was killed on the scene by Officer Banahan's fellow officers."

My BlackBerry continues to 911. I put it on the table so they can watch it ring.

Stone reads from his file. "Killed by officers Cullen Mahoney and Thomas Sobczak. Mahoney and Sobczak both worked for Jon Burge in the Area Two Violent Crimes Unit."

I tap my watch. "Race war? Red Summer? Blood ankle-deep in the streets?"

Stone doesn't look up. "Since we last spoke *formally*, Jon Burge has been convicted and sent to prison." Stone lifts a sheet from his file and shows it to me. "The City of Chicago has recently settled four of the Burge torture lawsuits for $20 million."

I stare at Stone and his spin.

In the early 1980s Jon Burge and his detectives were accused of "torture to elicit confessions" by 150 Blacks, including twenty-plus previously convicted murderers, all arrested for new homicides. After twenty-one years of trials, retrials, and Burge refusing to roll on his detectives, the G convicted Burge in 2010.

"The city settled *four* cases"—I show Stone four fingers—"of the *one hundred fifty* cases claimed and reviewed. The city *settled*—a settlement proves nothing more than risk/reward."

"You're saying Burge is innocent?"

"You convicted him of perjury and obstruction of justice. Nothing else—and those were flower petals—after twenty-one years of publicly saying he was the Antichrist."

Stone extracts another sheet. "Your brother—"

"My brother died on the line, Agent Stone. Not in an office. Not on TV. Not in a law office or think tank with secretaries and soft drinks. Three in the chest; bled to death in the ambulance."

Stone nods his condolences. "Must've been awful for you." Stone looks at the file. "The same year your deceased brother's service weapon was found at the death scene of Antoine and Odetta Starks . . ."

"So do your fucking grand jury." I jam my hand at the windows. "Can't you assholes smell the smoke? Leverage is one thing, but—"

Three of the four smile at me and my anger. The woman doesn't.

I suck a breath; point at their tape recorders. "Let me see Maureen Cane, *now*. That's a formal request from the Chicago Police Department. And relevant to the urgent investigation surrounding the Bayside bombing."

Stone looks at his team, then: "So, you know . . . about Maureen?"

"I know the FBI doesn't want to publicly impede the Bayside investigation. That the FBI doesn't want responsibility for encouraging a race war that could have been averted, merely to embarrass the Chicago Police Department and facilitate a federal takeover that will enhance your careers."

"Did you make this request in writing?"

My phone rings another 911. I stand, grab my phone, and point at the door. "Give me Maureen."

"Follow procedure."

"Okay, asshole. I got one for your personnel file. Pádraig Cane. He's your bitch, Agent Stone. Bad news is he's part of the clocktower murder, probably part of Cissy Noonan and Dill Reem. And probably took the shot on Loef Brummel two weeks ago. That's why you were at Maureen's; Pádraig's going off the rails; his felonies are gonna tattoo the FBI with the worst racial event since Selma."

"Whatever Pádraig is to us—"

"If you don't have Pádraig, or haven't killed him to shut him up, then he's ours. Give me Maureen, right fucking now—"

I glance everyone at the table.

"Or I go public; drop the bomb that your deal with Bathhouse John kept him on the street and murdering till he bought it in Florida. Just like you're doing with Pádraig Cane. If you don't know the Illinois criminal code, your Bathhouse John deal proves the FBI's 'prior conduct MO.' And that buys you Pádraig Cane's race war."

Agent Stone remains seated, unhurried. "Please put your Maureen Cane request in writing. I'll put the information I just presented in writing, as well. Adding that you stated your interest in saving your city, not just your friends, but when I requested your cooperation with the FBI, you declined."

1:15 p.m.

The female agent from the meeting escorts me to the elevator, then rides down with me. Inside the elevator, she stands shoulder to shoulder with me, like that's supposed to intimidate me. I call Leigha, my secretary; tell her to make the formal *urgent* request to interview Maureen Cane. The elevator stops at the second floor. The woman's sensible shoe brushes mine as she exits; the doors close. On the floor is a wadded paper or Kleenex. I drop my phone, pick both up with the phone on top.

In my car, I unwad the paper. It's typewritten, not computer printed, and undated; appears to be a transcript of a report or conversation between two unknowns, probably FBI agents.

> Maureen Cane is the widow of Sean Cavanaugh—a ranking member of the Ulster Volunteer Force (UVF) murdered in 1990 by a faction of the IRA. This photograph is an outdoor mural on a building in Belfast, Northern Ireland, at the corner of Shankill Road and Malvern Street where the murder occurred. The words above the three figures depicted with their rifles are: 'Ulster's Three Rivers.'
>
> In Northern Ireland this depiction represents significant adulation among the Protestant Loyalists and something close to sainthood among the UVF's ultraviolent faction.
>
> The other two men in the mural are John Bingham, murdered in his Belfast home, 1986; and Reverend Preston Howat, murdered in Chicago, Illinois, 1999.
>
> Great Britain's MI5 and MI6 report that Maureen Cane's father founded the UVF. Her pub in Chicago's Old Town is named "The Malvern." She should be considered to hold the same allegiances as her father, husband,

and brother, Pádraig, until proven otherwise.
Where CPD's Lt. Dennis Banahan's sympa-
thies align relative to Ireland's Loyalist vs.
Republican agendas is unknown.

I glance the FBI building. The woman who dropped this just risked
prison—*if* the document is real. The good news is, if it was the UVF
who killed the wrong "Claudy bomber" back in 1980 like R. Murph's
German says, it's not a reach that the UVF would want to kill the real
Claudy bomber now. And for Chicago, that would be some all-star
white-on-white.

The bad news is, it paints Maureen and her dead family as UVF
royalty.

I wheel out of the FBI lot, wait to return Jimmie's 911s until I'm on
Ashland—the FBI monitors all calls made on their property.

Jimmie answers, says, "Just made it home. R. Murph called—
Loomis Street Bridge. Two dead. R. Murph said he can see from
Augustine's window."

My eyes close tight, then open. "The dead; the banshees or us?"

"Banshees. Knocked off when they charged our police line. Both
drowned, unconscious. All of it on camera. Riviera's going nuts."

I say, "That it?" knowing it isn't.

"Ayatollah had trouble en route to Twelve."

"How bad?"

"One of our squads protecting his car, crashed it. The white officer
involved said it was the Ayatollah's driver. An argument ensued. The
officer and the Ayatollah's bodyguard threw punches. We arrested two.
Claims are being made that we purposely compromised the Ayatollah's
security in hopes of getting him shot. Again."

Not out of the question either time—coppers are people—but I
doubt it. "Pádraig Cane?"

"Ghost."

"Loef Brummel?"

"Same. They're not our only problem."

"Yeah, but they may be our only solution."

"Bishop Haswell Burke was one of my 911s to you."

"Tell me that cracker's dead."

"Announced he will be at Ogden Park to confront the Ayatollah and the mayor."

"Good. Burke dies before he gets within a block. One less gas-can to worry about."

"But a gas-can, nonetheless."

I tell Jimmie the FBI's news on Maureen's family, her dead husband's mural and the other dead men on it, and their ties to the "ultraviolent Protestant UVF." I add, "The Brits say her father was the founder. If that ain't bullshit, then Pádraig's gotta be UVF, was UVF even when he was the Irish police, and the perfect conduit to ID Augustine as Chesney."

Jimmie doesn't say *Same for Maureen.*

Jimmie says, "How'd Mahoney explain Augustine's phone number?"

"Said he brought Augustine over; all roads will lead back to Cullen Mahoney."

"Did he know? That Augustine was Chesney?"

"No, the church burned him, but that's not how it'll look, 'cause Mahoney won't roll on the church. I've known Mahoney since I could walk, and there's no way he draws blood on the Catholic church. None."

"We'll do it for him." Jimmie's voice sharpens. "That Protestant minister in the Belfast mural, Preston Howat, I remember him, ten years ago or so, Area Four side of the river. Beaten to pieces, found him buried under the bridge at Ashland."

"Beaten to pieces . . . same MO as Dill Reem . . ."

Jimmie's voice stays sharp, how he sounds when he's feeling it. "A homeless man's dog dug into Howat's body in 2003, remember? Howat had been missing three, four years; had a 1999 credit card receipt in his pocket. I'll pull the file. Odd the FBI had Howat's stats at your meeting . . . Howat's a foreigner, dead a *long* time."

"An *Irish* foreigner. Stone's looking at a dead Northern Ireland Catholic priest on our clocktower and a dead Northern Ireland Protestant minister under our bridge, both of them *here*, two miles apart. Stone's an asshole, but he ain't blind. He knows we're exhuming a story that's gonna bury him."

Jimmie says, "Howat dies in 1999 . . . And we have Renny-Mac's calendar on Augustine's wall . . . When'd she die?"

"What I said before—'98 or '99. About the same time as Howat. Just before, I think."

"Renny-Mac's father, Bathhouse John, was murdered in Florida . . . 2003."

"Yeah. I remember drinking a toast, several in fact."

Jimmie says, "Are we looking at tit for tat? Tie the murders by dates? Renny-Mac dies, then Howat, then Bathhouse John and his son?"

"Ten-fucking-four we can make a story outta that. Damn sure good enough for today. Tack on Dill Reem and Augustine/Chesney as the latest *continuation* of the same tit-for-tat chain."

Jimmie says, "All Irish, all the time. Whatever story we build has to have Mahoney's blessing or it'll blow up in our face. What's the Ayatollah's new ETA at Twelve?"

"Me and him. Right now."

Chapter 18

STEVEN

Ah . . . trophy time. And there he is, my infusion of color, elevating my client's all-white canvas out of the common and into the memorable.

Erudite, urbane Jimmie Daniels, *manhunter.*

The VV60 magnifies Mr. Jimmie—he's a bit smudgy from my rooming-house fire—but still quite unwrinkled after an early-morning start at the clocktower and a full day of homicide. I allow a grin and it pushes my cheek against the rifle—Mr. Jimmie and I are working together, a team, compadres secretly locked in a forbidden workplace romance.

I thought I'd have to follow Mr. Jimmie all day, but, no, he's quite considerate, committed to our romance. Sadly, I won't get to decorate the entire family, but the wife and one daughter will have to do, both home from church, all gospel'd up.

But, at three hundred yards, to do Mr. Jimmie the Manhunter justice, we'll have to "paint like a pro," as the buzz-cut SOG-wannabes say at the gun shows. A JFK is the answer, but I have only two windows of opportunity, and who knows if Jimmie will stay for the lunch his lovely wife is preparing? Window One is the dining room and perfecto Jackson Pollock–splattertology *if* Jimmie will nosh with the fam.

Window Two is an office, I'd guess, and by the looks of him, a troubling spot to spend your Sunday. Not much "Jesus loves us all" in there.

The Window Two shot would be buttah. Do I take it, forgoing the family portrait? The stars have lined up nicely so far. Let's give the universe a few more minutes to smell the chitlins. Jimmie looks up . . . and toward me. My phone rings. The client calling again, now that our trusty conduit, Pádraig Cane, is suddenly unavailable.

But Jimmie feels me! I answer my phone with an exuberant: "Yes?!"

"Where are you?"

I put the phone on speaker, lay it on the rooftop parapet, resight the rifle, and answer: "The steam room at the gym; people watching."

"Take me off speaker."

"Can't, my hands are full."

The connection ends.

My, aren't we temperamental. Those who have spent time in prisons and mental hospitals are, on occasion, prone to bouts of temper. Not me, my years in the hospital were swell. My client? Not quite so well adjusted. Not like Jimmie Daniels and his cutesy little family. Work hard, go to church on Sunday, and you live a long happy life.

Jimmie and I stare across the three hundred yards. Because I have the VV60, I can feel *and* see our relationship coming to its seminal conclusion, us together forever. Thank God, I brought the extra underwear.

I extract the last millisecond of Jimmie's life from my pocket, closing my lips on the long slender bullet as it enters my mouth, running my tongue its entire length as it exits. Mmm. *Turgid.* Jimmie's future loads nice and smooth into our .223-Magnum honeymoon. If everyone knew how good this felt there'd be no space on any rooftop anywhere.

Jimmie exits Window Two. He wants to help!

Jimmie enters Window One, bends to kiss his daughter, then turns for his wife. She brings a platter to the table, sets it in front of her family, and motions Jimmie to sit. Perfect. Edward Hopper couldn't have set the scene any better. I might get the daughter as well.

Jimmie apologizes to his wife using his huge hands, points at the door . . . then his head turns.

My finger tightens on the trigger. He looks out our window, then slowly focuses on the me he can't see. God, this feels good. He's so . . .

potent. We stay in the embrace, heart against heart, his brown eyes narrowing to the power of us. I exhale. Mentally whisper *Thank you*, and squeeze.

The rifle bucks into my shoulder. Jimmie's head explodes multicolor—

He didn't explode; he moved, at the last instant; the vase behind him exploded. Jimmie is scrambling his family out of the room. I didn't plan on a miss. Better exit, tout de suite; it won't be a hysterical wife screaming and screaming and screaming until a neighbor calls 911. It will be a professional, a hoodoo-manhunter. It will be any second.

This may not have been that good an idea.

Chapter 19

DENNY

TV cameras, microphones, and reporters wall in the corner steps of the Twelfth District's front door. Atop the steps, Alderman Leslie Gibbons clutches a noose above his head. His white shirt is blood-caked, not an ounce of fear in his face in spite of the fact that gunmen have tried to kill him at least once today.

Gotta give him his props, the Ayatollah's no coward. Leslie Gibbons *is* willing to die for what he wants, or who knows, maybe even for what he believes. That kind of commitment is for sure in short supply in this city; I wish the visual was: black man, bloody shirt, noose, police station.

Ten hours tops, the front page of everything in the USA that has ink and paper.

I circle the crowd to Twelve's back door, wad the noose from Keef's 5x5 in my hand, step through the shotguns and worried faces, hear one say: "The Riv's at the Loomis Street Bridge. Two dead. Gonna take an army to hold 'em on that side."

I drop down the steps and into Buff's lockup. RayLen Starks doesn't look as bold as last time, nor do his two partners. I walk directly to

RayLen, don't speak to the three uniforms or Buff, and toss the noose on the floor at RayLen's feet.

"White boys are fighting across the Loomis Street Bridge right now. Two of 'em dead. Because of you." I kick the noose onto RayLen's shoes. "Just cut that off a lamppost in Canaryville. The Ayatollah's outside; he has one, too. You heard the Irishmen shot him, right? Killed his badass bodyguard? I tried to move you but the Irish bosses won't let me." I wince at the decision. "So, even if we stop the banshees at Loomis Street, when the PNDH who tried to kill the Ayatollah an hour ago find out he's here with you, they'll roll up here, shoot the Ayatollah, then come down here and start in on you." I shake my head at unfortunate circumstance. "Camera's didn't stop the Ragen Colts and PNDH psychos on Halsted, and didn't stop the mob on the bridge. Damn sure won't stop any of 'em here."

The P-Stone next to RayLen says, "He was white."

RayLen slaps him with his free hand. "Shut up."

I hit RayLen between the eyes. His head bounces off the wall and goes limp on his neck. I turn to the carjacker who spoke. "I'm not sticking around to die saving your asses. Talk to me if you want to live till dinner."

"White man, tall as me, high-top hair. Had a bag he grabbed; fast ma'fucker, too."

"How old?"

Shrug. "Not old or he couldn't run like that."

"Weight?"

"Shit, ma'fucker, I dono—"

The other conscious P-Stone checks RayLen limp, then says, "Older than us, younger than you. Weighed, you know, one-fifty, one-seventy-five."

I show them the artist sketch of the hit-and-run.

"Uh-huh, face wider, though."

The first P-Stone says, "Ma'fucker scared, course he wider."

I wave the sketch. "But it's him? The same guy?"

Both P-Stones nod.

I yell for Buff. He's an inch behind me. "Get us a police artist." Buff pulls his phone. I turn back to the P-Stones. "Gentlemen, I wasn't lying about dead by dinner. Tell me everything about that white man you can remember."

"Then we loose?"

"I'll buy the plane tickets."

My phone rings with Jimmie's 911 ringtone. "Yeah?"

"Just dodged a bullet. In my dining room."

"No—"

"High caliber, rooftop—"

"*Sniper?* Get away from the windows!"

"Was at the table with Gayle and Sandy. Uniforms en route."

"Is Gayle, Sandy—?"

"Okay. Scared." Jimmie sucks a breath, then another. "Bullet was so close it burned Sandy's forehead and my cheek."

"Why? Why shoot at you?"

"Not just me. Pádraig Cane told us five hours ago he was gonna kill us. He knows we have his number and now he's MIA. The beating you gave him is probably why he missed."

I look at the P-Stones, tell Jimmie: "RayLen's boys just ID'd our hit-and-run sketch as the guy they carjacked for Chesney's car. That makes the hit-and-run and the clocktower the same sketch. Mattress fire, too. Fireman there said 'accelerant' and that ties in the Bayside. One guy for all four."

Jimmie's tone drops to the Jimmie Daniels who drank brandy and killed people. "And *that* perp's got no reason to shoot my daughter."

I step away from the P-Stones. "You okay, Jimmie?"

"No."

"Get Gayle and Sandy safe. Come to Twelve. The Ayatollah's here."

"Not where my problem is." Jimmie coughs. "I called Mercy again on the way here. ER found Pádraig Cane's file. Maureen picked him up, against doctor's orders."

"Come to Twelve."

"Can't protect my family at Twelve."

"Jimmie, don't. Pádraig fits in here perfect, but he isn't your shooter. He wouldn't—"

Click.

Being found guilty of almost killing Jimmie's daughter will have a high price for Pádraig Cane—and his sister, if Maureen is in fact free of the FBI, then defends her brother like I know she will.

I turn to Buff. "Separate these two from RayLen. Call me two seconds after you have their new sketch and sworn statement."

I run the steps and sprint to the back door. The door is blocked by civilians—if you can call the media civilians—they're facing the parking lot, their backs to me. At the crowd's center, shoulder-mounted cameras and microphones ring the Ayatollah, now standing high on the hood of a Pontiac. The car's protected by bodyguards and one woman who looks like Angela Davis. She would be my ex-wife, Renatta McCray. Who I still see and speak to on the first Tuesday of every month.

Renatta rushes me, pushing reporters aside with both hands. "I represent RayLen Starks, Cleaver Davis, and William Poe currently being held in your dungeon. I demand to see my clients. Now. No more bullshit, *Lieutenant*." She points at a Fox News camera and reporter. "Ten seconds, and I go public on the air; tell the world you have three innocent boys in there about to be lynched by an Irish mob of your—"

"Innocent? Are you nuts? These guys are—"

Renatta pivots, strides to the Fox reporter, points at his cameraman, then glares back at me, arches her back, her chin high and defiant.

The reporter repositions the camera so he has the Ayatollah's bloody image as background, then begins his intro for Renatta.

I bolt for the Malvern.

1:50 p.m.

It's a sixty-degree day and the Malvern is busy out front. I use the alley to get to the back. The same doorman from last night sees me coming and blocks my path, both hands up in apology.

"She's here, but mad, Dennis; up to her eyes with it."

I wait for him to get out of my way.

"Pádraig looks like a train hit him."

"It did. And it's about to again." I nod at the doorman to get out of my way.

He hesitates. "I can't let you hurt her. It's my job."

"If it comes to that, Sean, you have my permission to take your best shot." I force a professional smile. "There's a rather large Black sergeant coming here to put Pádraig, and maybe his sister, in a coma or a coffin. The sergeant is a close personal friend of mine, as is Maureen. I'd like to stop the confrontation if possible." Pause. "Pádraig's going to jail for murder, probably several. Get out of my way."

Sean steps aside. "Careful, Dennis, haven't seen her so full with it since her husband."

I stop. "You knew her husband? Her father? In Belfast?"

"I did."

"You were UVF, too?"

"I was, am." He touches the orange pocket square. "They'll not marry me to the Falls Road rabble."

"And Maureen?"

"She'd be the one to ask, Lieutenant."

"Am I missing something? I thought Ireland signed peace accords."

"Not the patriots. Bringing the murderin' IRA into the government is not a serviceable solution. I'll not forgive, nor forget."

The door bangs open behind him, Maureen framed in it. If she had a bat, I'd already be in the hospital.

"Jesus, Maureen—"

She leaps at me, throwing punches with both hands. Two land; I trap her arms and bear-hug her again. She rears back, headbutts me; kicks with her knees—I shove her back and into the bouncer. He hugs her from behind. She inhales to scream—

I yell: "Your brother's a snitch. That's why the FBI spent three hours here, why they came back for you and not him."

"A goddamn lie!"

"He is. And has been. He's selling you to them to get to me. Come to the grand jury, he'll be there. He's their 'witness.'"

Maureen fights to get loose. "A goddamn lie!"

"It's not a lie, Maureen. He's selling them our future."

"A lie!"

"And we better pray that Pádraig's so beat up he couldn't have fired his sniper rifle, or he'll be dead in five minutes."

Maureen stops fighting and stiffens to steel, eyes molten. "Stay away from my brother."

"Not me." I show her my hands. "A *sniper* just took a shot at Jimmie and his daughter. Pádraig told Jimmie he'd kill Jimmie as soon as he was able. Two plus two equals your brother. Jimmie's already lost one daughter to this job. He won't be gentle when he gets here."

"Pádraig shot no one! Was with me the last *two hours*!" Maureen fights the arms around her. "Out of the hospital, beaten half to death because of you!"

"*Because* he's an FBI snitch. And a sniper."

"A lie!"

"Do I look like I'm lying?"

Tires screech behind me. At the curb, a cold, resolute Jimmie Daniels exits the driver's side and loops the front fenders. I twist into his path, both hands up. "Whoa, Jimmie. Pádraig's too beat up to shoot a rifle."

Jimmie stops before he runs over me, looks at Maureen, the rage painted all over her and being held back by her bouncer. Jimmie says, "Get him out here. Or I go in."

Maureen screams: "The hell you say!" She bites her bouncer's arm; he releases, and she jumps into Jimmie's face. "Pádraig's been with me two hours." She slams her hand into her chest. "Me!" She glares, then pivots fast into my face. "Touch my brother and you never see me again." She spins to Jimmie—

I grab her, bring her face to face before she can hit him. "Calm the fuck down!"

Her glare hardens. Veins throb in her neck.

"The FBI told me about your husband and the mural; the name of this place is a street corner where the IRA murdered him. They think you're 'ultraviolent political-UVF' like your husband and father were. And based on whatever your brother told them, the FBI thinks—"

"Not Pádraig. Not me. Go see—" She stops midshout. Her eyes stay wide, lips peeled.

"What? Go see who?"

Maureen clamps her jaw, breathing loud through her teeth.

Behind her, Pádraig slouches into the doorway, two men in black bomber jackets and shaved heads support him. His head is ballooned and bandaged in the back. Both eyes are bloodshot surrounded in blue-black. I turn to Jimmie. He's staring hard at Pádraig's damage and doesn't charge. Pádraig sips from a bottle of Bushmills, winces as he swallows, and says: "Cullen Mahoney; ask him."

Maureen turns fast and glares at her brother.

So do I. "C'mon out, asshole. We're gonna ID you for murder one—probably two or three times. You can explain all the blood in Canaryville to Maureen, tell me who your crime partners are, then roll for us on the FBI. Maybe I can convince Loef to kill your partners instead of you."

Pádraig says, "The Catholics never quit the killin'. The murderin' papist bastards. Ask Cullen Mahoney, your sainted protector. He has the blood on him. Not us."

Maureen yells at Pádraig: "Enough!" then spins to me. "My brother has no hand in the FBI's witch hunt of you and the Starks. The FBI came after him, yes. And he should've told us. But he's no supergrass. And he'll not harm me—if it's my protection and not your own that has your mind."

A "supergrass" is a paramilitary who gives up his fellow partisans to the police; there are no lower forms of life in Northern Ireland.

I tell the bouncer, "Leave."

He doesn't. Maureen points him behind her and says, "Walk Pádraig inside," then squares up on me, two feet apart, teeth bared.

I check Jimmie again, ease off my tone, and tell her: "The FBI thinks—I don't know what they think. They like my priest on the clocktower as somehow connected to a UVF minister who's in your husband's Belfast mural. That alone puts you and your brother in the mix here—Dill and Cissy, the Bayside, clocktower, the shot on Loef, all of it."

Maureen blinks, tries to hold the glare, but her face shows conflicting emotions.

I add, "Howat was the minister's name—but you know that—and he was murdered here, in Chicago, and you know that, too."

Her lips tremble over the set jaw.

"So now that we *all* know that, how about you tell me what the FBI braced you with and why. Then, maybe I can protect you and figure out what the hell is going on. Why your brother just told me to see Cullen Mahoney for answers and you told Pádraig to shut up."

Maureen looks away, then at Jimmie, then at the concrete.

She swallows some of her anger, but not comfortably. "My husband, Sean, was a patriot. I'll not have his name dragged through the mud in my presence." She looks up at me. "Cullen Mahoney is your mentor. I know he's stood for you at least twice. I'll not have my brother insult him by bringin' him in just because Mahoney favors the church that murdered my husband."

My turn to stare. If this were a Homicide interrogation, it would be one of the moments where you either hink-up worse or start looking elsewhere for your perp. I know this woman; know her temper; know her protective instincts. And her brother does look hospital-bad. But Pádraig suggesting Cullen Mahoney is guilty of mass-murdering his own neighborhood and fellow Catholics is like saying I did it. And it's exactly the kind of shit an FBI rat like Pádraig would throw out to turn friend against friend.

I lie to calm Maureen further. "Okay . . . Who were you about to tell me to go see when Pádraig interrupted?"

"The FBI. They're buildin' fires under us all. For sins they'd rather see stay buried."

"Yeah, they are. What'd they offer you, threaten you with?"

She answers neither question. "They want you for the Starks." She looks at Jimmie, then shuts her eyes, wrestling with the experience. "Your old commander, Jon Burge, took the prison time, not their deal. They want public proof their case against CPD was righteous then, and now."

"What else?"

"That's the whole of it. You're the supergrass who can break the department. Agent Stone said that, and with my help, they think you'll do what Burge wouldn't."

"And what's the leverage on you?"

"They want me to pay for my husband's sins, for yours, for Ulster's." She points at the inscription she carved in her door the night we met. "In 1956 and 1968 my father and Ian Paisley founded political parties to protect the law-abiding from the Catholics and their bombers. The FBI and MI5 say my father's true face was 'a murderin' member' of the Ulster Volunteer Force—the UVF Loyalists who went eye for an eye with the IRA—not the lovin' man I knew."

"Come here." I wave Maureen to follow me.

She stays between Jimmie and the door to her brother.

I ask Jimmie, "We cool with Pádraig?" and point at the doorway.

Jimmie nods small.

"C'mon. *Please?*" I walk ten feet up the street. Maureen follows and stands so she can see her door. "I'm not saying Burge is guilty or innocent, but I worked for him for a whole month. Not one of those white-horse lawyers or innocent murderers ever used my name. And trust me, they used every name they could."

Maureen doesn't agree or disagree.

I tell her: "The priest murdered on the clocktower was Father James Chesney."

She steps back. "Claudy? The Monster?"

"Yeah. The only people who know that are my guys and Mahoney, and now you. Chesney's apartment had a book of matches from the Bayside, a yellow-pages page with Pádraig's company, a mimeograph of the Dublin bank standoff that Pádraig worked, and a flyer for the parade's VIP stand where Pádraig would be yesterday."

I don't mention Mahoney's number.

"Pádraig's a sniper. On the first Tuesday of every month I meet Loef Brummel and Renatta at a hot dog stand on Morgan. You know that. Possibly you mentioned that in passing to your brother. Two weeks ago, a sniper took a shot on Loef Brummel, blew the glass out of his hand. Your brother's a sniper. He's a crime-world player. He knows Cissy Noonan and probably Dill Reem."

Maureen gapes, blindsided.

"Pádraig is making a move on the crime business in the Riv. Maybe his move is the *why* behind this whole story, or maybe it's just Pádraig taking advantage of an unintended opportunity. Either way—"

"No." Maureen reddens again, then cuts to the door that protects her brother, then back. "No. Pádraig's not wantin' Loef Brummel's business. It's Brummel who's trying to move into the North Side."

I'm a Homicide guy, not organized crime. "Says who?"

"Ask your people, it's their job to know."

Maureen doesn't realize that she just explained Pádraig's motive to shoot Loef—Loef moving into Pádraig's territory.

"I'll ask. Either way, Pádraig has a private relationship with the FBI that he didn't mention to you until today. He's up to his eyeballs in this. If he rolls for CPD against the FBI, *maybe* he stays off death row, provided he comes clean before the city goes Belfast times a hundred."

"You'll not hurt him. Not and be my man."

"Even if he's trying to hurt me? Burn my city? Put me in prison for life?"

"I'll not allow that. And you know it."

"I do. But now you and I are in the box. I need to paint Canaryville 100 percent white-on-white and Pádraig can do that—"

"I'll see to Pádraig. Give me an hour." Maureen fights her anger and protection all the way down and steps closer. "I love you, Dennis. I want us and our horses more than you can know. But I have history to resolve—I told you, and you said okay. Don't forget that now when some of it may be upon us."

I try to read her, the history. "Your history can't kill Jimmie or his daughter. Or Chicago."

"No. And it can't kill you."

"Maureen, I don't have an hour. If your history's any part of Chesney or the Bayside, you have to tell me, now."

She shuts her eyes.

"Did you know Chesney in Ireland?"

Maureen shakes her head. "Alive here, all these years . . . Who but the Catholics would condone that?" She blinks at me. "I was little when Claudy . . . was barely a teenager when the Monster finally died." Her eyes close tight. "Father James Chesney was the modern proof. For all we children. The Catholics' church was the evil to fear in Northern Ireland, day and night."

"Maureen, look at me. Are you part of this? Any part?"

Her face is tortured. "We're seeing echoes, Dennis, the Troubles. We're all a part, will be forever. It killed my husband, consumed and killed my father, killed my friends." She dry swallows. "Your answer is no . . . I would not, could not, *ever* justify the Bayside bombing."

"What, then? 'Cause it's something."

"The Catholics have promised to kill my brother for his police work with the Garda—he lives with their death-promise every day. The Catholics murdered my husband, like the Blacks murdered your brother. Am *I* guilty—are *you*—because we'll not forget? For what falls on me from across an ocean?"

"And you think Mahoney's part of that?"

Maureen stiffens. "I'll not indict your mentor . . . for his religion or his history. Don't you indict me"—she points at Pádraig's shadow in her doorway—"for mine."

"You're trying to tell me something." I wait for a response she doesn't give. "Say 'David Rupert' to Pádraig. Ask your brother how he fits with Rupert and the FBI's program against the IRA—here and in Ireland."

"Pádraig had no part of Rupert. That story's been told."

"Pádraig's got a part in this. And *that* story's about to be told in more blood and fire. I'm *one* policeman. A whole bunch outrank me, and when they hear the whole of what I gotta report in the next few minutes, there won't be anywhere for Pádraig to hide." I tap my watch; point south. "Nothing anyone can do about it."

Maureen frowns hard, exhales, grips her fingers into my shirt, kisses me, and whispers, "Hold on to us, Dennis, and I'll see to my brother." She pivots for her door before I can grab her.

"Fast, Maureen. Gotta be now; thirty minutes tops. He can't run; there's nowhere left to go. For any of us."

She disappears behind her door. I walk to Jimmie and point us at his car. "Mahoney's office."

Jimmie shakes his head. "No. We grab Pádraig now, while we know we can. He's our white-on-white poster—"

"No. Maureen has to lean on him, convince him that he's trapped and we're his only out, or he'll just lawyer-up and tell us to fuck ourselves while Chicago burns."

Jimmie's face stays taut, worried with the same math that I am. He gets in the car, says, "There's something new here, Denny, and seriously wrong."

I call the Eighteenth District, tell them their citywide perp Pádraig Cane will be inside the Malvern in thirty minutes. "Come in soft. Has to be taken alive."

2:05 p.m.

Jimmie speeds south, dash light lit, siren on, looping traffic. "We're screwed if Maureen lets him run—"

"She'll make him explain, thirdhand through her, no lawyer. If Pádraig talks to us direct before he can cut a deal, he goes to prison. She's gotta convince him that lawyers or the FBI are not his out."

I call Buff to ask how far the Ayatollah show has gone off the rails at Twelve.

Jimmie makes the Outer Drive along the lakefront at North Avenue, then mashes the gas toward the skyline. His radio squawks multiple calls for assistance at all our flashpoints.

I tell Buff "Ten four" just as he cuts off, then turn to Jimmie and tell him what I just heard: "Ayatollah's still at Twelve. Mahoney's uniforms didn't shoot into the mob on the Loomis Street Bridge; mob just crossed into the Four Corners."

Jimmie winces. "Thirty blocks between that bridge and Twelve."

"Buff got the 'white male' perp sketch of the carjack/clocktower on the wire. Says it's pretty good."

Jimmie weaves into the Outer Drive's fast lane, light flashing, siren blaring.

I brace into the dash. "How's Gayle and Sandy?"

"Safe, far from me."

"What'd you tell Gayle?"

Jimmie shrugs, huge hands tight on the wheel. "She wasn't in a listening mood. Can't say I blame her. If I thought retiring would end the threat to them, I'd be downtown turning in my badge."

"We'll find the shooter. Whatever the fuck he's doing that made sense to him and somehow included you, he ain't done with the rest of it."

Jimmie looks at me; he's a father and husband defending his own.

I say, "You have my word. If Maureen is any part of this—she's not—but if she tries to save Pádraig, her and I will deal with it after he's faced the firing squad."

"And Mahoney?"

"He's a Chinaman, for chrissake; has to know everyone. Hell, he's your mentor, too. Now we jump his ass because Pádraig Cane—the Mick piece of shit—throws Mahoney's name around?"

"No. But Mahoney put Chesney in that apartment—"

"Mahoney put *Augustine* in the USA in 1980."

Jimmie shrugs. "Okay. How's Pádraig know Mahoney's name to throw around?"

"Pádraig knowing Mahoney's name is why we're going to Mahoney's office. Not because I think Mahoney blew the Bayside. Mahoney and I grew up together; he was Mike's training officer when Mike was killed. FBI would love to skin Mahoney if they could."

Jimmie looks at me. "Could Pádraig know about Mahoney bringing Chesney over?"

"Not from me."

"Odd."

I spit out the window and point Jimmie to speed up toward Deputy Superintendent Mahoney's office. "Mahoney's starting to show up almost as often as Loef Brummel. *Odd* isn't quite strong enough."

Chapter 20

2:25 p.m.

Before we're out of the car, Jimmie and I are mobbed in the headquarters parking lot. Reporter faces I haven't seen before jam microphones:

"Lieutenant Banahan! Did Black gangsters hang the priest on the clocktower?"

"Was the rooming-house arson a reprisal? By Canaryville?"

A young Black woman shoulders through the reporters, shouts, "Jon Burge! Jon Burge!" Her spit lands on my face and shirt.

"Sergeant Daniels! Will you march with Alderman Gibbons at Ogden Park?"

More shouts: "Antoine and Odetta Starks! Latoya Osborne!"

A white reporter jams a mic behind Jimmie and into my face. "Lieutenant, can CPD police people that you consider *monkeys*?"

A female reporter chest-bumps into Jimmie. "Two Ragen Colts were killed on the Loomis Street Bridge. Will CPD kill more whites to defend Black carjackers?"

"Rodney King! Rodney King!"

Headquarters uniforms pour out of the west doors and clear a path to Jimmie and me. The double doors inhale us; the shouts muffle to frantic faces at the glass.

On the fifth floor, outside Deputy Superintendent Mahoney's office, his secretary jumps up when she sees us. I've known Frances thirty years; she looks as grim as I've ever seen her.

I hug her gently, say, "We *will* handle this," then ask her for Buff's P-Stone sketch of the white man they admit they carjacked.

She nods, then ushers us immediately into her boss's office. There isn't time to sit, so we don't.

At his desk, Cullen Mahoney's white hair and reddish skin fit his corner office. The walls smell of the cigars he no longer smokes. His desk is large, old-school dark mahogany—not the new plastic—and worn at the back edge where he has sat facing the worst of the city's business for the last eighteen years. Next to the telephone that my mentor, Chinaman, and friend is using, is a silver-framed photo of his wife, Coleen—dead to cancer—sitting with their three kids, all grown now, two of them lawyers, the daughter a decorated police officer in the Twenty-First District who briefly worked for me in Six. She was good, and that surprised no one, she was Cullen Mahoney's daughter.

From this desk, her father runs the Bureau of Investigative Services (BIS)—the most powerful bureau in a very tough city. If it's bad, it ends up here. Two divisions—Organized Crime and the Detective Division. Cullen Mahoney has been my immediate superior or ultimate boss since I swore the oath.

Mahoney hangs up, glances out his window fifteen blocks west to the two helicopters hovering over the Riviera, then at the small TV on his desk.

He says, "Congratulations on securing the P-Stone's white-driver ID. Gael Gilmartin is drafting the media statement now. Pádraig Cane has been located but is not yet in custody." Mahoney turns the TV toward Jimmie and me.

The screen is a live aerial shot of Canaryville, five thousand whites massed from McInerney Park at Forty-Fifth and Emerald all the way across Halsted and onto the cracked pavement and rubble prairies of what used to be the Union Stock Yards. The camera focuses on two semitruck trailers parked side by side that form a makeshift stage.

On top of the trailers is a bright-white ten-foot Christian cross held by four men. To the cross's left is a white man with a bullhorn in each hand—Bishop Haswell Burke. Burke's face is red and tortured with the energy of his vocals: *"The ethnocentric, entitlement nation continues to murder the American dream, using entitlement-bought ballots, bombs, and babies!"*

Mahoney, Jimmie, and I react the same. Haswell Burke is one dangerous Florida cracker.

Our best answer is Loef Brummel on top of those trucks, telling Canaryville to stand down. Without Loef, we'll have to lure Burke out of the lights; grab and gag him before he can move his pitched battle to the three thousand Blacks in Ogden Park.

The shot changes to the two hundred banshees marching north from the Loomis Bridge toward the Twelfth District station, then cuts to a chaotic ground shot outside their destination.

Mahoney says, "Your ex is there now. Says she's filing formal charges against you, Sergeant Anderson, and the department." Mahoney taps a document stack in front of me.

Highlighted midpage on Renatta's stationary is: ". . . for the brutal beating of RayLen Starks and the threatened lynching of Cleaver Davis and William Poe. Banahan and Sergeant Anderson are partners in the 'Jon Burge culture of evil.'"

"Buff had nothing to do with anything. RayLen was in my face. I cocked my hand; he mistook it for a punch coming and banged his head into the wall. I didn't ask him shit before, or after. Be real tough to make that *torturing him for a confession*."

"And the noose?"

"Evidence."

"That was Special Agent Stone." Mahoney nods to his phone. "The FBI has agreed to investigate for a federal civil rights violation. With the blessing of the US Attorney. I'm afraid the time for your retirement has come."

"Don't do it, Cullen. St. Pat's is tomorrow." I point out his window at the helicopters. "Most of the South Side is gonna be a bonfire and my replacement will burn with it."

Mahoney starts to answer and I cut him off.

"Can't be Jimmie. Not after the shot on him. I'm already on fire and stopping this is the only way I dodge the grand jury."

Mahoney considers the reality as presented. "Anderson has to say you're innocent; that he witnessed the interrogation, and that Renatta McCray's charges are baseless."

Buff can't get dragged in on the record. Renatta's civil rights fantasy could last years after Buff's retirement, bankrupt him, put him in prison—unless he rolls and reads the FBI's script, which he won't.

"All or nothing, Dennis. I cannot keep you out front without corroboration that you are not"—Mahoney looks at his notes—"a brutal racist throwback to the Southern lynch-mob mentality of the 1960s."

"Has to be without Buff. I'll talk to Renatta."

Mahoney shakes his head. "All or nothing."

I look at Jimmie, then Mahoney.

Jimmie tells Mahoney, "The bullet trail burned my daughter's forehead." Jimmie touches the same burn on his cheek. "I, we, need Denny to find the shooter or there's a fair chance I could lose a second daughter." Jimmie points at Mahoney's family photograph. "That won't happen while I'm alive. Denny is the best horse for everyone. I need Denny; you need Denny."

Door knock. Mahoney waves Frances in; she has three copies of the sketch and hands us each one. Her hand is shaking. I reach for her shoulder. "You okay?"

She says, "No," to the floor and walks out.

I look to Mahoney. He says, "A grandson in the Bayside. The sketch, Dennis. *He's* who we can do something about."

The face sketch is quintessential American Caucasian. "Give Renatta a copy. Ask her how bad she wants to be responsible for any of the minutes after we leak that we have the bangers in custody who lynched a white *priest*—naked—*the bus driver at St. Gabriel's.*"

Mahoney smiles. "Dennis, we both know you lack the minerals for that. It's your city, always has been. No, it'll be Anderson or nothing."

"This ain't Buff's fight."

Frances walks in behind us, hands Mahoney three sheets of paper and leaves before we can say we're sorry for her grandson. Mahoney reads, then hands them to me.

It's Buff's statement, already signed into the record. Now I have to win or he'll face the same prison retirement as Jon Burge and the rest of us in 'Burge's culture of evil.'

Mahoney waves for me to return the pages. "I've stood with and for you, Dennis, have I not? Where we are now is no different. Anderson, Daniels, you, and I . . . Win, Dennis, and as always, all will be forgiven."

"Then we need help on things Ireland."

Mahoney waits.

"Thirty minutes ago Pádraig Cane spit your name at us like you have the answers, *here and in Ireland*, answers that Agent Stone inferred I already had, or could get, either from you or from Maureen."

Mahoney and I stare. When I don't continue, he curls his fingers for me to finish.

"I told you in the FBI parking lot that this was Ireland and the FBI, not Red Summer. The Irish mob in Canaryville and the FBI bought part of something *together* that's come back to bite them in the ass."

Mahoney says, "The mother and son on Fifty-Fifth were Black. Sergeant Daniels is Black, and someone—possibly the Bayside Bomber—just attempted to murder him."

I give Mahoney more Irish. "An FBI agent dropped this for me in their elevator." I hand Mahoney the unwadded document—Pádraig Cane's family history. "The FBI knows Maureen's dead husband is featured in a big three-man mural on Shankill Road in Belfast. One of the other guys is a UVF legend, Reverend Preston Howat. Why do we care? Howat was a Protestant minister, murdered right here in Chicago."

Mahoney's chin drops an inch.

"Yeah. That document says Pádraig and Maureen's *father* was a *founder* of the very same 'ultraviolent' Ulster Volunteer Force. And, no, I don't have proof yet, but either way, *Pádraig* Cane has pedigree, proximity, and ambition. He's in these murders big, with partners or an employer, or both."

Mahoney drums his fingers, looking at me sideways like I should've known, probably did know—

"I knew Maureen had been married. And her husband died in Ireland. But we don't talk politics *or* religion, heard all of that shit I wanted when you and I were kids."

Mahoney doesn't give me the look I'd give me.

He knows I helped her brother come over because she asked; worked it with his boss in the Garda—who I knew and who wanted me to help Pádraig, too. Hell, I know more about Pádraig's history than Maureen's. And for the record, the Garda didn't include any mention of the Ulster Volunteer Force–Loyalist father or brother-in-law stuff. Not a word.

Mahoney frowns. "Hard to imagine the *national* police force of Ireland omitting Pádraig's history, and his father's, accidentally."

"No shit. No way the omission is an *accident*. The Garda should've told me and they should've told the FBI—*they* had to vet Pádraig. And if the Garda didn't tell them, the FBI should've come up with the information on their own."

I lean in at the desk.

"Because the motherfuckers have all of it now. The Garda works with our FBI every day. Hell, Americans clear USA *entry* customs while they're still in Dublin; only place that happens. I think the FBI and the Garda partnered to grease Pádraig Cane into the USA from *go*—Just like they did David Rupert."

Mahoney processes the implication.

I tell him what he already knows, that Pádraig's on the opposite side of the IRA fight from Rupert—Pádraig's with the Protestant Loyalists who are the bomb throwers these days. "Trust me, Pádraig got jammed over in Ireland on something criminal. The Garda and FBI flipped him, sent him here to inform on the UVF and Protestant Loyalists."

Mahoney nods . . . "Assuming you're correct, the FBI would've focused Pádraig on a specific target—"

"Maybe Pádraig was informing on some UVF plot that the FBI kept secret from us. Maybe that was the FBI's *original* target. Then maybe, because of me being with Maureen, they see a chance to use Pádraig to nail CPD—we are the FBI's goddamn life mission. Me with Maureen would be the perfect conduit, Pádraig the perfect instrument—and if I roll, this whole place comes apart."

Mahoney nods again. Waits for me to continue.

"The FBI's fingerprints are everywhere under the umbrella I just built, right? What if the FBI set a 'legal,' sanctioned FBI operation in motion, but their centerpiece-snitch Pádraig went way off the rails? Pádraig's felonies would make every FBI crewcut who touched him radioactive. Just like Whitey Bulger did in Boston."

Jimmie leans way back.

Mahoney laughs small, but not at me. "Well, Dennis, if this is a 'Whitey Bulger,' then that would mean your sins are no longer top of the charts."

He's right. Whitey Bulger murdered at least ten people *while* he was an FBI Fed. If Pádraig Cane is Chicago's Whitey Bulger, then Agent Stone and his crew are facing *ownership* they can't afford, all of it dying to go live on MSNBC. And in Chicago, it will also include Bathhouse John. Who probably killed just as many as Bulger.

Agent Stone worked Rupert; might've been Rupert's control here. Either way, it's absolute fact that David Rupert took money from the FBI, almost a million dollars. Rupert was a serious career criminal *and* a Fed; they paid him—that makes Rupert a Fed.

I look at Jimmie, then back to Mahoney. "Carve this in stone: Rupert, or Bathhouse John, corrupted the Chicago FBI during that case—same as Whitey Bulger did the Boston FBI."

Mahoney's eyes narrow. "Could be. And could be that Pádraig Cane has corrupted the Chicago FBI yet again—"

I point at Mahoney. "'Rupert, Bathhouse John, Bulger, Pádraig Cane,' sounds like 'a pattern of prior conduct,' because it is. Or even better, a 'culture.' No fucking way Stone and his crewcuts can survive that kinda mud where they live."

Jimmie taps the perp sketch. "Pádraig Cane is the one hand that probably touches everything in the here-and-now." Jimmie looks at Mahoney. "I'll be the devil's advocate. Why does Pádraig Cane know you? Why does he throw your name at us? Why is the FBI using your name on Denny in the same paragraph with Jon Burge and Denny's brother?"

Mahoney smiles. "And you're the ASA now?"

"With all due respect, sir, I have to understand what Cane and the FBI are inferring and so does Denny. He just won't ask you."

Mahoney smiles wider. "It's not that Dennis won't ask, Sergeant Daniels, he already knows the answers."

"*I* don't." Jimmie holds up the perp sketch. "Pádraig and this killer are connected. He missed my daughter by a single breath. I'm past subtle."

Mahoney nods. "Understandable. I can't speak for Pádraig, but he likely knows my name and relationship with Dennis; his sister, Maureen, would have discussed it. And if Pádraig Cane knows nothing but that small amount about me, then he will know I am a tireless supporter of the Catholic church's mission here, Ireland, and Northern

Ireland. Should Cane be a criminal as you and Dennis believe, as well as a political as the FBI implies, then Cane will hate all things that I, or any other active Catholic, touches."

My phone goes off. Gael Gilmartin texting me: "911. What's your 20? 911."

"As for what the Federals may be implying, they've been interested in my demise since I declined to join their Jon Burge witch hunt, then survived the purge they and their friends threw at me. The fact that I twice snatched Dennis here from their grasp—and he was innocent both times I might add—further convinced them that I am not the devil's advocate, but his handmaiden."

Jimmie says, "When the FBI puts you together with Chesney for bringing him over, they'll light up the media like the Fourth of July." Jimmie chins at me. "Us, too," then stares at Mahoney. "You'll say the church set you up, right? Keep us all out of Marion."

"No, Sergeant Daniels. Until we see *conclusive* proof to the contrary, the man on the clocktower was *Father Augustine*." Mahoney leans in for punctuation. "Between *us*, we think the man is Chesney. Between us. Understood?"

I nod. Jimmie doesn't.

Jimmie says, "And if we run into the church as an active player? Like the FBI is."

"We all have sins, Sergeant Daniels, including the church. You yourself, it has been said, have been touched by the devil." Mahoney waits for Jimmie to push "church" further. When Jimmie doesn't, Mahoney points us out his door. "You know what has to be done. Unfortunately, there isn't sufficient buy-in to accomplish it. Do what you can, then we'll smoke the pipe with Alderman Gibbons."

"Crack pipe sounds pretty good right now."

"Peace pipe, Dennis. Peace."

3:00 p.m.

In the car, I call Leigha. "You remember David Rupert, the FBI snitch?"

"Think so. The IRA-Canaryville guy?"

"Yeah. Get his IRA court-case transcript and search it for all mentions of Bathhouse John, Preston Howat, Loef Brummel, and

Renny-Mac MacGrath, then locate our CPD file on Preston Howat's murder, and bring me everything you find wherever I am."

She says, "May take a decade or two on the Rupert transcript—those channels will require FBI cooperation."

I put her on hold, call R. Murph. Jimmie's phone rings. He answers his when R. Murph answers my call.

I explain to R. Murph the Rupert transcript we want, then ask if he can get it from his German.

"I can ask. Already kinda asking him a lot on proving Chesney for you."

"Has he? Is it Augustine in Chesney's grave?"

Detective Murphy tells me that Norbert the German has seen the DNA. Says it's Augustine in the grave. *Someone* will share a sample with us if we don't know how we got it. No chain of evidence, just him telling R. Murph that if we exhume the grave later, the DNA sample that someone will send us now will match Augustine, not Chesney.

"Good enough for me. Ask him for one more favor. A-sap. Get the Rupert-IRA transcript, electronically if you can, so you can search—"

"I know, Den. I'm the guy who spent a week teaching you to use your BlackBerry."

Jimmie stops us at Harold's Chicken for food we needed five hours ago. My phone bings with another 911 text from Lieutenant Gilmartin.

I text back that Jimmie and I are at Harold's.

3:20 p.m.

The alley by Harold's Chicken has no reporters, no FBI wires, and lousy sniper angles. Chi-Town Bega powers through a $6 quarter dark at our Crown Vic's rear tire. Her dog food's in my car and I'm in Jimmie's.

My BlackBerry is charging on the hood next to our eight-piece fish bucket. Jimmie and I watch the alley's mouth while we inhale food and coffee. The coffee tastes better when I add the cocktail sauce. I hit redial for Maureen. Her phone goes to voicemail. By now, Pádraig will have answered Maureen's questions. He should be in custody, but isn't. She should've called me. But hasn't.

Screech.

I drop Bega's fry and go for my gun. Jimmie's already aiming at the car blocking the alley. The driver's door pops. A truck horn blares past.

Gael Gilmartin doesn't jump back from the horn, rounds her fender glaring at me. Bega barks once and runs to Gael, successfully protecting me from untold vitriol and bodily harm. Jimmie holsters his .45.

Gael bends to pet Bega's face and neck with both hands. "Hello, pumpkin. How are you today? Miss me? Ready to come home?"

Bega yips and licks at Gael's face. Gael pulls a treat from her pocket. My dog inhales everything but Gael's fingers.

I say, "Nice to see you, Lieutenant."

Gael stays with my dog, but glares up at me, her white teeth biting together into the smile she's known for just before you see her ferocious temper. Gael strokes Bega's head and neck twice more, then stands, staring *Hospital visit* at me. "If Mahoney lacks the balls to replace you, I'll go direct to the superintendent, replace you both. Retire—right now—or I swear to God I'll file charges against you two myself."

I smile. "Never happen. That was me who got you the 'white' ID for the clocktower. They won't replace me and you won't file."

"I'm warning you, Denny, the world is about to fall on you. That grand jury's not a rumor." Gael jams her hand at the FBI car watching us from the other side of her car.

I answer, "Like I don't know that?"

"You can't assault a defenseless handcuffed suspect. You can't put their necks in a noose. Your ex-wife has dressed you for the FBI's Most Wanted list. That's prison forever, Denny. Exactly what Agent Stone's been looking for."

I wince small and shrug *No biggie.*

"Don't give me that goddamn look. You and that bitch are gonna break the department you say you love, hand us to the federal takeover as racist thugs in capital letters."

"I'm not a racist and you know it. Defend me, that's your job."

"Me? I can't defend you from your marital ramifications; we did that once, remember?"

Bega barks between us. Her head swivels and she barks again.

"Renatta lost her temper; you can calm her down, and if you can't—"

"I *tried*, asshole. She's not having it."

"—the Ayatollah can."

Gael balks. "Then you better call him. Because CPD can't afford Denny Banahan anymore. We're better off naked than having you out front with your ex-wife screaming 'Jon Burge' and 'culture of evil' every five minutes."

"What's the Ayatollah's number?"

Gael provides a different number than the one I have. I punch it in my phone, make sure my ID is live, and hit call. I show Gael that the phone is connected. Jimmie stops scribbling in his notebook. "Jesus, Denny, be careful. It'll be on tape, maybe on speaker, maybe on broadcast."

Gael glares.

Crowd noise answers first, then the Ayatollah. "I *am* surprised."

"Yeah, well, it's one of those days."

"I was unaware that days such as this were mandatory."

"Could you muzzle my ex-wife?"

"Excuse me?"

"Renatta went nuts, basically said I shot Malcolm X and Medgar Evers and should be burned at the stake. I'm kinda busy trying to stop people from killing you, Jimmie, white priests, and, basically, the entire South Side."

"And you'd like my help."

"Yes." I grimace a smile for Gael.

"And what are you offering?"

Gael punches my shoulder; glares *Behave* at me.

"At this point, pretty much whatever you want. Get Renatta to back it *way* down; you stay out of the Riviera, and—"

"Not as long as these boys are in custody. Their lives are at stake, gangsters they may be, but symbols they also are."

"How about I move 'em way north?"

"Release."

"They're carjackers for chrissake. Driving a murdered priest's car. Did you miss that?"

"They're young Black men *like* the young Black men hung on the lampposts during our original Red Summer."

"Sorry. Can't do it. Never fly."

"Release them. To me. My custody."

"To you? Are you nuts? You know who they are. RayLen's murdered and raped at least four people, probably twenty."

Crowd noise. "One of us understands the politics of the moment, the inherent combustion and what it will bring. Release these boys to me; do it now, and *possibly* we avert *today's* explosion . . . at least at Ogden Park."

I look at Gael, then Jimmie, surprise written all over his face same as mine, then say: "I gotta make a call—"

"Give Deputy Superintendent Mahoney my best wishes." Click.

Gael flips out her phone and covers mine with her other hand. "No. I'll call Superintendent Smith. He'll authorize it if I explain. Stand over there and wait."

"Is that an order, Lieutenant?"

"Fuck you." She backpedals five steps, already talking to her phone.

Jimmie doesn't vote, but he cocks his head, a salute to the Ayatollah that he deserves.

I lift my BlackBerry to answer a call—

Gael glares at me from her call with Smith and the possibility I may make an unsupervised telephone call. Gael walks up, pointing my phone down. "You're lucky Smith loves you. Anyone else and he'd cut you loose *yesterday.*"

"Yeah. God bless him; you and him put your boy RayLen, that murdering piece of shit, back on the street, instead of on a lamppost where he belongs."

Gael exhales through her teeth. "Always the hard way. If you had more dick, you might be able to think like an adult," she ramps volume, *"who has the city's life in his fucking hands."*

"Tell your dad I said, 'Hey.' Put plenty of water in his fire trucks."

She chins at the welt above my eye. "I heard."

"Hope you heard he swung first."

"Like I said, if you had more dick, you'd be dangerous."

"Thanks."

Gael points between my eyes. "Fuck up again today and you're gone—that's straight from the top." She fans at the city behind us. "Alone out there for whoever wants to clock your stupid ass." She turns to Jimmie. "Don't let him take you down with him. He isn't worth it. I found out the hard way."

Gael storms off and Bega follows. Jimmie watches Gael walk to her car with my dog. My phone rings again.

My secretary says, "Hope you're sitting down."

"All I do."

Jimmie points his phone at me. "Mahoney just got a twenty on Brummel."

We jump in the car. Jimmie fires the engine. Leigha tells my ear: "The file on Reverend Preston Howat's murder/slaughter was checked out today by the original investigating officer, Detective Timothy "Fruit" Baskett—"

"What?"

"And neither the file nor Detective Baskett are currently findable."

"Call you back."

I tell Jimmie what I just heard.

Jimmie fisheyes me big. We've discussed Howat with three people—Agent Stone, Maureen, and Mahoney. Two hours later the original investigating officer beats us to the file, then bails with it?

My teeth grind. "Where's Loef?"

"Inside the Riv. Mahoney's verifying the tip."

"*Finally.*" I slap Jimmie's shoulder.

"Why'd Fruit take the file, Den?"

I don't know. And it can't be good. We'll get our answers from Loef. I'm betting he can recite Rupert's court testimony from beginning to end. Loef knows who killed Dill; he knows they aren't Black, that this whole goddamn thing is Irish.

"We read that transcript; use it to leverage Loef, put him on top of those semis in an hour; the Ayatollah will see Loef backing the Riv down."

Jimmie states the obvious. "If Loef doesn't make us kill him."

Chapter 21

STEVEN

Food sounded like a good idea. The waitress stops short on her reapproach, her rodent eyes fixed on my rebuilt harelip and hands.

I bend my neck to snake up at her. She jolts and quickly finds somewhere else to be.

I'm a customer, you . . . *floozy*. I don't have to be happy *all* the time; it's not like a *law*.

I return to the $8 cheeseburger oozing through all my fingers. *What?* I should eat with my fingertips like a Japanese princess?

I plop the remaining ooze-burger onto the plate. Catsup, bun, and meat goo cover my fingers. I resist painting my face. Wonder if Ms. Prim Apron would like me to fist this goo up her big fat ass?

Because I could. If I wanted. No problem.

Her and Voodoo-Hoodoo Man.

Voodoo Man taunted me, waited until the last eensy-teensy bit of squeeze, then—*casually*—leaned out of my line of fire. Forced me to run like a cowered house pet.

Where's the bill? I must paint. Now; today. I'm not a house pet, tongue out, tail wagging, waiting for a client's modification. I don't do tricks. BITCH.

I'll do our agreed Target Three, but I'm not spending my downtime with mongoloid humanity, toilet paper on their shoes, clutching their new TV Guide.

I AM AN ARTIST!

Half the restaurant is looking at me.

Oops. Must've said that out loud.

***

I don't use spray cans. Or recreational drugs. Outside in the elements, I use latex, not oil-based, and large brushes, all purchased from the all-American hardware store across the street from Ooze Burger, even the paint. God bless me, economic powerhouse, multiplier effect.

Painting "semiprimitive" is similar to peasant cooking—use the materials of the proletariat, food or art. This piece is a homage to the "ethno-outsider" fast-art that's all the rage with the modern dilettante bourgeoisie, the latest generation with no taste and all the money.

The woman watching says, "My God, you're talented."

I don't smile or turn around. I know I'm talented; I am here to paint, not bask. Not a mural, though. Yes, yes, I'm working life-size, and on an alley brick wall, but this is portraiture—my gift to Chicago on the eve of their immolation.

The woman says, "But why here? You should be out where people can see your work, where they can appreciate it . . . like the Picasso and Chagall."

Picasso was given the grand spectacle of Daley Plaza; Marc Chagall got an outdoor basement and three homeless benches. Both men are default French communists. Picasso's from Spain, but Chagall's a Jew, so naturally he goes to the basement. The gatekeepers of the public art commission will deny it, but why play the game? Do your work where it fits, and let the grand marshals of the soulless society do what they will.

I paint; they exist.

The woman says, "What's your name? Where do you show?"

The flash behind me is wholly unacceptable.

The latex gloves, I'll take with me, and all my supplies. The woman, I'll leave behind.

To pose or not to pose? Sexual imagery or political commentary? Does the woman add or distract? I ask the painting; it will tell me. The painting says, "Fuck Maureen Cane. To death."

Well. That certainly would be a statement. And earlier today we were only a few feet from her warm-and-wet when we were sidetracked by government men and ingrate hoodoo-man Jimmie Daniels and his perfect little sitcom-ready family.

Hmmm. Maureen Cane in her sexy underwear and boots, panting and screaming and—

"And if she's not available, fuck her boyfriend to death."

I step back from the painting. "My, we're sexual today."

Not to be outdone, I add, "Why not both? One could watch and enjoy."

That's it! A ménage à trois. French! A tribute to Marc Chagall—Russian Jew marginalized by the Anglo-Saxon colonial oligarchy. Continuity! My phone rings with the apropos "client" ringtone—the Fiona Ness–Nina Hagen anthem: "Damaged and De-ranged."

"Yes?"

My client's voice is icy. "Did you—Are you responsible for any other activity since Father Chesney?"

My client is likely referring to the mattress fire, not hoodoo-man Detective Daniels. I refocus Corrissa the Crazed on our Target Two and her Freudian breach: "Do you mean since Father *Augustine*?"

Icy silence, then: "Yes. Are you responsible for any other activity?"

I lie. "No. I don't work for free."

More icy silence, then: "I have changed your third target. Tomorrow, a rifle shot in the Stock Yards. If you agree, I will deposit half the payment now."

Hmmm. Don't like this, but . . . "Deposit the payment. But we have no contract until I know the specifics."

"You know the name. I will confirm it tomorrow morning. I suggest you locate a perch, east-facing, that commands the demolished four square blocks from Morgan Street along Forty-Fifth Street to Halsted.

There will be five thousand, possibly twenty-five thousand people in the crowd by noon."

"My acceptance is conditional, on the perch and the name."

"Your activity outside the original contract has jeopardized its overall success. Your acceptance is already booked." Click.

Frown. The boundaries of the original contract were and are: settle a Protestant-Catholic score from the old country, wrap it all up in one cataclysmic urban fire that shields her and the UVF from blame in the USA.

Exhale. And like the art critic taking my unapproved photograph, using *tone* with me is not acceptable. I look at the painting, then Corrissa Howat's number on my phone. I think we know who we should fuck to death. After we're paid in full.

But we should practice.

Find the perch. Then bring a friend. Practice. Practice. Practice.

I smile at the crumpled art critic. Okay, if you like redheads, you can come, too.

Chapter 22

DENNY

4:00 p.m.

I pop the siren again and again. The Riv crowd ripples back as Jimmie weaves us toward Loef Brummel. Two blocks from him, I punch my BlackBerry, then draw my Smith.

Our radio squawks a series of updates—eight blocks from us, Bishop Haswell Burke has massed two thousand to cross Fifty-Fifth Street and attack the Blacks at Ogden Park. The governor has called out the National Guard. The mayor agreed.

Jimmie acknowledges the radio, "About damn time."

Maureen's new ringtone rings in my hand. I answer: "Are you alright? Where are you?"

Her voice is cold. "Pádraig's mates took him away before he and I could speak. He collapsed in their car. They brought him to St. Mary's. I'm here. Pádraig's in their ICU; his heart . . ."

I sit back in the seat, angry faces craning to see inside our car. "How bad?"

Maureen says, "Don't know."

I look at my bruised knuckles now wrapped around the Smith. "Sorry."

"The FBI's here. And detectives from Area Four with a tape recorder. And two investigators from your Bureau of Internal Affairs. They want Pádraig to say you beat him." Maureen chokes. "They want it to be his deathbed statement . . . that you beat him to death. For cooperating in a federal investigation."

My eyes squeeze shut, seeing a future my temper bought. "I hope it isn't."

"Goddamn you, Denny." She chokes again. "You didn't have to."

I want to answer but can't, not on the phone, not with who knows who or what listening. Maureen doesn't hang up and neither do I.

"Maureen. I, ah . . . I'll explain—"

Jimmie's hand raps my arm, his head shaking hard at me instead of watching the Riv's crammed humanity that surrounds us.

I tell Maureen, "I love you, okay? Keep me posted. I don't want Pádraig to die. I . . . we'll talk when you're ready."

Maureen stays silent . . . and clicks off without answering.

At the intersection, Jimmie wails the siren nonstop. I tell him the hospital news on our star witness–white-man perp. "Pádraig's in St. Mary's ICU; not good. Feds want a *deathbed* that I beat him to shut him up, keep him away from the FBI."

Jimmie stops hard, short of our destination. "Mahoney will know Pádraig's there. Mahoney knows Pádraig's our key. No better guy to play our cards." Jimmie hard-eyes me. "You and I have Loef in front of us. Our antidote for Red Summer." Jimmie draws his .45 and lays it on his lap. "Don't want to die because your mind's on Pádraig. Focus on Loef. After we have him, we deal with Pádraig's *deathbed* and wherever that goes."

My phone rings in my hand. I know the number; hit speaker.

The female detective who's been chasing all things Dill Reem tells me: "Dill's teeth finally came back. Dill's real name matches the passport: Darragh O'Brien, born Belfast, Northern Ireland, 1962. Serious record over there, mostly IRA with the one biggie—the 1998 Omagh bombing. Killed 29 and injured 220. Was an IRA attack on Protestants."

"And the CPD files on him as Dill are fakes."

"Ten four, Lieutenant. Somebody on our side faked his prints and—"

"So, we got *two* IRA-Catholic bombers hiding in the Riviera? In some kind of quasi witness protection program?"

"Would appear so, Lieutenant."

Jimmie adds, "And both Catholics die in Canaryville one day apart. One gutted at the train tracks, the other hung naked from the clocktower."

I say: "Whose protection program were they in?"

Jimmie says: "CPD's files are fakes. For sure, some of us are involved—"

Midblock, a white man steps up into the bed of a curb-parked pickup and faces us from above the crowd. Early forties, acne-scarred cheeks, flat nose, sunglasses, black leather car coat.

Jimmie raises his .45. "Know him?"

"Maybe. Fits Loef's crew." I tell my female detective on the phone, "Give the 'Dill is Darragh O'Brien' revelation to Mahoney; tell him 911. Make sure he knows about the fakes in our files, whatever proof you have; I'll call you back."

The Irishman in front of us waits till we inch closer, then jumps down into the street. He shoulders through the crowd toward our head-lights. Jimmie pops the siren to stop the guy. He stops. Jimmie lowers his window, then extends his .45 outside on top of the side mirror.

I step out of the car and stop at our headlights. The crowd pulls back from the confrontation. The man has a phone in his hand. I have my Smith in mine.

The Irishman says, "The message I have for ya is—"

"No. The message is, I'm putting you in the car, driving you to Ogden Park, letting you explain race politics to our Black brothers."

He eyes Jimmie's .45. "Won't help. But let's go, if we're goin'."

"I'm going inside." I point at the building Loef's in. "Get Loef on your phone; time to stop Red Summer."

The Irishman punches a number and hands me the phone.

Loef answers. "Chasin' me instead of the Bayside? Never fuckin' changes, does it? You and your fuckin' niggers."

"Ain't me who's hiding. Either you help me stop this goddamn war from incinerating your neighborhood and my city, or . . . or maybe that's what you want? Cover up all the Irish blood I keep wading through."

"We've waded through all the Irish blood we're gonna. It's your team's turn."

"You're one of this maniac's goddamn targets—"

"I been a target since I was twelve. It ain't Irish; it's ghetto. Always has been."

"Five hours ago when I had you handcuffed in the car, I told you Father Chesney could be the motive for all the blood, that it might go back to Bathhouse John and his crew—and that would be *you*. But you didn't stick around to help me out. Since then, our *white* sketch has taken a shot at Jimmie. In his *house*, missed killing Jimmie's daughter by a breath. That's not how the game's played. So now the gloves are off for everybody and that includes you and this Mick standing in front of me."

The Irishman doesn't move, but he's paying attention.

Loef remains silent on the phone. I continue.

"Since Dill and Cissy yesterday, we put together an interesting story, goes back a long way. You wanna tell me you didn't know your top guy was the Omagh bomber, Darragh O'Brien?"

Silence.

"Didn't think so. No Black in this story, all orange versus green, Protestant versus Catholic, and you've been in, or near it, since it started on this side of the Atlantic."

Silence.

"The story is Catholic IRA versus Protestant UVF—killing each other, tit for tat, there and here." I lie: "I'll have the Howat file in ten minutes, but I already know Reverend Howat was UVF, probably wearing orange knickers when Bathhouse John had you and Darragh O'Brien grab Howat off the street in 1999 right here in Chicago. Don't figure you for slaughtering him, that would've been Bathhouse John and his psycho son."

Silence.

"2003, Bathhouse John and his son get slaughtered just like Howat. Sound like tit for tat to you? Any Black in there I missed?"

Siren. Loef's guy steps back, looking both ways.

"Answer me, goddammit."

Loef says nothing.

"Write this down, motherfucker. You're going into the Riv with me, standing on those goddamn trailers, and telling our friends and neighbors to stand down. After they do, you and me gonna nail down this shooter who's killing your world."

"You fuckin' know that, huh?"

"I know you and me are gonna make the Bayside and clocktower *white*. You and me are gonna stop the napalm before the South Side is ashes."

Silence, then: "Tell ya what I'm gonna do, Denny. I'm gonna hang Cissy's shooters in the rubble of the Bayside. Her shooters are Black, all of 'em, and I know who they are. And I'm prayin' the Ayatollah and your project bangers wanna fight about it after they see the lynchings on TV. And you're right, the South Side—*the fuckin' ghetto*—is gonna be ashes. All your bangers are leaving town, one fuckin' way or the other."

"It's *white*, Loef; *Irish*."

"No. The five-decade war between the IRA and the UVF has nothing to do with this. Let that shit lie, Den. That's *me* talking to you, two kids from the same block. The guy who looked after Mike's—"

"Don't throw my brother in here. That rooftop was a long time ago. You and me were insane-angry, young, and stupid. And we aren't now. Renatta's got her name on part of that rooftop, too, but it didn't stop her from handing me to the Feds as the next James Earl Ray."

"Renatta we can deal with; same for her aggrieved fuckin' client—I been sayin' that for a while. I done payin' their ma reparations for two murderin' pieces-of-shit who deserved what they got."

"And the answer on Renatta's shortened future is still *never gonna happen*. What you and me have to do is stamp *white* on the Bayside, the clocktower, and the train tracks. Today. Now. And loud."

"It's Black. Open your eyes, man. You can't survive any other answer."

"Excuse me?"

"You're either gonna be deaf and dumb, retired out at your racetrack, or at Mount Carmel next to Mike. Ain't no other choices, and nothing you or I can do about it. Leave the cat in the fuckin' bag."

"Motherfucker, this is *my* city. You want to run, be my guest, *after* you get up on those trailers and tell these Irish banshees to stand the fuck down. I'm in too deep to run. Everybody I fucking *know* is in too deep for me to run."

The bells at St. Gabriel's begin to peal.

Loef and I both listen till they stop.

Loef says, "Hear them bells, hero? Come on in to me, then. *Alone*; I'll tell ya, me to you, face to face, what you can't survive hearing. Then I'll *show* you the ghetto-fuckin'-bangers you wanna die for. Might even keep one alive; let you decide, him or you."

"You *have* Cissy's shooters?"

"And remember them bells you just heard when you're cryin' your fuckin' eyes out. You'll be lookin' down the barrel like your brother, Mike, did."

"Goddammit, Loef. Don't hang them. I'll get you past everything so far; just help shut Red Summer down. Don't do anything; wait till I get inside—"

Loef disconnects. Jimmie's .45 jumps up off our Crown Vic's outside mirror. The Irishman in front of me freezes; his hand is halfway into his leather coat. Jimmie's 230-grain bullet will blow the man's hand off his arm and most of his stomach into the street.

I lower the Irishman's phone.

He smiles behind the sunglasses and acne scars, eases two fingers the rest of the way into his coat, extracts a photo, extends it toward me, says, "Cissy. For your wallet."

Behind Loef's building, shapes snake past the openings—black body armor. SWAT is closing from both sides. They shouldn't be closing. Two SWAT snipers appear on the adjacent rooftops. I spin, look up behind me. Two more SWAT snipers. The Irishman's phone rings in my hand—

Loef says, "Figured you for smarter."

"Not my doing. Keep your head down; I'm comin' in." I grab the Irishman, say, "C'mon," and shove him in front of me.

A bullhorn booms: "Stand down."

The rooftop snipers all fire flash-bang grenades. Four windows shatter on Loef's second floor. The grenades explode loud and blinding. I twist away. SWAT charges the doors, front and back. Gunfire explodes inside. Loef jumps out a first-floor window, a pistol in each hand.

"Don't, goddammit!"

Loef fires behind him at a shape following out his window. I charge to tackle him. Two SWAT shooters rip Loef with their MP5s. He blows backward, spins off his feet, and pancakes the grass.

I reach him, drop to my knees, flip him over, rip at his bloody jacket and shirt—Loef's eyes are white. "Get EMTs!"

A SWAT guy knocks me off my knees, jams his MP5 in my face.

"Homicide!" Jimmie runs up with his badge out. "Homicide!" He rips Loef's jacket farther back. No blood's pumping from five holes.

"He was our only chance!" I jump up to punch the SWAT guy. "Mahoney told you we had to take him alive!"

Jimmie bear-hugs me.

The SWAT commander steps between me and his guy. "He was shooting at us, Den. His decision, not ours."

"Lemme go, goddammit."

Jimmie does. I step back to Loef. "He could've stopped Red Summer. And he . . . would've." I don't see the gangster, I see us as kids; me, Loef, Mike, and Cullen Mahoney, the white T-shirts, teacup ears, my first Pepsi bottle. My hand wipes at my eye and mouth.

Jimmie says, "Tough . . . fucking . . . town, this one."

I blink back to the race war bearing down on *the tough fucking town*, and ask: "Now what? No local heroes left to stand on the semis."

Jimmie says, "Pádraig Cane knows the perps' names. We grab 'em, stand 'em on top of the Canaryville semis, up there with Haswell Burke's cross."

Jimmie and I bolt for the car. I pull my cell and call ICU—

My detective there says Pádraig is still alive, surrounded by Feds who will never let me near him. My detective doesn't see Maureen there, but she has to be.

I hang up, call Maureen. She doesn't answer.

A 911 rings through my call. I hang up, answer Area Four Homicide, and say: "Tell me we have Fruit and the Howat file."

"We got a dead woman across from the Malvern. Under a mural. It ain't good, Denny."

***

Jimmie's screaming through traffic, dash light flashing, siren wailing. Leigha rings through my death grip on the BlackBerry. I answer; she says, "You've spoken to Area Four? About the mural?"

"We're en route. Pull the file on Bathhouse John's murder; him and his son. Bring it to us."

Leigha says, "They told you who's in the mural—"

"Yeah."

"Have you spoken to her? Is she—"

"No. No one can find her at the hospital."

"Oh my God . . ."

Chapter 23

STEVEN

Leaving old friends behind is painful. Fans and patrons of the arts, even harder, but there are situations that call for self-deprivation. I did bring the woman's camera, though. And a hand; it was the best I could do. She and I will hold hands with the affection of artist and patron, our fingers laced, while I work with my new girl, Maureen Cane.

Maureen Cane stares at me wide-eyed.

Pleasure? Wouldn't that be swell. No, I think it's fear, terror. Maureen knows me. Maureen intended to talk about me. Maureen has been a bad girl.

I walk past her with my nose elevated, hand in hand with my most recent patron, and peek out the window. We're much too far from tomorrow's target area to be effective, but then, I'm not at all sure Chicago will last till tomorrow.

I pivot fast. "And you, Maureen? Will your *man* save Chicago, *hog butcher to the world,* from its race toward a final fill-up at the Sinclair station?"

Wide eyes, but no verbal. Clear plastic packing tape compresses the luscious red lips and bunches her hair.

"Petrol station? Upton Sinclair?" I wave out the window at the remnants of Upton's playground, currently packed with two-legged feed animals. "*The Jungle*? Hog butcher to the world? City on fire?"

Nope.

I walk back to her and smooth at her hair. Her head jerks away.

"Maybe you'd just like to fuck, then? I'd like that. From behind? Oh, yeah. Wait, you like horses; maybe you were born to ride?"

I fetch my recorder and bring it to her so we don't miss any of the action. "I wonder, maybe you'd rather talk? You know, foreplay. We could talk about Corrissa Howat, then fuck later. That's a bit of a risk—maybe I'll find my client more alluring. Sex at the office is de-lish. What do you think?"

Maureen looks too terrified to talk or fuck.

I always have to do all the work. It's just not fair.

Chapter 24

DENNY

Jimmie and I step into the blind alley across from the Malvern, fast-walk fifty feet, then duck under the yellow tape.

A decapitated woman is posed on her knees beneath a graffiti-style mural. Her right arm cradles her head in its crook. The other arm is pressed into the wall as if the missing hand has reached inside the painted bricks. The clothed, headless body is drenched in blue paint to match the background behind it.

The mural's background is the outline of the Chicago skyline on fire. Charred infants in white diapers fill the sky as ashes. The entire foreground is a rutting satyr with the outsized face leering toward us. The satyr's face is a distorted version of our sketch from the hit-and-run and the Augustine/Chesney carjack.

The satyr is mounting a female deer. The doe has a long spindle neck with two large faces, both drawn quickly, but distinctive. One face is in shades of orange—I don't recognize her. The other face, done in shades of scarlet red, is an unmistakable likeness of Maureen.

My forearm trembles against my Smith. "Why paint Maureen?" I stumble backward into Leigha, my secretary, arriving and R. Murph arriving right behind her. Both stare at the death scene, then the mural behind it.

R. Murph looks at me. "But we know where Maureen is, right?"

Jimmie grabs my shoulder. Lowering his phone, he tells me: "FBI says they don't have her. A nurse says Maureen answered a call on her cell inside ICU. The nurse made her step out into the lobby. Five witnesses saw her turn the corner. The parking lot attendant *might* have seen her enter a cab." Frown. "Doubt it. Maureen Cane's not a woman you *think* you saw."

Jimmie keeps ahold of my shoulder.

Leigha chokes, shies, then feebles me the 2003 Bathhouse John death-scene file from Florida. I take the file, hiding the tremble that has moved down into my hand, then wave for R. Murph to bring me the Rupert-IRA court transcript he's holding.

R. Murph is fixated on the mural, eyes cutting from left to right across the painted bricks.

Jimmie punches his arm.

R. Murph says, "*The Destruction of Eden.*"

Jimmie squints at him.

"A painting in the main hall downtown at the Art Institute; just change the faces and skyline."

I squat in front of the headless woman. The decapitation cut is fairly clean, definitely not angry, not hacked like Darragh O'Brien. Maureen could be alive. This murderer might want something rational. It could happen that way. It could.

"Denny?"

It could. I can find this guy. I can; will. I'll use the FBI if I have to. My eyes squeeze shut. *I'm coming, Maureen. Believe it. I promise. Stay alive.*

"Denny?" R. Murph touches my shoulder. "We don't know he has her."

I stand fast, pivoting into R. Murph. He jolts backward, pushes me the IRA-Rupert transcript. Parts of the transcript are highlighted FBI notes:

> Reverend Howat had a family—wife and one daugh-
> ter. Howat was murdered in Chicago, 1999. Wife was

murdered in a mental hospital, also 1999, in Carstairs, Scotland. Bathhouse John killed them both. The reverend first, then the wife.

The tit for tat hits me like a train. R. Murph nods. I keep reading.

Also 1999: Previous to Howat's murder, Renny-Mac, Bathhouse John's daughter, was killed sharing a bed with the actual target, IRA bomber Redmond Lynch. Renny-Mac was collateral damage.

Bathhouse John "proved" it was Reverend Howat who ID'd Lynch, then he slaughtered Howat in Chicago, then killed his wife in Scotland.

I ask R. Murph, "What happened to the daughter?"

"Corrissa Howat was in the Carstairs institution as well. Lost a hand in the attack defending herself and her mother but didn't die." R. Murph glances at our dead woman under the mural with no hand. "Carstairs wouldn't talk to me, but when you run 'Corrissa Howat' through the Interpol database there's a bunch of hits. She's major-political, Ulster Volunteer Force pedigree like her father, so *orange* she glows; prison twice—Northern Ireland and Cuba—"

"When? What years?"

R. Murph points at a handwritten page on top of the transcript. "Did seven years in Cuba, on piracy and weapons charges, 2003 to 2010, but I haven't confirmed—"

"Pull her up on Interpol."

"Den, they don't like cell phone access—"

"Now, goddammit."

Jimmie nods at R. Murph's notes. "Cuba timing would be perfect. But . . ."

I jam the transcript at the mural. "The face next to Maureen's is *orange*, Jimmie. A violent Protestant activist who graduates from a mental institution. It's her. Corrissa Howat is Pádraig's crime partner."

R. Murph hands me his phone. I look at five photographs, two of which could easily be the face in the mural, then read Interpol's pedigree for Corrissa:

Well educated. Political activist; revolutionary. Court
ordered to psychiatric hospital. Daughter of . . .
Traveled with father throughout Ulster and Scotland.
Joined the UVF at university; rises to senior position
in the most violent faction of the UVF. Imprisoned
twice and committed once to the hospital at Carstairs
in Scotland.

I slide down the Interpol report by date:

1999. Father murdered in Chicago, USA.

1999. Mother murdered in the State Hospital at
Carstairs; Corrissa cut and stabbed, loses right hand
fighting off the attackers.

2000. Released from the Carstairs hospital due to
groundswell popularity. Makes three-year bid for control of the UVF, advocating against the 1998 peace
accords signed while she was incarcerated.

2003. December. Arrested on boat piracy and weapons
charges in the Florida Straits. Incarcerated seven years
in prison Manto Negro, Havana, Cuba.

I stop, stare at Jimmie. "See it? The arrest date—2003—the
location?"

Jimmie nods. "Bathhouse John and his son were murdered on a
houseboat in the Florida Keys in 2003. Son was *slaughtered.* Same
month Corrissa is popped ninety miles away in Cuba for piracy and
weapons. Gotta be her. She hunted 'em down, killed 'em, then rolled
to Cuba."

2010. Thirty percent of her body burned saving female
inmates in a prison fire. Survives in a Cuban burn
hospital.

2011. Deported to Northern Ireland; hero's welcome in Ulster, remounts her campaign for control of UVF, stating that their leaders have betrayed the cause, citing the current leaderships' 'peace stance' and the crumbling economic conditions of Ulster. Demands a return to the armed attacks on Catholic Nationalists and moderate Loyalists.

I toss R. Murph his phone and use mine to order a citywide, statewide, a fucking *worldwide*: "Corrissa Howat, white female, born 1965, Belfast." I add all the details I have, and finish with: "Interpol photos to follow. Artist photo to follow. Wanted for homicide and kidnapping. Armed and dangerous, use extreme caution."

Dispatch answers, "Ten four."

I tell R. Murph, "Call INS; run her passport. Tell them it's urgent; a hostage situation." I point Jimmie back to the mural—the orange face, the missing right hand into the wall.

"Corrissa's our story to stop Red Summer—white-on-white—just out of prison, here to mount an extension of her Irish war. She slaughtered Darragh O'Brien—an IRA bomber—then hung an IRA priest. We find her, we find Maureen. How do we find Corrissa?"

Jimmie works through it out loud, then: "Corrissa Howat doesn't have Maureen."

"Wrong! Corrissa's perfect—"

"Corrissa *bought* the Bayside. She didn't *do* it—or the hit-and-run after, or the clocktower or the mother and son on Fifty-Fifth. Or the shot on me. That would be a man, a sniper-bomber, a white male professional, controlled . . . with some issues. *He* did this painting. *He's* got Maureen."

R. Murph says, "Jimmie's right. If someone grabbed Maureen, it's this guy. He's a sniper—Pádraig's a sniper. They know each other . . . from sniper-assassin world or the military, Iraq-Afghanistan. Pádraig's the bridge between Corrissa and her sniper-bomber."

I stand Leigha square facing the mural. "Use your phone; take a good photo of Corrissa's face, the orange face, hunt the internet for any photo more recent than what Interpol has, then get the best photo of her to every car in the city."

"Den, everyone's working the riots and the crime scenes—"

I inhale to yell at her . . . and stop. She's so pale she might faint.

I cut to the mural. "Either Pádraig, or somebody who knows Pádraig, ID'd Chesney and Darragh O'Brien in Chicago, called Corrissa, and she came over here to kill both of 'em. Pádraig's her conduit to the shooter. Pádraig knows who has Maureen, this fucking . . . painter."

Jimmie repeats, "Painter," then taps R. Murph. "While you have Interpol, run 'sniper, bomber, painter,' emphasis on Ireland, Iraq, and Afghanistan."

I push Jimmie toward the car. "Go to St. Mary's. Get a doctor to clear Pádraig's room, then make him talk. No, I don't know how. Tell that motherfucker his sniper-world buddy has Maureen; Pádraig gives us the name and location, or I kill him in his bed."

Jimmie and R. Murph roll hot.

Leigha finishes her call, starts to tell me something—

I interrupt her: "Call Stone at the FBI. Tell him I'm on my way to his office. I want whatever they have on Corrissa Howat, her father, and a sniper-bomber who paints."

6:00 p.m.

In the FBI lobby I surrender my weapon. Police or not, it's the only way to pass through their security. The elevator opens at the sixth floor. Agent Stone faces me. He enters, pushes the "B" button and says, "Corrissa Howat, her father, and David Rupert. Can I assume you intend to publicly implicate the Bureau as somehow complicit in the current—"

"And your bitch, Pádraig Cane."

Stone doesn't react. The elevator begins its drop.

"Corrissa Howat's crew has Maureen." I jam my finger in his face. "You motherfuckers empowered that bitch, made Rupert a millionaire to attack the IRA, then put Pádraig Cane on the same orange-versus-green program."

I lower my finger and clench my fists white so I don't use them.

"Chicago's about to burn because you DC motherfuckers consider us pieces on a board game. Imagine Maureen is *your* wife. How's that feel? All those bodies at the Bayside, *your* goddamn family; the bodies on both sides of Fifty-Fifth Street, *your* friends and neighbors."

Special Agent Stone stares, relaxed, unmoved.

"Motherfucker, if they hadn't taken my gun it'd be in your mouth. Your shrinks have done a profile on the Bayside Bomber. And now you know he paints murals and can snipe. Give us his profile, track Corrissa into the US, and I'll forget I want to kill you. And I'll forget I've read the sealed Rupert testimony that proves you DC assholes knew the risks to the rest of us civilians and you took them anyway."

Stone monotones, "Assuming you know something that could be construed as damaging to the Bureau, how did you—"

I slam the "Stop" button. The alarm rings and I go nose to nose. "I'm not gonna live a long time without Maureen. Neither is anyone else who doesn't help me." I lean the last inch until our noses touch. "Decide—part of my problem, or part of my solution."

"Other than threatening a federal officer, what are you offering?"

I ease back. Feds don't die for the cause. "You want me to roll. Tell me on who?"

Stone doesn't smile or think about his answer. "Deputy Superintendent Cullen Mahoney."

Chapter 25

STEVEN

6:00 p.m.

"Corrissa Howat has become a problem." I smile at my new girl, Maureen, mouth taped and bound to her chair. "Had Corrissa been less dysfunctional, I doubt you'd be . . . here. I'd like to discuss her future, *and yours*, if you'd be amenable." I smile my good smile again, the straight razor behind my back.

My new girl, Maureen, nods that a chat is in the cards. I intend to stroke the fruit and veg for her, but we'll cover the important ground first, before we all go off to summer camp. I keep the razor hidden and stroke her head gently with my other hand. "Okay, MC, I'll remove the tape so we can talk. But if you scream, I'll be, like, Jack the Ripper unhappy. Do we understand?"

She nods, eyes not quite so wide, plotting no doubt. Useless, but it does keep their blood pressure up. I've had a few go catatonic. Not easy to enjoy that, no matter what their equipment.

I brandish the straight razor for that wake-up jolt, then cut the tape at the back of her head instead of her throat. Her red hair fluffs, but extricating the mane from the tape will be a mission, and I'm not in the mood for a mission. Plus, I prefer my girls with the boyish cut.

Slice. Slice. Slice.

Re-coiffed, lips untaped, it's talk-show time. I sit directly across from her and can still smell a bit of the ether mixed with her otherwise intoxicating perfume of sweat and fear.

"Before we start, I do appreciate your brother's recommendation of me. I'm sure your stumbling upon Father James 'the Monster' Chesney *alive*, sharing a street corner in sunny Chicago with Mr. Brummel and the Omagh bomber, Darragh O'Brien, dampened the old panties." I grin for agreement, all of us holding hands on our yellow brick road—

Maureen stays home, wary.

Hmmm . . . I thought we just agreed.

I'll toss in a few more accolades. "Instead of you shouting '*Der Weisse Engel! Der Weisse Engel!*' and fainting like the old Auschwitz survivor did in *Marathon Man* . . ."

I give Maureen the double thumbs-up.

"You called your dead hubby's UVF compatriots in Belfast." I bob my head and pump my thumbs. "Bet that was a big day in orange world."

Maureen declines to acknowledge her participation or share the joy in orange world. She stares—possibly at my surgically repaired lip and palate.

Really? Heat tightens my face. I switch the straight razor to the other hand.

"But things became messy, *didn't they*, Maureen? Pristine-perfect Maureen has a change of heart after poor Cissy Noonan at the railroad tracks and the Bayside goo . . ." My face prunes at Maureen's societal discomfort. I add baby-talk voice to cover the anger I don't seem to be managing as well as I'd like. "Prissy-perfect Maureen wishes to quit."

The muscles in Maureen's shoulders contract ever so tiny, then relax. Her eyes focus on the straight razor, not me and my show of injured temper.

I lean closer. "Sorry. Where were we? The guilty, yes, that was it. Mr. O'Brien was not my doing; his soupy mess was courtesy of your partisan friend Corrissa. That girl really does not know when to stop. And the pretty handmaiden Cissy?" I make a pistol finger between Maureen's ample breasts. "Cissy died at your brother Pádraig's hand—a greedy, troubled young man, your little brother. Politics are not his driver; he wants to be the new boss of Irish crime in Chicago."

Maureen's eyes widen at her brother's indictment. Poor thing didn't know. A good sign for the proposition to come.

"As I understand it—and please correct me if I'm in error—you reported Father Chesney and Darragh O'Brien to the faithful back home, hoping for a public trial of some sort. My client, the grandiose-barbarian-patriot Corrissa, visited Chicago and verified the two bombers' identities, then asked you for an 'extradition' contractor. Yes? You don't know such people, so you asked your loving, security-specialist brother for a recommendation. Unfortunately, Corrissa was a tad deceitful with you—she had no intention of *kidnapping* anyone for a trial. So, after the introduction you provide, Corrissa tells Pádraig privately that she wants a contractor for wet work. And voilà, Pádraig produces *moi*."

The muscles in Maureen's shoulders continue their ever-so-tiny contract and relax—ahh, she's working her hands taped behind her. Yes, it's an insult that she'd even try, suggesting I know that little about my craft. But, again, I'll not be sucked into an argument that under-mines my larger goal or ruins our potential satin-sheets holiday. Nor will I be painted as a villain who should not be affectionately serviced.

"Also, for the record, Corrissa's become a bit of a problem herself. I'll not bore you with the details, but Corrissa the Crazed has to go. I really can't afford her negativity on the CV."

Maureen stops working her hands. She senses a bit of hope.

"So, Maureen, here's the proposition: My client trusts you. You lure her to me. I rewrite my CV to match the outcomes achieved, we all go home happy—well, you and I go home happy. Corrissa, not so much."

Maureen partially slurs something that might sound like an ether-clouded "And you'll harm no others?"

I bask in our first words together; that moment on a first date when you know it's going well. "Did you say, 'When and where for Corrissa?' Right this minute, and anywhere you can convince her to meet."

Maureen's chin lowers. She breathes through her mouth. "Then you'll harm no others?"

"I'll let you go. And I won't kill your brother or your man, Dennis."

Maureen reads me for the lies that deep down she knows are there. A smart girl, tough no doubt, but in this type of situation the brain has to believe in something or the terror melts the synapses. Often, this is the moment when some collapse and begin to mess themselves.

But not our Maureen of Belfast. She has her men to protect; her betrayal by Corrissa the Crazed to avenge; this will keep my Maureen vibrant, searching for the sword, and all her erectile tissues functional.

I straighten in my chair, a man in full. "Other than my lip, would you say I'm attractive?"

Chapter 26

DENNY

Agent Stone gave me the Corrissa Howat pages. I'm in my car in the FBI lot, searching pages that can/will/might locate Corrissa or her white shooter.

"Maureen's alive—if I am, she is."

"Maureen's alive."

Jimmie calls from Pádraig's ICU. I hit speaker; keep flipping pages.

Jimmie says, "No doc will clear the room. Pádraig's semiconscious, in and out. Won't talk to me or R. Murph. His lawyer says Pádraig knows nothing that will save his sister or stop Red Summer."

I grab the phone. "You told Pádraig? No way he survives if Maureen doesn't. You told him."

"I told his ear, Den." Jimmie coughs. "I told him we know he's the conduit in a three-way involving Corrissa Howat and the assassin who did the Bayside and clocktower. I told Pádraig we know he was making a private move on Brummel, that the FBI will cut him loose—deny they've ever heard his name—ten seconds after we go public. I told him we're all he and Maureen have if either intends to see Monday."

"And he won't talk?"

"His heart's beating sideways. The docs allowed me three minutes with him, and only because I knew one of them and gave the FBI agent my .45. I'll leave R. Murph here; if Pádraig lives long enough to help—"

"He's got the goddamn answers—"

"Denny. He's dying. There's four suits here from IAD and the FBI who want to make you his killer. Murder One. Okay? Are you listening?"

"He's got the goddamn answers, Jimmie. He *knows* who has Maureen; knows the goddamn phone number—"

"His mouth doesn't work, Denny. Listen to me."

I fall back into the seat, drop the phone on the papers, and take a breath.

Jimmie eases off his tone. "INS has Corrissa Howat into the US twice this year. Both times she cleared customs in Chicago, not Dublin. Last time was eleven days ago. Hasn't left."

I slam the car in gear. "What address did she give?"

"Hyatt. On the river."

"On my way."

"Don't. Her room hasn't been slept in since Friday night. No luggage or personal items; but she hasn't checked out."

"Somebody's seen her there, spoken to her. Have 'em run the cameras. We want every picture of her they have; every time stamp on her room lock. Every—"

"We're on it, Den; we know what to do. Did Stone give you anything?"

"Looking at FBI pages now. Nothing in them on Corrissa's pro bomber-shooter-painter. We won't get the FBI's profile of him until I sign up to roll."

Pause. "On who?"

"Mahoney. They want Mahoney and his 'network.' He's their lever to take down CPD."

"A *trade*? They know it's Maureen on the other end?"

"She's the lever on me. They drop my grand jury and give me federal immunity, I give them CPD on a plate. Stone helps us save Maureen and whatever part of the city that isn't burning."

"But you won't roll. And Stone knows you won't. Not for real; he's smarter than that. He's playing you. If Stone had something that would help Maureen, you would've already seen it."

"So, we'll play his ass back. Corrissa Howat, too."

"How?"

"Go big, get everybody's attention, slow 'em down. I'll go on camera, dump our story like we have hard proof; make it all white-on-white and the FBI responsible. Name everybody—Corrissa, Pádraig, all of 'em."

"And the pro who has Maureen?"

"I'll tell him direct—me to him on camera."

Jimmie says, "Won't stop the Blacks in Ogden Park. Mayor McQuinn had to damn near fight his way out. Four of his security detail are being treated in Mercy's ER."

"Fuck. Mahoney was right. This is a war that wants to happen."

Silence, then Jimmie says: "Maybe team up *with* Gibbons; smoke the pipe like Mahoney said. Announce a concert. Like in Boston the day after Martin Luther King was assassinated—James Brown saved the city. They broadcast his show on live TV; three-quarters of the population stayed home to watch instead of burning Boston to the water."

"I remember."

"Sounds stupid, but it worked. On an assassination day that couldn't get any worse."

"Gibbons could announce a show way south at the ball fields at Foster Park. Get McQuinn to cut the red tape, cover the costs, steal it from the school budget. Together, they could mount a show in four or five hours; hell, Oprah lives here, who's turning her down? Announce hip-hop/Motown Woodstock right now. Start flying in headliners from—"

"It could work, Den. Out of left field . . ."

"I'll call the Ayatollah."

Jimmie says, "Call Mahoney first. Don't let Mahoney hear you went to Stone from someone else. Right up Stone's alley to leak that you switched sides."

"Meet me at the Bayside cameras."

I hang up, drop Corrissa's FBI file on my lap, and mash the gas out of the FBI lot. I hit Mahoney on speed dial, get voicemail, call back, and leave a 911, then call the Ayatollah and get voicemail from him.

Mahoney calls. I tell him what Agent Stone offered, then, "I can go on camera. Hang this on the FBI and the Northern Ireland players. Because it's true. That'll slow down the white side of Red Summer till we find—"

"*True* doesn't matter." Mahoney's tone hardens. "*Believable* matters. White-on-white—names and proof that sound good on TV."

"I can do that."

"Then you have my blessing. The price, Dennis, will be high."

"I'll pay it. You call out every fucking dog you've got; find Maureen."

Mahoney waits a moment, then says, "In six hours it will be St. Patrick's Day. The Chicago chapter of the Orange Order intends to move their traditional rally to tonight, the location as yet undisclosed. If you were campaigning to become boss of the UVF as the Interpol research suggests—to rise-up your fellow Loyalists from their 'disastrous peace stance'—where would you be six hours from now?"

"That's our story. Corrissa Howat tracks the men who killed her parents across the world, finds them here and in Florida, and kills them all. Then, after being burned half to death in Cuba, and all alone, she uncovers and executes the supreme, modern symbol of Catholic treachery, Father James Chesney *and* the Omagh bomber, Darragh O'Brien. They'll make her queen, the goddamn Morrigan come to life."

Mahoney nods. "The Celtic goddess of revenge, war, and witches. A formidable opponent, and if mythology serves us, no less unstable."

My phone rings. On the screen: "Jimmie Daniels 911." I tell Mahoney, "Jimmie's got something; call you back."

Mahoney says, "I know your answer, Dennis, but take a moment to decide. If we lose a public confrontation with the FBI, your future will not be the horses; it will be courtrooms, and likely federal prison for a very long time."

"You want to talk me into running away, you should've said that."

"I'll call Lieutenant Gilmartin; she'll organize the on-camera."

"Ten four." I button off, dodge a stalled car in the third intersection, hit redial on the Ayatollah's number. He rings to voicemail again. I tell his voicemail Jimmie's concert idea, say I'll help, even if I have to steal helicopters. I don't say we'll blackmail McQuinn, because I don't want that recorded and fed back to me in a courtroom. But I will do it. The mayor has history and I know some.

Jimmie 911s again. I answer; ask what he has.

"Interpol has a possible: File name: 'Painter.' Early thirties, might be an American; an independent contractor believed to be the assassin who killed the IMF deputy minister in Montreal last winter—showy, lots of drama, not unlike our clocktower. Interpol has him connected to three professional murders but doesn't know his name. Interpol came to attention big, though, when I detailed the Bayside. They credit 'an individual fitting the Painter's file' with a C-4-and-thermite explosion—like the Bayside—in a Kingston, Jamaica, synagogue, and the gunshot murder of a Greek casino boat operator at the dock in Hollywood, Florida. Operator and his wife, thirty-five seconds apart, one round each. Someone sent flowers to the funeral; the card had an abstract drawing and *Revelation 22:1-9* on it."

"Which means what?"

"Interpol says those passages are something about 'beyond Eden.' I told them about the *Destruction of Eden* mural; emailed the photo. Interpol emailed a sketch back; maybe 50 percent, but might be our guy."

"*Might be?* I want to talk to the German. Tell R. Murph to get him on the phone—"

"R. Murph's talking to the German now, but he hasn't changed. They don't cowboy. He's sorry, but he's not using his system off the record; Augustine's DNA is as far off the board as anyone he knows is going."

"Will he talk to me?"

"Hold on." Jimmie puts me on hold. I keep driving, weaving traffic while trying to read FBI pages that have yet to yield shit and won't. Jimmie pops back on. "Herr Bleses will talk. But do it calm, Denny. *Erster Kriminalhauptkommissar* Norbert Bleses is a London Fog guy, okay? Has his own helicopters, gadgets we haven't seen yet, hunts fugitives all over the world."

"He's the police, just like us. Get him—"

"Twenty-eight letters in that title, Den, and R. Murph says Herr Bleses deserves them all. If he decides to help, he can bring a ton of weight our way; Ninety-ten he won't help, but you never know. Calm, Denny, okay? Calm. Herr Bleses is calling you now."

Traffic snarls to a stop. I hit the siren, try to inch, veer—My phone rings: "WITHHELD" on the screen. I quit the siren, shut my eyes tight. *I'm coming, Maureen. I promise, and this man's gonna help us.*

I lift the BlackBerry to my ear, hit the button, and say, "Her name's Maureen. You're the police; you know what it's like . . . She saved me, Herr Bleses. Please. Help me save her."

Chapter 27

Erster Kriminalhauptkommissar Norbert Bleses has no German accent, precise English, and the wrong answer. "Culturally, this is not an accommodation I can make."

"Maureen Cane is everything I have."

"I'm sorry."

"She's gonna die, Norbert. Badly. Along with a whole bunch of this city. The pro who has her is international, that's what Interpol thinks. He could be coming your way. Another Munich Olympics, Berlin train station. You could call your help 'preventative'—"

"Violating the rules that I have sworn to abide is a criminal act. It is, for you and your culture, a crime that can be theorized and justified. For me, for German policemen, it is a clear abuse of power. Given World War II and our National Socialists' atrocities, abuse of power by German authorities is not condoned, nor should it be."

Lights flashing, I loop into oncoming traffic.

"Don't hang up, okay? Listen, we have the FBI; they're kinda like you from what R. Murph said, and I'm sure you've worked with them somewhere, but here they've played both ends against the middle. They helped create the problem, knew it was boiling—killing people here back when Corrissa Howat killed one of our local gangsters—and did nothing about it."

Horns blare; cars swerve.

"R. Murph said you were hunting a guy in Glasgow and Belfast who'd killed one of your guys. You'd go off the board for that, right? I mean, some shit just requires harder answers. Not clean, not good, but there's just no way to stand down. Either we—the police—get in the line of fire or shit like this never stops."

No response.

A van misses me by inches. I jerk back into my lane.

"You've been there, Norbert, or you wouldn't have helped with the DNA. You and yours stood up for the oath you took, but the elected-and-anointed rewrote theirs whenever it was convenient. They burned you, broke your fucking heart so often it became the standard. But you stayed on the job. Why? Same as me. Those little victories, when we matter. And I don't mean matter to those motherfuckers in the capitals—I'm talking about the faces on the street, tears in their eyes 'cause you saved 'em, 'cause you didn't run."

Silence.

"Norbert. I need help. Please."

"Perhaps there is someone. I will see. Should they assist you, it has been my experience they will require payment in kind. And they are not shy in asking."

"Deal. Anything. Gotta have it now. *Right* now."

"We shall see. Remain by your phone. *Auf Wiederhoeren.*"

6:42 p.m.

I dump my car as close to the Bayside crime scene as I can get, snake through the crowd, then duck under the yellow tape and approach the microphone array Lieutenant Gilmartin arranged. Twenty-two minutes and Norbert Bleses hasn't called. The Ayatollah does.

I ask, "You recording us?"

He says, "No."

"Sure. Like the last time. So, remember, there's things I'll say and do in person that I'm not saying on this phone. Understand?"

"Understood."

"You listened to my voicemail?"

"We've considered a concert, are exploring the logistics, the possibilities, the risks."

"Good. Here's the deal: concert, money, helicopters, that's what you get. And a formal TV announcement from me that the Bayside and clocktower perps are white, not Black, not from Chicago, and completely unrelated to Red Summer."

"And you suddenly have the power to accomplish a commitment of that magnitude? The credibility?"

"That story is the truth. You add one lie; say the shooters who clocked you on Halsted were not PNDH or Ragen Colts; they were from Northern Ireland, not the Riv."

"Northern Ireland."

"Yeah. This is about the FBI and Northern Ireland, all of it. And when I catch the killers, I will personally perp-walk them down the middle of South Halsted."

Pause. Gibbons goes silent while he calculates the possible outcomes. "Why should I believe you'll do as you say? Even if you survive your grand jury, publicly indicting the FBI and committing the city and police department to your plan will likely cost you your pension and your freedom."

"Are you in, yes or no?"

Gibbons tries to see the trick. "Your plan could easily be viewed as blackmail. If I willingly join you, then you disappear or recant, or we don't deliver the cease-fire, it will be me left to face the consequences—"

"Lorraine Motel, April 4, 1968. Remember who you were then. Let *that* Leslie Gibbons decide; I'm doing my part right now, as if *that* guy's my partner."

I pocket the phone. Jimmie's back from Pádraig's hospital and staring at me and what I just said. "Your FBI speech is scorched earth, Den. No going back after you light up the FBI. Threatening it is one thing, doing it . . . They'll have no choice but to crucify you."

"We win, all is forgiven."

Jimmie doesn't bite.

"Gimme another option."

Lieutenant Gilmartin waves me to the microphones piled in front of her, a crescent of cameras behind them, and reporters of every shape, size, and color behind them. She's slept the same four hours I have in the last thirty-three. Her expression is tense; so is mine. Every minute Maureen is . . . is—I bury the images, praying that Mahoney or a faceless German policeman will deliver a miracle. *Run this game, do it tight, big, and we win.*

Lieutenant Gilmartin stops me as we pass. Through taut lips she says, "Don't screw this up, brain surgeon. Whatever it is you and Mahoney are doing better pour cold water from here to Fifty-Fifth."

At the mic pile I say, "I'm Lieutenant Dennis M. Banahan, Area One Homicide. I grew up here. And I know who's killing our neighbors." I lay out my indictment of the FBI for David Rupert, Pádraig Cane, and the Bayside bombing. Four minutes into the stunned faces absorbing my indictment of the FBI, my phone rings in my hand.

The screen reads: "WITHHELD." Heart in my throat, I step back from the mics and answer.

Norbert Bleses doesn't ask who he's speaking with. "In Cincinnati, Ohio, there is a fourteen-year-old German national named Annika Elter. She is a cancer patient in the Down Syndrome unit at Children's Hospital. Annika would like a racing silk autographed by Arlington Park's jockey Earlie Fires."

"Huh?" I cut to Jimmie and Gael staring at me. "Yeah. We can do that."

"Please see to it quickly, Detective, Annika is terminal. Your information is en route."

"That's it? En route?" I spin 180. "I need it now."

"The information will arrive before you do."

"Arrive? I'm in Canaryville, at the Bayside—"

"We know where you are."

Gael steps in front of me, her eyes wide at what I just told the media, and hands me an iPad, then nods small over her shoulder to a black-haired woman melting into the crowd. "She said to tell you your username is 'Earlie Fires.'"

Blink. I tell the iPad, "Norbert?" then my phone: "Norbert?"

No answer.

"Norbert? . . . Thanks."

My phone screen blinks a stream of green. Never done that before. And he's gone.

Gael cups my phone to get my attention. "You've lost your mind. You're, you're . . . dead. You can't say what you just said—"

I pop the iPad on. It asks for a username. I enter "Earlie Fires." The screen connects to the internet, then splits into two sections. One is a photograph of Corrissa Howat—burn scars redden half her forehead, temple, and cheek. Her hairline has a bald crescent above her right eye that she doesn't hide. Not pretty, but it's her eyes—the fire, the intellect, the *commitment*. Be a very bad day to see her in the cockpit of your airplane.

The screen's other section is a grid-collage of nine sketches, including our two from Chicago and a blank. Each sketch has a date and the originating agency stamped across it. I enlarge the first sketch; the screen blinks to half sketch, half data lines. Six of the nine sketches produce similar results.

Reporters yell from the crowd. My back is to them. I look up. Jimmie's reading over my shoulder. Gael is staring, mouth open, somewhere between fury and neighborhood-girl pride. I keep reading the iPad.

All nine sketches are the professional assassin who Corrissa Howat hired. The pro is referred to by numbers in some grid sections, code names in others. The three sketches that have no data are the two from CPD and the blank labeled "FBI."

The data lines with each sketch are minimal—notes, references, *possible* connections. Nothing to jump on *now*. I switch back to the Howat photo, dated last month, her face burned on the right side same as depicted in the mural.

Reporters keep yelling questions and demands.

I tap Corrissa Howat's photograph. A UK cell number appears at the top of the page with "(current)" after the number. Beneath the UK number are eight headings, obviously a lot of information.

I look up at Jimmie, inhale big, and dial the number.

Voicemail. Mechanical, not her, no use of her name.

"Corrissa, this is Denny Banahan. I'm a Chicago Homicide lieutenant. We know you're part of our problem. Either you, or your associate, has my girlfriend, Maureen Cane. I want her back. Alive.

"I understand you have political aspirations with the UVF in Northern Ireland. Being tagged there with Chesney and Darragh O'Brien are career builders. But the mass murder of innocents at the Bayside won't serve those aspirations; I'm sure you know that. I'm facing a sea of cameras in Canaryville, ten feet from worldwide microphones. Beyond them are five thousand white people ready to go to war over Red Summer. What I say next is gonna matter to you. I have to save my girlfriend and stop the war. Tell me what you want from me."

Exhale. Lower the phone. My hands are shaking.

Gael steps up, then chins at the microphones behind us. "You intend to continue? Or just fall on the knife?"

"There's more." I cut to Jimmie asking his phone about cell-tower traces. He gives me a thumbs-up.

Gael says, "Every word better be true or you'll never get out of prison. Hell, even if it is true—"

Shrug.

Her jaw drops. "How goddamn dumb are you? I'd tell you to enjoy prison, but you won't live that long."

"What do you want me to do?" I show her my hands, my phone in one, the iPad in the other. "*Run?* You're from here, Lieutenant. I saw you on Halsted, being who your da raised you to be. You think I'm gonna do it different?"

I turn to Jimmie and give him the iPad. "Read that thing. I'll be done preaching in five, then take two questions I already set up." I show Jimmie my phone. "Corrissa will call back. Be ready to triangulate her cell tower."

Jimmie dry swallows; lets me hold on to hope he doesn't have.

"She will." I start toward the cameras and mics. "Can't let me shape the message."

Jimmie comes with me. "Eyes on the crowd, Den. Your name's on a bullet, likely several of 'em."

Chapter 28

I will Corrissa Howat to be watching this, then reapproach the mic pile and waiting faces. Tracy Moens—formerly with the *Herald*, now with the *Sun-Times*—shoulders an MSNBC celebrity correspondent off balance, then elbows in front of him. She and I have known each other twelve years. Her mic is not part of the pile. She shoves hers forward: "Lieutenant, why are you speaking for the department, and not Lieutenant Gilmartin?"

"She'd like to have her job tomorrow and not go to prison." My jaw clenches—*tone and delivery, goddammit.* Media spokesman, spin doctor.

The media wall crushes inward. Moens stumbles forward into the microphone pile, knocks five mics off the top reaching for her balance. "We're supposed to believe the FBI is culpable in the Bayside bombing? And Red Summer?"

"The FBI isn't a TV show; they're federal police with an unlimited budget; people with career aspirations—just like you guys—some of whom step over the line, way over—just like you guys—and just like you guys say the police do. Remember the FBI's COINTELPRO?" I point at the Bayside rubble. "Our rubble is the result of the same FBI misconduct; maybe the very same program. Unintended consequences then, unintended consequences now, but it belongs to the FBI nonetheless."

Reporters shout and yell. I wave them down with both hands.

"The Church Committee said COINTELPRO was forcibly ended in 1971 when it was exposed. Right? Some of you remember that. But then you found out they had mob boss Whitey Bulger under contract in Boston till he ran in 1994—that's twenty-three years *after* the COINTELPRO program supposedly ended. That very same year, the FBI replaced Bulger as their star informant with child molester David Rupert here in Chicago. The FBI ran Rupert undercover until he went public in Dublin in 2003, testifying against the IRA. And now that Rupert's done, the FBI has Pádraig Cane—yet another protected, continuing criminal partnership kept secret from the local police, the courts, and the citizens while these criminals infect our communities."

Reporters yell from every direction. One uses Maureen's name.

My phone rings. Corrissa Howat's UK number is on the screen. I point at Jimmie, turn away from the crowd, and jam a fingertip in my other ear.

"Denny Banahan."

Corrissa Howat says, "I am not your Bayside murderer and I'll not be your sacrifice. And I'll not have Ulster's Loyalists dragged through blood that is not ours. Blame me if you will for Omagh bombers Redmond Lynch and Darragh O'Brien, and Claudy bomber James Chesney, mass murderers all three, and guests of your city, all three. To be charged as their executioner will be an honor. I welcome the court proceedings you threaten. Your courts will rally my clan and bring the endless horror of the Catholic church in Ireland to light, and in the end, exonerate me."

"The Bayside—"

"The Bayside Inn has Catholic fingerprints; gangsters killin' each other over their turf. The murder of innocents is their constitution."

"I want Maureen. Either you or your pro have her. Give her back; tell me what you want."

"Maureen Cane is yet another Loyalist murdered, or to be murdered, by your Catholic gangsters. Look to them for her safety." Howat's voice ramps. "As your city should have looked after my father's safety . . . instead of funding the murderin' IRA paramilitaries."

Click.

"Looked after my father" and "funding" rings in my ear. Her murders were aligned at the borders of Canaryville where lots of IRA money was, and is, raised. She won't be shy about killing this neighborhood.

Jimmie waits, then makes a short inch with his thumb and finger and shakes his head. My phone rings.

Corrissa says, "Inform the cameras it was the Catholics of Ireland, *and Chicago*, not the FBI or me, who murdered the Bayside."

"Nobody will believe it was Catholics who blew the Bayside."

"The Blacks will believe it; the racist, murderin' Catholics are not news to them. You'll inform the cameras now, or I'll not help your Maureen. Protectin' the Catholics, their bankers, and their imperialist theology is why I've cried over my family and friends for thirty years. You'll help now; you'll tell the truth, or you'll cry over yours as well."

Click.

I cut to Jimmie. Jimmie shakes his head. Gael's at the mic pile, her back to me. I wave Jimmie over.

"Howat thinks she can beat this. And she knows we're tracking her." I point at the iPad. "Anything on there that—" My phone rings. I tell Jimmie, "See if R. Murph can email Corrissa the mural shot, but do it so she has to stay connected to see it. Tell him how long you'll need to track her."

I answer my phone. Corrissa says, "I see a woman speakin' to the cameras. I don't hear you tellin' the world the truth . . . if it's Maureen's screamin' you plan to stop."

I inhale to threaten her back—

Jimmie points to a data line on the iPad. "CONFIDENTIAL: Carstairs Hospital."

I read the line and remember what Bathhouse John and Darragh looked like slaughtered to their spines, who and what I'm dealing with.

I tell Corrissa: "Your portrait's on a mural with Maureen. Two faces on *The Destruction of Eden*. Revelation 22:1-9. I'm emailing a JPEG so you know it's true. Your face is orange, Maureen's is scarlet. Your pro painted it; he left a one-handed dead woman as part of the show. I doubt your face on a wall was part of your contract. Right now, I can't prove you hired him, and won't try real hard if I get Maureen back. But if I don't get her back, be absolutely positive I will stand up and blame you and the UVF Loyalists at every Bayside funeral till they're over.

The IRA and their 'Catholic bankers' will need armored cars to handle the contributions."

"I'm to be surprised by a mural? Or Chicago's love of Loyalist blood? Your mural is the Falls Road way; it's their public high mass, rejoicing in their slaughters. The Catholics mean to murder me, as they have my family and Maureen's family, and unless you shout the truth at them—*right now*—they will murder your Maureen, the Blacks, and likely your golden city."

Chapter 29

STEVEN

My client has personal issues. I believe we've already established that. For this attempt at false calm, Corrissa the Crazed has forgone her Irish accent and now speaks a bland, scholastic version of our common language. Her words, however, are not bland, nor are their implications.

"A mural? With Chicago on fire and my likeness?"

Oops. I grin and don't answer.

"My appearance is timed to temporarily quell the Black-versus-Catholic clash. Do you understand? The UVF in Ireland and the Orange Order in Chicago want credit for *attempting* to *stop* the conflict—not cause it—*in spite* of Canaryville's continuing financial support of the IRA. Red Summer will happen, but we will not be the cause. You will do nothing other than what I instruct. Nothing."

I make a bobblehead face. Me, professional as a marionette.

"If Maureen Cane is not alive and not where I instruct you to place her, I will make it clear to anyone who might employ you in the future that you are an incompetent psychopath, uncontrollable in your personal appetites and not to be trusted under any circumstance."

I glance at my girl Maureen. *My* girl. *My* trophy. I want to giggle, but I am a professional, blessed with a turbo IQ and—one would hope—the ability to outmaneuver those driven by the cross, be it of religious issue or otherwise.

This moment is why I grabbed Maureen; why I chose the subject of the mural; the potential ejaculations merely a bonus. I've seen the problem from the moment my client began to rewrite our conversations. I knew then that before this contract was complete, I would (a) have to rewrite the intended outcome of said contract to protect my résumé, and (b) be obliged to unpack the old rod 'n' reel to complete said rewrite if it was to be sans dissenting witnesses.

"And one must never fish with the wrong bait"—those immortal words belonged to my original teacher and purveyor of the best sex I've yet enjoyed. I wink at Maureen and massage my genitals. She doesn't massage hers, but I bet she would if she could.

I tell my client, "As it happens, I do have an ongoing relationship with the young lady you mentioned"—pucker, smooch—"not that it's any business of yours. And if you wish to reserve rights relative to my personal choices, those should be negotiated prior to pricing your contract, not after. And . . . and I'd be *very* careful whom you threaten with career slander and libel."

"Do you have her? Is she alive?"

I glance at my girl. "Why, yes, ma'am, I do, and she is."

"Has she seen your face?"

I float a fib at my girl's savior. *"Please."*

"Yes or no?"

"No."

"Give her your phone."

"I think not."

A chilly silence descends.

My client continues, "Perhaps you'd prefer I refer your details to the authorities . . . in Canada, Jamaica, and elsewhere? Would that help you decide to not further injure a project you were well paid to accomplish?"

Me-*ow*. I walk the phone to my girl, press the speaker against Maureen's full breasts, and tell her: "Say only: 'This is Maureen.' Are we clear?"

Maureen Cane nods, I put the phone to her luscious lips. She says a hoarse: "This is Maureen."

I walk back to the window that frames thousands of angry white persons who can, and will, start my fires. *Mine.* Always have a second exit strategy, especially good if the backup exit can be in front of a wave already headed for shore. My CV will suggest I was hired to push Chicago into a burn-down race war (the "Red Summer" it appears it wanted anyway). And gosh, it appears I'll do a really good job.

Corrissa Howat continues her threats. "Are you capable of completing this contract?"

"As I explained when last we spoke, that will depend upon the target, time, and location."

"The time is being decided now. The location is the UVF–Orange Order rally in the Stock Yards. The target is me."

Chapter 30

DENNY

Jimmie says, "Got her. The half-mile tower, west side of Arrigo Park in Little Italy; Leigha and R. Murph are emailing another set of her photos into Twelve."

We bolt for the car, sprint past the Bayside rubble, duck the yellow tape, and run up Emerald into the crowd. My phone rings. I answer, tucking in behind Jimmie shouldering through people who hard-eye him and don't want to move.

Corrissa Howat tells my ear, "The Catholics have Maureen. They hold her and her brother responsible for the Bayside. If Pádraig has not yet died by their hand, he soon will. Speak to the cameras *now*, as I instructed, and I might be capable of trading for your Maureen."

"Nobody will believe the Catholics bombed the Bayside, but I'll say it for you. Wait thirty minutes. Give these maniacs time to pull back and veer toward the Federal Building now that I've blamed the Feds. Thirty minutes and you get everything you want."

"If that is your decision, then I suggest you call the Catholics and ask them for their mercy."

"Wait. Where is she? Who has her? Who're you trading with—"

Corrissa Howat's gone. I grab Jimmie's shoulder to stop him. He waves his phone: "C'mon, Mahoney's diverting a helicopter."

I say: "A half-mile cell tower covers sixteen, twenty blocks. Needle in a haystack."

"So what?" Jimmie grabs my arm. "You can read what the German sent while I drive." Jimmie pushes the iPad at me. "Very scary material in here."

"Corrissa wants me on camera, blaming the Catholics, not the FBI, for the Bayside. If I stay by the cameras, at least stay in the frame, maybe she'll—I'll explain to Gael, call Mahoney, and—"

"You won't be blaming the Catholic church with Mahoney's blessing." Jimmie chins at the crowd surrounding the reporters and cameras. "Blame the Catholics and we'll never get off this block alive. Might not anyway."

"Gotta do something."

"You already committed suicide with the FBI. Call Stone while you're on camera, see if he has an offer to make. I'm going to the cell tower." Jimmie bolts for the car, his badge around his neck the only thing that might keep Canaryville from killing him.

I shoulder back to the yellow tape, duck under, and walk toward Gael. The reporters are yelling questions at her from all sides. I touch her shoulder from behind. She half jumps, glares, and turns back to the lights and cameras.

I tug her away from the microphones and show her the iPad. "We might have the crew responsible. For all of it. We need your help."

Gael cuts to the iPad, then me. "With what?"

I explain Corrissa Howat and her pro assassin, then, "Over here, Corrissa believes she can deny killing Darragh O'Brien and Father Chesney, but still take the credit back in Ireland, and not go to prison. And she may be right, who knows? But she's got Maureen, or her pro does. Corrissa says she can save Maureen and the city if I go on camera, now, recant the FBI story, and say it's the Catholics—here and in Northern Ireland—who did all of—"

"Are you blind? Look around, everyone dead is Catholic."

"I didn't say it made sense, Gael, or that it'll work. I said that's what I have to do."

***

Corrissa Howat wants me, Steven L. Sociopath, to shoot her.

God Almighty, where do I find these people? I realize most of you don't do what I do for a living, but imagine your boss has been trying to gain access to your privates since you took the job, then one day instead of offering more candy, he says, "Hey, could you give my wife a call? Tell her I masturbate at your desk while you're at lunch?"

You'd pie-face, right? Nine-one-one the Human Resources counselor? Something?

Not me. I'm supposed to forget my difficulties and trust issues, then place a high-velocity projectile at three thousand feet per second through the upheld handless arm and whatever it's waving. At five hundred yards. Or more—that's three city blocks—and there isn't an oversupply of properly elevated platforms in this neighborhood. The clocktower would've been perfecto, but why think a step or two ahead, you know, if you'd like the "big plan" to actually work?

Hmmm.

Frown. I glance at Maureen Cane, a responsible party in the dilemma du jour associated with her brother and Corrissa Howat.

If I misjudge the glare, windage, or elevation, Corrissa Howat's head is goulash . . . all that risk so she might win another Girl Scout merit badge to go with her lost hand and burnt face. But in this case, I'm all for the risk. An unfortunate "miss" will be the perfect endgame for *moi*; goulash solves my CV problems.

Except, Ms. Grandiose Patriot tossed me a curve—if I "miss," a file Corrissa has clandestinely compiled on me goes to the world police.

Now I have to kill her *and* retrieve the file. That's pressure, let me tell you.

I frown at Maureen Cane in her chair; my unfortunate introduction to Corrissa Howat is sufficient reason enough to kill Maureen's brother and her as well. Not that I require a justification, I'm a sociopath, some decisions come naturally.

But the life of a professional requires restraint. I step behind Maureen. Her bound wrists are bloody from her quiet, courageous, ongoing battle to escape. I run a finger through Maureen's new haircut, then lean in to sniff her head from behind. Hmmm. We've had sufficient foreplay. And our satin-sheets camping trip has always been on the agenda . . .

No. First things first. Stop and smell the roses—something is amiss here in the garden. I step to my rucksack, remove the Zeiss VV60, and walk to the window. At maximum amplification I can see the corner of Forty-Fifth and Halsted and the several thousand crazed white people massed everywhere.

In order to take my shot, I have to be within three, maximum four, blocks from there, preferably forty-feet high . . . And Corrissa will know that.

Hmmm. I would have to be in—I scan the available perches—one of three locations. In roughly three hours.

Corrissa believes I have harmed her grand political plans. Do I smell treachery?

I spin to look at my girl Maureen. Women are devious, my mother a perfect example. Not even a goodbye! I circle Maureen, then plop down cross-legged in front of her. "So, dearly beloved, the reason we're gathered here today . . . *is* . . . your fellow freedom fighter has threatened me with a file, one she contends contains copious amounts of information about *moi*." I point at me with both index fingers and beam George Clooney on a babe-day. "Now, how would our Corrissa come across this file if it didn't exist?"

Maureen stares, scared to death, but hiding it with every inch of her potato-famine stoicism while her little muscles fight.

"But what if? Well, if you must know, some form of this information could have existed, but only through your little brother."

Maureen's lovely face flushes. Maureen doesn't agree, defend, or enjoy. My nose runs and I wipe it with my hand. She is pretty, but cold; and this should be the fun part.

"How, you ask? We've already covered that—after you stumbled on Brummel, O'Brien, and Chesney together, you phoned home to Belfast. Corrissa popped over, verified the targets, then asked for help."

Maureen doesn't help this time either.

I slap her, hard. "Yes?"

She nods. "Yes."

"Better, thank you. So, as we previously discussed, Corrissa wants a professional already operating in the old USA. Corrissa lies to you, agreeing that she also wants a public trial for Chesney and O'Brien. You don't know people who might arrange a kidnapping, but your brother would. You ask."

Maureen shuts her eyes tight and *again* does not agree to indict her baby brother.

I slap Maureen on the other side of her pretty face. She doesn't agree or open her eyes. I slap her again, and again.

"My, aren't we brave, and for a little shitter like your brother. Such a waste."

Her shoulder muscles are working harder than ever. She might cut her wrists so deep she'll be listed as a suicide. I stand up and circle behind her. Her muscles stop.

Call me the Red Cross.

"Unfortunately, Pádraig sees financial opportunity as outweighing patriotism. Pádraig sees the chance to replace Loef Brummel as the new Irish crime lord of Chicago."

I check Maureen's wrists but pretend I don't, then step back in front, bend my knees so we're eye to eye. "And possibly, it appears, Pádraig also generates a personnel file of some sort. So, first things first. Pádraig has to go. And since Corrissa the Patriot won't be around to do the job—"

"Don't hurt my brother; I will organize Corrissa any way you wish. And I'll see to Pádraig. He'll be no threat to you."

"He won't? And your other boyfriend, Lieutenant Dennis? He's no threat to me, either? I kill Corrissa and we're all eatin' Banbury cakes by the Liffey?"

"Dennis and I are done with this fight, that's the whole of it. I made a mistake; this fight's no longer mine. I don't know who you are and it won't serve me to know."

"Really? And your crimefighter-lieutenant? And your brother? They wish to quit the contest?"

"Yes. Allow me to ask."

Maybe Maureen could live on, but I doubt it. But Pádraig has to die—we all know that—the question is when and how. I lean back, say, "Okay," and make Maureen a happy face. "Let's make the call to

Corrissa. If the call doesn't go the way I'd like it to go, we'll hang up and call your lieutenant or your brother. I'll kill the loved one you don't call, first."

Her eyes harden.

"And by the way, you never did say if you thought I was good looking. Other than the lip."

Chapter 31

DENNY

"In goddamn fantasyland you can switch from the FBI to the Catholics." Lieutenant Gilmartin shoves my shoulder so I'll look beyond the microphones and cameramen to the Bayside's gaunt, ghost faces and sentinels. "You can't change your story now, say it's all Catholics. No one—Black or white—will believe another word out of your mouth or anyone else in a uniform."

I can't, but I will.

And she knows it. Gael exhales and says, "Stand next to me and shut up." She doesn't wait for an answer and storms back to the microphones. The sun is down and the TV lights brighten in our faces. Gael points at me.

"Lieutenant Banahan has developed subsequent information regarding the charges made previously against the Federal Bureau of Investigation and their COINTELPRO operations. Lieutenant Banahan's new information further demonstrates COINTELPRO's extensive roots in the lawlessness currently engulfing Northern Ireland and Chicago."

Gael pauses to drama the crowd, then points over my shoulder.

"The John Doe found hung from the Stock Yards clocktower at 4:00 a.m. this morning has been identified as Father James Chesney, the Catholic priest believed to be Northern Ireland's infamous Claudy bomber. Father Chesney was declared dead thirty-one years ago, but has for the last twenty years been driving the school bus at St. Gabriel's under the assumed identity of Father Augustine P. O'Dwyer."

The reporters go nuts.

"Detective Banahan has irrefutable proof that the perpetrators of Father Chesney's murder are *white*, and *completely unrelated* to Red Summer. The motive for Father Chesney's murder was political, as was the motive for the murders committed at the train tracks of the Forty-Seventh Street yard yesterday. We will make more details public as they are verified."

Reporters yell, "The Bayside! What about the Bayside!"

Gael says, "Yes," then grabs my arm and jerks us away from the shouts and demands for clarification. She stops us twenty feet back, squares up, and stabs her finger in my chest.

"That's as far as I can go, and that was any-promotion-I'll-ever-see too far." Her phone rings. "I know politics; you don't. The Ayatollah will sell you the instant he sees the benefit." She looks at her phone screen, then glares up at me. "He's a snake. Do. Not. Go." She pulls the phone to her face and turns away to talk. I start to say thanks, that she did the uniform proud no matter what the fuck they say in the boss's cafeteria, and my phone rings.

I answer. Corrissa Howat says, "Insufficient."

"Give me Maureen. I'll help you reach whatever audience you want. Don't give me Maureen, or give her to me hurt, and when you walk out to make the big play tomorrow morning—yeah, we know that's where you're headed—I'll put a bullet in your fucking head before you say word one."

She doesn't answer.

She should've folded when I threatened her political aspirations the first time. But she didn't. The phone goes dead.

I call Jimmie at the cell tower. He says, "Not there yet, but Twelfth District uniforms are stopping cars and pedestrians, showing Corrissa's photo."

"Gotta find her." My head pounds. I button off, remember the iPad in my hand. Jimmie said, "very scary material" in there; I start to look and my phone rings again.

Special Agent Stone says, "We had a deal, Lieutenant."

"Me rolling on Mahoney will never happen, and you knew that when you offered to let Maureen die if I didn't. In FBI world, that's in the fair-play manual. In mine, it reduces your life expectancy."

"Like the Starks?"

"Help me save Maureen and Chicago and I'll tell you all about the Starks. Nothing to do with Mahoney."

Silence. "You're certain?"

"Save that shit for your TV show."

"Have you read all the files I provided?"

"Fuck your files. Maureen Cane's all you need to care about. If she's hurt or dead, make sure I am." I duck away from the mic stand to a Fox TV van with its dish up and two techs outside. "Open up."

They do. The guy inside with all the equipment and monitors has a headset and draftee-foxhole posture.

"Have you got cameras at Ogden Park?"

He points at three monitors. One has Reverend Jesse Jackson on a makeshift stage in the center of the shot.

I call the Ayatollah. He answers; a PA drowns him out, booming with Jackson's anthemic voice, an appeal for a "positive focus."

The second monitor is a crowd shot. Thousands of fists pump at the dark sky. "RED SUMMER! RED SUMMER!" drowns out the PA. Police helicopters thump overhead. The monitor pans the huge park. At the western end, a bonfire explodes.

The camera on Reverend Jackson pans the makeshift stage. Thirty people are up there with him, including Leslie Gibbons, RayLen Starks, and my ex, Renatta. All stand braced or squirmy, talking to their phones, and generally look scared shitless.

Gibbons looks the least rattled, but then he's been eyeball to eyeball with bullets before. Gibbons reacts to something on his left, then says, "Mayor McQuinn has declined my request that he assist your concert plan."

"He will."

Concussion. Gibbons flinches, says: "Why?"

"I'll blackmail him with his Riviera history. And you'll help. Win or lose, we go down together."

The Fox van tech wide-eyes me.

Gibbons says, "What history?"

"Not on the phone."

"Noble of you, Lieutenant, but our goals are not the same. You wish to halt the rage, maintain order, the status quo. My people want America, land of the free. We fought for it; we died for it. Tonight is one more unfortunate night in our battle."

Renatta is at Gibbons' shoulder, hears "Lieutenant," and cold-eyes Gibbons.

I tell the phone: "It won't just be Canaryville on fire. Gonna burn from here to you, then all the way to Seventy-Ninth Street. No city money left to rebuild it like last time. No federal money either. No housing equals no constituents. Daley pushed a bunch of your flock out of the city limits and McQuinn's using you and Red Summer to finish the job. Take a good look at your bonfire. A week from now, all the power you had will be outside the city limits in Lansing and Berwyn."

Another *concussion.*

Gibbons flinches again but stays face to face with the fists and fires. He points into the crowd. "Find a TV. *That* is power. *TV* is what America respects. *That* is what African Americans are forced to wield in order to gain what you were given freely at birth."

"You're not gonna help me?"

He waits, still in the camera shot. "I didn't say that."

I stare at the screen, at a professional politician in America's most politically corrupt city, a guy who could play cards heads up with the devil and be fifty-fifty. I tell him: "One of the two perps has my girlfriend. The FBI says they'll help, but that's TV talk. Either I catch the perps or Chicago burns and my girlfriend dies. I want your help. I'm offering mine."

"And you can catch the *white* perpetrators . . . in time?"

"We're close, real close."

"You won't succeed unless you are prepared to reexamine your past relationships."

Renatta stares bullets at Gibbons.

"Who?"

Gibbons adds, "Cullen Mahoney."

STEVEN

My client is on my phone and . . . unhappy-*er*.

Corrissa Howat says, "Maureen Cane does not belong to you and will be found, alive, immediately prior to my appearance at the Orange Order rally. *Immediately* prior."

"Sorry, she's seen my face."

"Deal with your failures after my contract is complete. For now, her release is the only acceptable outcome. Ten minutes before you complete your contract by wounding me, you will call Lieutenant Banahan and provide him Maureen Cane's location. *Alive*."

"And the file we spoke of? It goes the way of the polar ice caps?"

She works hard to find her inner Greenpeace. "Yes."

I roll my eyes for Maureen and point at Corrissa the Crazed on my phone. "I'm to trust your veracity?"

"What choice do you have?"

"Take a listen." I remove the stick recorder plugged into my phone, and play back our previous conversations. When Corrissa's and my history is done repeating itself, I plug the stick back in and say, "Thought you'd want to know."

"Do your job correctly, if you comprehend the term, and neither of us will suffer penalties."

I smile at Maureen. I am now certain that Maureen's fellow patriot, Corrissa Howat, intends to kill me later this evening. Before I can kill her.

Hmmm. So, it probably goes like this: I leave Maureen here, drugged, taped up, but alive. In two hours, I'm set up in one of the three perches, I call Banahan, his people go to Maureen's location, verify she's safe, then SWAT descends on the three perches simultaneously. When Corrissa knows I'm dead, she walks out on stage for her big political moment—her 'attempt' to save Chicago from the Catholics—and Red Summer anoints her as Joan of Arc.

Not bad. Her targets are dead, Canaryville is ashes, she's a hero in Belfast, the Blacks and Catholics are guilty here.

Actually, quite an accomplishment. *If* the Catholics don't tear her to pieces.

So . . . what do I do?

In the distance, the Stock Yards clocktower shadows against the night sky. Hmmm . . .

I pocket my phone, turn to my girl, Maureen, and kneel at her knees. Her knees tremble under my palms. I apply pressure spreading the knees an inch and look up through my eyebrows hoping for a 'Yes.' It is prom night, after all.

She swallows but doesn't resist. I spread another inch. Then another. She relaxes back. I smile and look down to find the edge of her skirt. *Finally*, someone wants to help.

The thighs flex in anticipation . . .

Maureen explodes out of the chair, knocks me flat, bangs my head into the concrete. Fingers claw into my eyes. I hammer her head. She shrieks and gouges. My teeth rip at her face. Both my hands batter bitch flesh.

Chapter 32

DENNY

Deputy Superintendent Mahoney ducks under the Bayside yellow tape and walks fast to me at the mic stand. Mahoney's face is solemn, creased, and ashen in the emergency lights. He pulls me away, squeezes my shoulder, says: "Keep the faith, Dennis. We'll not stop until we find her."

Sirens wail and echo.

"The UVF–Orange Order have reorganized their rally for *tonight*— arriving in the Riviera as we speak. They'll be the fuse for our destruction, and our chance to stop it."

"Where? How many?"

Mahoney shrugs. "Could be five hundred orange. Could be two thousand—it's word of mouth, no permit. The number's irrelevant—we lack the manpower to keep the Ayatollah's ten thousand on the Black side of Fifty-Fifth. Nor can we keep the Protestants and Catholics apart on this side."

"I talked to him, the Ayatollah. Promised him we'd back him with CPD and city money if he'll take a chance on the concert, use his juice to—"

"We've covered your concert idea, Dennis. Barbeque and water-melon are tools of the past. And Mayor McQuinn will decline to make a hero of the alderman."

"Who gives a shit if Gibbons is a hero?"

Mahoney grabs my shoulders, looks at me like a forty-year project he'll never finish. "Because, Dennis, it will also make the alderman our next mayor. A power shift that would dramatically alter the city's position on the issue of 'urban revitalization' and people of color. And that is not our current mayor's direction."

Mahoney locks eyes with Lieutenant Gilmartin to our left but keeps talking to me: "Within the small part we pawns are allowed to play, focus on the UVF–Orange Order. Corrissa Howat's capture offers us a chance to save Maureen and possibly affect tonight's outcome. I'm here to support your efforts, our efforts, in any way possible. Find Corrissa Howat; *win*, Dennis, and tomorrow the FBI will be making apologies, not brandishing our heads." Mahoney's lips flatten. "Excuse me, I have a willful, petulant child to reprimand." Mahoney storms toward Gael Gilmartin.

They square up on each other, ringed by shouting Ragen Colts and lesser madmen, and reporters who weren't smart enough to leave.

The headache throbs across my temples. A fifty-five-gallon drum fire ignites behind me on Emerald, probably a hundred more drums being filled with flammables up and down Halsted and in the Stock Yard prairies.

Think, goddammit. A helicopter thumps overhead, one of three with splash lights sweeping the Riviera's flash points. Another two sweep Ogden Park to the south.

I run across Emerald to a ladder leaning against a building, slap the ladder to the fire escape, climb both to the third-story rooftop.

Fifty-Fifth is lined and lit with truck-mounted klieg lights. Military vehicles have blocked off a mile from the tracks to Racine and filled Fifty-Fifth with guardsmen. I can't see the fixed bayonets Gael said they've deployed.

Think, goddammit. Maureen's out there with a white man, a pro-fessional assassin who came here to kill two IRA bombers he's already killed. Why grab Maureen? Why be here at all? Professionals don't stick around—

Because . . . because *the assassin's part of the show isn't over.*

I look east, west, then behind me, north. *He has another target.*

Who? What?

I look south toward Ogden Park's drum fires and helicopter splash lights. Someone yells: "LIEUTENANT?!"

Beneath me, a tense Ninth District patrolman is at the ladder waving me to come down. He points to the yellow tape on the north end of the Bayside crime scene.

I yell, "WHAT?"

The patrolman waves harder, frantic.

I climb down to the pavement.

The patrolman points through the flashing lights, truck engines, and helicopter thumps to the yellow tape. Standing there is Bishop Haswell Burke, six foot, rail thin, wearing the same cheap black suit and shirt he had on at St. Gabriel's steps.

The patrolman says, "The older guy there—with the Bible. Says it's urgent."

Burke is sided by five large men in similar clothes. Two of the men elevate the ten-foot cross Burke had on top of the semis. Three bodyguards react to something in the crowd behind them. Burke doesn't. I flashback to the TV at Malvern, the battle scene in Arizona, Burke bloodied and in the middle of it.

I tell the patrolman: "Only Burke under the tape, none of his backup. Keep him midstreet and don't let him touch anything on his way to me."

The patrolman helps Burke duck under from the crowd side, then brings him down Emerald to me. A woman screams somewhere deep in the crowd. Somewhere Maureen's with Corrissa's assassin, so scared she can't scream, or think. My eyes shut tight. *Who is his target?* Real terror has no true survivors; the longer the terror lasts, the less of you that's left.

Bishop Burke stops short, keeps eight feet between us.

He says, "As a founding member of the Christian Identity movement, I've been asked to lead the prayers at tonight's peace vigil." Burke checks a $20 Timex on his wrist. "In approximately two hours."

"Peace vigil?" I close to three feet. "Prayers and 'peace vigils' ain't gonna do shit in Canaryville. You need to rein in these parishioners;

stop lighting fires under their asses. And do it *now*, not in two hours. Most of 'em won't be alive in two hours."

Burke adds more orator to his posture. "*Catholics* have *parishioners*, ecclesiastical geography to control their minds and money. True Christians have Jesus Christ. And while the true Christ never intended we lay down our swords when defense of his word was required, He did not intend for the slaughter of innocents. Ever. Under any set of conditions. It is the standard worldwide used to identify true Christians from Muslims, Catholics, and Jews."

Burke reads my eyes. "You've known Satan, walked with him. He returns to exact his toll." Burke narrows his eyes, intensifies his stare. "The races were not meant to merge. The Blacks have their place in the plan and we have ours—"

"Believe whatever you want." I point at the Bayside rubble. "That's mine." I point south and west. "And all those stupid motherfuckers out there who aren't dead yet, they're mine. All colors. Help with that or get your cracker-ass outta Chicago."

Burke doesn't fold. "Should you survive the test Jesus Christ has put before you, do not forget that it was He, not Satan, not chance, who put me in front of you tonight."

I wave the patrolman back to—

"Corrissa Howat has contacted my church. She wishes to join my peace vigil tonight. More specifically, she wishes my fellow Christians to ring the stage along with her Orange Order Protestants. We are to keep the Catholics at bay so she might show Protestant solidarity with the church of Christian Identity."

I point the patrolman to stop. "Where?"

Burke points southwest. "On the corner, the semitrailer stage at Forty-Fifth Street and Halsted."

"When?"

"Ten o'clock."

"Why tell me?" I show Burke calm I don't feel while I 911 for Jimmie. "I'm a Homicide lieutenant, not tactical; I can't stop the bloodbath you and Howat will start with your peace vigil."

"Because, Lieutenant, while you lack the faith, it is a fact that some of us can sense Satan's presence. He is with Corrissa, *inside* her, building his house. A grand, cavernous palace, filled with her hatred."

Burke looks beyond me and extends his Bible at the silvery emergency light. "We are surrounded now by Satan's work, his armies, and she is a commander. If her advance can be stopped, *his* advance may be thwarted. For a time. The police have their mission; the reformation of Christianity around the true Christ is *mine.*"

I stare, reading Florida-cracker Bishop Haswell Burke like I do a suspect with blood on his clothes and a story that *might* explain it away.

I tap my BlackBerry. "Show me Howat's phone number."

He does.

I nod around us to the faces and body language vibrating beyond the tape. "Meet her now, somewhere close. We don't have two hours."

Reverend Burke raises his phone.

I stop his hand. "How many of your true believers are here, now?"

"One thousand. Within walking distance."

"Okay. Call her; don't mention me. Get her somewhere, anywhere, to talk, plan, whatever. Out in the open."

Burke punches her number, raises his phone, waits, then begins talking.

I answer Jimmie calling me back. "Got a twenty on Corrissa—the trailer stage at Forty-Fifth and Halsted, ten o'clock. Haswell Burke's here with me, says Corrissa's a minion of Satan. Burke will help us grab her somewhere before ten, before the crowd there can protect her. Has her on his phone right now. Hold it—"

Burke lowers his phone shaking his head, tells me: "Ten o'clock at the semitrailers, not before. Persons are there now, wiring lights and a powerful PA system. I will mount the trailers at ten o'clock and introduce her. Corrissa Howat will climb to me, and together, we will begin to pray." Burke frowns deep creases into his hollow cheeks. "But she won't come to pray, not to Jesus Christ."

I hold up a finger, turn away, and tell Jimmie on my phone: "Come straight here and hold on to Burke. He goes nowhere without us in his pocket. I'll keep Patrol with him till you get here."

"Denny, I looked at the FBI files Stone gave you on Corrissa Howat. You went through them?"

"Screw the files. I'll recon the trailers. We gotta grab her before she gets there."

"Jesus, don't scare her off."

"Don't think we can."

I wave the patrolman to Burke and me, tell him that he goes wherever Burke goes.

The patrolman says, "Ten four."

I grab a CNN cameraman. "C'mon. You and me gonna make Pulitzer TV."

Chapter 33

STEVEN

My elevated clocktower crime scene has been abandoned to the bugs and rats, no longer of interest to the undermanned police or fans of high-quality executions. Art is often fleeting, and one must make peace with that.

Inside the cupola, I dial the Zeiss VV60 for clarity, using my left eye. I'm not sure my right eye will be repairable even if I went straight to an ER and lucked into a master surgeon. Two semitrailers fill my lens, both logo'd with "Allied Fastener" and that cute Christian fish logo. Just above the fish stands a troubled police detective searching low and high, unconcerned with the sea of angry white people roiling in every direction beneath him—

Our Moses at the Red Sea. Lieutenant Dennis surveys the wonderful world of white power from the stage of destiny. His nose is oddly unshriveled—very stinky down there; my brief visit confirmed that white-power world does not use deodorant in sufficient quantities.

I track lower to Lieutenant Dennis's shoes, then along the narrow space between the two semitrailers to a gift that can be enjoyed by many: six pounds of C-4 pre-shaped, detonator attached; and wedged beautifully to avoid detection. Unfortunately, when it's time to part the Red Sea, I'll be the only one who gets to enjoy the countdown drama.

My hand without the broken finger salutes bye-bye to my soon-to-be-deceased lieutenant.

I finish setting up my rifle's tripod. Then, with great affection, I attach the Zeiss scope to my rifle and my rifle to the tripod.

The rifle is set back far enough from the window to be believable when "we're detected," but close enough that when Corrissa tips the police on my whereabouts, they can locate this perch in their mad dash to save the day.

Or they will locate the rifle after they have run all their other options to no avail—down there in the roiling Red Sea, a decent detective will do a panicked spherical spin, and: *Oh my gosh, there's the clocktower*, the only remaining option.

If I were any better at this, I'd have my own mountain in Tibet.

At the clocktower's stairs, I take a last look at my chessboard. In one hour, we will be playing *Come out, come out, wherever you are.* But now, it's on to Mercy Hospital and Pádraig Cane's long journey into night.

Down the stairs and out the door, my head down, I drunk-stagger into the crowded alley. Twenty feet into Halsted, I phone my client. "Your special friend is alive and well, *as instructed*, and waiting for her knight in shining armor. Use this link on your phone or computer and you may watch her rescue live." I provide Maureen's location, then the web address for the camera rig I installed. "I'm set up; ready for your martyr-shot. Where is my file?"

"All traces of the file will be destroyed when I am released from the hospital and not before. Where are you located?"

A smile creeps across my field-bandaged, semi-shredded face. My, my, my, Corrissa the Crazed is a good liar under pressure. "It's better you don't know."

"I must know. I must present myself in that direction to ensure the safest possible shot. I will establish at a spot looking directly at your location after I have made the primary statement. I will then begin a long statement to the cameras and crowd. Do not shoot until I am facing you directly. Do you understand?"

She really is quite good. "Yes, ma'am. I am in the clocktower. Thought it would be a nice touch." Pause. "Should the file ever surface, anywhere, under any circumstance, I hope you realize all our business will also be made public. Before I kill you. Cheerio."

Corrissa clicks off. Now, she'll call for Maureen Cane's rescue. And shortly thereafter, my murder.

Oh, woman, thou art treachery! Like the good ol' boys say, *If they didn't have a pussy, there'd be a bounty on 'em.* My better hand touches the bandage that holds my eye in the socket. Pussy or not, a bounty is likely the way to go.

I click on the video link, the show should go like this—pretty Maureen is rescued, two seconds later, Corrissa, being an anonymous tipster, tells the police: "The Bayside Bomber is back in the clocktower plotting mischief and mayhem—*stop him, oh, please, stop him!*"

Chapter 34

DENNY

I hoist the CNN camera up across the Allied Fastener logo to the top of one semitrailer, then the cameraman. He shoulders his camera—

"PNDH!"

"FOR GOD AND ULSTER!"

—slowly 360s it at five thousand combatants ramping for war, then focuses on me.

Pulitzer TV time. I put a finger in my ear, my words drowned out in the roil, and yell into my phone: "Yeah, *the* Denny Banahan, the Homicide lieutenant. Let me speak to the mayor."

The mayor's chief of staff says, "You've been suspended. Ten minutes ago. Turn in your badge and—"

"Tell the mayor I'm standing on top of two semitrailers at Forty-Fifth—"

"We're watching you on CNN. You're the subject of a federal warrant. Everything you say will be part of your trial."

"In an hour, both sides of Fifty-Fifth are gonna be graveyards. The mayor and your FBI alma mater can stop it. Help the Ayatollah; give Gibbons whatever he needs to divert his people south."

"Surrender to the FBI when they arrive. You no longer represent the Chicago Police Dep—"

"See this?" I pick up and wave a microphone that's being attached to a three-stack PA. "Everything I know about the mayor's DWI stops, his family history in Bridgeport, the city contracts, is going on the record."

"We'll add blackmail to the charges—"

Corrissa Howat's number tries to ring through.

I tell the mayor's chief of staff, "Help the Ayatollah or I bury McQuinn. You got three minutes, then I go live on CNN's mic. Tell Gibbons to call me with the deal."

I pick up Corrissa Howat's call and yell: "Banahan! This is Banahan."

The screen reads "CALL LOST." I squeeze the BlackBerry. "C'mon, call back."

No call.

No call.

I *will* the BlackBerry to ring. It does, but it's Jimmie. I yell to tell him: "Corrissa's not doing another bomb; doesn't want to own the first one. Has to be a sniper shot . . . on someone; why he's still here."

"Yeah, but who?"

"Don't know. You? Me? Burke . . ."

"PNDH!"

"NIGGERS DIE HERE!"

I plug my ear. Jimmie says, "It's her. A martyr-shot—"

"A what?"

"What you said the Ayatollah probably pulled on Halsted. Corrissa's a hero in Ireland if she kills Chesney and Darragh—you said that, too. A martyr-shot is how she takes credit but gets off the hook for the Bayside."

I 360 for sniper perches. "Could happen . . . Bitch *is* crazy."

Jimmie adds, "Bullet misses her, hits Burke, lotta blood; there she is in the TV lights with the cross. Story sells itself. *Especially* if you're crazy."

"Makes sense with what she said on the phone, blaming Canaryville for funding the IRA and killing her father. She pulls the martyr-shot trying to stop Red Summer from burning Canaryville to the ground. It burns anyway. She hits the fucking trifecta."

I 360 again, keep yelling into my phone.

"Have to be a long shot. I make three buildings that are high enough—the Morris, the Armour, and the clocktower. We could splash all three rooftops with the helicopters—"

"He'll pick line of fire first"—Jimmie's phone goes static—"then height and distance, then cover."

"Then my three are it. Clocktower's best. Everything else is compromised; probably still usable, but nowhere as good."

Jimmie says, "Can you get SWAT and uniforms? Now?"

I plug my ear tighter. "No. The city's a battlefield. Call Mahoney, maybe he can—Wait, he's buried here; call the superintendent. I can't, the FBI has a warrant for me; mayor's chief of staff says I've been suspended—"

"Did you read their files, the FBI files? About Mahoney?"

"What?"

Jimmie's voice ramps. "The files Stone gave you. He mixed in two pages on Mahoney."

"No. Shit was worthless. I'll take the clocktower—"

"Alone? Jesus, don't. You can't—"

"Don't let Patrol lose Burke. Keep trying for backup on the other two buildings. Make sure they know Maureen's a hostage. Make sure."

A siren blares over Jimmie's phone, then: "Mob's on my fenders. I'm at Thirty-Sixth; can't get any closer in the car. I'll take the old Armour building; Patrol will have to handle Burke. By the time I get to him, it'll be too late."

Fuck. "Ten four. Stay alive."

I lower off between the two trailers, drop the last five feet, and land next to the tires. The CNN camera will try to track me in the mob. I force my way out, into the shouts, elbows, and twisted faces.

"GOD AND ULSTER!"

"NIGGERS DIE HERE!"

My phone vibrates in my hand. I plug one ear and answer.

Corrissa Howat says, "Maureen Cane is on the second floor of the Swift and Company building, east side. I have emailed you a video link. I cannot vouch for her safety or her rescuers' safety when they arrive; the kidnap was not of my doing." Click.

I curl around my phone, speed-dial SWAT, fight my fingers calm to email SWAT the video link, no idea if the camera in the link works or why it exists.

Dispatch answers, doesn't mention my suspension, says all SWAT units are currently deployed—

"Send uniforms, anyone. I'll be in the building." I punch 911, call in an EMT helicopter to the roof of the Swift building, then pull my Smith, yell, "POLICE!" and fire twice at the night sky.

The crowd shrinks.

I sprint toward Maureen four blocks and three thousand combatants away, firing the Smith empty as I run.

9:26 p.m.

Th Swift building is spalled brick and boarded windows. The front door's ajar, the chain lock broken. I reload the Smith, toe the door open, and jump to the side—

Quick look: The first floor is black-dark to a stairwell. Dim light spills where the stairs pierce the ceiling. There will be, or should be, trip wires with explosives. Blind, I walk inside. Trash crunches. I make the stairs alive, drop to my knees, and pat the first tread.

I fingertip along the tread's face, then its top, raise one knee onto the tread, then the other. Deep breath. I repeat onto the next tread, and keep repeating until I reach the second floor, Maureen's floor.

Dim light spills from an open doorway. I pat the floor one-handed to the doorway. Check for trip wires, creep inside—

Mostly shadows—no Maureen visible by the nearest windows. No Maureen by the—

There, a horizontal shape, a small light focused on it. A mummy of clear tape, only the head exposed. Short hair, not long like Maureen's. My heart begins to pound. I squint shadows for the trip wires. The mummy doesn't move.

Still on my knees, I feel and crawl toward the light. My left hand touches the mummification, stained and fouled—terror underneath in the clothing folds. It's Maureen; she's breathing. I smell ether. I'm afraid to move her; afraid she's the trip wire.

I lean over her to look at her face. Battered; white, too white. "Maureen? It's Denny."

She blinks. Her eyes close, then open, then roll to white.

"No, baby. Come back—" I grab her to me before I can stop—

She doesn't explode.

I holster the Smith, grab the light, then scoop her to my chest. "We're good, baby. I got you. Hundred percent. You're safe."

I focus the light on the floor . . . for trip wires I don't see, hug Maureen to my chest, and mince-step too fast to the stairwell, then climb two flights to the roof. "Stay awake, baby. We're going to the hospital. Helicopter, short ride, piece of cake. You're safe."

Her eyes roll to white, then back, then blink tears. I kiss her. "Work with me, Maureen. You're safe; I promise—" Lights in the sky, then the thump-thump-thump of the Mercy Hospital trauma transport. I ease back into the roof access doorway as the helicopter lands.

Two EMTs jump out and run to us illuminated by the forward lights.

One EMT leans into Maureen's face, shines a penlight in her eyes, and touches her cheek. Maureen blinks, tries to speak but can't. He says, "Easy. We're here to take you to the hospital. Do this all the time. Nothing whatsoever to worry about." He looks at me and nods hard at the helicopter's bay door.

They help me load Maureen onto a slide-out gurney. I put a foot in with her, but the EMT pats me back. "No; runnin' on fumes; too much weight for the fuel left." The EMT pushes my foot off the deck. "We got it; she's got a chance, let us go."

I grip Maureen's arm until she blinks. "Got one stop to make and I'll be there with you. Spend the night, then it's you, me, and Bega at the farm. We made it, baby."

The EMT pushes me farther back. "She's in deep shock, Officer. We can save her, but we gotta rock."

I step back; he climbs in, and they're in the air. The lights rise fifty feet, then veer hard east.

I sprint the rooftop, then four flights of stairs, then shadows, and out into the crowd, phone to my ear, running for the clocktower.

Jimmie's breathing hard, says, "Ayatollah tried to call you. Mayor called him; said he'd back a show for tonight and tomorrow. What'd you do?"

"Threatened him with Oprah." I sidestep a pack of men with bats. "I'm killing this motherfucker. He's all done."

"Maureen . . . ?"

"He thinks he killed her; she's got a good chance. Inbound to Mercy." I run behind the Swift building to loop east. A bright-white light flashes the night sky to the east. "Jesus, you see that? What was that?"

Jimmie pauses, pants for breath, then says, "Scoreboard at Comiskey. P-Stones and GDs said they'd blow it again"—pant—"light up Canaryville and signal Red Summer."

"Fuck."

Jimmie adds: "R. Murph and I just cleared the Armour building, no shooter; headed to the Morris." Jimmie's phone goes static. "Who's your backup for the clocktower? Shooter's either there or ours."

The clocktower looms at the north end of the mob. "No time. ETA in three. Don't get R. Murph killed; you'll need him when you're boss."

"Don't do the tower alone. Grab uniforms out of the crowd."

"Roll hot, Jimmie! We can still stop this!"

9:35 p.m.

Inside the cupola, I'm panting from adrenaline and too many clock-tower stairs. Everything is deep shadows. Rifle's here, but no shooter.

I call Jimmie: "Got the rifle."

"He's *dead*? You got him?"

"No. Guy was here, perfect line of sight to the trailers. Got a text halfway up the stairs, anonymous, that he'd be here. His name is Steven—"

"You ran him off?"

"Not here. Coming back, though. Any minute. I'm waiting in the dark; he walks in, party over. We win."

Jimmie says something I don't hear—I notice the rifle . . . it's closer to the window than it needs to be, visible if someone were looking. This guy's killed fifty people and hasn't scuffed his shoe. Now he sets up for the big finale and makes a mistake?

I tell Jimmie: "Wait a sec," then look down the rifle barrel to the trailers where Burke and Howat will be in fifteen minutes.

I back off the rifle, aim my Smith 360 at the shadows, and tell Jimmie, "Think we've been tricked."

STEVEN

9:50 p.m.

Outside, Mercy Hospital is buzzing, so active it's amazing they can treat anyone. The outdoor triage center isn't full as I pass through, but they obviously expect a customer rush. And they now have the added concern of being bombed from the sky.

Smoldering metal dots the lawn and driveways, the full circle of a story well told—the fragments of their trauma helicopter that exploded fifteen minutes ago before it could land.

Pretty Maureen had seen my face, so giving her the C-4 suppository seemed like the only way. She and Dennis did get their teary reunion, though; I'm not heartless. Well, actually, I am. And I prefer French noir, where the hero can die. Duh, it's *noir*, stupid.

I manufacture shock and dismay to go with my bandaged face and hand as I snake through the ER to the ICU.

The ICU is busy as well, but not overwhelmed. Probably difficult to overwhelm these girls and boys. Poise under fire would be part of the credo. So, we'll give them a bit of fire—the old grenade into the waiting room trick used so effectively by our Semite brothers since the 1940s.

Walk in, nod respectfully to the black CPD bomber jackets; then the scared, the hopeful, and the vigilant look for a chair, then a magazine, a trash can for the nonrecyclable NR423 grenade in my rescued Wendy's bag. Pull pin, deposit bag in the receptacle—

Three.

Step out.

Two.

Around the thick concrete corner wall.

One.

KA-FUCKING-BLAMMY.

I fake-stagger through smoke and the blown-out double doors into the ICU, bump shoulders with stunned personnel in the dark. Emergency lights click on. This place could have been built better. I slide down the ICU glass and doorways until I see my "agent" for this fiasco du jour, Pádraig Cane. The FBI man standing at his bedside wears a suit and stunned expression. He has his automatic pistol out, but doesn't get the shot off before I shoot him in the heart. He blows backward into the lights and lifesaving devices.

Pádraig blinks, wide awake. I wink back, press down on his arm rising to stop me, put my pistol in his ear, and blow most of his brain onto the dying FBI man spurting blood through his suit.

As I turn to exit, an attractive nurse covered in concrete dust is right behind me, horrified and trying to back up. I hook her around the neck, shoot her in the heart, hold on till she's done absorbing the shock, then let her fall. Her blood further marks me as one of the victims. The rest, as they say, is—always walk off stage while they're still applauding.

I keep the eye putty, cheek cotton, and wig until I'm in Chinatown five blocks away.

***

Wow, smells great . . . if you stay away from the sewers. I'm always ravenous when a job's over—like after you've been swimming or to a funeral. I'd say we have time for an egg roll before we detonate Corrissa the Crazed. Then it's destroy the toolkit, pick up our luggage, and make for the airport.

BERLIN CALLIN'!

After an eye-hospital visit in Switzerland.

I will be a one-eyed painter. There are worse possibilities; Maureen the she-witch of Belfast could've killed me.

Inside the Hong Kong Palace, I order an egg roll, remove the phone-detonator from my pocket, and check the Jolly Shandy beer clock on the wall. Give or take a few minutes, and it's part of the Red Sea in Canaryville.

Should I call Lieutenant Dennis and Jimmie the Ingrate? Tell them it was a pleasure? You *know* that call will be in the movie whether it happened or not.

Above the cheap tables, a TV materializes in the wall clutter. This place is so garish that I missed the Sony mounted in the dragon heads and "decor." And the TV has a live shot of my semitrailers! Oh my God. I have a front row seat.

I squint my one eye at the flat-screen. A man with a white beard and a microphone, a huge crowd of people . . . fighting or dancing? The screen is angled to benefit the kitchen help; I move closer. Oooh, big fight going on, a riot. Lots of orange.

The TV cuts to a similar shot, except everyone's Black—the other half of my CV rewrite. They look unhappy, too. Possibly the gang nation is having words among themselves.

The TV cuts to an overhead showing the distance between the two camps, then back to the Blacks, no correspondent in the shot. Probably a voice-over I can't hear. Drama is always best when direct, no talking head in the way.

The screen runs a tape at the bottom announcing . . . a concert? Big names, too. Eminem, Kid Rock—damn, De-troit comin' out for the peeps! West Coast too—Snoop, Dre—gosh, I may have to stay for a show like that. The tape keeps running. Not *a* show, but two, beginning in three hours and running through Tuesday. Hmmm . . .

Homies' "We Are the World."

Boogaloo instead of burn. Not good; I smell an Irisher in the wood-pile, yet another Mick throwing potatoes at my CV.

There's a limit to my self-control. I remove my thumb from the detonator button. I wouldn't taunt me; I really wouldn't, not after all the work I've put in. I thought we covered that. Not to mention being disfigured for life.

I set my egg roll on the paper plate and dial Lieutenant Potato Famine.

Banahan answers, I use a Sony phone app to mimic my voice to Howard Cosell: "A concert?"

"Who is this?"

"Do I hear a bomb threat? Stampede? Dead Black children piled at the exits?"

Silence.

"I didn't have sex with Maureen; let's get that out of the way first; you and I are professionals. If the jigaboos have a concert, do we honestly believe they'll no longer covet white women?"

"Don't know, Steve, but why would you care? Hunting polar bears with a scope from a mile away doesn't seem all that . . . virile."

He used my name. I scan the slanted eyes around me glued to the TV. Banahan used my name. "I understand the value of recreation; a concert is good, but better to wait till after the inevitable, then have a *benefit*, like Katrina or WTC."

"I'm gonna find you."

"I doubt that. Seriously."

"I promise."

Egg roll reapproaches my lips. My repaired lip fails to move. He used my name. And he taunted me. Quick trial for the lieutenant—blah, blah—verdict: guilty. Sentence: death penalty.

"I'm in a good mood, Dennis. Call me generous. You're waiting for me in the clocktower, yes?"

Silence.

"Use my rifle—it's already sighted—remove Corrissa from the trading floor and I won't detonate the bomb underneath her." My egg roll bobs approval. "Dennis the Hero saves five hundred Christians from the lions, thereby gaining absolution for the rooftop forty years ago. I smell a big opening weekend and red carpet."

DENNY

"Saves five hundred" vibrates in my ears.

I reapproach the rifle and scope. If the bomb's scaled for this event . . . I look through the scope. Most of an Allied Fastener logo is visible. I bend back—if the trailer's full, the shrapnel will be like a million razorblades. I tell Steven, "If I kill your boss, you'll blow the trailers anyway."

"Certainly a risk. But what choice do you have?"

I re-look through the scope: Makeshift footlights glow up at Bishop Haswell Burke and the ten-foot cross behind him. At his shoulder, dressed in black and orange, is Corrissa Howat, a twenty-foot pole banner is tilting up behind her. On one side it reads "FOR GOD AND ULSTER" on the other, "NO SURRENDER."

Steven adds, "Execute the woman who any death-penalty state would happily kill, or abdicate your newfound hero status and allow more innocents to perish. *Lots* more."

"What the fuck do you want?"

"Honestly, Dennis, I have everything I want."

"Then pull out. Disappear."

"Sorry, not professional; no can do."

"Alright, I'll shoot her. Convince me you won't blow the trailers."

"Convince you? Hmmm. I hadn't intended on more effort."

"Be generous."

"Good one! Okay, by my watch I make it 10:07. You have eleven minutes; maybe you could fight through the crowd, remove the timer, and defeat the evil Bayside Bomber." Pause. "But if you're too late, *poof*, hero Dennis goes to Heaven with five hundred friends and neighbors."

I'm already at the stairs. "And if I'm not too late?"

"Call me if you get there in time. We'll make this a game show."

STEVEN

10:08 p.m.

I massage my lip, then bite the tip off my egg roll. *Timer? Game show?* I'm so Hollywood. This much talent in one man is, well, a stunner.

Lieutenant Dennis knew my name; excellent *professional* reason to add him to the detonation. Another good reason to wait the eleven minutes is Lieutenant Dennis will be unhappy when he learns his Maureen fell out of the sky. Leaving adversaries with a singular life mission is unwise.

I check the TV; ah, death rallies, competing shots of Black drama and white drama, America at war with her own image. Hope they film

the hip-hop show live; East Coast gangsta versus West Coast gangsta—
Puffy and Suge won't need me to bomb their "unity" show; nor will
they require a primer on how to blame Canaryville for the carnage—
white or Black, hillbilly/gangbangers are currently above criticism.

DENNY

10:08 p.m.

Phone to mouth, I run the last of the cupola's stairs, telling Jimmie:
"Killing me with Corrissa was an afterthought when I used his name.
Steven's his name. But he won't wait beyond his timer. Ten minutes is
it. Get the helicopters to broadcast something, disperse the crowd—"
    "*That's* your plan?"
    "Bomb has to be underneath the trailers. Probably prebuilt it, but
not well hidden; he had no idea on the location until Corrissa chose. I
get to the bomb unseen, jerk the detonator, and hope for the best."
    "I'll call for the helos; you run the other way."
    I bang out the door; am instantly crammed shoulder to shoulder,
chest to back in the crowd. "Right. Let the FBI take care of it."
    "Run the other way. We got a possible on 'Steven.' A nurse followed
him from Mercy to Chinatown—"
    Jimmie's call drops.
    A fifty-five-gallon drum spills fire on my left. The crowd surges
away; I yell "BOMB! BOMB!" and sprint the gap. The crowd retightens,
blocks me—
    I jerk shoulders out of the way. Elbows slam me. I yell "BOMB"
again. The crowd lurches. I run the seam, shove and fight through to
the next barrel fire, spill the barrel, yell, "FIRE!" The crowd surges away.
I sprint the gap. My pant leg ignites. I slap the flames out, take an elbow
in the head as a baseball bat slams past me to the pavement. I duck left,
drop my head, and ram forward.
    Three hundred feet from the trailers, Burke and Corrissa are
surrounded by melee—orange versus green—fists, bats, hammers.
Fighters trample and surge. Bodies fall.

I pull my Smith and fire three rounds in the air. "FIRE! BOMB! RUN!"

The crowd roils, stumbling over the fallen. I fire the last three, jump, bounce, crawl, fight the last twenty feet to the trailers, then half circle to the long backside.

Eye wipe. Try to catch my breath.

Bodies litter the pavement. Bricks litter the trailer tops. Burke has been knocked down. Corrissa holds a mic, facing the clocktower, telling the crowd: "Look to the Catholics for your murderers! Not the Blacks! The murderin' Catholics want Red Summer!"

I yell up at her: "BOMB! Tell 'em to run!"

Corrissa sees me and disappears toward the trailer's center. A baseball bat crashes near my head—

STEVEN

10:14 p.m.

Hmmm. The TV coverage is a bit shocking—I hadn't imagined that the crowd would panic and run *away*. The fire, gunshots, and helicopters look good, but . . . my good eye cuts to the window of the Hong Kong Palace.

Police cars are outside on Wentworth? Several cars, men exiting. Chicago does not have extra police tonight. I dig for my phone with my good hand. Two of the waitstaff huddle behind a drink machine, looking at me?

I bolt out of the chair, leap behind the counter, grab the first girl by her hair, and bang us through the back door—

"POLICE!"

I shoot him in his vest, pivot with the girl tight to my chest and fire three times running backward. She falls; I sprint right, wedge into a stinky, garbage-littered wall break, scrape dark bricks till a light adds a shadow-silhouette, jump through a makeshift door and crash into an old man bent over a basket.

DENNY

Above me, Corrissa yells into the PA system. I duck under the back trailer and crawl the trailer's width past a set of rear tires to the space between the two trailers.

Crouched, I try to stand, but only my head will fit in the narrow gap. Hands on the edges, I duck-walk the first fifteen feet toward the front tires.

Above me, visible in the narrow space between the trailers, Corrissa Howat incites the crowd. Above her, helicopters splash-light the melee and broadcast my bomb alert.

Midtrailer, my feet trip over a partially unseated manhole cover. I fall to both knees, jump up, bang my head, and—

Blink. Stars. Pat. I crouch again and inch farther down the trailer, keeping both hands on the metal above me. Five paces and my left hand strikes—a package . . . something. I fingertip a tube or a prong extending from the center but can't see it. I jerk it out, expect to explode . . . and don't. I throw what might be a tube/timer/detonator under the back trailer, rip at the package's tape until it tears, then rip the package away from the trailer. I make five steps back the way I came, trip over the manhole and lose the package—

STEVEN

The old Chinese man veers back off his stool. I run through a maze of rice kettles and steam, find a door, then another. I'm out, into an alley, I run under the L tracks, jump a fence, and dive into weeds.

Panting, I pull my phone. *Fuck.* That was close. Time to part the Red Sea and space-shuttle my friends Corrissa and Dennis.

DENNY

10:18 p.m.

Manhole lid. I know these, played in them with Mike and Cullen. I tug the iron lid aside with both hands. My BlackBerry rings. I grab, answer, "Banahan," then drop the phone on the ground and grab the package.

"Well, Dennis. Did you make it?"

"Fucking right I made it. Got your bomb right here."

"And you removed the timer?"

"Now I'm coming for you. Lights-out, motherfucker."

"Bad news, Dennis. Your concert may lessen Chicago's body count, but your girl Maureen didn't make it. And neither did you."

"Tell that to your tombstone." I throw the bomb into the manhole. "In the comics, you motherfuckers are better than me."

A small pin light blinks red. The world goes *deafening, blinding white.*

THE ETHER

Chapter 35

Eighteen days later

Bleak, desolate . . . gray. Opening my eyes won't make it better. I'm here, but I'm not, and don't have to stay. Up to me.

Twenty days later

Death is a process, a partnership. If I thought I'd be less sad, I'd die, but the glorious white light others experience is not what's being shown to me. The water ahead is gray, the reeds wilted, no horizon. Not fear— just sadness. I thought I'd done more good than bad. I stood when others wouldn't; I was tidy, consistent, fair. That's what I thought.

Twenty-one days later

As it turns out, the big lesson is: the cosmos does not grade on a curve. Denny Banahan's account has payments unmade. I have unfinished business with the living. And the dead. I don't get to die, happy or otherwise.

I open my eyes.

A reprint of Buz and Tod's Route 66 map is taped to the ceiling. The charred corner of Mike's and my map is fitted to it. Wires and IV tubes snake to me on a bed. Monitors blip. Warm hands hold one of mine. Above the hands is a beautiful woman; sad, too, but beautiful.

She squeezes. "You've been in and out for three weeks, like you were deciding." She squeezes again. "I want you to stay."

Twenty-two days later

In layers of fog, a voice deep in the ether says, "Yes, yes, you were right, my name is Steven. It was business; people die, get over it. Die, Dennis, like Corrissa and Bishop Burke, blown skyward atop the IMAX volcano your manhole created.

"Okay, not *all* business, there were moments: the waitress in the Bayside, Jimmie Daniels about to decorate his family; our brave, astonishing Maureen throwing herself on the pyre to save her lieutenant . . . bonus rounds in what you have to admit, was a bravura performance—mine. Go ahead and die; you'll never catch me and I won't stop . . . because the money won't stop. And if you die, you can watch."

An hour later

I open my eyes.

Next to the monitors, tubes, and wires, a giant Black man reads a copy of *GQ*. He cuts to me, then smiles. His head is smaller than a refrigerator. He shows me a copy of the *Daily Racing Form*, rolls it into my hand, and points at the Route 66 map on the ceiling.

I shut my eyes . . . then open them, and tell Jimmie: "Maureen's dead."

Jimmie nods. Squeezes my hand.

"Saw her in the ether. She told me what happened."

Jimmie swallows, squeezing my hand. Tears mist his eyes.

"Maureen didn't mean for any of it . . . didn't know it would go . . . like it did."

Jimmie says, "We know." His voice cracks. "We found a journal at the Malvern."

I shut my eyes and wait till the images pass. They don't.

I open my eyes. "Mahoney?"

Jimmie shakes his head. Fumbles for words he can't find, not that they'd matter.

Mahoney and his pages . . .

A flash of black and white bumps past Jimmie, bends, grabs my wrist and stares into my face. A Black nurse; she makes a professional smile.

"What's your name?"

"Denny."

"Hello, Denny."

I smile but it doesn't happen.

"Where are we?"

"Hospital."

She leans back and points at Jimmie.

I say, "Sergeant Daniels."

She nods. "I live south of Fifty-Fifth Street. My sons were in Ogden Park. It would've been . . . Red Summer." She swallows. "You're a hero, God bless you, a living-breathing hero, no matter what the FBI or anyone else says." She swallows again. "Every room on this floor has flowers because of you; twenty people a day, sometimes twice that. Black, white, sending baskets. You're a hero, Lieutenant Dennis."

Jimmie says, "Gibbons dedicated the concert to you, the second night. You living was ninety-ten against. No reason to think you'd screw up being a martyr by opening your eyes." Jimmie smiles, shrugs, not hiding the pride. "I quote the Ayatollah standing in front of a Bud Billiken banner in Washington Park with Chicago's media and sports stars on his left and right."

Jimmie reads a paper. "Dennis Banahan told me to remember who I was at the Lorraine Motel, who I was with, what the stakes were. I remember. And I want all of us to remember a white policeman who valued his oath 'To serve and protect' above his life, his color, and our color."

The nurse pats my hand. "You are lucky to be alive, Lieutenant. That bomb imploded half a city block of sewers. Incinerated Corrissa Howat and Bishop Burke."

I glance past her to the window.

She pats my hand. "*Very* lucky."

The window is gray, like the water and the reeds. "Compared to who?"

Route 66

Buz and Tod's time machine has two lanes.

If you decide not to die, and your insurance covers the required surgeries, the westbound lane runs from Chicago to the Pacific Ocean, through Prohibition, the Dust Bowl, the Great Depression, WWII, and the ghosts of millions of American migrants trekking west to start over.

Every hundred miles or so, there's an old motel with a lunch-counter restaurant, and Lana Turner—from *The Postman Always Rings Twice*—waits tables in all of 'em. The motels look like the 1950s, fifteen or twenty doors surrounding a heat-rippled parking lot and a fenced swimming pool with no water.

Inside, the rooms have asbestos ceilings, nubby carpets, nubby bedspreads, a recycled TV, fluorescent bathroom lights, and freshener that hurts your eyes. The first, and last, one I stayed in was in Joplin.

Since then, I've slept in the Banahan's 1960 Chevrolet Biscayne happy ship. Somehow our car seems less . . . empty. At night I lie on the hood, propped up against the windshield, sipping Maureen's Tullamore Dew from the bottle, looking at the stars. Lotta stars above this road; but so far, not many answers.

Next gasoline will be Cassiopeia, Arizona. Maybe that's where the answers are. They weren't in Chicago.

Four days ago I was discharged from the rehab facility—one less kidney, a prosthetic shoulder, and three steel rods in my leg. I wasn't in a federal prison or on death row at Stateville—big victories, both—but I had to trade my pension, and with it, the horse-farm dreams that belonged to Maureen and me. As it happens, "heroes" who don't roll for the Feds have to pay their own way when the story moves on to the next headline.

I picked up Bega.

We go straight to Maureen.

She's outside Chicago's city limits, at Mt. Hope Cemetery by Morgan Park. The grave is in the back, next to her brother's. Green spray paint and excrement smears cover Maureen's headstone. Not right, seeing her like this, but not unexpected. I kneel close, on the grass. Both hands fingertip her name.

"Hi."

My palms flatten on the stone, then grip the sides like I would her shoulders.

"I know I've been sayin' this every night, but . . . I'm so goddamn sorry"—swallow—"I promised . . . I was sure we could . . . Then . . . I thought I'd saved you or I'd never have let you fly . . . And everything woulda been okay. We're us; we'd have found a way."

Choke, inhale.

"So, so . . . I'm here, me and Bega. You can talk to me again. Okay? You can. It's important. To me. Us."

Wind rustles the elm trees. Rain drifts in with it, soft but cold on my hands and face.

Somewhere in the wind is Maureen's lilt. Her voice says, "Seems there's a way of things that has to be. Bringing Chesney and the church to justice was proper and I'll not suffer that. Someone had to do it. Destroyin' so many innocent lives in the process was, and is, unatonable."

The wind and rain pick up and silence Maureen's voice. I rub her name clean, want to comfort her, to disagree, but can't, she's right about unatonable. We both had sins we couldn't outrun. And they cost us our future.

Bega leans into my hip, yips at Maureen's tombstone. The rain goes deeper gray and rolls over the three of us like a curtain. I hug Bega to me and tell Maureen, "I'm sorry. Every way . . . possible."

Maureen whispers, "I love you fierce, Dennis, always will; then and now and forever, and don't forget me. The blue of my eyes will be in the first light of day."

I whisper back . . .

But she's gone.

My eyes blur with rain and tears; wait to hear her again but know I won't. I push two acorns into the earth beneath her birthdate. Seeds from the oak tree that shaded the barn we almost owned in Darien. Seeds that don't have much chance, but then neither did Maureen. Cut deep into all four sides of the granite headstone shipped from Belfast is:

WE CLAIM HER PROUD: FOR GOD AND ULSTER.

Because you can't outrun DNA. And visible or not, Maureen's DNA has been front and center since the night I met her carving the epitaph above the Malvern's door: *Every country gets the circus it deserves.* Freezing cold and she didn't care; she was consumed with the murder of her exchange student/employee—one of the four homicides I was working—who, it turned out, was her dead husband's daughter, newly arrived in America to outrun the Troubles before they became part of her life.

The grass puddles my knees and jeans.

And DNA is what revenge becomes, before it grows into flags and monuments and murals, each displayed with pride, each one a promise to spill more DNA. I never solved the four homicides.

Bega starts to shiver. I tell Maureen's tombstone, "So . . . baby, we kinda gotta go. I'll be back . . . that's a promise, someday. We'll make it out, you and me. We're supposed to." I kiss her name in the granite and prop up the tiny doll we made from barn hay and our unworn racing silks that I wore on my belt as a talisman, set it there with the acorns. And cry like a little boy all the way to the car.

Wiping my eyes, I keep a promise to Jimmie and go by the graves of Antoine Starks and his sister, spend an hour on my crutch circling their markers trying to forgive them and say I'm sorry, but can't do either. If they could get up and walk, I'd kill them again and they both know it. All of us still have some karma ground to cover.

Bega stays at my leg as I shuffle back from the Starkses' grave sites.

Three FBI agents wait there at the Banahan's Chevrolet happy ship. Agent Stone blocks my door, eyes the mud on my clothes and hands from Maureen's grave.

He says, "A promise from me to you. The pass you received from the US Attorney doesn't have my signature. When the public discourse shifts back to law and order, I'll have full-time staff working to put you in front of another grand jury. We will keep bringing prosecutions until you're locked down in Marion. Twenty to life."

I remind Stone, "My Smith's in the Chevy behind you."

Agent Stone doesn't demonstrate concern or worry.

"I begged for your help to save Maureen, help you could've provided, but didn't."

Agent Stone keeps his "fuck you" face.

I'm surprised; I'd given him more credit for survival instincts, and lean into him. "I'll be off this crutch, one of these days. That's a promise for your file. Serve your fucking warrant in person." I thumb over my shoulder at the tombstones. "We'll see how you like law and order."

Stone has one of his agents open his Cullen Mahoney file on the hood of my Chevy. The agent reads out loud from the two pages Stone had mixed into the worthless Corrissa Howat pages. Pages I hadn't seen before the explosion, but that Jimmie had.

Stone waits for his agent to finish, then manufactures a sympathetic wince. "Now, we're all on the record about Mahoney." Stone waves for the pages, then tosses them in my front seat. "Keep this copy. Might want to read them again when you stop by your brother's grave."

***

It's been three hours and twelve minutes since I didn't kill Agent Stone.

I'm alone at the intersection where Route 66 begins at Lake Michigan. I'm alone because Bega decided to stay, as I knew she would.

On the visor is my favorite photo of Maureen, Bega, and Jimmie. Behind the photo is where I put Agent Stone's Mahoney pages. They're in a sealed envelope with the *Herald* clipping that says the unlikely partnership of me, Mahoney, and the Ayatollah stopped Red Summer. The clipping of Cullen Mahoney's suicide is in there, too. Used his service revolver the day he was to appear at his grand jury. His femme fatale Lana Turner was the Catholic church and the Irish politics that bridged the ocean.

Like me, Cullen Mahoney had sins. His were bad, even by Riviera standards. Hard to believe he could live with them.

Mahoney went in behind my brother, Mike, and killed one of the three shooters in the liquor-store armed robbery that killed Mike. Mahoney couldn't ID Antoine Starks and his sister solid enough to charge them, but he was positive—him to me—that it was them. The FBI file says they have proof Mahoney set up Mike, used Antoine and his sister to protect Bathhouse John's guns-for-money pipeline to the IRA in Catholic Northern Ireland.

Mike was talking to the FBI about it.

Mike had to go; Cullen Mahoney became a star.

With my back to the lake, I repeat Mike's and my pop-bottle promise: "You'll see," to the nonbelievers, put the Banahan's shoebox comfy on the front seat, and head west into the sunset.

We do a quick dip into the Riviera to the ghost of the Byrne's Building. In the parking lot that used to be our apartment, I make sure 'everyone' has their seatbelts on, write down the number on the odometer, pop my returnable Pepsi, and hit the gas.

Cassiopeia, Arizona

We're sixteen hundred miles from Chicago. The "answers" aren't here either.

I pump the last of my fill-up. A four-foot ball of tumbleweed blows through the service station and stops at the adjacent café's glass door and chain. Duct-taped to the dirty glass is a sun-bleached, unreadable sign.

Yep. Lana Turner has definitely left the building.

But Cassiopeia still has presence, a dusty echo of how this exact spot felt on the Banahan's nineteen-inch Motorola when Buz and Tod rolled through a bunch of lifetimes ago.

I do the Bana-Plan's one-nod lock that Mike and I did at Koonce's after every Pepsi haul, tell the tumbleweed: "You'll see."

Cassiopeia was the last mile Mike and I tallied on the Bana-Plan before the Byrne's Building fire ended the dream.

A new Ford pulls in and stops at the farthest of the four gas pumps. No dents, a rental with California plates and serious road dust. Another tumbleweed blows into the Ford's bumper, bounces, then rolls to the rear tire.

An early-thirties man exits the new Ford, kicks the tumbleweed away from his tire with a stylish slip-on boot, nods hello to me at my pump, then turns to read the prices and octane choices.

He has wavy red hair, an eyepatch, and a scarred cheek and fore-head. He's a shorter version of Conan O'Brien after a car accident or plate-glass window. Nothing about this guy is FBI or threatening, but I keep looking anyway. A cop thing you never shake. Same for bartenders when the street-door opens.

The stranger inserts a credit card in the pump, puts premium gas into his new Ford, caps his tank, takes his credit card receipt, and drives away.

I go back inside, grab two packs of beef jerky, turn the postcards wheel, pick the one with an Indian gunfighter, address it to Jimmie, Homicide's new LT; drop it in the box, pay the disaffected Indian girl working the register, take a last look for "answers" hiding in the tumbleweeds, then head west, away from the sun.

At twilight, I pull into Needles, California, Dwight Yoakam on the radio. Gas is not cheap in Needles. Dwight and I finish at $62.

A car bumper stops two feet closer to the back of my knees than is polite. The guy gets out, apologizes, and turns for the gas pump.

Same Ford, same guy from Cassiopeia, Arizona.

Okay. Could happen, a coincidence, one tank of gas for us both. He has California plates, we're now in California. I stare. He doesn't. Still not threatening, just Conan-familiar. I step between our cars to the pump island, the length of his car between us.

"Same route, huh? Not many stations."

He looks up—maybe he does kinda resemble someone other than Conan, someone I can't place; a coma for three weeks, surgeries, and rehab will do that to your cognition.

He says, "Excuse me?"

The voice sounds familiar, sorta . . . maybe. Doesn't fit the cadence . . . I point at our two cars. "Arizona, we got gas in the same place."

He squints the one eye. "Never been in Arizona, sorry."

I look at my watch. "Ah, eight hours ago you were in Arizona."

He shakes his head.

I begin to feel less pleasant. Look closer for any sign of Steven, a mass murderer/assassin who's made the FBI's Most Wanted list but is still out there.

I don't see anything and say, "Okay. But so you know, when we do this next time"—I point west at the sunset—"I'm not saying boo; you go direct to the hospital, capish?"

He finishes pumping his gas, twists on the cap, and closes the fender lid. "I don't enjoy being threatened. Should there be a next time . . ." Small smile. "You'd never see me coming."

I step to my car, reach inside, withdraw the Smith, and hold it against my leg. "Not real big on games of chance. What do you want?"

He shrugs. Both hands are visible. "Gasoline."

Okay . . .

I pull out first. The oddball stranger is in my mirror. Guy felt like one of those highway transients who end up on the news with a trunk full of murder tools and shovels.

The lights of Needles fade behind me. No headlights follow me into the Mojave Desert. Shapes materialize at the outer edges of my headlights. Tired eyes mix bad memories of bad dreams and harsh voices from the ether. I put the Smith on my lap, back off the gas, adding reaction time that a mirage or a nightmare won't give you.

Not good enough; I pull over, exit the car, and allow two hours of headlights to pass. The Ford isn't one of them.

Maybe that guy didn't feel like a transient with shovels . . . More like a feral cat playing with a mouse it hadn't decided to eat. Maybe that's the same thing.

***

Back behind the wheel, the Banahans' first California sunrise hints near Barstow. I stop to see Maureen's eyes, and stay with them until they fade and become sky. The final 120 miles of Route 66 is downhill.

And there it is, the Pacific Ocean. The finish line. Buz and Tod leaning against their red corvette; Dinah Shore singing *See the USA* in the background. Everybody there waiting for the Banahans of the Byrne's Building.

Just like Mike and I planned it.

I lean over to tell Bega how good this is—right, she's not with me. I point for her anyway. "Hollywood Park racetrack is that way, Santa Anita that way, nothing but beach, sunshine, and happy in between."

I park, walk to a breezy, sandy bench, sit facing the Pacific, place Mike's shoebox on my knees, remove the lid, and lean it against my stomach.

First out is my ma's photo, then Da's, then Mike's—Mike looks as proud as I've seen him, all of them placed gently into the lid and turned toward the waves.

I extend both arms at the coastline. "Cal-i-fornia."

For an hour, the Banahans sit on the bench, smelling the spindrift and salt water; no drunks pissing in our mail, no animals dying at the Stock Yards, no building supers stealing our money. The waves are green-blue, bluer and longer than Lake Michigan's. The larger curls support surfers in wet suits. Chicago's waves in the winter are big enough to surf, but you'd freeze to death.

The Banahans sit, communing with our new West Coast life. The waves and sunshine will tell us the rest of the plan, the part Mike and I didn't figure. *Getting here* was as big as we could envision.

We commune for another hour.

The west end of the continent isn't all that talkative.

I look at my family aligned in the shoebox lid, then turn us all back to Route 66 that we just came in on. "Twenty-five hundred miles in the Chevrolet Bana-Ship, okay? That's the part I promised."

The Banahans aren't satisfied, wait for me to articulate what's on their mind.

I don't want to.

They wait—Denny, you're the youngest; it's your job.

Okay, fine. You want me to say it? I'll say it: *"Now what?"*

Waves splash the pier.

Wind rustles palm trees. The Banahans remain silent on "Now what?"

I look north up the coast, then south. "Okay. What would Buz and Tod do?"

My phone rings—either voodoo at work or my karma has realigned to provide life-answers. This is Hollywood; I'm going with voodoo.

Lt. Gael Gilmartin says, "We're at Harold's; Bega wants to know where you are."

"Pacific Ocean. Lemme talk to her."

I imagine the phone at Bega's nose. "Hey, movie star, how we doing?"

Bega barks.

I flash on the hospital, the girl in my dream holding my hand in the ICU, a dog with her—and tell Gael: "That was you, on the bed, in the hospital telling me to come back."

"Dream on, tough guy."

"You were decked out in nylons and heels; I remember. And happy, for a change. Wanted me to stay, spend the night."

"Yep. You and I did a naked four-pile with two of the teenage nurses. Only way we could save you."

"Man, that would've worked."

Small laugh. "For you, maybe."

Gael's laugh mixes with the waves. In the mix, I hear Maureen's laugh, want to feel her heart beating, but can't.

Gael says something I don't hear.

I ask, "Why'd you want me to come back?"

Silence, then, "Complicated."

Gael Gilmartin and I were always *complicated*. "Yeah. Tell Bega I love her. And take care of Jimmie. And yourself."

Silence.

Then: "You, too, Den. Call home now and again."

"Ten four, Lieutenant. Tell Bega she'd like the ocean."

Silence . . .

I button off, gently replace Ma, then Da, then Mike in our shoebox, and close the lid.

The Banahans all walk under the pier.

I dig a hole three feet deep, open the shoebox a last time, add my BlackBerry and the Smith I carried for forty years, then lower the shoebox to the bottom of the hole. I take a last look, then cover the Banahans of the Irish Riviera with California sand.

My first day in uniform with Mahoney, he told Mike and me, "Some of the fights you'll win; some you'll only survive. You'll commit sins you can redeem; the others we have to live with."

I want to believe that, I really do.

Author's Note

To heighten the pace of the story, the day of St. Patrick's Day in 2011 was modified to reduce the time between Chicago's two "quintessential" St. Patrick's Day parades.

Dedication

DENNY BANAHAN. Early on, an editor told me, "Only Russians need a thousand pages." He didn't know Denny. This novel required twice the time as the previous ten, and twenty-one passes. If I somehow conveyed the Lieutenant Dennis I know and love, I owe it to $8 Berlin vodka, soul communion with English-speaking, four a.m. televangelists, and the inherent intellectual cruelty of Calvin Coolidge.

JIMMIE DANIELS. A gentle, urbane, erudite gunfighter. There aren't enough seasons to call SAC Daniels a man for all seasons.

GAEL GILMARTIN. The no-shit police. The muse. The beguiling Canaryville *one* who almost was.

JIM LOEF. It wasn't my intention to have Jim die in this novel, let alone the way he did. But as in his life, shit happened. Jim lived fearless and fast, and when I was with him, when we were pals and he looked after me, he was as tough and as good a kid as I ever knew.

And CANARYVILLE. My first serious car accident at age sixteen and my first Guinness as pain medication.

Acknowledgments

BRIAN RODGERS and MURAD SIAM. Princes of the Cosmic River. If not for them, *Canaryville*, *Privateers*, and all that follow die in New York City.

SHARON BENNETT and DON McQUINN. Never tire of thanking them. Have yet to write a book they didn't make better.

MEGHAN HARVEY. Publishing's Magellan. The girl who searched for and found the strait and had the nerve to sail it.

LESLIE "LAM" MILLER. Editor, empathy counselor, Lost Girl, *chef de Cosmic River.*

SIMON LIPSKAR. A bog wind blowing from three directions and yet he's still here.

RAB HOWAT. For sharing his neighborhood, the Gorbals in Glasgow, and his song "The River Runs Through It." They inspired Corrissa of Belfast.

And, ARMANDO STILETTO. "'Cause he always delivers."

About the Author

Charlie Newton is a Chicago native and a writer known for his global life on the road and extended MIA absences. When he does publish, Newton's heart-pounding, gritty, and witty realism has been a starred-review favorite of the critics and a finalist for the Edgar, the Ian Fleming Steel Dagger, the Macavity, and the International Thriller Writers awards. Newton is the author of *Calumet City* (Simon & Schuster, 2008), *Start Shooting* (Doubleday, 2012), and *Traitor's Gate* (Thomas & Mercer, 2015). His acclaimed book *Privateers* (BlackType Press, 2020) was the winner of American Book Fest's International Book Awards and the Goodreads Readers Favorite Award, both in the thriller category.